FAREWELL, MY SWEET

FAREWELL, MY SWEET

Walter Reutiman

ISBN: 978-0-9976950-0-7

First Edition: August 2016

Pre-press by North Star Press of St. Cloud, Inc.

Printed in the United States of America

Dedication

This book is dedicated to my grandchildren:
Katie, Tyler, Lauren, Henry, and Miles.
They are the joy of my life.

~•~

PROLOGUE

O N AN EARLY summer's evening, a Twin Cities television news broadcast was in progress when the newscaster said:

"This bulletin is just into our news room. Minneapolis police this afternoon reported discovering the body of well-known local bank executive, John Payton. Payton was the chief financial officer of Orion Bank of Minnesota. No details surrounding the death are available at this time, but police say foul play is not suspected. No one from Orion Bank has been available yet for comment. We will bring you further details as they become available."

~ 1 ~

OUT OF THE PAST

I ADMIT TO BEING a creature of habit, a person who does not like change. My desire is to have everything move along smoothly day to day, with no hiccups or bumps in the road. That's why if I could have foretold the turmoil my life was about to encounter, I never would have gone to work on that fateful Monday morning.

My name is Michael Connelly, and I have resided, worked and played in the quaint little City of Excelsior for most of my thirty-eight years. Nestled on the south shore of Lake Minnetonka, this one-time Minnesota outpost has had a storied history as a vacation Mecca dating as far back as the late 1800s.

Today the town still draws residents and visitors of all ages, either playing hard or relaxing in quiet luxury. Plenty of activities abound here for the outdoor enthusiast of any age, and large numbers of those folks take advantage of the ambiance during the warmer months, especially on weekends.

As a small-town attorney of no distinction, I've practiced in these environs nearly my entire professional life. After a time away from here for higher education, I returned to my roots to work at my chosen profession. Both the work and the surroundings have suited my temperament and lifestyle. So much for me.

It was late on that fateful Monday morning while I was trying to adjust to a new workweek that I received an unexpected phone call. When my business partner, Janet Brown, announced the call was from a Katherine Williams, I momentarily was stumped. I sat back in my chair thinking about the name, having no clue who that was. Staring at Janet with a bewildered look, I raised my hands in the *I don't know* gesture, and Janet responded by hollering, "She says she's an old friend who's known you for years."

That little tidbit of information was of no help, and I truly was perplexed. It wasn't as if I knew that many people or had so many friends I could start forgetting some of them, and certainly I wasn't that familiar with so many women I wouldn't recognize a name. Nevertheless, I scratched my head trying to recall the face that might go with the moniker. No such luck there.

I decided to take the call, the gears of my brain clanking and grinding while I attempted to identify the caller. What did I have to lose? Maybe I had won the lottery. Better yet, maybe some hot babe had heard about me and wanted my body! I chuckled at the thought as ridiculous as it was.

"Hello," I said in my most professional tone. "This is Michael Connelly."

"Michael, this is Katherine Williams."

When I didn't immediately respond, she followed up by saying, "You probably remember me as Katherine Brancel."

Brancel, Brancel. At first the name didn't ring a bell. I knew some Brancels, but no Katherine. Then Katherine translated to Katie for me, and I made a connection to both the voice and the name. Katie Brancel.

"Certainly I remember you, Katie, err Katherine. How are you?"

"Fine, Michael, and you?"

"Just fine. Gosh it's good to hear from you. It's been a long time, hasn't it?" How long had it had been since we'd last seen one another?

She answered, "Yes, it has been a long time, Michael."

Memories started to surface. I had not even entered high school the last time we had been in contact. Actually I was a little surprised she even remembered me. I had not thought of her much in the intervening years.

I began to recall her more vividly, at least a version of her I remembered as a young girl. Katie had been a babysitter my folks hired for a couple of years who occasionally sat for my little sister and me. Gosh, what a crush I had on her back then. Katie had been my fantasy girlfriend just when I was beginning to realize girls were different from boys. She looked awfully good to me back then, and I wondered how she looked today? How old would she be now? Mid-forties, tops.

Katie interrupted my thoughts. "Yes, it's been a long time, Michael. Too long. How's your sister Mary?"

I had to change gears rapidly. "Mary. Mary's doing fine. She's living in California, in the Bay Area, actually. Married with kids. Husband's a great guy."

"I miss her," she said. "She was fun to sit for."

"Not me?" I asked expectantly.

She paused. "No, as I recall, not so much. You were a brat."

That might have set me back, but I could hear the smile in her voice, so I chuckled as I said, "And all this time I thought I was being so cool."

She laughed. "Yes, real cool, for a ten-year-old."

"I had hoped you might have a shorter memory," I said submissively.

My mind was wandering back to those days when I'd look forward to the babysitter's arrival. Instead of going out to play I'd hang around the house just to be near her. She had looked and smelled so good.

"Don't worry," she said, drawing my thoughts back to the present, "I won't tell anyone any of your secrets." She paused for a moment as if reflecting, then, "Actually you were pretty nice to me."

So she had noticed my attempts to woo her. I had understood the difference in our ages then, but hoped she would wait for me as I matured. I suppose I had the same dreams of most pre-pubescent boys.

The next question from her jolted me. "You said your sister has a family. Are you married, Michael?"

Why did she want to know that? Had she heard I was divorced? I laughed inwardly. Was this the first step in making a play for me? *Yeah dream on, big fellow.* Would I ever grow up? I finally answered. "No, not at the present, Katherine."

She let my response go at that, and I was grateful. I had no desire to discuss my brief, unhappy marriage.

There was a pause in the conversation, so I asked. "What can I do for you, Katherine?" The name, Katherine seemed way too formal to me.

I had known the girl as Katie, but since she had become had introduced herself as Katherine, I would accede to her wishes until such time as she instructed me to do otherwise.

Though I was not intimately familiar with her, Katie's current public persona began to clarify itself for me. Katherine was Katherine Williams now, wife of Larry Williams, president of the Orion Bank of Minnesota. Orion was the largest independent bank in the State of Minnesota, if not the five-state area, and, from what I had heard and seen, the Williams family had done well for itself over the years. I was happy for the woman.

The only reason I had kept up at all with her affairs was because of an occasional mention of her in the Minneapolis paper for her charitable work. Chairwoman of this or chairwoman of that, it was all very proper activity within her elite circle. That had been my only connection with her in those many years, and I wouldn't have been surprised if it had been all one-way.

Katie spoke. "Michael, I know we haven't seen one another for a long time, but I need a favor from you. I was wondering if you might be able to help me?"

That statement, frank and direct as it was, surprised me. There was a slight hint of pleading in her voice, a certain neediness I wouldn't have expected to hear from her. I vacillated before answering. Maybe it had something to do with an upcoming charity event. If not that, then I certainly was puzzled as to why she would be calling me. Her family and business certainly had a battery of high-priced legal talent. I wondered what it was that could I bring to the table?

I answered hesitantly, not sure what I might be opening myself to. "If I can, Katherine, I will."

She paused momentarily, and I wondered if she had changed her mind. Then she said in a soft voice, "I wonder if we could meet and talk about it in private?"

Now I was flummoxed. Why she didn't she want to talk over the phone? What reason could she have for that? Was she concerned with being overheard? It was the only reason I could fathom.

I answered in a controlled tone. "Okay, sure. Where? When?"

"Are you perhaps free for lunch tomorrow?" she asked.

"I can be," I said hesitantly.

Katie pounced right on that. "Would one o'clock be all right?"

"Let me check." I knew I didn't have anything scheduled, but it never hurt to appear busy.

After a short pause I said, "Yes, I can make that work. Do you want me to pick you up somewhere?"

There was a slight pause and then, "No, I'll meet you. Say down at the city dock at one. I'll be there with my boat."

I puzzled at the rendezvous, but replied, "Yes, that's fine. I'll meet you then. One o'clock at the city dock. How will I know you . . . your boat?"

"It's a very ostentatious boat, Michael."

I almost laughed. She always did have a sense of humor. "Fine, one o'clock, then."

We rang off. I sat there wondering at the conversation. After all these years to hear from a former crush. Yes, Katherine to me had been Katie, and she had been our sitter for about what—two years when she was in high school? Later, when she went off to college, I lost track of her, which was unfortunate for me. I remembered how I once had dreamed of marrying her. I closed my eyes and reflected. She had the smoothest peaches-and-cream complexion I think I ever had seen. That set against her dark hair and small pink lips had made her irresistible to me.

I shook myself from my reverie. I guessed I'd find out tomorrow what she wanted.

I thought I could just forget about it for now and get back to work, but no sooner had I had gotten off the phone when I turned to find Janet leaning against the frame of my office doorway with her arms folded in front of her chest wanting the scoop.

"New business for us?" she inquired.

When I blushed, she shook her head and said, "New girlfriend I don't know about then?"

I looked down at my desk trying to look professional. I was ill at ease but didn't know why. Guilty conscience, I guessed.

7

Janet continued. "You know I have to look out for you to keep you on the straight and narrow. I'm tired of you showing up for work with your face beat in, leaving the heavy lifting here for me."

There was little I could do but nod in agreement. That very thing she was referring to had happened to me twice the previous summer so there was nothing I could say in my defense. I just waved at her to leave me alone, and Janet went back to her desk, smiling.

I made it through the remainder of the day with occasional random thoughts of my impending meeting creeping into my head. I was unable to figure out what Katie had wanted to require a personal meeting. On that I was totally in the dark. Shit, why hadn't I inquired when I had the chance? I shrugged as I realized I had been so flummoxed by her call that my mind had not been working. Did it ever?

Pondering the question, I realized there could be a million reasons for her contacting me as she had. Obviously she was in some sort of trouble, but why scrape the bottom of the barrel when looking for help? There was plenty of mystery about that, but I was just going to have to wait until tomorrow to get an answer.

~2~

A Delayed Task

I WRAPPED THINGS UP at the office that Monday afternoon and walked home after my rather singular day. Once settled in, I considered my options for dinner. I had done my weekly grocery shopping on Saturday. This early in the week there remained quite a selection from which to choose. I waffled at the decision.

Then while staring out my patio door, I sighed, remembering with consternation the chore I had committed to for this evening: cleaning the deck. I shook my head because it did look scuzzy, and though I had planned to clean it over the weekend, I had let the chore slide, promising myself to do it Monday when there was nothing else to do. I had been having too much fun over the weekend to get all my work done. I hung my head in disgust because now I had to pay for that dalliance.

Would I commit tonight or find another excuse? I went out onto the deck in my stocking feet and once again perused the sky—a few patchy clouds with no rain in sight. That left the question; should I clean the deck before or after dinner? If I were to grill, it made sense to grill first, but I really didn't want to eat this early. In addition if I were to let the chore go until later, I might just skip it again, leaving it entirely until the weekend. Heck, would that be so bad?

No, shithead, get it done. Though if I cleaned up first before eating, then everything outside would be wet, and it would be difficult to use the deck at all this evening. Without direct sunshine, the deck could take hours to dry completely. Then I considered doing it in the morning before heading out to work, but no, that wasn't likely to happen. Dammit, it should have been done last weekend. I sighed once again and decided I might just as well do it now.

I went back inside and checked my refrigerator for possible menu items. I spied the package of brats I had left there after Saturday's shopping. The thought of sizzling brats wetted my appetite, and right then and there I committed to grilling. I would both grill and clean the deck. Somehow I would make it work.

Those were the kind of decisions I had to be prepared to make moving forward. They had not been so easy for me over the winter months. Moving forward I didn't want any more indecisiveness in my life. Whether it was work or my personal life, I had to take charge. And that went for my meeting with Katie also. I wasn't going to roll over for her just because she battered her eyelashes at me. No sir. I would help her if I chose to do so, and not unless I did.

Resigning myself to the immediate task ahead, I changed into shorts and a tee shirt, dragged out the garden hose, attached the nozzle and sprayed everything down. It wasn't as effective as using a power washer, but it did the job. I also sprayed the patio doors and wiped them dry with newspaper. Then I stood back and admired my job. The chairs were dripping, but they were clean. Now my grill stuck out as being a bit grimy. I decided to wipe it off before I used it for dinner.

I became aware of someone's presence. When I looked up, I saw my next-door neighbor, Sherrill, watching me from below the deck. She apparently was walking up from the docks. I smiled at her and playfully pointed the spray nozzle in her direction. That was when she asked me if I wanted to do hers. I had impure thoughts at that statement and just smiled at her before I turned away to store the hose. Then I carried my wet shoes inside, putting them in the laundry tub to dry.

Once I had moved indoors off the wet deck, I wondered if I should invite Sherrill over for a drink? I looked at the state of my housekeeping and decided tonight wasn't the best of nights for that. Maybe tomorrow. I could come home from work and tidy up and then give her a call. I snickered at her statement that I could do hers? Yes, I certainly would like to clean her deck.

I recalled a Twins game was supposed to be on the tube tonight, so I checked. One was. I decided to go ahead and cook a couple of brats on the grill despite the deck being sodden. Maybe by the time I was ready to eat, the wood would have dried some so I could hop scotch about it. I decided on having baked beans with my brats while I watched the boys of summer labor under the lights. Of course beer went well with both brats and beans, so I'd need a couple of those. I made sure I had enough cold ones in the refrigerator, then I started the beans on low heat.

After starting my dinner, my thoughts returned to my impending meeting with Katie. I suddenly remembered the shoebox of pictures my mom had given me awhile back after cleaning out her place. I'd never looked at them. Now I wondered if, perchance, there might be one of Mary, Katie, and myself in the bunch?

Now, where had I put that box? I first looked in the back of my closet with no luck, but I found it on the shelf of the closet in the spare bedroom. Sitting on the bed, I began to go through the pictures one by one. The task went quickly until I began to relive memories. Here was one with me in my t-ball uniform, one of me holding my golf trophy.

Finally I found one with Katie standing with Mary to her left with me on the other side. She was wearing a skirt, blouse, and knee-high stockings with tennis shoes. A ribbon crossed the top of her head and kept her hair off her face. She was absolutely gorgeous. What a smile. I decided with an ache in my chest I once again was in love.

I put away the remainder of the photos and carried the singular picture downstairs with me. I watched a couple of innings of the game. The Twins already were two runs down. It seemed like a good time to fire up the grill. The deck was dry in spots, with puddles in others. I was able to navigate those and started the fire, leaving the flame heating on low. Once the grates were hot, I would place two beer soaked brats onto them. I like to cook the meat slowly at a medium temperature so the skin didn't split. Otherwise they lost all their juicy flavor.

I puttered in the kitchen until the grill had heated. Once I had the brats on, I needed to turn them frequently to get the skin crisp all the way around just the way I liked them. I grabbed a beer and waited outside in my bare feet while my dinner cooked, watching the lake while I did so.

The activity on the nearby bay had increased a hundredfold since this morning. Boats were piling in at the waterside restaurants like ducks into decoys. The drone of their engines was a familiar and pleasant sound.

I saw smoke rising from other backyard decks further down the line of lakeside houses, indicating I wasn't alone in my decision to grill tonight.

When the brats were done to my liking. I plated up my meal. I wasn't eating buns with my meat because I did not want the extra calories. I laughed at that thought, knowing my two brats alone carried enough fat grams to meet my weekly limit. And it was only Monday! I carried my dinner into the living room with me to watch the rest of the game. By then the Twins were three runs up. I had missed some good action. Maybe it would be better if I didn't watch. Maybe I was bad luck. They seemed to do better when I was absent.

My dinner hit the spot and my appetite was satiated. Once I had finished and was comfortably situated, I nearly nodded off. The game lasted until nearly eleven, and I stayed up until the conclusion. Occupied as I was, I had given no more thought to my impending meeting with Katie. There just was no way to anticipate what was on her mind.

Not knowing particulars of her current life was no help to me at all. After the baby-sitting years, Katie and I had maintained no further contact. Our worlds had been in different orbits. By the time I started at Minnetonka High, she already had graduated. I met new girls while there, and then met Grace my junior year. That was a tragic story. The bottom line was that I'd paid little attention to Katie and her life in the intervening years.

Whatever Katie wanted, it couldn't amount to much, and it made no sense worrying about it. I'd find out everything I needed to know tomorrow. I picked up the photo of her and looked long and hard. Then I laid it on the living room table and went upstairs to bed.

~3~

A Fresh Season

THE FOLLOWING MORNING I woke early after a restless night. I sleepwalked through my usual morning routine, finally waking up enough outside on my deck to enjoy the late spring weather while savoring a hot mug of coffee. Still a bit chilly early in the day before the sun cleared the tree line, the cool fresh air felt good. A misty cloud rose from the lip of my mug as the hot java contacted the cooler air. It reminded me that true summer warmth had not yet arrived in our region. Mornings and nights still remained chilly near the water. That would soon change.

I normally would have waited for my caffeine fix until after arriving at the office, but today I needed the jolt. Along with it I decided the cool, fresh lake air might help me shake my lethargy. That and the liquid stimulant would provide me the bump needed to begin another day. I assumed my condition was the result of playing hard this past weekend and not concern over my impending rendezvous. I guessed from my activities I was just a kid at heart, though at thirty-eight no longer a kid.

While I remained immobile, enjoying my warm beverage, the sun finally topped the trees facing me along the east shore. Even with the bright orb at a low angle, I needed to shield my eyes against the reflection as it danced on the water and burned a hot path toward me across the bay before ultimately dissolving into the nearby shoreline. I could almost see heat rising from the water where the rays had singed the surface. Nonetheless, it was a sight to behold. It lightened my mood.

Humidity levels were surprisingly high this morning. I could feel it kissing my bare skin. Folks would need no moisturizer today. Humidity levels generally were higher near the water, but they abated somewhat

13

after I abandoned the water's edge to walk uptown to my office. Then too, as temperatures rose, the relative humidity would drop. That was my little meteorological note for the day from Mr. Weather Fact Man.

I was fortunate to live where I did. My townhouse overlooked the lake and also was located just a few dozen yards from Water Street, the main drag through town. This setting kept me near the hub of town activity, but distant enough from the main center of action to afford me some peace and quiet on those raucous summer weekends when visitors overwhelmed the town. I lived alone, but I enjoyed my location and the amenities provided therein.

Being a creature of habit, I did as I wanted, had a routine, and generally enjoyed my peaceful, tranquil life. That was the great thing about being a bachelor; no one told me what to do or when to do it. I was my own boss.

Scanning the water a final time, I realized not a single boat had as yet ventured out onto the bay this morning. The only visible activity was a large raft of seagulls lolling on the water's surface near the end of the boat docks. It was early still and only Tuesday. Everyone else probably was as physically spent from the weekend as I was. The out-of-towners would need to recharge their bodies and bank accounts before returning again in a few days, allowing the locals to have the lake to themselves for a while. Though with school out, there would soon be plenty of activity, especially at the beach.

With the sun now surmounting the green barrier across the water, and with few clouds marring the pristine sky, I already could feel the air heating up. The building to my back acted as a reflector. With little wind I was confident it already might be seventy degrees where I stood. Down on the dock where I kept my boat would be another matter. The cooler lake water would moderate the air over it and let the temperature rise but slowly throughout the morning.

Looking at my watch, I saw I had plenty of time, so I sauntered on down to the dock where I sat on the end facing the open water. Dangling my wingtips just inches from the water's surface, I pulled a cigar from my jacket pocket, prepared it, and brought it to life.

Coffee and a good cigar—there was nothing better than that combo to begin the day. I rolled the tube of fine tobacco between my fingers and expelled the inhaled smoke. The breeze had stirred just enough to pull the plume away from my face, and I watched it as it swirled and curled like a diminutive tornado.

When the gray ash had grown long enough, I flicked it onto the water and saw a school of sunfish come to the surface to investigate. *Don't eat that little buddy. It'll stunt your growth.*

The relaxing atmosphere had almost allowed me to forget my troubles, including the forthcoming meeting with Katie Williams. I pondered that event for a moment, then tried to put it out of my mind. It was a riddle yet to be solved.

Later, with my cigar half gone, and my cup empty, I decided to return inside. I could finish my smoke on the walk to work. Pushing myself erect, I walked the length of the dock and climbed the steps leading up to my patio door. While I had been savoring the morning solitude, my neighbor, Sherrill, had come out onto her deck adjacent to mine. She wore pajamas and slippers and had the morning paper. I waved and she returned my greeting with a wave and a smile. She was a cute little dark-haired beauty, but, alas, married. Yes, I should have invited her over last night. No, maybe it was best that I had not.

To anyone reading my thoughts, I appeared to be waffling, unable to reach a conclusion.

My life had been a lot like that lately, more or less left alone to drift aimlessly. Decisions, even simple ones, had not come as easily as they once had in times past. Throughout the long cold winter I had been in a funk, and I admitted to that now. Maybe that in of itself was a sign of improvement—me recognizing where I had been. I realized that things had begun getting a bit better with the coming of spring, and I believed I perhaps had now turned the corner toward personal redemption.

Almost a year ago I'd had a disastrous encounter with a former lover of mine, from which, at the time, I could not imagine I'd ever recover. When Gracie Adams left my life and disappeared from town in late summer without a word, I had felt betrayed and vulnerable. As a consequence,

I had lain low socially and had not been seen by others as that normally energetic man about town. Friends had been supportive though, and pretty much left me alone to heal at my own pace. I slowly had begun to realize I had to find my smile again. I was working hard on that.

Minnesota can be a cold, lonely place in the wintertime, and reflecting back over that frigid timeframe, I recognized that my personality perhaps also had been a reflection of the weather, causing me to sink into depression along with the deepening cold. Fortunately, as I said, that began changing with the coming of spring. I had gotten myself outside more, and I had been burning plenty of marine gas pounding around Lake Minnetonka. I was using the excuse that I was looking for a new place to live. In actuality I merely was enjoying the out of doors and the beautiful lake. Yes, things definitely were looking up for me.

Throughout the winter months, my solitary life consisted of going to work each day, then returning in the evening to my cave where I sat by myself and brooded. I saw few friends during that time and made no effort to be convivial. I tried to amend that attitude most recently with my actions. I even had a couple of dates with a gal named Jill Philippi, who had been a friend of my long lost love, Grace. It turned out to be a healing experience, as I remembered how much I enjoyed the closeness of a woman and her soft, gentle touch.

But, hey, life must go on, and I was making progress with that mantra.

I looked again into my empty coffee mug before returning inside to finish preparing for work. I was about to pack a lunch when I remembered my luncheon engagement. One less task for me on an ambivalent morning.

I headed out the door, wearing nothing more than my lightweight suit. It was approaching late spring/early summer in this part of Minnesota. The ice had long left the lake and water temperatures had risen to a tolerable level. Also, springtime thunderstorms seemed to have abated and we'd had no recent tornado activity.

As I said, I was committed to getting out and enjoying life again, so I had spent this past Saturday morning fishing with a buddy over near

Tonka Bay, and on Sunday had taken two friends for an early evening cocktail cruise along a few of the 225 miles of Lake Minnetonka shoreline. We viewed the variety of castles that had risen along the shore while we sipped beers. That had been a good day. I had not had to drink alone.

I walked to work most mornings, even during the winter. It wasn't far. Today, the early morning sun was comforting. It should be, since in only another week it would begin its long six-month retreat southward.

Excelsior had its charms. As I moseyed along the street, I glanced up at the sun reflecting off the upper reaches of the building directly before me, producing a golden hue on the brick facades. Across Lake Street the marquee of the movie theater glistened as if a hundred spotlights danced on the smooth surface. Landscape painters should be here this morning capturing the scene. Why would they go to Paris to paint when they had the Lake Minnetonka and the town waiting for them right here?

It was only a five-minute walk to the office, about three short blocks. The sidewalks generally were empty before eight o'clock, especially on my end of town. Other than the coffee shop, which drew a crowd, none of the other businesses were yet awake.

The bookstore, salon, and pet store would be the first to stir, followed by the liquor store; but the theater and ice cream parlor would not come to life until later this afternoon. Thus I had the street pretty much to myself as I walked the length of the block toward Second Street. I owned the town this time of day.

Looking further up the main drag I saw some activity, but easily avoided that by turning left at the corner. Then I momentarily paused to critique the newest arrangement of the shop window presented before me. After perusing the display, I continued along a few dozen more feet and turned right down into the alley toward the long-term parking area. Here was where my office was located, on the lower level of a building that fronted Second Street.

It was time to go to work and see what trouble, if any, lay ahead for me that Tuesday.

~4~

An Unusual Meeting

JANET ALREADY WAS in the office when I arrived. After we exchanged our usual pleasantries, I advised her of my late luncheon appointment.

"With the new girlfriend?" she asked.

"Don't I wish." I bit my lower lip. Looking off into the distance, I said, "I have to admit she was my first crush as a kid, but I don't think she even knew I existed back then. I'm a lot younger than she is."

Janet suddenly got a funny look on her face. I could tell she was about to say something, then held her tongue.

The woman had peaked my curiosity. "What?" I asked.

"Nothing," she said, lowering her eyes.

I knew that wasn't the truth. "No, what? Tell me." I was pleading. I valued Janet's opinion and wanted to hear what she had to say. I had plenty of misgivings about this meeting myself and didn't want to go forward without knowing what Janet had to say.

Janet sighed. "I just hope you're not going to do something foolish. I mean with what happened last year. You're very vulnerable."

My eyes began to mist. I was surprised at her comment. Then I realized she was spot on in her assessment. Chewing my lip some more, I thought for a moment, then said, "Thanks for caring, dear, but this is just a business meeting. I hold no illusions. I'll be careful. I'm only bantering about her being an old girlfriend. She merely was a childhood crush."

"That may be so, but I know how those things can hang on."

"Not in this case. I barely remember the woman."

"Okay, good. You be careful."

Janet turned toward her keypad, and the conversation was over.

Once at my desk, I worked through until twelve-thirty, with just a short break for a snack. I left the office then because I wanted to go home to change clothes. I didn't think I needed to wear a suit for our meeting, but that wouldn't have been a big deal. But I knew better than to wear hard-soled shoes onboard a boat. I needed to change those for sure.

While I was at it, I decided to dress down from my work attire. I settled for a soft-blue knit shirt, khaki slacks, and the soft-soled shoes I wore when on my boat. Then I threw on a light-blue sports jacket just to dress up the outfit a little. I decided against wearing a hat, but I did locate a pair of sunglasses, which I dropped into my jacket pocket.

No briefcase, I thought, though this was supposed to be a business meeting. Instead I placed a small notebook into my jacket pocket and made sure I had a working pen.

I ran a comb through my hair. I could have used a haircut. Discounting that, I swiped the comb left and right through my neatly groomed mustache, and poked at my rather large nose, which took a couple of jogs down my face. I suppose I could have had those breaks fixed, but figured they added character to an otherwise plain mug. I should learn not to lead with my face. Shrugging, I realized this was as good as it was going to get. At the last minute, I brushed my teeth again and dabbed on a smidge of cologne.

I felt I had a decent Minnesota tan for this early in the summer, one acquired solely on weekends. I was fortunate I colored easily because it still was early in the season. However, in a little over a week the days would begin to shorten. Summer didn't last long in this northern climate. Minnesotans had to enjoy it while they could. I gave one last look in the mirror and approved my outfit. With the tan, I thought I looked better than the pale edition of myself back in the winter months. Perhaps my rediscovered smile helped also.

I had been working hard lately trying to get into better shape. I committed to the program last winter when I joined a health club. The routine of attending, and the goals I set helped me to get my head on straight and get over that disastrous love affair. As a result, I had lost ten pounds and firmed up a good deal. I didn't look half bad in a bathing suit for a man in his late thirties.

My weight was down to one-ninety, which was nice for my six foot three inch frame. I wore the mustache to balance an otherwise unremarkable face. I'd heard it said my hazel eyes were my best feature.

I should have worked out last night. Golf league was tonight and I'd miss the club two days in a row. I tried to maintain a regimen of exercising every other day. I wasn't sure why I had become distracted last evening. I guessed it was okay if I hit it hard the remainder of the week. I felt better when I worked out consistently.

Before my low mood last winter, dating never had been a problem for me. I never had trouble meeting girls, but that may be due more to my personality than my looks. Or it could have been, as my nephew said once when I asked him to tell me which of my many fine personal qualities he liked best, "Your boat."

I applied some sunscreen to my face and arms, rubbing it in well. Then I proclaimed myself ready to go. I had my wallet and keys. At the last minute, I decided to bring a bottle of wine. It seemed a nice gesture. Pinot went with almost anything. Too bad it hadn't been chilled.

Then I stopped short. Suddenly I realized how I was acting. Why was I fussing so? This was a business meeting. I normally didn't stress like this even before a big meeting. Sure, first appearances counted, but I was who I was. I always had confidence in myself. What had changed? Perhaps Janet was right. I was letting myself in for something troublesome. *I'll have to be careful, that's all.* With that inward inspection, I felt I was fully prepared for whatever lay ahead.

It was five before the hour when I walked onto the municipal dock at the end of Water Street. A large cabin cruiser was maintaining station thirty yards from the end of the wooden platform, and as I walked toward the dock's end, the boat began a slow lateral approach.

There was a slight chop on the water, though nothing to cause a problem. I noticed on my walk over, however, that clouds were building far to the west. The weather report had forcast a chance of rain later today. I shrugged. Whatever happened, happened.

The cruiser was big, I had to say that. I was impressed. It appeared to be a fairly new Sea Ray, and I'd put it at about a fifty footer. I couldn't remember what lengths they came in, but my guess was that its length would make it a yacht. I knew of two such boats on the lake, but until now hadn't seen either of them or known who owned them. In all my sorties about the lake, I never had seen one docked at a residence, so I assumed both were kept and maintained at marinas to be delivered on call. I recognized this craft as a monohull, twin engine Troller, which is much more common in locals such as Florida and the Caribbean than on an inland lake in Minnesota. *Well, I guess if you've got it, you flaunt it.*

The yacht's hull was painted black, contrasting to a molded white superstructure. Freshly polished chrome sparkled in the sunlight. The aft deck was mostly covered with a hardened canopy and the bridge was elevated so as not to impinge onto the large aft deck space.

A light breeze blew on shore, so to dock the pilot merely had to let the boat drift to the pier, while he maintained lateral position to the aft end where I presumably would board. The skipper appeared to have the task well in hand.

My quick perusal showed a small woman in a brightly colored dress and oversized sun hat standing on the aft deck looking toward shore. Her head moved from side to side as if watching for something or someone. Perhaps she hadn't recognized me, but why would she? The woman's face was in shadow, but I assumed it was my hostess, Katie.

Suddenly I realized I was becoming nervous. I had wanted to guard against that. Was it the anticipation of this meeting, or that I was about to encounter a beautiful woman? Perhaps all my childhood fantasies were about to be quashed and I was getting into something over my head. Then why this secluded rendezvous? Was Katie in trouble? *Cool it, big guy, you are about to find out.*

Just before the boat made contact with the pier, the driver shifted the twin engines into neutral and left his elevated console to drop two bumpers over the near side. He then threw a short stern line over the near post and positioned a portable ladder over the side for me to step onto. Even carrying the bottle of wine, I could have made the one-foot step up without the aid of the ladder, but he was doing just as he had been trained, and I chose not to make a fuss.

Once aboard, I nodded in the man's direction, then walked over to my presumed hostess. She stood in a sailor's stance with her feet splayed slightly apart to maintain her balance on a slightly rolling teak deck. She reached out a petite hand and said, "Michael, I presume. Thank you for joining me." She gave me a large smile.

"My pleasure, Katherine," I replied as I grasped her hand lightly. A jeweled bracelet graced her wrist. I glanced at her brightly colored nails as they rested in my large palm. They were the color of a ripe plum. She gave my hand a slight squeeze.

I looked into the woman's eyes. Even in shadow from her wide brimmed summer hat, they were bright and lively. Although her face was still in shadow, I could see it well enough to now remember the younger version. I tried to liken this face with the teenager I'd once known. The resemblance certainly was there, but today I was looking at a much more refined and sophisticated continence. Her presence overwhelmed me.

I felt as though I was partaking of a dream. Everything moved in slow motion. No sound other than Katie's voice reached my ears. I even forgot my admonition about not being taken in by this woman and was prepared to accede to her every wish, when suddenly a gust of wind whipped across the deck. Just like that, the spell was broken.

My shirt ballooned out, and Katie had put her free hand up to the top of her hat to still its flight. Behind me I heard the sound of the ladder being retrieved and laid onto the deck. I reluctantly released Katie's hand and took a half step back.

She smiled at me as she said. "Shall we go below, Michael?"

Everything around me appeared to have returned to normal. My hostess half turned toward the door leading below deck. From my vantage point, I was able to study the woman's slim frame clad today in a brightly colored, sleeveless sundress, with scoop neck, and hemmed just above the knee. A colorful, jeweled belt cinched a tiny waist. She wore decorative sandals with a low heel that matched her belt. It was a well-coordinated ensemble.

In addition a brightly colored necklace with matching bracelet appeared to showcase rubies. If they were real, they were expensive. No doubt they were real.

Several rings adorned her fingers, while a ruby ear stud was visible on the side where her short hair was pulled behind her head. No doubt it had a partner. She looked both sophisticated and very Caribbean. I was in the presence of a very beautiful woman. Though I had known her in her youth, I felt somewhat ill at ease now, uncertain if I belonged in her league.

As I inhaled the woman's scent, I heard the engines spool up, and felt a slight bump as the boat pulled into the wind. I glanced up toward the control console as I walked. I had to hold my free hand up to shield my eyes, and I could see that the driver had moved the control for the port engine to reverse and now was engaging the starboard engine forward. The man was looking down at the dock as he piloted the craft. I guessed he was going to pivot the boat away from the dock so as not to scrape the starboard side. He had left the bumpers in place. It was a difficult move with the wind trying to push him back onto the structure, but he gave the starboard engine just enough power to overcome the wave action. Once he had achieved an angle of about sixty degrees to the dock, both controls were pushed forward and we moved slowly out into Excelsior Bay. The man knew his stuff.

Katie interrupted my observation. "As I was saying earlier, it's a little breezy today, Michael. I thought we might eat below."

I found the breeze refreshing, but said, "That's fine. I think it might storm later."

That settled the question of where we would eat. We were to have our own private meal aboard the boat. I wondered why? Obviously Katie had wanted privacy. Was that the only reason?

She said, "Charles will take us around the point to the lee shore and out of the wind."

I nodded, then said. "I brought you this. My mother taught me never to go anywhere without a gift."

Katie smiled and took the wine. Then we climbed below. The salon was a space equal to the size of my boat. It had a table and bench seats for eating along the port side that I suspected converted into a sleeping berth. I confirmed that when I saw the overhead tracks for a draw screen to isolate the space. There were comfortable looking chairs in which to lounge in the free space, and a kitchenette along the starboard side. The windows had curtains, and the deck was carpeted. It was a space as plush as my living room and slightly more up to date.

Katie removed her hat and placed it onto an open space on the counter. Her dark hair was parted in the center and pulled toward the back of her head. She walked over to the cooking area and placed the un-opened wine into a bucket before adding ice. Turning toward me, she indicated a chair with her open palm and said, "Please be seated, Michael."

"Thank you. After you."

"No, I'm waiting on you today," she said with a smile. "Would you care for a drink?"

I thought momentarily and then said. "Do you have any diet soda?"

Katie looked in the refrigerator before turning to say, "Sprite Zero okay?"

"Yes, that's perfect."

Katie removed an insulated tumbler from the cupboard and dropped ice into it with shinny tongs from a counter top ice bucket. Then she handed me the can and glass. Returning to the refrigerator, she took out a pitcher and poured brown liquid into a tall glass. After putting in a slice of lemon, she joined me.

"Iced tea?" I asked.

She nodded.

We sat facing one another.

"Do you mind if I smoke?" she asked.

"No, go ahead."

"Will you join me?"

I thought of the stink a cigar would make below deck and declined. Besides, I had neglected to bring any. "No, thank you, not just now," I replied.

Katie walked over to the counter, tapped out a cigarette from the pack sitting there, and lit it. Then she returned with an ashtray, which she placed on the small table between us. She sat and crossed her legs at the knee letting her limbs stretch out alongside the table. I tried not to be obvious while looking at her shapely legs, but my thoughts drifted to where they should not be headed. The soft fabric of her dress clung to her body and I followed the shape of her leg all the way to her hip. I could feel my face heating up as I visualized what lay beneath, so I poured my soda and took a quick drink. Katie smiled and I smiled back.

I observed that Katie still had the same peaches-and-cream complexion that had enthralled me when I was ten years old. A few beauty lines had formed around her eyes and the corners of her small mouth, but nothing to diminish her looks. Actually they made her face more interesting. Her dark hair was uniform in color, either natural or from a bottle and today was fastened in the back with some sort of comb.

It was the woman's makeup that caught my attention, though. It was done so perfectly it looked more like a painting. I wondered if her eyebrows had been tattooed on, they were so uniform. This truly was a beautiful woman, and obviously she took the time to display herself in the best possible light.

Seeing her as she was today rekindled all my childish fantasies of nearly thirty years ago. Now more mature, I was left to wonder if I ever thought I would have had a chance with her? Perhaps not. More realistically she always was out of my league. I laughed inwardly as I grasped that I may finally have to resign myself to that realization.

Katie began the conversation, and we chatted briefly, catching up on the recent past.

"You certainly have grown, Michael. You never were very tall when I knew you."

"Well, I was pretty young then. Plus, I think I was a late bloomer," I answered. "I never shot up until sophomore year in high school."

"Play basketball?"

"Freshman and sophomore years."

She nodded that she understood.

"Did you go to Minnetonka, then?"

"Yes."

"I assumed you had. So did I. Did you have that weirdo Schultz?"

"No, I was lucky, I had Skoy."

"I suppose you went to college, since you're an attorney."

I nodded.

"Local?"

"Yes, and law school out of state."

Katie smiled. She stood and walked to the refrigerator where she secured me another soft drink. I thanked her. We had talked exclusively about me. I wasn't sure if that was by design, but I figured she would tell me what she wanted me to know. I had decided not to inquire about her background as I felt I was being interviewed for some purpose. However, the mild banter had put me at ease. In the dip in the conversation, my anticipation grew as I waited to find out why I was there.

Then Katie suggested we eat. "I've prepared chicken salad. I hope you like it," she said.

"Yes I do, but I haven't had it for a while. My mom used to make it."

"That's where I got the recipe."

"Really?" A whole range of thoughts and motivations slammed into my brain. This was a simple business meeting. Why would she contact—

"Yes. Your mother gave it to me when I went away to school."

Oh.

She smiled and stood. I stood with her, but remained where I was as she went to the galley. There she removed a bowl from the refrigerator and slipped off the cling-wrap cover. She placed a sterling serving spoon into the bowl, and brought the crystal bowl to the table along with bread. Tableware already was in place. The china plates had a black-and-white design mimicking a zebra pattern. The flatware also was sterling, and the stemware was crystal glass.

I walked over near the table. "Is there anything I can help with," I offered.

"No, why don't you sit there," she said pointing to the side closest to where I stood. "Would you like to open your wine?"

"That would be nice."

Katherine walked over to the refrigerator and returned with the wine, two wine glasses, and a corkscrew. Then she made a second trip for glasses and a pitcher of water. After placing the wine glasses before us, she poured water in each of our drink glasses.

We both sat. When I placed the napkin on my lap, I noted it was linen. After this, I definitely need to upgrade my personal dining experiences.

"I hope you like my version of chicken salad," she stated.

"I'm sure I will. How do you make it?"

"I cook small rings, mix in a blend of Miracle Whip and cream. Then add celery bits cooked chicken and sliced green grapes. Sometimes I'll put in apple bits instead of grapes."

"I like it with grapes," I answered. "It's a complimentary taste."

Katherine nodded.

The salad was delicious. Katherine had taken just one spoonful and when I did the same, she reached over, took the serving spoon from the bowl and plopped a heaping spoonful onto my plate.

"I was hoping I wouldn't have to take any home, Michael. No one else at my house likes it that well. You'd be doing them all a favor if you finished it."

I laughed and that brought out a smile on her face. I did my best, but didn't succeed in finishing it.

Our conversation through lunch was friendly but non-personal. Katherine seemed adept at conversation and making whomever she spoke with feel important. I wondered if I really was important to her. I supposed I'd find out after lunch.

I could feel the boat beginning to roll a little now and wondered if the wind had switched. Soon after that, the captain started the engines and retrieved the anchor. He was heading for quieter waters, and I hoped that soon Katie and I would get to the purpose of our meeting.

~5~

An Unusual Request

A FTER WE FINISHED LUNCH, Katie and I bussed the dishes to the sink and put away the food. Then we moved back to the lounge chairs.

Before we sat, Katie asked. "Can I get you anything else, Michael?"

I still had my glass of wine and said, "No, thank you, I'm fine for now. The lunch was delicious, Katherine." She had barely touched her wine. I figured maybe it was not up to her taste. It would probably go down the drain after I left.

"Thank you," she responded graciously.

I remained standing until she sat. She seated herself in the armchair resting one arm on each rest. She then crossed her legs at the ankle and tucked them under her to one side, the typical finishing-school posture. Unconsciously she tucked a finger over an ear to put her hair in place, though I could see nothing amiss. It must have been habit.

Katie's small breasts rose and fell with her breathing and captivated my attention while I waited for the next act in our performance. Finally I realized I had been staring, and I moved my gaze up to Katie's face. That was a pleasing picture for me. She must have been accustomed to ogling by now. I couldn't be the only man to find her attractive.

Her large, hazel green eyes were wonderful to look at, and I was doing just that. Always maintain eye contact they said in the sales classes, and that was just what I was doing. That was not a problem here. The entire view was magnificent.

I leaned forward, placing my nearly empty glass onto the small table between us. Then I leaned back in my chair and crossed one leg over a knee, being careful not to point the bottom of my shoe toward my hostess. I was trying to use my best manners.

Neither of us spoke. The sound of sloshing water through an open window only disturbed the silence. I watched while Katie fidgeted with her hands. Apparently she was working up the courage to ask me something, and I was becoming nervous with expectation. Was something emerging to disturb my tranquil life?

Finally, when she had twisted one ring several times, she stuck out her chin and said, "Michael, I suppose you're wondering why I asked you to meet with me?"

The words leapt from her mouth in one fast, long string, revealing her level of tension. Just hearing her speak seemed to pop the balloon of expectations for me, and I somehow felt relieved, even though I yet had learned nothing.

Looking her straight in the eyes, I nodded. My hands remained on the armrests of my chair, and I sat back, feigning relaxation. I hoped my posture would put her at ease.

Katie smiled a little smile, then cleared her throat, placing one hand over her mouth.

Then she began to speak, very slowly and softly. I had to strain to hear her. She momentarily looked down.

"I don't have much of a private life, Michael. With my husband, Larry, as prominent as he is in banking, I seem always to be in the public eye."

Here she paused as if looking for affirmation. I couldn't tell if I was supposed to say anything so I just nodded, stupidly. I was good at playing stupid; it came naturally.

Then Katie continued, "You may not be aware, but expectations are high for me to live a certain lifestyle. In addition I get very little privacy." She paused for a moment to collect her thoughts. "It's necessary that I attend all the correct events and volunteer my time to the proper organizations. It's all done to help further my husband's career. I need to be the perfect wife." Here she looked up at me and punctuated her statement with her hands.

Her declaration awaked me for the first time to her lifestyle. I had never considered that there were people living like that. I didn't think I could. I briefly wondered if she would trade her material possessions for more privacy?

Katie remained silent as if expecting me to say something. I didn't. I was waiting for the punch line. I shifted in my chair, putting both feet on the deck.

"I don't know if you can understand?" she said finally.

I chewed my lower lip. I had to be careful to say the correct thing since I wasn't sure where Katie was headed. "I think I do, Katherine. The wife behind the man so to speak."

In my adolescent mind, I privately hoped this was the prelude to a come on. Did she want a fling with me to break the monotony of her life? My heart began to beat faster. I was up for that. Better on her boat than on mine.

She nodded at my brief comment and continued. "Good, you understand. That makes what I'm going to say to you easier for me." Her chest rose and fell, causing her necklace to dance against her ivory skin. "My position you see, that's partly the reason for meeting as we did on the boat. This way we wouldn't be seen together. The boat picked me up at my home, and with me aboard, came to Excelsior."

I wondered why the two of us should not be seen together. I was not exactly white trash. The only thing I could think of was to further my adolescent fantasies. I attempted to put those thoughts out of my head and instead asked, "You mean you expected to be . . . followed?"

"Not so much followed as being constantly in the public eye."

Her response was so ambivalent it confused me. "Who? Why?"

"I'm afraid I'm not expressing myself very well. Who would see me? Everyone. People gossip, you know. What am I wearing? Who am I with? I didn't want to subject you to that kind of scrutiny just for being seen with me."

I tried to understand what she was saying. Maybe I was white trash in her circles. That would be the reason for her not to be seen with me. I tried to grasp the significance of what this strange woman was saying. I couldn't. Her world was not my world. Katie probably saw the confusion on my face and said, "Maybe if I continue."

"Sure, go ahead." I was getting a little peeved.

"My husband, Larry, always has been capable of separating his work life from his family life, such as that is. When we are on our private time, as I call it, he always had been affectionate and loving. However, over the last few months all that has changed. He's now more guarded in his conversations with me, and he appears to be completely self-absorbed. We talk very little at all, and when we do its totally trivial. Plus he won't discuss work with me at all."

I was troubled at this point. If Katie went the direction I thought she was headed, we were talking about her husband having an affair. I didn't want to be discussing that. If it involved her and me okay, but I didn't want to get dragged into some sordid affair of her husband's. I raised a finger and interjected. "Do you think it's another woman, then?"

Katie frowned and slowly shook her head. Her eyes pinched in thought. "No, I don't think so, Michael. If that were the case, I believe he would try to cover himself with false affection." Here she paused and reflected. "No, he's terribly distracted. Something's bothering him, and he won't confide in me what that might be. You don't know what it's like to be excluded like that." I was uncertain, but it almost looked as if a tear had formed in Katie's eye. She quickly snapped her eyelids shut and shook her head.

I felt better after hearing the rest of her explanation. I did not know why, but the thought of Larry cheating on this fantastic woman infuriated me.

She now continued. "It's not his health, because I've spoken to his physician. I was coming around to the conclusion it must be work related. You see?"

"You've asked him then? I mean about how things are at work?"

"Innumerable times. He merely says there's nothing wrong. For me not to worry. Everything's under control."

I thought for a moment, then asked, "Is there no one else at the bank whom you can ask? Who will talk to you?"

"Michael, I have tried, but with no success. The people I know at the bank won't talk to me beyond the superficial, and that's what leads me to believe it relates to the bank. It's as though Larry put the word out not to communicate any bank business with me. I know I could be completely paranoid on this, but I worry about him."

I took a deep breath. She appeared sincere; she was concerned for her husband. "Tell me about the bank."

"Okay. Larry's president of Orion Bank of Blaine. It's done very well and is the largest independent bank in Minnesota with a capitalization of over a one hundred million dollars. Over the past five years it's grown tremendously. Larry's been very proud of the growth."

What she was saying appeared was all good news. I needed to dig deeper. "Do you think the pressures of work are weighing Larry down?"

"I don't know for sure, Michael, but it would appear so. Though, I can't get anyone to confide in me. That's why I decided to contact you."

My surprise must have shown. "Why me?" I asked, bewildered. I couldn't fathom where any of my diminutive skill sets could come into play.

Katie exuded confidence when she said, "I saw you were elected to the board of that new Excelsior bank a couple of years ago. I surmised that, perhaps, with your knowledge of banking you might be able to help me. You know, give me some advice."

Oh, shit, now I was done for. If Katie only knew how little I knew about banking, and how much more I didn't comprehend. I didn't wanted to mislead the lady, so I replied, "You have to understand, Katherine, being a bank director isn't the same as being a banker. I provide some oversight, but I'm not expert in any particular banking area."

A frown clouded her pretty face. That troubled me. Katie's shoulders sagged a little, and she again played with her ring.

I quickly interjected, "But perhaps I could ask around and see if I could find out anything?"

That brought out a smile. "Oh, Michael, could you? That would be wonderful."

I momentarily felt good. Then I realized what I had done. Why had I said that? Trying to be the big shot. Now I'd surely disappoint her. Damn. But . . . in for a penny, in for a pound.

I sighed and said, "Let me ask you, though. Are you a shareholder of the Orion Bank?"

"Yes, I am."

"Large, small, what?"

"I personally own ten percent of the outstanding common stock in the bank holding company. Then, I'm the beneficiary of a trust that owns thirty percent of those shares."

"Does your husband own any shares?"

"Only a couple of hundred. He put most of the stock into the trust."

"Okay. Any idea what that ten percent's worth?"

"Oh, I'd say about close to twenty million book value, maybe."

That just about knocked me off my chair. I was astounded, but I regained my composure to say, "Good, that gives me something to look into." My heads was swimming. I barely could comprehend amounts such as those.

I stared across the table. Now Katie became more her old self, and we continued our visit discussing multiple topics, none of which related to her personal life. I listened to her but the idea kept creeping into my head that I was making a mistake with my involvement. What could I hope to accomplish? Well, maybe another visit with Katie. She was awfully good looking, and if she ever had a drink, she might even loosen up and become the fun-loving kid I remembered. But we all change. I wasn't the person she remembered, so why should she have remained the same?

Soon thereafter, the boat took me back to the city dock, and I departed with the warning to Katie to hurry home before the storm broke. The sky to the west held billowing clouds and was growing increasingly dark as they climbed higher into the heavens. The breeze had picked up, and I feared that, once the boat got through the narrows and into the upper lake, it would encounter rougher water. Maybe it could gain safe harbor behind Howards Point.

I briefly stood on the dock and watched the boat depart. Then I recalled my earlier admonition to not get myself involved. I had absolutely failed in that regard. I stuffed my hands in my pockets. Shit, what had I got myself into?

I walked slowly home to my townhome at 116 Water Street and changed clothes. As I did so, I had time to reflect on the meeting. It was nothing I could have expected. Katie totally surprised me. Then I thought about her request. I wished I could be as certain as she was that her husband was faithful. I knew guys and how they acted, or I thought I did.

Once I had changed, I decided to drive my Mustang back to the office on the assumption it would be raining by the time I needed to return home for the evening. Sometime even I can make a good decision.

It already was three o'clock by the time I removed my coat and sat behind my desk. I had changed into a pair of slacks, but had left on the casual shirt.

Janet came to my door and asked. "Lunch with the new girl, how'd it go?"

"Not good," I smiled. "I found out she wasn't after my body, just my brain."

Janet broke out into uncontrolled laughter. "She's aiming really low then," she managed to choke out before more laughter.

I just shook my head. Janet continued laughing. I had to bite my lip to keep from breaking out in laughter myself. What a card Janet was. I tried to feign indignation, but she just waved it off. Slowly we regained our composure, through Janet had to wipe the tears from her eyes.

I looked at the printouts set before me and acknowledged to Janet that we could proceed with the work. The sky had darkened by now, though no rain seemed imminent. I preferred sunshine, as it brightened my mood, but I'd muddle through what remained of the afternoon somehow.

I realized I was fidgety and didn't quite know why. I didn't thought it was something I ate. Maybe it was the scenario laid out before me by Katie. I had to give that some thought and see if I could get my head around it. My legal training caused me to approach things analytically. If she had told me a fairy tale, how would I deal with that? How *could* I deal with that?

I would have to try, though. I had given my commitment. Shit, how could I have been so stupid? Then I briefly reflected on the scenario. A woman I barely knew, whom I had known when we were children, asked me to lunch. She asked me to help her check up on her husband, whom I had never met. The man was distant and uncommunicative, but she thought he still loved her and wasn't playing around. She thought a lot of things, but she had nothing concrete to offer.

I shook my head. Why hadn't she just hired a competent private investigator? That would have been the smart thing to do. Of course, I could have pushed her in that direction but I hadn't. Why not? Because I was stupid.

I gave the matter a few more minutes thought, and the longer I sat there staring at the gloom outside, the more I began to fear my answer. Could it be I wanted to see Katie again? Did I harbor feelings for her that my childish dreams had conjured up years ago? I hated to keep harping on that subject, but it seemed to be true. Was Katie the rebound woman after my disastrous affair last summer? Only time would tell. I shook my head in disgust. What was I thinking to say I would help? What could I do now to salvage the situation?

~6~

GOOD NEIGHBOR MIKE

WHEN THE AFTERNOON RAIN finally came, it was no surprise since the sky had been growing ominous for the previous several minutes. What surprised me, though, was the intensity of the rain once it began. Blustery winds drove heavy raindrops against the office's plate glass windows in a loud staccato. At first I thought it might be hailing, the rain impacted so loudly. Maybe there was something to the discussion about climate change.

Leaving my sanctuary behind my desk and standing in front of the window, I had a sense of being trapped inside a giant carwash, while huge sheets of water cascaded down the expansive glass. I walked closer to the partition to look up at the threatening sky. A loud clap of thunder caused me to flinch. I saw no lightning flash, though. Perhaps the worst of the storm had now passed by, moving behind us and to the east. Yet, I could see no further than ten feet into the remaining gloom, the sky was so dark and moisture laden. I watched the heavy runoff flow across the blacktop outside. This definitely would bring up the lake level if it rained this hard throughout the watershed.

Glancing at my watch, I wondered if Katie had made it home before the storm struck. I imagined it might have gotten pretty wild out on the water for a bit. I considered calling her before deciding she should have made it home safely. It would only have been about a twenty-minute cruise from Excelsior to her place. She would have motored past Big Island, through the Narrows and on to Howard's Point. The mate could have opened the throttle on that big boat and roared across the water. Whether he got the boat back to safe harbor after that before it rained was another matter.

36

Looking off to the right, I saw a swelling pond where the street had been. The huge grated drain must have been temporarily overwhelmed. Our front entrance appeared to be safe, although I wouldn't want to be in the vicinity of the alley where the drain was. The water there could be as much as three feet deep, with a pretty good vortex over the drain. That was enough depth to stall any car that might try to get through.

I went back to my desk. The rain soon began to abate, yielding to a soft drizzle. Nonetheless, there went my golf game. With so much rain having come that fast and heavy, the course would now have several small lakes not previously there, and I was not going to play in hip boots. I felt confident the greens keeper wouldn't want golfers stomping and tramping on the soggy greens, anyway. I sighed. I was just getting into summer form, and now I'd miss a week. I decided I'd go some night this week and drive some balls at the practice range just to get my swing in shape.

Sometime later, when it was time to head home, I bid good night to Janet and rushed out to where I had left my car, which was high and dry. I hardly got damp, and since I parked in an underground garage below my place, I was relatively dry entering my living quarters. Once home I decided to change clothes and drive out to the Shorewood Center to exercise. I would not miss my workout after all. This is one of those few occasions when I did need my car, though I could make it a one-mile bike ride. Not today though. Not in the rain.

I arrived at Snap Fitness just before six and my timing couldn't have been worse since it once again was raining hard as I pulled into the parking lot. I couldn't find a nearby parking spot, so I waited in my vehicle, hoping the downpour would subside. Looking about my vehicle's interior, I was unable find the umbrella supposed to be in there. I must have left it in the house. That certainly was a good place for it. Oh, well. Stupid is as stupid does.

When the onslaught seemed to have eased up somewhat, I dashed for the door with a towel over my head. Damp all over, once inside I felt the full effect of the air-conditioning, which appeared to be on full blast. Suddenly I felt chilled. Life does have its inconveniences. I would have to heat up with my regimen.

I did an hour on the elliptical machine, listening to my iPod. I finished very tired, but I felt good, if that makes any sense. I was hot and sweaty, so now the air-conditioning was more welcome.

When I had left the club, it didn't appear much warmer outside than in the air conditioning. A cool front must have passed. At least the humidity level had dropped. Perhaps that was what I felt. That was Minnesota for you. If you didn't like the weather, wait five minutes and it would change. The skies probably would be clear tonight. A great night for stargazing.

I drove home through soggy streets, and went down onto the dock to check my boat. Even with canvas covers on, some water was going to seep in. The back cover tended to dip in the middle and collect water. That was why I stuck a pole in the middle under the cover. The cover looked like a tent, but it shed water.

Unzipping the back cover, I saw no water on the back deck, but I reached inside and turned on the power key. Then I turned on the sump pump. It spit water for a few second and then ran dry. Good. That had been working. It never hurt to be safe.

My boat is a twenty-three-foot Chris Craft Catalina outfitted with a 300-horsepower Yamaha outboard. It has a center console. It had a canvas canopy strung within stainless tubing for shade. My craft couldn't hold a candle to Katie's yacht, but it was pretty special to me. I used it mainly for fishing, but it cleaned up quite easily when I needed it for those romantic cruises about the lake.

Being reassured the boat was okay, I closed everything up and headed back up to my place. As I was climbing up to my deck, I heard a shout from next door. "Mr. Connelly . . . Mike, could you help me?"

I looked around the partition over toward the adjacent unit and saw Sherrill Thompson through a partially open patio door. I wondered what was going on? I was sweaty and stinky and not dressed fittingly for anything but a workout. I was certainly not fit for company, thus I hesitated.

"Please," she pleaded.

I resigned myself to at least find out what was wrong and approached her, conscious of my appearance. "Hi, Sherrill, what's up? Sorry how I look. I'm just coming from a workout at the health club."

"You look fine, Mike." She pointed at her patio door. "See, I can't get this damn door closed, and it's been raining in on the carpet the last two hours. My carpet's all wet here. When I called the maintenance company, they said they'd be out tomorrow morning first thing. I don't want it raining in all night. Plus animals might get in."

Sherrill appeared to have been crying. Her eyes were red and glistened, so I hesitated to suggest she just close the screen. I didn't think that would mollify her. Keeping critters out wasn't her only worry. Security also could be an issue. And more rain. Where was her hubby?

She and her husband had lived in their place since the previous November, though I hadn't seen much of them. Moving in during the middle of winter generally did not invite camaraderie, and I hadn't been very socially oriented during those winter months myself. So few tenants here used their front doors, I seldom saw anyone that way. It usually was in the garage where I might run into someone. I'd bumped into Sherrill's husband that way a couple of times, but I didn't remember his name.

Looking over the situation, I quickly saw that the door was hanging kiddywampus. It was open wide enough for me to slip through, so I shed my shoes and entered the room. The bottom wheels had come off the track. There was no danger of the door falling into the room as long as the upper wheels were in place, so I checked that right away and was relieved to find them still in place.

Having the bottom wheels come off the track had happened to my door once, and I had fixed it myself without too much trouble. It was relatively easy for someone strong enough to lift the door. I had used a heavy twelve-inch screwdriver to pry the door up and hold it in position while I had maneuvered the bottom wheels back onto the track.

I looked over Sherrill's situation and saw it could be fixed without too much bother. Why not then play the hero?

"Sherrill, let me get my tools. Meanwhile, why don't you get some towels for the carpet. Maybe you have something I can stand on without soiling the carpet. Wet carpet picks up all kinds of crap."

The woman stood nearby, her fragrance floating over to me. She held her hand clasped together under her chin. She said, "Okay, Mike.

I'll do that. Thanks. I really appreciate you helping." She sniffled and I turned to go.

I then went home by way of the deck, dug through my toolbox and found my large screwdriver, a pair of channel locks, a small block of wood, and gloves. I also threw on a clean pair of shorts and an old sweatshirt. Then I slapped on cologne, so I wouldn't stink up her place. With my hardware in tow, I returned by way of our decks. I was barefoot, but at least my feet were clean, and I'd create a minimum of a mess with my efforts.

The door fix took only about five minutes. I had Sherrill pull her curtains all the way to the other end and out of the way. Then I set the wood block next to the bottom rail and used it as a fulcrum with the large screwdriver as the lever. With one hand as high up on the glass as possible to steady the door, I pried up the right end and popped the bottom wheels onto the floor rail. The upper trolley remained in place. Good. Then I repeated the procedure on the other end of the door.

I felt good. Neither upper trolley had come off. I stood, relieved.

I flexed my back. "How'd it happen?" I asked.

Sherrill looked toward the floor with a sheepish expression. "I opened the door too hard. When it hit the end, it fell off," she murmured. "I tried to move it but . . ."

I realized she must have shoved it pretty hard, but did not think I should ask any questions.

Sherrill looked awkward and vulnerable. Not wanting to make her feel worse, I laughed aloud and boisterously. When she looked up at me with a shocked expression, I said, "I've wanted to do that myself a few times." Her mouth curved up into a slight grin.

I previously had speculated that the woman was about thirty years old. She had no children I knew of. She wasn't a large woman but was heavy hipped. Previously I'd noticed that her walk was enticing. I had once heard her walk described as "her giddy up had a hitch in it." I thought that perfectly described her movement. She was fun to watch.

I got my mind back on the subject at hand. "Something must have made you angry," I casually suggested.

She hesitated, and then said, "I talked to that deadbeat husband of mine. He's making things difficult. He infuriates me."

Before my brain kicked in, my mouth said, "Why?"

I instantly felt foolish for intruding, but the scuttlebutt I'd heard about her husband was that he'd apparently begun to play around. That was the gossip anyway. I hadn't paid any attention to it until now. It must have been true.

She answered me by saying, "I asked him to move out. He was . . . well, he was fooling around."

So she'd given him the ultimatum to stop it or get out. He'd gotten out. Good for her, though I couldn't figure out why he'd do what he did. She was easy to look at. Brown, curly hair, parted in the center and just reaching her jaw line. A round face, big eyes, and full lips. She looked a little Irish. Besides, she had that come-hither look in her eyes. I guess they call them bedroom eyes. If she wasn't married . . .

Sherrill shifted her weight from one foot to the other. I watched her hips, then said, "Do you have an attorney?"

"Yes."

"Let me suggest you do your talking through him. Less aggravation for you."

She agreed.

"We have to do something about this carpet," I said. "It has to dry out or you'll get mold."

Now Sherrill looked concerned. I could see she had no answer so I asked, "Do you have a hair dryer?"

"Yes."

"Can you get that and a small frying pan?"

She looked puzzled, but responded, "Um . . . okay."

I used my screwdriver to pry up a bit of carpet, which I grabbed with the channel locks. Then I opened about a three-foot length of carpet and pad and supported it in the middle with the wood block I'd used previously. When Sherrill returned, I laid the pan half under the carpet angled against the glass. Then I put the hair dryer into the pan with the snout shoved under the carpet. The pan should insulate the heat of the dryer motor from burning anything. Then I turned on the switch to low and plugged in the dryer. The fan spooled up and gave out a constant whine.

"There," I said. "This'll blow warm air under the carpet and dry out the backing and the pad. The top will dry easily. Leave it go until the maintenance man comes tomorrow. See if he'll put the carpet back. If he won't, I'll stop over and do it tomorrow night."

"Gee, thanks, Mike. You're real handy."

I smiled at her and gathered my things together.

"Would you like a glass of wine before you go?" She had taken my elbow into her hand.

The idea sounded good to me, but I was a mess. "Look, Sherrill, I just got back from a workout. I'm pretty stinky and need a shower."

"That's okay. Take one here."

I looked into her beckoning eyes. We showered together until the hot water ran out.

~7~

LOOKING FOR A PLAN

I WOKE THE FOLLOWING MORNING feeling strangely euphoric, which had not been the case the previous evening. After returning from Sherrill's house and disposing of my dirty clothes, I had stood before the bathroom mirror and done a self-examination as I studied my reflection. Outwardly I'd been in need of a shave, but that wasn't what had concerned me the most. I had appeared okay on the outside. It was what was inside that had caused me consternation. I was concerned I'd taken advantage of the situation with Sherrill Thompson.

Though I hadn't been the aggressor, since she had come on to me, I understood the situation . . . knew she had been vulnerable. No question that lately she'd been having a tough time with her husband. I knew that. What should I have done under the circumstances, run away? I was a full-blooded male and couldn't just ignore women, could I?

Then I got my head on straight and decided I was getting too moral for my own good. The woman should have been thankful I was able to help her with her broken door. If and how she had wanted to thank me was her business.

I wanted to fire up a stogie outside, but felt strangely uneasy about running into Sherrill. Thus, I hung by my door hoping she'd slept in this morning. Maybe I was ashamed, after all, of my actions last night.

Looking out over Excelsior Bay, I realized how lucky I was to live in such circumstances. I had lived in the Excelsior area my entire life, most recently enjoying both the quiet suburban life and the festivity that often accompanied weekends. It was a nice combination. The town was well known in the Twin Cities area and had a storied history. Steel rails that once snaked through the village in yesteryear had some time ago yielded to a well-used recreational trail, though in the heyday of casual living, several daily trains marked the Lake Minnetonka area as a resort destination.

That period would have been a sight to see. Ladies decked out in their summer finery with delicate parasols to protect their fair skin; men in lightweight suits strutting along the lakefront, sporting spats and straw hats. It must have been a grand time for the well-heeled gentry.

Back in the resort's heyday whole families had flocked to the lake area for weeks on end to enjoy summers promising milder temperatures and lower humidity than in the visitor's hometowns. Most guests were from sweltering regions far to the south, but there were plenty of visitors from the East, as well as a few all the way from Europe. Lake Minnetonka indeed had been the place to be in the summertime.

Oddly, in my perusal of the town's history, I seldom saw mention of our state bird, the mosquito. Perhaps its presence back then simply was taken for granted, or maybe our variety was smaller than that which had been left behind by those intrepid travelers.

Grand hotels, many along the railroads, had been scattered about the lake, and streetcar boats ferried passengers over the water between destinations. One boat, the *Minnehaha*, remained yet today, having been raised from the lake bottom in 1980 and restored by a group of volunteers working with the Museum of Lake Minnetonka. Boat enthusiasts would appreciate that legacy for years to come thanks to those worthy volunteers.

From the deck of my home, I was able see the *Minnehaha* moored across from me at a dock on the waters of Excelsior Bay. During the summer season, she had a regular schedule of sailings on weekends. I could recommend the ride to anyone who would enjoy the lake experience.

I still remembered being on hand for that first public voyage in 1996. It had been quite an emotional moment for many of us in the community. I was told her restoration took almost six years, lots of money, and many hands. She had been built in 1906. After years of service she had been deliberately sunk in 1926. Apparently that was how they got rid of unwanted material back in those days, just sank it in the lake. I was amazed that after lying fifty years in the mud, the restorers were able to accomplish what it did with the wreck. It truly had been a grand effort.

I looked at my watch and saw it was time to head out. Going back indoors, I grabbed my lunch and put on my coat. Then I was out the door to work. It was a nice morning. It took me just a couple of minutes to cover the short distance to the office.

When I wasn't enjoying my boat on this fourteen-thousand-acre majestic lake, I practiced law, with most of my work being for insurance companies, banks, and realtors. My office had no need for public exposure. It was accessed by way of the municipal parking lot.

The parking lot was mostly empty at this time of the morning, except for Mondays when scattered debris was left behind by weekend visitors. That untidiness was a cross to bear for the inflow of funds into the local economy from our short-term guests and generally was cleaned up quickly.

My office facade had an abundance of glass. Once the sun moved around to the west, my place was bright and cheery. I appreciated that especially in the winter months. We had blinds for days when the sun was too intense and could overpower our decrepit cooling system.

After arriving at my door, I lingered outside a couple of minutes, enjoying the remnants of my Tobascos Baez stogie. The cigar was made in Nicaragua and had become an old habit of mine. I originally became acquainted with them in my youth while doing a six-month college foreign studies semester through an exchange program with Augsburg University. Janet Brown, my partner in crime, didn't appreciate the cigar smell indoors, and I complied with her wishes.

After a couple of minutes standing in the shade, I began feeling a chill. It was remarkable what a difference there was between standing here in the shade and being in the sun on my deck. I shrugged. Soon the sun would be spreading its magic here as well. I dropped my stub onto the pavement and crushed it out with my foot. Then I picked up the remnant and carried it inside.

Surprisingly, I was first into the office this morning. Janet beat me nine days out of ten, so today I could gloat. Good thing I remembered my key fob. After opening the window blinds, I started the coffee pot. The coffee was easy to make since we used the prepackaged coffee packets. Neither of us drank much, but what would an office be without the smell of fresh brewed beans?

Janet would stop by the post office and pick up the mail, such as it was, since she drove to work. We didn't get a whole lot of mail since most everything we did now was electronic. If everyone was like us, it was no wonder the postal service was in trouble.

Janet was not an attorney, but still she was my partner in this practice. She worked hard and deserved to share in the profits. I could only spend so much money anyway. My lifestyle was set, my wants were few and simple, and I was not about to change. I had the diploma; she had the street smarts and the work ethic. We made a good team.

I had practiced law in Excelsior for thirteen years, while Janet and I had worked together for seven. Her children were raised, and she enjoyed this opportunity to be useful. Never slim, Janet maintained her full-body look for as long as I'd known her, which was many years.

Janet liked to keep her hair short, favoring perms. She apparently colored her dirty-blond curls because there was no hint of gray. There was a smile, however, on that round face, and a quick wit to accompany it. Her smile generally brought a twinkle to her hazel eyes, opening a window to her personality. To me she looked like everyone's grandmother should look. But it was important not to let looks fool you. It was well not to underestimate Janet.

Now me, I was entirely a different story. Pushing forty, I had been lucky to avoid needing to color my hair, nor had I begun to lose any. Both the dark-brown, wavy hair up top and my well-trimmed mustache were full and natural. I looked at my reflection in the office window; I was tall, dark but maybe less than handsome. I laughed at myself. Maybe rugged was the word?

Once Janet arrived, we relaxed and discussed our respective evenings over a cup of coffee.

"So, handsome, bed any beauties lately?" Janet wasn't known for her subtlety. She managed to keep a straight face.

I wasn't sure if she was referring to Katie or if somehow she'd found out about Sherrill. I decided to remain coy. "Not so lucky. You need to do some recon for me."

"I can do the recon, but you'd just chase them away. Girls around here are too sophisticated for you. Plus, they like good-looking guys."

I laughed. "No doubt, no doubt."

Then I meditated, my tongue working the inside of my cheek. "Not so easy meeting girls at my age," I mused.

Janet nodded, pursing her lips. Then she patted the back of her hair with one hand. Nodding, she said. "I suppose not. I mean a person has to work at it a little more, I guess. Make oneself available. Let folks know you want to meet people."

I thought about how I'd hid in exclusion the previous winter and was nodding agreement as she spoke. "I think on some level I know that. I mean, high school grads are way too young for a man my age and college girls seem to match up before graduation. All that's around are retreads."

My statement brought a grin to Janet's face. She said, "You mean like you?"

"Yeah. Like me," I said dejectedly.

Janet perked up. She pointed a finger at me. "Hey, buddy boy. There are some nice ladies out there. You just have to look harder. Sitting home in your darkened room won't find them."

The truth hurt and a wave of depression enveloped me like a heated blanket. I bit my lower lip and squirmed in my seat.

Janet interjected, "Maybe I'll have to fix you up. I have this friend with a tremendous personality . . ." She barely got the statement out before laughing.

"Whoa. Stay away from me with the personality girls. I'm not that desperate."

We both laughed. Then we got down to business. Part of that discussion turned toward impending deadlines. Then we dug in and went to work. She handled the mail, then printed out and dealt with emails.

In our discussion, Janet had reminded me that this coming Friday was the annual firefighters fundraiser dance. We had received a booklet of tickets, and I had written a check to cover the expense. That would go out in today's mail. I took one ticket for myself and gave the rest to Janet to do with as she chose.

The office was utilitarian, but was bright and cheery, thanks to Janet. Last winter she insisted we brighten things up, so we painted the walls an off-white. It made a real difference. I was glad she had insisted. During that endeavor we'd had a few hilarious moments, usually caused by my ineptness. Maybe that was supposed to be therapy for me.

My office space was partitioned off from the main area, while Janet commanded the remainder of the interior. A door blocked off my office, if desired, but two interior walls were glass from three feet up. A small reception area up front faced the parking lot.

In my office I had a large picture on each of the two solid walls depicting the latest Air Force jet fighters, gifts from a friend of mine in Colorado who I had helped out on an art fraud case the previous year. They were purchased at the Air Force Academy near Colorado Springs. I enjoyed them immensely.

About mid-morning I began to sag. I leaned back in my chair and closed my eyes. I tried to clear my head of everything not concerning work, but yesterday's visit with Katie slipped into my head. That was a pretty nice boat she had. I wondered what I'd do with a craft like that? It wouldn't be much good for anything other than a party boat. *I think I will keep what I have.* I laughed as I thought of fishing in that monstrosity.

I reflected on the thrust of Katie's request for a couple of minutes but couldn't find an easy solution to her dilemma or for that matter even a plan of attack. I shook my head. Whatever had possessed me to get involved? Had I been thinking with my dick? It had been my whole adolescent approach to her request for a visit. My youthful fantasies had overwhelmed logical thinking. Instead of taking a thoughtful, rational approach to the situation, I'd blundered on in without thought to the consequences. Big hero. Now look what it had got me. I said I'd do something. The only thing I'd be able to accomplish would be to make an ass of myself.

I ran my fingers through my hair and smiled as my thoughts turned once again to my rendezvous with Sherrill. What was I thinking there? Well. Of course she was sexy and available. Dawh. Maybe it had been a response to the pent-up fixation with Katie. I hoped not. Sex through proxy. Not a good idea.

I went back to work, but the issue with Katie kept reoccurring in my thoughts. Finally, about eleven o'clock, I looked up and found Janet in my doorway. I was startled, as I must have been daydreaming.

"What's up?" I asked.

"That's what I'd like to know."

My expression must have revealed my confusion because she said, "You've been staring out the window half the morning. What's going on?"

Now I felt guilty. There was no point trying to keep anything from Janet; she'd eventually wheedle it out of me anyway. I said, "I'm stumped as to how to help on this Williams deal. I don't even know where to begin."

"Talk to me."

I gave Janet a brief outline of what I was up against.

Janet stood leaning against the door jamb for a few moments thinking, and then said, "Why don't you look the bank up on the Internet? You know Google it. There's bound to be a lot of information there. At least it'd give you an idea what you're dealing with. Then too you could go to the *Star Tribune* website and search Orion Bank. That'd give you any newspaper articles they may have run. There's bound to be a ton of public information available."

"That's a good idea, Janet. At least I'd learn something about the organization."

"Yes, you would. But do it on your own time. You're still planning to go on that fishing trip, aren't you?"

"Yes."

"Only if you have your work done." Janet said that while giving me a stern look and shaking her finger at me.

"You sound like my mother," I retorted. But she was right. I had been suitably chastised.

I typed in Orion Bank of Minnesota to my search engine and got three pages of possible search sites.

Janet looked over my shoulder. "See, I told you. You'll find out everything there is to know about the bank and the people involved," Janet quipped.

"Looks that way," I said. I signed off and went back to work.

Janet went back to her desk and I thought briefly about what I'd found. I still didn't know what I'd do with the information, but I decided to educate myself first and then make a decision. There was bound to be something there to lead me somewhere. Something, anything, because as of right then I had nothing.

And if there was nothing, the worst that could happen was I would tell Katie I was unable to help her. I said I'd try. I never promised any results. Then too there was that name thing. The girl I had known as Katie had become Katherine. Was that some sort of social thing? Katie was not sophisticated enough; it had to be Katherine? I decided it was not my place to pass judgment. I'd better get used to calling Katie by her new moniker, Katherine, at least to her face.

~8~

SOMEBODY NEW

THE WEEK DRIFTED ALONG. Friday night I attended the Firehouse dance. I drank a little too much beer, which caused me to sleep late on Saturday morning. As a result, I decided not to go out on the lake fishing as I had planned. Normally I would have left before six, but because of the dance, my buddy and I had decided eight would be plenty early this time around. When I called Jack Benson to say I was unable to make it, he sounded relieved. I remembered he'd had a pretty good time the previous evening, himself.

With nothing else planned for this morning, I decided to do some research on Orion. I ate a hearty breakfast to settle my stomach, then spent two hours online reading various websites. What I learned was that I was not knowledgeable enough to glean any insight from the information presented. Sure there was plenty there. Golly, they had their whole balance sheet posted, but what could I do with that? I was sure if anything was problematic, it would be buried.

Because of my realization I was feeling a little down in the dumps. I wished I'd never told Katie I would help. As I reflected on the subject, I stood staring out at the lake. I had made the commitment, though, so I'd have to make some attempt to follow through. I had made some sort of attempt, at least, though it had got me nowhere. I was just not knowledgeable enough in this area to be able to glean anything from the outside looking in.

Perhaps the whole thing with their relationship was related to sex anyway. I'd end up spinning my wheels, and in the end I'd find out the guy was sleeping around on her. That was probably the case nine times out of ten. Then a picture of that lovely woman came to mind, and I thought why would he? She was a beautiful woman. Seemed to be in great shape. She was well-educated, respected in the community. Why would he cheat on her? I had no answers.

Well, if I were going to help, I needed someone smarter than I was to show me the way. That might very well be Bob Lindgren, president of the Bank of Excelsior. The bank, new to the community, had formed four years earlier by a group of local businessmen who no longer wanted to deal with large banking institutions. I put up a few grand and owned a few shares and also sat on the board. That was probably why Katie thought I might know something, which I did not.

I called Bob at the bank. Not surprisingly, he was working this Saturday morning. After explaining what I was looking for, we agreed to meet at my place Monday night at six for a drink. I would see what happened next. I felt a little bad because I had not told Bob the whole truth. Was that a euphemism for lying? Anyway, I didn't want to talk about Katie, so I said I had a friend who wanted to buy stock in Orion. I asked Bob if it would be a good deal?

With that concern off my shoulders, I decided to go for a walk. It was a beautiful sunny day, and I was not about to get trapped any longer indoors. But first I decided I'd better eat something more, since my stomach was still doing flip-flops from the night before. Maybe it would settle down with more food in it. Then I might put in a load of laundry. That could run while I was gone. At least I was good at planning.

After I finished those chores, I put on my sneakers and began walking down to the Commons. This parkland located to the north of me comprised several acres of open land held in trust by the city. It was quite a jewel.

Activity all along the lakeshore started just past my place. The sidewalk was crowded, and groups of people were scattered all over the green space. Bar B Q grills were smoking and picnickers were enjoying the beautiful summer day.

Further along I saw that the ball field was occupied. The game announcers were perched on top of the concession stand calling the action. Apparently a softball tournament was scheduled for this weekend, and I decided to stay and watch several innings of a game already in progress. The breeze was blowing in off the water, which made it comfortable for us spectators to sit and enjoy the activity, but the same breeze made it more difficult for the batters to reach the outfield fences.

After a while, I got up and climbed over the hill behind the bleachers to walk towards the beach. That had to be busy on such a pristine day, and I wanted to see what was shaking there. On the near corner a mobile stand was selling all kinds of refreshment, which I reluctantly passed by. The popcorn smelled terrific, but I wasn't going to work out for an hour to account for one guilty treat.

The tennis courts also were active this afternoon, as was the playground equipment. Numerous loud children ran about under the watchful eye of a parent or guardian. When I passed by that area and reached the beach, around the point facing Gideon Bay, I found it nearly overwhelmed with bodies, with nary a square yard of vacant sand available to me. Umbrellas staked out valuable territory and lent shade to some of the occupants. Toddlers sat at the water's edge constructing their temporary monuments.

The water looked inviting, with plenty of people splashing and playing together in the cordoned off area. I managed to find a spot to sit on the sand and relaxed, enjoying the sun for about an hour. This was a great people watching location, and I saw plenty of bare skin to watch.

I had neglected to bring water with me, and before long I became thirsty. Feeling overheated, I got up and brushed at the sand clinging to my legs. It wasn't easy removing damp sand from all that hair. A hot shower would have to aid me with that when I got home. I could go in the water, but then I'd have soggy feet for the walk home. No, I would deal with the sand later.

Beginning my journey home, I had intended to take a different route, just to do more sightseeing. A house being remodeled along Linwood Avenue, and I wanted to see how that work was progressing.

As I passed by the playground, I noted fewer children playing on the equipment than earlier. Nap time, I guessed. It really was a nice day; too bad they had to nap indoors. I recalled the forecast had been for highs in the low eighties, and it had to be near that now. What a day!

Before I had traveled much further, I heard someone calling. "Excuse me. Can you help me?"

At first it didn't register that someone was speaking to me. Then I looked around to see who might be talking and to whom. A woman off to my right stood next to her open car door with an anxious look on her face. She was looking directly at me.

I couldn't see anyone else nearby, so I responded, "Yes. Can I help you?"

The woman was young, maybe twenty something. Short in stature, no more than five-foot-two, she had a beautiful head of red hair. I wondered if that was natural or if it came from a bottle? I had not seen many redheads around town. Her hair was somewhat windblown and her fair skin was tinted with color from the sun, at least what I could see on her face and arms.

The young lady took a step toward me, walking around her open car door. "I was wondering if you maybe could help me?"

Her question refocused my attention. "What seems to be the trouble?" I answered in my friendliest tone.

"I'm not sure. I mean my car won't start. Is there a service garage near here? I'm new here and not sure who to call."

Red had a cute, turned up nose, and nice cheekbones. Her bare skin was covered with sunscreen. I could see it glisten.

I took a step toward her, careful not to invade her space. "It won't start you say?"

"No."

"Maybe the battery's dead. Want me to try?"

I thought maybe a battery cable might have come loose or was corroded. I wasn't sure what I could accomplish, since I did not know much of anything about cars. It was just something about a woman in trouble. They were so vulnerable.

The woman hesitated. "I don't know. Do you know anything about cars?"

"Not much about Audis, but I'm willing to take a look."

The woman was dressed in blue cutoff shorts and a white top with spaghetti straps. Colorful straps clung beneath the thin, white ones. She wore tennis shoes. It was obvious she had been at the beach and had thrown clothes on over her bathing suit.

"I guess it'd be all right," she said hesitantly.

She stepped back out of the way as if afraid to be too close to me, and I approached the driver side door in as much of a non-threatening way as possible.

"Does it turn over?"

"I can't get the key to turn," she replied.

A thought struck me. Before I climbed into the car, I looked at the front wheels. They were turned about fifteen degrees to the left. She had pulled into the parking space at an angle and left the wheels turned.

I entered the car and tried the key. She was right; it wouldn't turn. I wiggled it in and out slightly to make sure the key set was not getting sloppy. No. It wouldn't turn. With my left hand on the wheel, I pulled it slightly to the right until I heard a click. Then I tried the key. It turned and the engine fired up.

I looked toward the woman. Her face expressed first shock and then pleasure. "What did you do?" she yelled excitedly through the partly open door.

"Just some of the Connelly magic."

I climbed out of the front seat and reached out my hand. "I'm Michael Connelly, local superhero."

The woman began to laugh, but took my hand. I'm Sandra. Sandra Grose."

"Well, Sandra, I think you're okay here. If it happens again, just turn the wheel a bit. Without getting technical, there's a stop you were turned up against. Turn the wheel a bit and it releases so the ignition can engage.

"Thanks a lot. I was imaging a tow and a large repair bill."

"Luckily for you not today."

"Were you leaving the beach?" she asked.

I nodded. "Heading home. I've had enough sun. I have a load of laundry in the washer to deal with."

"Domesticated guy huh?"

"I smiled. "Hardly. It's either that or take it to the professionals. I only do that with my shirts. They're too hard to iron."

She smiled—a beautiful smile at that.

"Are you walking?" she asked.

"Yes."

"Do you have far to go?"

"Just a few blocks."

"Then I'll give you a ride."

"Don't bother. I enjoy the walk."

"I'm sure you do, but it's no bother, and I'd enjoy your company. I do owe you something for getting me out of a jam."

I shrugged and said, "Okay." There was no point in arguing on such a pleasant day.

I got in on the passenger side, since I didn't believe she was going to kidnap me.

"Put on your seatbelt. I'm a stickler for that."

I did as commanded. I would have anyway but saw no point in making an issue out of it. This woman had a commanding presence and spoke her mind. That was different from a lot of women I knew.

"Are you visiting us here?" I asked.

"No. I live here now."

"Oh, really. What does 'now' mean?"

"I'm staying at the apartments by Christmas Lake. It is Christmas Lake isn't it?"

"That's right."

"I bought a house here in town, but it'll be another month before I close. Which way do I go?"

"Do you know where the liquor store is?"

"Yes."

"Head for that."

She looked at me funny. "You going to try and get me drunk?"

I laughed at that. She had a sense of humor.

As she turned left onto West Lake Street, thin wispy clouds momentarily crossed the sun, dimming the sky slightly. Sandra wasn't running her air, so I opened the window and rested my arm on the frame.

"Do you work near here then?" I asked.

"Yes. Right in town at that professional building on Second Street. You know it?"

"Yes. Really?" I wondered what she did there.

"Yes," she answered.

"What doing?"

"I'm a dentist."

"A dentist," I replied. "That's swell."

There was a lot of traffic along the lakeshore this time of the day. I probably could have walked as fast as we were traveling, but then I would not have had the pleasant company.

A couple of minutes later I indicated a good spot to pull over. Sandra pulled to the curb in front of the dry cleaners on Lake Street, and I thanked her for the ride.

Turning toward her, I said. "I'd love to show you around sometime."

"Sure. Let's do that sometime."

"Then, how about tomorrow afternoon. I'll pack a picnic lunch and we'll take a boat ride. I'll show you some of the sights. I'll bring the wine. Do you prefer white or red?"

She thought momentarily. "Probably white."

Okay, I'll pick you up."

"That's not necessary. I'll drive over."

"Then you'll probably have to park over by your office."

She nodded. "Where do I go?"

"Oh, right. I'm across the street in 116." I pointed. "Say about four?"

"Aye, aye, sir. See you at four."

I closed the car door, and Sandra drove off.

I went inside and decided to take my shower. But first I threw the damp clothes into the dryer and started another load. When I was cleaned up, I felt better.

I went down and fixed myself a scotch and sat out on the deck with it. The sun had gone back around to the other side of the building, and it felt comfortably cool next to the water. I lit up a cigar and put my feet up. There was no one outside next door, so I did not have that to avoid, in case I had wanted to.

In fact, I had not seen Sherrill Thompson since I left her on Tuesday night. Had I really wanted to avoid her? Of that I wasn't certain. The other night was great, but . . . I didn't think she was looking for any commitment. She was vulnerable, and I wasn't about to mislead her. I think she worked a day job, though. That was pretty bad, live next door to someone and not even know them well enough to know what they did. I had no idea what her husband did either.

My thoughts turned to my run in with Sandra. It obviously wasn't planned, but she ended up offering me a ride. What was up with that? Just being polite, I guess. She looked young, though. She had to be at least ten years younger than I ws, maybe more. So what? It wasn't a date. I was just showing the gal around. Then I thought about fate. If I had not had so much beer last night at the dance, I would have gone fishing as planned. If I had gone fishing, I wouldn't have met Sandra. Was this something ordained by the gods? The thought left me with a creepy feeling.

I paused at what I was doing and reflected on Sunday afternoon. Now what did I want to bring on the boat? I had no idea what she did or did not eat. I should have asked. That would have been the polite thing to do. I didn't have her number, so I was out of luck calling to ask. I would have to take a chance. If I brought sandwiches, would she eat them? No way to know for sure. Cheese and crackers might be nice. Add a little chunk of meat and a nice loaf of Italian bread. Maybe some chocolate for dessert?

I set my drink down, retrieved my wallet and proceeded to walk across the street to the liquor store. The street was full of traffic, but I waited for a break and hustled across. Every checkout was busy, and the aisles were crowded. Beer appeared to be the preferred choice of the discerning weekend visitor. It appeared that most if not all the customers were new to town. That was great for the local economy.

Eventually I caught the eye of one of the storekeepers. He knew me and helped me select a bottle of Santa Margarita Pinot Grigio, and a bottle of Chateau San Michelle White Riesling for dessert. I had glasses at home, so I was set. I carefully negotiated the traffic so as to not jeopardize my package and placed the wine in the refrigerator. I would grocery shop for the rest of what I needed in the morning. Better yet, we could boat over to Wayzata tomorrow and choose the cheese together at their local cheese shop.

I took my drink out of the refrigerator, plopped in some fresh ice, and went back onto the deck where I relit my cigar. That first little bit of a relight tastes skunky, but I hated to waste the remainder. It did not take long to burn through that little bit of burned tobacco. I then put my feet up onto an adjacent chair and relaxed, leaning all the way back in my chair. Smoke rings climbed above my face as I thought about the new women in my life.

Sandra, I just met. She was a young professional. Really cute too. Maybe a bit too young for this old stud. I was surprised she wanted to meet me, but I would ride that horse as long as it would carry me.

Sherrill I had known without really knowing her, though I now knew her in the biblical sense. She was in tough shape emotionally just now, and I felt a little ashamed for our coupling last week. Had I taken advantage? Perhaps not. Perhaps I could help her through a difficult time. I remembered what it had been like for me this past winter and how I had felt more alive once I had a woman to hold. It didn't have to be anything permanent, just to give her comfort.

Both those women's names begin with S. Did I have a fetish? I didn't think so, just a coincidence. Would I only date women from here on whose names began with S, or would I work through the alphabet in proper order. Good luck with X.

Katie now was the enigma, just a friend, though not even that. Yet, I was doing the most for her without even the prospect of sex involved. What a swell guy I was, a real humanitarian. I thought about what I knew of Katie's life. Then I realized I knew next to nothing.

What kind of life did a woman in her position have? She was a slave to her husband's career. That seemed apparent from what she had said to me on our one visit. I had not learned if she had interests beyond that.

Certainly she couldn't want for anything material, but did that make her happy? The saying goes that you can't buy happiness, but most people would be willing to try, especially those of us without real money.

I probably would find out a little about her life if we met some more, but for the purposes of my assignment, what more did I need to know about Katie? We would have to see about that. If I were unable to learn anything concerning Orion Bank that might aid Katie in her quest, then our next meeting might be our last.

Of the three women, Katie appeared to be the one most cut off from a support group. Like Sherrill, Katie could not depend on her husband, nor did she have a job where she might have friends or associates. That put her a head above Sherrill. At least Sherrill had a job and probably friends where she worked. Katie's husband had seen to it no one at the bank would speak with her, so she was cut off there. Then too she had not seemed to have any friends in which to confide, or else why would she have sought me out? I would have imagined a couple of close girl-friends would have been the first place to turn for advice. Perhaps she had. I had never asked and she never said. I just assumed. I was too busy mentally undressing her to ask the proper questions. Some detective I'd make. *Don't worry, Sam Spade, you'll get no competition from me.*

Then I realized that, with no contacts at the bank, Katie had no access to the accountants and attorneys who advised her husband. Where was she to turn? It was as if she were stranded alone on a deserted island. Under those circumstances, I guess it had been logical for her to turn to me. I was someone on the outside whom she perceived had knowledge of banking and could help her to find the truth.

For now, I would let things take their course and find where that led me. I just hoped it did not lead to trouble.

~9~

A BOAT RIDE

WHEN DAWN BROKE on Sunday morning, I opened the bedroom blinds to hazy sunshine and a few scattered clouds. A mild breeze rippled the surface of an otherwise empty bay. I opened my window wide and took in the sounds and smells as well as the view. The lake always looked pristine early in the morning with boats lined up along each shore like tanks ready for battle. There surely would be fishermen out this early, but they were frequenting their favorite haunts, not the wide-open water of the bay.

I turned, aware the current quiet would change all too soon. The lake would end up being crowded today, fed by an insatiable line of boats at every boat launch. It always was busy on weekends, with plenty of boats already docked on the lake, and those ramps disgorging many more. The launches would begin getting busy by nine and would stay that way until well after dark.

Looking out at our dock, I spied a neighbor puttering with his boat. He probably was readying it for later today, as I would have to do soon, though mine was pretty much prepared.

I wandered into the bathroom where I brushed my teeth and shaved. Then I slipped on a pair of shorts and came downstairs to make coffee. Putting in two scoops, I added just four cups of water. I wasn't a big coffee drinker on weekends.

I stood and daydreamed while watching the ebony water slowly drip into the pot below, wondering about my forthcoming rendezvous. I wouldn't be at all surprised if my new acquaintance didn't show. She hadn't wanted me to call for her at her place, and neither of us had the other's phone number. What was up with that? Besides, she seemed awfully young for me. If

61

she hadn't told me she was a dentist, I might have guessed she still was in college. I could feel myself tensing. Then I stretched my neck and shoulders. That felt good.

After pouring a half-cup of coffee, I went out the front door to retrieve the Sunday paper. Momentarily standing on the front stoop, I scanned the street for activity. Nothing much yet had stirred. Returning downstairs, I was enveloped in the aromatic smell of brewed coffee, which stirred my olfactory senses and enticed me to eat something.

What was I hungry for? I decided on toast, so I made two slices. My friend Bev Johnson had made homemade jam earlier this summer and she gave me a jar of her strawberry. I decided that was what I was having on my toast today. I considered buttering the toast first, but went with just the jam. That was flavor enough. I have got to watch those excess calories.

No sense working out for nothing. I had done so well over the winter on my exercise program, I wanted to watch my calorie intake as well. I allowed just the one vice on pizza night.

Once my toast was ready, I stepped out onto the deck with the morning paper under my arm, a plate of toast in one hand and a mug of coffee in the other. I was greeted immediately by the piercing cries from a flock of seagulls stirring near the water's edge. They were flapping their wings and thrusting out their heads and beaks. At first I thought it was the sound of my screen door opening that had agitated them, but then I realized my neighbor had tossed something onto the water, causing a feeding frenzy. He stood on his boat and, looking up at me, waved. I set down my plate and waved back.

After emptying my arms, I slid the screen door closed. My chairs didn't have cushions, but were made from some synthetic material that shed water, so the overnight dew was no problem. The table was wet, however, so I had to go back inside to get a roll of paper towels. Wiping the table dry would clean it, which I would have had to do later, anyway. Finished, I looked around to see if anything else needed attention. Everything appeared to be in order for my afternoon company.

I didn't have a green thumb, so I had no flowers here on my deck, or in the house for that matter. I had considered artificial for inside, but never got around to it. For that I would have needed someone with taste to help me choose what looked good, and I never had gotten close enough to someone to impose on her for that task. Outside plants would look nice, but only for the first week or so. Then I'd forget to water them and they'd no longer would look good. I marveled at my laziness.

With my immediate chores completed, I sat to read the sport page, while working my way through the toast and coffee. It took another mug full to drain the pot, but I persevered to the end. I had spend most of the time on the sports page and then hurried through the news. I already had heard most of it anyway on the radio or TV. I would save the crossword for later.

This was a normal Sunday morning routine for me, unless I went out fishing. My activities later would be normal as well. I often entertained on my boat, so any consideration of the work ahead to prepare for my date was not daunting.

However, I felt strangely ambivalent about this date, if it was a date. I was not sure why, but maybe because I'd had such brief contact with the woman. I had seen her for what, ten minutes. That was not even enough time to lust after her. I barely could remember what she looked like. That red hair was something, though. Our encounter was so brief, I never had a chance to admire her from afar before pursuing her. Or had it been the other way around? Had she pursued me? It had been kind of a quick meeting, and then follow up engagement. I again wondered if she would show?

I had better not overthink the whole thing. Just let it play out and see what happened. At least she wasn't married, I felt fairly confidant of that since I had not seen a ring. I seemed to have gravitated to the married ones lately. Somehow they seemed safer. A fear of commitment on my part? I had better save the psychoanalysis for another time.

It was cloudier now than at sunrise. That gave me a moment's concern. It was not supposed to rain though, according to the weather gal. Some cloud cover would be welcome in the middle of the day. I was certain it was going to be a glorious afternoon.

With that thought, I returned inside where I cleaned up the kitchen, and ran the dishwasher with its bi-weekly load. After that I pulled out the vacuum and worked on the living room floors and the stairs all the way up to the second floor. I left the vacuum up in the spare bedroom to do that level sometime later, or not. After cleaning the lower bathroom, I spent a half hour in mine getting that ready to meet another week. I had a cleaning woman who came in once a week on Wednesdays, but I could never let the bathrooms go a week, especially not mine. The toilet would get awfully gross. The last thing I did in the downstairs bath was open a new air freshener. The old one was kaput.

While putting away my cleaning supplies, I realized I had not thought last night about needing crackers for the boat trip. If I were going to have cheese for snacks, I would need crackers. I checked the pantry, and found I had three different kinds, but I was uncertain how fresh they were, since they all had been opened. I decided I had better get fresh ones. We should be able to get some at the cheese shop.

Wait a minute! Were they even open on Sunday? I bet they weren't. That would be a fine kettle of fish if we motored all the way to Wayzata only to find the store was closed. How smart would I look then? My superhero status would quickly diminish.

I decided to head for the grocery store out in Shorewood, and since I was going to be out that way anyway, I chose to go next door and work out for a while. That would help get rid of my lethargy. Better yet, I could do my shopping first, then get sweaty. I got dressed in something fit for the public, threw a cooler into the trunk of my car, and headed off to the store. I couldn't make up my mind what I wanted to purchase, so I bought six kinds of cheese and four kinds of crackers. I almost forgot the Italian bread, but included that, and the chocolate, as well as a block of ice. It all went into the cooler. I needed my cooler for my fishing trip anyway, so it was just as well I dug it out and cleaned it up. I used a much smaller one for the boat.

As it was Sunday, I noticed a lot of my fellow health nuts were at church this morning. Unlike during the week, the club wasn't very busy. Consequently the resistance part of my work was done in rapid time. After ten minutes warming up on the treadmill, there was no waiting for machines. I finished with twenty minutes on the elliptical.

When I returned home, I once again put on some grubs and went down onto the dock with cleaner and paper towels. After pulling off the canvass covers from the boat, I wiped them dry and rolled them up, storing them in my port storage area. Then I spent an hour cleaning the boat. The carpeting was a little musty from being closed up for a week and from old-fish smell, so I went back up to the house and retrieved a can of carpet cleaner. I did the best I was able with what I had to work with. Then I sprayed everything with an air freshener. I believed the smell was somewhat mitigated. The sun would help freshen things after the boat was exposed for a few hours.

My craft had nice stability, and its 300-horsepower outboard had plenty of power to do almost anything. This model was fairly easy to keep clean, as it was made of molded composite material. I also use an electric trolling motor for fishing, which I kept in a stored position when not in use.

Chores completed, I had nothing to do until Sandra arrived but clean myself up. After a long and luxurious shower, I remembered to check the rest of my plug-in air fresheners. They were working. I left my upstairs windows open, so the house should be aired out.

With plenty of free time, I sat on the deck and decided to review the bank materials I had printed off the Internet. No light bulbs went off, but the task turned my thoughts to Katie. I reflected on my planned excursion later this afternoon and compared it to my luncheon aboard her boat. Talk about two different worlds. I was but a poor cousin to Katie's lifestyle.

I sat back in my chair wondering if she was happy living the way she did? She certainly had not grown up that way. I could recall the small rambler she and her three siblings had lived in. Much like mine, with one bathroom to fight over. No, she had not come from wealth, but she had it now. It was no wonder she had found it, though. She was an extremely beautiful woman and had a terrific personality. *You deserve it, Katie.* But wait, this was Sandra's day. I'd better be thinking only about her or I might find myself calling her Katie. That would be embarrassing.

At three thirty I put the cooler aboard the boat with the bottles of wine and all the cheese inside. Plastic plates, flatware, and glasses were clean and aboard. I'd even remembered napkins. Maybe they weren't linen, but paper worked. This was no sloppy affair.

My gas tank was nearly full, and the motor had been running fine. We should be all set to go. When I went back up to the house, I carried up my two life vests, which were a little old and somewhat soiled. I brought back down two new belts still in their plastic packaging that I'd purchased this spring. I stowed those under the center console. Now I was legal.

I thought I was ready to go.

When Sandra arrived, she was sporting a pair of oversized sunglasses. They reminded me of what the Hollywood gals wore. Her red hair was wavy but cropped short. I wondered what was up with that? With hair that beautiful it should be allowed to grow long and luxurious. My attention was drawn to full lips colored to compliment her hair. She was outfitted in a sundress and tennis shoes. The dress, predominately a white affair, was strapless and gathered about her bosom. It was very fetching. I had not remembered her legs from the previous encounter, but as I followed her down the stairs, I saw they were lightly tanned and shapely. Her dress swayed with the movement of her hips.

"So this is where you live?" she said, standing at the bottom of the stairs. "Can I leave this here?" She sat a large beach bag onto the floor.

"Sure."

She looked left and said, "Nice size living room you have here."

She then wandered into the kitchen. "I bet there's beer in the fridge," she said with a lilt in her voice.

I smiled. "Of course. This is a guy's pad."

"What's upstairs?" she inquired looking back up the stairs.

"Two bedrooms and a bath."

"So, a bath down here and one upstairs?"

I nodded.

"Sweet. Bigger than my current place."

Sandra was wearing two sets of studs in each ear, plain but colored. Her only other jewelry were rings on the fingers of both hands. I double-checked and saw that her fourth finger on the left hand was bare. But of course it would be or she wouldn't be here. Her red hair was held in place by a plastic band.

I looked at the bag, and quipped, "You moving in?"

She smiled and replied, "Sunscreen, hat, and a sweater."

I nodded. "We'll come off the water before it gets too cold."

"Okay."

"Ready to go?"

"Can I use your bathroom before we go?"

"Sure, right in there."

I was glad I had done a once over earlier today.

"I'm surprised," she said upon exiting the bath.

"At what?"

"The bathroom. It's not only clean, but there aren't any girlie magazines in it. And you have guest towels."

I think I was blushing when I said, "Men aren't all slobs you know."

She laughed at that and picked up her bag. I took it from her, and we walked down onto the dock where I attempted to help her into the boat. Instead, she took one leap and was aboard.

"Want me to drive?" she asked.

I laughed. "Not right away. You're my guest. It's a luxury cruise."

We sat together on the wide seat behind the steering console, our shoulders touching.

When we left the dock, I kept the motor at closed throttle, and we just crept along slowly along the near shore. I cruised past the docks for the adjacent condominiums and approached Maynard's Restaurant.

"Have you eaten here?" I asked.

"Yes. It's good. Nice place to sit and watch the lake." Then she gave me a funny look and said, "But you have a better view, don't you?"

"Yes, I really enjoy my place. I agree, though about Maynard's. Fun place, too. Lively crowd."

We could see from the water that the deck and outdoor bar were crowded to near capacity, as I assumed the interior was as well. It appeared to be a typical weekend crowd, loud, fun, and well-mannered.

I waved my arm along the shore. "This whole piece of land all along this shore and up almost to my place used to be the Excelsior Amusement Park. It closed down back in the seventies, and Valley Fair was built in its stead."

"Really? An amusement park here?"

"Yes."

"You must never have seen it before it closed."

"No. Just pictures."

Then we turned about and cruised along the Commons and toward the beach.

"So, how long have you been practicing dentistry?" I asked.

"Almost three years."

I quickly tried to calculate her age. "Where did you practice before coming here?"

"I was in the Navy."

"Really?" I said, surprised at her answer.

"Yes, really."

"How'd that happen? I mean, why the Navy?"

"I did R.O.T.C. in college in Dakota, and the Navy put me through dental school. I served my hitch after graduating, and then came here."

"Are you a trained killer?" I made sure I was smiling as I asked, and also made a point of leaning away from her.

She started to laugh a marvelous laugh. She removed her glasses, and I saw that her eyes sparkled when she laughed. They were a lovely hazel color.

"I hope my patients don't think so," she answered. "Only sometimes the way they shrink away from me I'm not too sure."

"I can't imagine anyone shrinking away from you."

"You haven't seen me holding a drill."

"Touché. How'd you end up here in Excelsior?"

"There were openings in different parts of the country, but this was closest to home, so I chose here."

"Where was home?"

"Langdon, North Dakota. Ever hear of it?"

I shook my head.

"Not many people have. Pretty small town," she said.

"Want a glass of wine?" I asked.

"Sure."

"Do you want to drive or serve?"

"I'll serve," she suggested.

"The wine's in the cooler, glasses are also. Pick some cheese, and we can let that warm up a bit. I've got several kinds. Keep the Brie for dessert, if you wish."

Sandra spent a few minutes setting things up. Then she handed me a glass of wine.

"Here's your daily ration of grog, matie," she roared.

I laughed. She had a nice sense of humor.

So, what's your story, Mike?"

"Nothing special. Grew up locally. Went to the U. Out of state to law school. I have a small practice here in town."

"You're an attorney?"

"Yes. You act surprised?"

"I am. You aren't up-tight enough, I'd think."

"What did you think I did for a living?"

She thought a little while. "Oh, a writer, maybe. I don't know. We just met, so I don't know you well, but first impressions, you know. You just seemed to me to be a fun-lovin kind of guy."

I laughed. "A writer, huh. I can't even spell. But you're correct. I like a good time."

We both smiled at that.

"I can see that. This is really a great boat. They run these along the East Coast. Very stable craft. This is what I'd have if I could afford it."

I was uncertain if she was patronizing me or not. I did not know her well enough, but she seemed to know her watercraft.

"Did you spend any time at sea?" I asked.

"Three months. Have to have sea duty. Loved it. I was on a guided missile frigate. Communications officer."

"I'm impressed."

"I'll be in the reserves until I'm a grandmother."

For the remainder of the afternoon, we worked on the cheese and crackers while I pointed out homes along the lakeshore, and oriented Sandra to where we were by land. We traveled as far as the Narrows separating the upper and lower lakes, and then motored back home. It was nearly seven when we docked.

"It'll begin to get cool on the water. Let's have dessert on my deck."

"Okay."

I put the chocolate into the microwave for the allotted time and then took the green grapes out of the refrigerator. I put a small bowl of those onto the tray and added the fresh strawberries. When the chocolate was done, I added that to the tray and carried it all outside. We uncorked the dessert wine and start dipping the fruit.

"Sorry I don't have any toothpicks," I said. "I knew I forgot something. Do you want a fork?"

"That's all right. This way I get to lick my fingers."

The wine went well with the chocolate.

The only thing that would have enhanced the evening would have been a sunset. We managed without, and enjoyed our time together.

At eight Sandra looked at her watch. "This has been a delightful afternoon, Mike. Thank you so much."

"Do you need to go?"

"Yes, I have some things to get done tonight."

I was a little surprised by her leaving, and not sure what to make of it, but that was fine.

I said. "I'll walk you to your car."

"That's all right, Mike. It's plenty light out. I can make it okay."

We walked up the steps to my door, and I opened it for her. Then I asked. "May I call you?"

"I don't have a home phone. How about if I call you?"

"Sure."

I dug out my wallet and gave her my card. She looked at it and shoved it into her bag. Then she stood on her tiptoes and gave me a kiss on the lips. It lasted about three seconds.

"Bye, Mike. Thanks for the nice day."

I took her free hand and squeezed it. "Good night, Sandra."

I watched her leave until she had turned the corner by the liquor store.

When I was alone, I cleaned up and wondered what to do. It had been an afternoon ballgame for the local boys, so I was forced to watch the network Sunday night game. While I watched the action, I analyzed our departing kiss. Sandra had broken it off. Obviously she likes to be in control. She didn't jump into bed with every Tom, Dick, and Harry that came along. How about a Mike, though?

Was that lack of a phone tale true, or was that another way for her to remain in control? There was no way to tell. I didn't even know if we would see each other again. She was kind of cute, though. We'd have to see what happened next.

In between innings, I ran upstairs and folded the clothes I had not gotten to earlier. When the game was over, I hit the sack. Tomorrow was another workday, and I still had my problem with Katie to solve.

~10~

SEARCHING FOR INFORMATION

WHEN I WENT INTO THE OFFICE on Monday morning, the last thing I had on my mind was dealing with the Orion case. I'd be meeting with Bob Lindgren later this evening to hash that out.

That good intention got blown out of the water almost immediately when Janet opened our morning conversation by asking, "How was your weekend?"

I poured her a cup of coffee before taking one myself. Then I stood before her desk when I answered, "Good. Yours?"

"Nice." She took a sip of coffee. "I didn't get around to making any coffee at home this morning. This hits the spot. Say, did you look up anything on that Orion Bank we talked about?"

I ran my fingers through my hair in a nervous gesture before saying, "Yes, quite a bit. Thanks for the lead." Every time this subject came up, I felt a sense of being overwhelmed.

Janet looked up at me over her cup, sensing my disquietude. Nonetheless, she said, "Did you get to the newspapers?"

I shook my head. "Not yet. There can't be anything there of much use." The minute I had said that, I felt as though I had walked into a trap. The smile on Janet's face was a clue.

"Oh?" was all she said in reply.

I knew by the inflection in her voice that I had erred.

She reached into a folder on her desk and handed me several articles dealing with the death of John Payton, former financial executive with Orion Bank. "Read these," she said. I read through them carefully while Janet watched. When I looked up, Janet had stood and was leaning against her desk, her arms folded across her chest.

There had been an obvious point in her collecting this information, but I was uncertain of the relevance. I would have to think about it further. Thus, I asked, "What do you make of this?"

Janet pursed her lips and slowly nodded several times before saying, "I thought about it quite a bit," she said while fingering her necklace. "The paper says he committed suicide. If that's the case, the question would be why? Supposedly, from what was said, his married life was contented. If that's true, that leaves work or something going on outside work. Unless the man was a gambler or involved in criminal activity, I think a person has to ask what was happening at work to cause such an act of desperation? I lean in that direction because of your girlie's concern with her husband. It sort of ties together." Janet shrugged and sat back down.

I had to digest what she had said, so I took a stroll toward the front windows. I looked out, watching a man park his car and walk toward the rear of a main street store. Then I turned and said, "I don't know much about suicide. Does anyone know what someone's home life really's like?" Stroking my chin, I said, "I mean, as you said, there could have been a dozen reasons for him doing what he did. I think we should be careful not to jump to conclusions. At least the police let it lie. They must be satisfied."

Janet took in a deep breath. "I know, Mike, but I approached the subject with the idea in mind that something was bothering the husband. The wife thinks so, anyway. I think we can agree on that. Couple that with something also bothering the right-hand man and that's maybe not a coincidence."

We stood looking at one another for a moment. Then I nodded. "I suppose the papers got their information from the deceased's wife."

"I suppose." I looked at Janet's expression to see if she believed what we had been saying. Her face was inscrutable.

Janet took a sip of her coffee. "Think about this possibility, then. What if it was a staged suicide?"

I scrunched up my face into a frown. "I don't get you."

"Murder. What if someone wanted him out of the way?"

Janet's theory had knocked me back onto my heels. She was all over the map with this new hypothesis. I hadn't even digested her previous supposition, and now this. I answered somewhat hesitantly, "No, I wouldn't think so." I said it, shaking my head. "The police would've tumbled to that by now, wouldn't they?"

Janet ran her tongue over the front of her teeth. Then she said, "Maybe, maybe not. Why not murder? Put yourself in the victim's place for a minute," she said. "Here you are sitting in a car in a closed garage while the motor spews out carbon monoxide. That's not an easy thing for someone to get his mind around. What if it was made just to look like an accident?"

I turned and looked at the wall. What Janet said was too fantastic. Then I turned back. "I don't know, Janet. You could be right. But either way, the death could be troublesome for the bank. You don't lose a key employee and just sail smoothly along. There's bound to be some hiccups. Plus there's the physiological trauma involved. This is great information, though. You may have put your finger on the problem. Thanks."

"No doubt you're right, but it would be good to know which it is," she said.

"I'll go with suicide," I commanded.

"Okay, you go with that, but I'm going to keep an open mind."

I smiled at her before walking into my office.

Now I couldn't get the subject out of my head. Janet may well have found the solution to what had been troubling Williams. Losing a key employee was one thing, but trouble at the bank causing that employee to take his own life was a totally different thing. If it was suicide due to problems at work, I might be able to put this whole mess behind me. I just had to figure out how to pursue it and come up with a reasonable answer.

In light of Janet's information, I almost called Bob to cancel our afternoon meeting. Finally I decided to let it stand.

That afternoon I got an unexpected call from Katie Williams.

When I picked up the phone, she said, "Hello, Michael."

"Good afternoon, Katherine." I was dreading this conversation as I was feeling squeezed. As of yet, I knew nothing concrete. I was only beginning to speculate. I wondered if I should say anything to her about the suicide.

Before I could decide, she said, "Michael, I was wondering if we could get together and talk."

Get together and talk. Shit. I didn't have time for this. I was leaving town on Thursday for my fishing trip, and I had to get a lot of work done before that. Plus I had the meeting with Bob tonight and golf league tomorrow. That only left Wednesday night. Damn.

I explained my problem to Katie. She ignored me entirely. Obviously she was used to getting her own way with things. She said with authority, "I realize that you're busy at work, Michael. Shall we say Wednesday at your place? I won't take long."

I shook my head in amazement, but relented. "Okay, let's say five-thirty. You sure you want to come to my place?"

"Sure, why not?"

"Well, you had said people would talk."

"Oh, that. Since we know each other, it'll be all right."

I wasn't following the logic. "Fine, see you Wednesday. You know where I live . . . 116?"

"Okay, I'll be there." Then she disconnected.

I somehow made it through the remainder of the Monday workday without further distraction and hurried home for my appointment with Bob Lindgren. I wasn't certain if Bob drank and I did not know how complicated our conversation might become, so I considered holding off having a cocktail myself. I relented, however, and fixed myself a scotch. Just a short one, though.

Then I set about to prepare a couple of snacks for the conference. Afterwards I picked up the living room and fluffed the couch pillows. The afternoon had become cloudy, and the room had taken on a gloomy feel, so I turned on all the lamps. I decided to leave the patio door open, since it was a warm day, and my place had heated up in my absence. With my bedroom window open upstairs and the patio door open, we could enjoy the fresh breeze off the water. Then, too, we always could sit outside. I'd let Bob decide.

I looked around the room, satisfied. Then I awaited Bob's arrival.

I heard his car and greeted Bob at the door. "Thanks for stopping by," I said. Bob was a spare man, six feet tall, but weighing less than one-fifty. His thin frame made him look both tall and small at the same time. His hair was light and cut short, which helped minimize the thinness on top. Blue eyes dominated his thin face, while a narrow nose looked hawk-like with his other features.

"No problem, Mike. Glad to help out."

"We could sit inside or out," I said. "What's your preference?"

"Inside's fine."

"Okay, then have a seat." I motioned toward the living room. Once seated, we spent some time on chitchat. Then Bob asked, "So what is it that I can help you with, Mike?"

I briefly considered telling Bob the whole thing was off, but then decided my newfound analysis could be wrong. I opted to go ahead with my original story.

I said, "Remember when I said I knew someone who was asked to invest in the Orion Bank Holding Company stock?"

Bob nodded.

"I really don't feel qualified to advise him, Bob, but he thinks I'm knowledgeable since I'm a director of the bank. And because of that relationship I must have this unique knowledge of banking. I don't want to let the guy down with a bad answer."

Bob had a serious expression on his wrinkled brow. "Do you want me to talk to him for you?"

I had to squash that notion. "Well, that'd be one way, I suppose, Bob, but I was hoping to use this as a learning experience for myself."

"I see." Bob smiled. "I run into situations like this all the time, Mike. I'm expected to be a financial genius in areas I know nothing about, because of my occupation. So you're wondering about Orion's financial health?"

"Yes. I was doing a little research so I printed this off the Internet."

I handed Bob the two dozen pages I'd copied. Bob looked over my sheets. "This gives a snapshot picture of year end financials from last December, but it leaves a lot out a lot of important information."

I leaned back in my chair. "How so?" I asked.

Bob picked up a cracker with cheese. "Let's talk about our own situation for a minute. That's something you're familiar with. The F.D.I.C. and Minnesota Department of Commerce came into our bank last September and did a review."

"They do that every two years, right?"

"Well, actually they usually alternate, but with the banking crisis, they're doubling up, coming in together."

"Oh," I said.

"We're pretty small potatoes, so they were able to review eighty percent of our loans in short order. They also reviewed our method of calculating our need for providing funds for any possible loan losses. They tore everything apart, remember?"

"Yes. They were in the bank a couple of weeks."

"Right. When it was all said and done, they criticized us for making some loans without having adequate collateral. Remember that?"

"Yes. Well, I mean we talked about that, yes."

"And do you remember why we supposedly didn't have enough collateral in those couple of instances?"

I thought for a minute. This was like a spot quiz. I said, "In the case of the building loan on the carwash, the latest appraisal estimate done by the examiners said the building was worth less now than when we placed the loan three years ago."

"That's correct. Real estate values have dropped across the board in the last couple of years. It wasn't a surprise to anyone that this particular building would also be worth less than when we originally loaned money on it. Also the feds didn't do an actual appraisal. They guestimated the building to be worth less now than when we put on the loan, just because of how commercial property has declined in value in general. Right?"

I nodded. So far this wasn't anything new to me.

"Okay, so then they told us that, because of the reduced appraised value of the property, we were in violation of our loan policy as it pertained to how much we could loan on the building. See, we loaned more than we should have on that building since it's now worth less than it had been worth before. Of course at the time when the loan was originated, we'd loaned less than seventy-five percent of the actual new building cost. That didn't matter to them, though, did it? They also questioned the ability of the owner to repay the loan because times have been tough and he hadn't been able to make a profit this past year."

"But I thought he was cash flowing because of his depreciation, even if his financial statement didn't look good?"

"He is, but the auditors wanted us to show proof of the company's future ability to pay."

"Right," I said, "and yet John's never missed a payment, has he?"

"No he hasn't, but the F.D.I.C. said we had to downgrade the loan and put more into our capital base to guard against a possible loss on that particular loan. Do you remember all that?"

"Yes," I answered, somewhat hesitantly.

"Well, that's what's happening to banks all over the state, all over the country for that matter. We're small potatoes compared to a lot of them. We just opened four years ago and are pretty much a retail bank doing small loans and small lines of credit to businesses here in town.

"We've never gotten into real estate development loans. Our lending limit isn't high enough for those boys. We caught a break. That good fortune protected us in this economic downturn.

"A lot of banks tried to grow fast by taking on real estate loans, either commercial or residential development. They were chasing loans all over the country. Many of those banks got burned when the real estate market crashed, and the owners of those developments ran out of cash to make payments. We were lucky not to have been into any of that.

"I suspect Orion has a good many of those loans because they were selling off portions of some of them the last couple of years," Bob said.

"To spread the risk, right?" I replied.

"That's right. Plus, they can only lend up to a certain amount to any one borrower." Bob placed the papers down onto the table. "Here's what I'm hearing in general, Mike. In the last six months, every community bank examined in this state, but one, has been downgraded, many to a four rating. That means they had better come up with a plan to fix their loans or get more capitol or both real quick or they'll be shut down by the banking authorities and taken over by some other bank."

"I hadn't realized things were that tough," I said. "By the way. What was our rating, I forget?"

"We are lucky. We retained our two rating. As to the other, the news really hasn't gotten out. The F.D.I.C. doesn't go out of its way to publish bad news, but it's there to be found when they issue their Consent Order to a non-performing bank."

"Which is what exactly, the Consent Order?"

"That's their findings of the examination and what the bank has to do to come into compliance. The Consent Order is the list of requirements."

"Oh. Do you think Orion is in trouble?" I asked.

"I don't know, Mike. However, I do know someone I might be able to speak with at one of the branches. We started out together at US Bank. Let me nose around and see what I can find out."

"Okay, but before you go, what do you make of this?"

I handed him the newspaper articles Janet had passed to me about the suicide. He scanned each article in turn, then said. "Yes. I saw all these when it occurred last November. Quite a tragedy." He shook his head.

"Bob. Could this in some way be tied to some hidden problems at Orion?"

Bob thought for a moment. "I guess anything's possible. I'll keep it in mind as I'm researching."

"Thanks Bob. I appreciate it."

"Anything else?"

"No, that'll do it, Bob. I really appreciate your help."

"Glad to help. Well, I'd better get home to dinner."

I said good-bye to Bob and wondered about dinner for myself. I ordered in a pizza.

Then I tried to analyze what Bob had told me. If banks all over the state were in trouble, maybe Orion was also. Could that have been the reason for the executive officer's suicide?

~ 11 ~
A MISSING PERSON

I HAD NO SOONER WALKED back downstairs after showing Bob Lindgren out when the doorbell rang. I considered ignoring it but then went back upstairs after the second ring. Who was selling what?

I was surprised to see Officer Bill Rehms of the local constabulary standing on my front stoop.

Officer Rehms smiled at me and said, "Mr. Connelly, may I come in?"

I hesitated for but a moment and said, "Sure. Come on down."

I was surprised at the visit and wondered what it was about? I was certain I was in the clear on anything involving the police. I closed the front door and led the way down to the living room, my mind continuing to grind on what the officer could want.

Officer Rehms spied the prepared food sitting neatly on a platter, and my work papers strewn about the table's surface and said, "Expecting company?"

"No. They've just left."

Bill nodded.

I pointed an open palm to the couch. "Help yourself. Care for a drink?"

"No, thanks I'm still on duty. Water would be nice, though. It's warm out today. Mind if I have one of these cracker things?"

"No. Go right ahead. You're right about the weather. It's been a really nice summer so far, just the right amount of rain."

"And a lot coming at night," he replied.

I had met Officer Rehms for the first time the previous summer when he was investigating a fire in a local art gallery. I found him to be a real bulldog once he set his mind to something, even if he had been on the wrong track. Since I had no idea what had brought him here today, I decided to sit back and let him take the lead.

I went into the kitchen and got him a glass of ice water. Then I freshened my drink.

When I had passed over the water, Bill said, "Have you been out on your boat much?"

"Quite a bit. Maybe about three times a week.

"Good. Do you want to sit in here or outside," Bill asked.

"Which would you prefer?"

"Outside okay?" he asked.

"Let's do it, let me get this platter."

I was pleased to be outside, because now I could light up. "Care for a smoke, Bill?"

"Never touch 'em."

We were seated facing the water enjoying the view when I asked, "What can I do for you, Bill?"

Bill swallowed the cracker he had in his mouth and said, "Do you know the woman who lives next door?"

I pointed to the unit to the north of mine. "You mean Sherrill Thompson?" I picked up my lighter and lit my cigar.

"Yes. That's her."

I drew in two quick puffs and then blew the smoke skyward. Fingering my cigar, I said, "As a neighbor, yes. I see her on her deck once in a while. Couldn't tell you much about her."

"Do you have a key to her place?"

I shook my head. "Sometimes neighbors exchange keys, just in case, but we never have. I keep an extra key for my house at the office. That's not far to go if I get locked out."

Bill nodded.

Bill Rehms was a powerfully built man, only slightly shorter than I was. He had dark hair, cut short, and a swarthy complexion. Wide set, dark eyes compliment an oval-shaped head.

When Bill reached for his water glass, I noted that he bit his nails. Must be a nervous sort. I took a drink of my scotch and waited.

"When do you think you last saw her?"

I grew anxious, wondering where this conversation was headed. I did what I often did in those situations, I took my time. Rolling my cigar between my fingers I drew a puff and exhaled. Did Bill's question mean something had happened? I thought long and carefully before answering. Bill sat all the while looking at me.

"Let me think. When did I last see her? I don't believe I've seen her since last Tuesday."

"You sure about Tuesday?"

I pushed my tongue into my cheek and then moved it side to side. Then, "Yes. That's the day it rained really hard."

He nodded. "You did see her then on that day?"

I thought back to the climax of that evening, but decided to begin at the beginning. "That night actually, Bill. After coming home from a workout at the club, I was checking on my boat and was just returning up here from the dock when she stuck her head outside and called out to me."

"Just saying hello then?"

"No, not exactly," I said. "She needed a bit of help. Her patio door had come off its track and was stuck open a couple of feet. She couldn't move it. You can't move those doors when the wheels aren't rolling."

Bill nodded his understanding.

I continued. "If you remember, it had rained really, really hard that afternoon, and with the door stuck open, it had been coming in on her carpet. She was desperate to get it fixed, and the association guy couldn't make it until the next morning. The woman appeared distraught, so I said I'd take a look at it. Fortunately I was able put it back on its track for her. It had rained pretty good in on her floor. She had a mess."

I explained everything to Bill, but left out the shower scene. I didn't think he needed to hear about that.

Bill continued. "The super says he was called to fix the door, but when he arrived the next morning, it already was fixed, and Mrs. Thompson wasn't there. Her workplace hasn't seen her since Tuesday last."

"You're kidding."

Bill shook his head.

Officer Rehms's statement had caught me by surprise. Sherrill had expected the man to show up, and she was the one who had wanted things fixed promptly, so why hadn't she been there to see the job through? I thought about that but could come up with no good explanation. I could tell Rehms I thought the woman might have been depressed, but I was no authority on that subject. I dummied up, since all I could accomplish would be to get myself involved in something that did not concern me.

I shrugged. "I guess I haven't seen her either, but of course that doesn't mean anything. I probably only saw her on an average of once a week, if that. Have you been inside her place?"

"Yes. Her husband, Jack, is on the contact list in case of emergency, and when she didn't show Wednesday or Thursday, work called his cell. He got to thinking about it, and when he wasn't able to reach her this weekend, he called us. We just left there before I came over here."

What did things look like over there?" I asked.

"Bed was made, everything cleaned up. No dirty dishes. No dirty laundry. Her car was gone."

I shrugged again. "She's left then. What's the big deal?" I asked.

"Just that we've been asked to look into it. Hard to say what's going on. Maybe she went on vacation, but if she had you'd have thought she'd notify her work."

"Yes. That would be the normal thing."

"Can you shed any light on it?" Bill asked.

I was surprised by the question, but shook my head. "I don't think so. I don't know anything about her personal life. I kind of wondered, though, why her husband wasn't around much."

"They're apparently separated, or in the process of divorce," Bill said. "I didn't dig too deeply."

I nodded. "That explains it, then. What happens next?"

"We'll put a B.O.L.O. on her car. Maybe talk again with her husband. See where he was last week." Bill looked at me hard. "So the last time you saw her was Tuesday evening?"

"That's right. I'm pretty sure I didn't after that."

"And she didn't say anything about her plans?"

I reflected for a moment, trying to remember. "Mmmm, no. I remember she was quite upset about the door. She stood there sniffling while I fixed it. But no, she didn't say much."

"Okay, Mike. Thanks." He looked around the barrier over at the neighboring patio.

I walked him up to the door.

Then I went back outside and looked next door myself. She beat it, then. Nothing to keep her here. I wondered if they would check on her bank account.

THE FOLLOWING NOON after lunch, I set out on my daily walk. My intention was to walk east along Lake Street past my place over to the recreational trail and then follow that back to Water Street, making one large circle. As I moved briskly along, my thoughts were on my upcoming fishing trip. Our group would drive up to Baudette after work on Thursday, fish Lake of the Woods Friday, Saturday, and most of Sunday before driving back late Sunday night.

I turned the corner by the liquor store and glanced up at my building just in time to see blinds in an upstairs window close. Wait a minute, that was the Thompson place. I stopped in my tracks and wondered if I saw what I thought I saw.

Now I wondered if there was something unusual about someone being in that unit. Sherrill was supposedly missing. It could be her, though. I could just go over and ring the doorbell, see if someone answered. What if it was a break in?

I crossed the street and rang the bell. I waited, then rang it again. When no one responded, I went through my unit and around back to look in the patio door. The blinds were drawn, and I couldn't see a thing. I tried to remember if those blinds had been closed the previous day when Rehms was here. I could not remember.

Returning inside my place, I wondered what to do. I'd hate to see the place trashed. Thinking about it a bit longer, I turned the decision over to someone else by putting in a call to Bill Rehms. When he returned my call about fifteen minutes later, I was on my walk, but told him of my suspicions. "Bill do you want to take a look?"

"I'll call Jack Thompson and see what he knows."

"Okay."

I put away my phone and continued on my walk, wondering if Sherrill Thompson had returned home? I got my answer later at my office when Officer Rehms dropped by. I offered coffee, but he declined.

"Learn anything, Bill?"

"It was Thompson in there."

"The husband?"

"Yes."

"Well, I suppose he has a right to be there. It is his place, right?"

"So far as I know. I think I'll check that out, though."

We chatted for a couple of minutes and then Bill left, and I returned to my work. If I wanted to beat it out of town later this week, I had to finish my work and not let outside influences distract me. Good luck with that.

~12~
ANOTHER VISITOR

LATE WEDNESDAY AFTERNOON I rushed home after work and prepared cheese slices on a small decretive plate my mother had given me. Then I grabbed a handful of crackers, put them in a bowl and stuck the bowl and plate onto a plastic tray.

The wine I had placed in the refrigerator before going to work that morning certainly was chilled adequately, so I tried to remember what I had done with the corkscrew. I knew I had used it on the boat, and thought perhaps I had left it down there. No, I remembered bringing it up with everything else. The dishwasher, of course, I had never taken it out. Now I was set.

Then I had a new thought. I put two wine glasses into the refrigerator to chill. Yes, this was a high-class operation. No linen napkins, though. I didn't own any. I thought maybe I should ask for some for Christmas?

Since I didn't drink much wine when I was alone, I wasn't always prepared to serve it properly, but I thought I was prepared now. When Katie arrived, I would put out the goodies. Until then I had the cheese covered with wrap.

Running upstairs. I removed my jacket and tie. I decided to change my shirt, using fresh deodorant and cologne. Then it was back downstairs, where I opened the patio door and closed the screen. I wondered if we should sit in or out? I decided to leave the decision to Katie.

I grabbed some paper towels from the kitchen and quickly wiped off the patio table just in case we sat there. By now I was sweating, but I thought I was ready. It was important I make a good first impression with my place.

Then I realized I had no idea why we were meeting at my place. She previously had not wanted to incur unwanted publicity. Was that just bull shit? Did I really know what was going on with this woman?

The doorbell rang. If it was she, Katie was right on time, and I leapt up the stairs two at a time to let her in the front door. She was a vision. Her hair was put up with some sort of jeweled thing in it, and she accented it with dangling earrings and wore a clingy, little black dress with a scoop neck. A choker necklace of diamonds lay against her soft tan. A small clutch bag rested in her left hand. I took it all in within a second.

"Katherine. Welcome to my humble abode."

She smiled when she looked at me. "Michael, looking at the stairs, this must be a split level."

The landing wasn't that large, and we stood quite near one another. Her fragrance was intoxicating. I wanted to reach out and hold her. Instead, I said, "Yes, it is. We'll be going down."

I crossed in front of her and led her down to the living room.

We stood between the kitchen and the living room. I asked, "Would you be more comfortable inside or out on the deck?"

"Inside, I think. I don't like bugs much."

Katie was looking around my compact room. "Yes, inside would be better. So we can talk."

I nodded.

"Would you like the couch or a chair?"

"I'll take the chair, thank you. I don't like looking into the bright light."

"I can fix that," I said, and partially drew the blinds. That dimmed the room considerably. I turned on a couple of lamps.

Katie sat picking at the arm cover of her chair with two fingers like she was afraid it might carry lice. It probably was a nervous habit. Imagine her being nervous to be here in my home.

I excused myself and walked to the kitchen to garner the refreshments. When I returned I put the tray onto the coffee table and poured a half glass of wine, which I placed before my guest. Then I sat facing her.

When Katie crossed her legs, I noticed her black shoes, medium heel and sandal like straps. Very elegant. Her legs were bare, but smooth. Nicely tanned, a professional job.

While I watched her, Katie was looking around the room.

So this is your home then?"

"Yes," I said with a smile. "Home sweet home."

"There's an upstairs area, then? Bedrooms I would guess," she said as she looked toward the stairs.

"Yes, and a bath."

"She nodded. "Compact, isn't it?"

I felt like I had just been slammed to the mat. I guess this wasn't what she was used to. I attempted to shrug it off and said, "It's perfect for a guy who lives alone."

She smiled at my comment.

I tried to recover my aplomb by saying, "You look nice tonight, Katherine. Going somewhere?"

Katie smoothed the dress on her legs and said, "Thank you, Michael. Yes, I'm on my way to a dinner."

"Would you like some wine?"

"I'd better not. I'm driving. I don't have much tolerance for alcohol."

"Oh." I had always liked girls like that. Cheap dates. Katie's cheeks had a glow to them without alcohol. I couldn't tell if it was makeup or the heat of the day. I'd like to think it was from her proximity to me.

"Katherine, is it hot in here for you? I could turn on the air."

"It is a little warm."

I rose, and went to the wall that separated the two rooms. I turned the rheostat that controlled the ceiling fan and set the fan on low, followed by the air conditioning control. The thermostat said it was seventy-nine inside, so I turned the setting down to sixty-five, just to make sure it kept running the whole time Katie was here. Then I crossed the room and closed the patio door. I liked fresh air, but it did get hot in here in my absence during the day. I should have realized that, but I spent so much time out of doors, I never considered the interior conditions. I had assumed Katie would want to be outside. Now I knew.

When I was once again seated, I said, "So, I guess you'd like an update of what I've been able to accomplish?" I said.

"Have you found anything?" She brightened as she looked at me expectantly. Katie nervously re-crossed her legs, laying them to the side. I couldn't help watching.

Then I awoke. "You realize I'm just getting started on this whole thing, Katherine. Based on your suspicions, I'm looking into the operations of the bank. On that subject, what do you know about the death of the Payton employee?"

Katie's head jerked back and she looked shocked. After not saying anything for a moment, her face took on a more placid continence and she answered, "He committed suicide. It was tragic."

She was playing with her hands. Then she touched her hair. Finally, she brushed her dress down to her knees. Her face began to color. I wondered what was going on in her head. Was she leveling with me? It was bad enough working in the dark, but if she was holding out . . .

I pressed on. "Hear any rumors as to why he would do something like that?"

She sighed. "Just that he'd been depressed."

"Yeah, I suppose. There's a lot of that going around." I recalled what I had gone through the past winter and wondered if at any time I had ever contemplated ending it all? I could not recall.

I said, "Did you know his wife well?"

Katie shrugged. "Just to say hello."

That answer surprised me. Here was one of the chiefs of the bank. I would have thought there would have been a lot of interaction between the couples at required events at least. Apparently I was wrong on that score.

"You haven't talked to her about his death, then? I mean after it all happened."

"No."

Katie seemed ill at ease with this discussion, but I had to get to the facts. I continued. "No idea what she's doing now, or how she's getting along?"

"No, I don't . . . I mean human resources at the bank have been in touch. They're handling everything."

I realized Katie had no real involvement with the company. As such it wasn't her responsibility. At the same time, I found it strange she never reached out to the poor widow. Her husband had been an employee of their bank!

I dropped that subject and took up a new course. "One thing I want to caution you about. You'd like this to be a case of work influencing your husband's behavior, but I wouldn't put all your eggs in that one basket. For instance, if there is another woman—"

"I said there wasn't," she interrupted defiantly.

I put my hands up in a defensive gesture. Then I waited.

"Look, Katherine. If you want me to help you, we need to enter this investigation with open minds. We don't know where it'll lead. We can't make it turn out one-way or another just because we want it that way. What we find, we find. If you want me to continue, that is."

She looked at me with surprise. "What are you saying?"

"I'm saying that we, or rather *you* need to take precautions. For example, say your husband is fooling around. What's your reaction? What would you want to do about it? Would you want a divorce? Are you financially independent in that event? Do you even have anyone you can trust and depend on outside the bank people to advise you on financial matters?"

My voice had risen and now I softened my tone. "There are a lot of things to consider, Katherine."

Her face took on a pensive look. She was staring over my shoulder, not really seeing me. I wondered at her thoughts.

"Yes. Yes, I see," she finally said. "You're being very professional, Michael. I think I made a good decision here to work with you. You don't pull your punches, do you?" Here she smiled, and absentmindedly reached for the glass of wine sitting before her and sipped from the glass.

I continued, since I had her attention. "If I'm working for you, Katherine, I have to keep your best interest in mind. That covers a whole range of possibilities. I don't know what kind of estate planning you and your husband have done, but I want to look out for you, personally. Understand?"

"Yes, I'm beginning to. I'll have to think about this. What you are saying about my personal affairs. I've generally left that to Larry. Maybe I need to take a hand myself. Like you say, protect myself just in case."

Katie swirled the wine in her glass. "Is that what you're saying? That he's fooling around."

"No, absolutely not. I have no evidence of that, but I don't know your personal situation, finances and all that, and I don't want you to be caught unawares. Who owns the house? Who's responsible for payments? Where would you get the cash to live on if you were on your own? Do you have access to ready cash? Those sorts of things."

I let that sink in for a moment and then said, "Do you think anyone at the bank would come to your aid?"

She slowly shook her head. "You mean if there was a marital split?"

"Right."

"Probably not. After all, their bread is buttered by their employer, not me."

"Even though you're a majority stockholder?"

"They wouldn't know that. No. They'd fear Larry and stick by him. They've got phantom stock. They want to cash that in some day."

"What's that?"

"What's what?" she asked.

"Phantom stock."

"Oh, it's like a bonus they get every year." Katie leaned forward and placed the wine glass onto the tray. "Stock instead of money, but the shares can't be cashed in while they continue to work there. They do it when they retire. It's part of a non-compete deal designed to keep key employees, somehow. I don't know the particulars. Like I said, it's all part of the non-compete agreement each executive officer has."

"Okay. I think I understand. So you may want to find someone not involved with the bank to advise you on all this, Katherine."

"Besides you?"

"Yes, experts in areas I'm not trained in. You know, it's a good idea anyway. God forbid, but Larry could have an accident any day and you'd have to cope. It's called estate planning."

She didn't say anything then. She obviously was thinking, and as she did so she started playing with the hem of her dress. When it rose inch by inch above her knee, I stared.

"Okay then," I said, startling her. She jumped slightly, and smoothed out her dress.

I went on to explain what I have been researching so far, leaving Bob out of it. Then I laid out the plans to get to someone inside the bank in the next few days. I didn't know if she was paying attention, she seemed to be far away. If she was thinking about what I had said, good.

I finally said, "Do you know anyone with whom I could converse? Someone working in the bank." I thought I sounded extremely erudite.

She contemplated my question for a bit and then said, "I'm not sure. I'll think about it, though."

"Good." I felt a degree of relief. Perhaps I was getting through to her on some level.

Katie was silent for a minute before saying, "I don't know if you can understand our life, Michael. It's all wrapped around the business. We basically only go out together to community events where we need to be seen, and money is at stake. It's not the life I once envisioned. Even when we go to the symphony or ball games, it's to bring customers or regulators. I don't know when the last time we went on a picnic together, just the two of us or the family? Gosh, that luncheon I had with you was a real treat for me."

I hadn't expected Katie to open up to me like this after our previous discussion, so I let her speak without interruption.

"When we entertain at home, it's the same thing. At Christmas the decorations inside and out are professionally done. We have an officer party with them and their wives. God forbid if one of the children wanted to hang a homemade decoration on the tree. I have all these old world German ornaments from my family, and I can't even use them"

"Can't you put up a small tree somewhere for the kids?"

"I guess . . . I hadn't thought."

"Maybe let them do the decorating. What did you do when you were a kid?"

"Dad put up the tree, and Santa decorated it. We never saw the tree until we got up Christmas morning. That was great."

"A lot of work for your folks."

"It must have been, but it sure was great."

A tear came to one of Katie's eyes. She dabbed at it with a finger.

"You've got rewards, though the rewards are material," I suggested.

"Yes. That's all nice, but it gets lonely sometimes."

"The kids live a normal life though?"

"Yes, we send them to the public schools. The schools in the Minnetonka district are really top notch."

"That's what I've heard," I said. "You know, I'm not a marriage counselor, but maybe if you spiced things up a little."

"You mean have an affair?"

"Heavens no. I mean with your husband."

She smiled. "Like wearing one of those little French maid uniforms when I served him a drink?"

I had a mental picture of her dressed like that. "Oh, la la, oui, oui."

"Do you think he'd notice? I'm over forty. Oops."

"I'd notice," I blurted out. "My heart would be pumping like crazy." I began blushing.

"Thank you, Michael. That's nice of you to say," she said, smiling.

She looked at her watch. "Michael, I'd better go. Thanks for everything, so far."

When Katie stood, I did as well and took her elbow. I walked her up the stairs. When we reached the landing, she turned her head and glanced up to upper level.

"Thank you," she whispered.

Then she stood on her toes and bussed me on the cheek. I must have been crazy, because I put my hand behind her back and held her there. With my free hand, I turned her jaw until our lips were aligned. Then I kissed her. She didn't resist. Her breasts pressed into my chest, and blood raced through my groin.

Suddenly, I came to my senses, relaxed my grip and said. "I've wanted to do that since I was ten."

"Who says dreams never come true?" she said, smiling.

Then she turned, and I opened the door for her, watching her leave. I stayed there until she had reached her car. Then I sighed and returned inside.

I had packing to do. I wouldn't have time tomorrow, since we'd be leaving right after work. I decided to put it off. Instead, I fixed a drink, grabbed a cigar and went outside. Then I returned inside and turned off the air. Once back on the deck, I relaxed, and had a daydream that Larry was fooling around, and he and Katie got divorced. Then Katie thought I was the coolest thing since sliced bread and married me. God, she was hot. For the next half hour I fantasized on ways to get her into bed.

~13~
A RETURN TO NORMAL

JANET HAD LET ME GO FISHING, and it was quite late on Sunday night when my fishing buddies dropped me off in front of my place. My part of the six-hour car ride was over. After unloading my gear from the back of the Suburban, I watched as the red taillights vanished down the quiet street and into the night.

The conversation on the trip home had been more subdued than the raucous camaraderie Thursday night on the way up north. We fished hard and played hard for three days, and it was beginning to tell. We all were dead tired.

We'd driven through rain from Blackduck to St. Cloud, but here the sky was only partly cloudy. I was able to see a few stars despite the glow of the nearby streetlight. A northwesterly breeze felt refreshing after being cooped up in the car for so long.

I almost tripped going up my front steps. Instead of making two trips, I tried carrying everything at once. I was that anxious to see my own bed.

Once inside my place, I left everything but the cooler on the landing. The cooler went into the kitchen where my walleye fillets found a place in the freezer. Since the nighttime temperature outside was cool, I turned off the air, opened the patio door and locked the screen door. A fresh lake breeze washed my wind-burned face. I was dried out and tired. In the kitchen, I drank a glass of cold water and brought a second along with me upstairs.

I planned to leave my unpacking until Monday night after work, I was that beat. I did a half-ass job brushing my teeth, and then I staggered around opening all the upstairs windows. After setting my alarm, I fell into bed. I was asleep within five minutes.

When morning dawned, I had to drag myself out of bed to the sound of the alarm. I was more than a little stiff. Rocking around in a boat for three days will do that to me. It was a good thing I had a job to go back to, so I could rest up for the remainder of the week.

I stumbled through my morning routine, and then I was out the door ready to begin anew. I had promised Janet a package of fish, and I carried it along with me to work. It would just fit into our dainty freezer there.

My mind had been away from reality for so long I didn't even remember if I had any commitments for the week. When I looked at my schedule, it was bare. Janet said nothing was pending as far as work was concerned, and I was pretty sure I had nothing on my personal agenda. Mid-morning I looked up the number to the dental office and asked for Dr. Sandra Grose.

"Mr. Connelly. I didn't think you were around any longer," she laughed.

"I've been out of town for a bit," I answered.

"You sound like you have a cold."

"Just a dry throat. How have you been?"

"Good. You?"

"Tired. I just returned home from a fishing trip."

"Boys will be boys."

I laughed. "Say, would you like to go to dinner with me Wednesday night?"

"Wednesday. Let me think. No, I'm free. What did you have in mind? How should I dress?"

"Casual but nice. I'm planning on taking you over to Lord Fletchers."

"I've heard of it. Isn't it fancy?"

"It can go either way. We can eat in the dining room if you're dressed up or outside if you're more casual."

"Will we being going by boat?"

"I planned on driving. Otherwise the ride home on the lake gets chilly."

"That sounds fine."

I arranged to call for her at her apartment.

There had been a lot to do the last week, but Janet kept up well with my absence on Friday. I worked in hyper drive all day and was glad the day went by quickly, so I didn't have a chance to get tired.

BY TUESDAY NOON I was back in sync. I had skipped my walk on Monday to work straight through. Then I did weights at the club after work. It felt good after having had no real exercise for five days. Today I needed the exercise of a nice stroll. While I was walking, I thought of Bob Lindgren and wondered how his inquiries were coming. I speculated I must be back in the groove to be thinking about that.

Thus, when I returned to the office, I called Bob, leaving him a message. He returned the call at four-thirty.

"Hi, Mike. Welcome home."

"Good afternoon, Bob."

"How was the trip?"

"Lots of fun. You're going to have to make one sometime."

"Sometime. I suppose you're wondering if I've found out anything on Orion?"

I laughed. "Of course."

Bob paused. "Yes and no. I talked to my buddy Jim Owens, who manages Orion's Anoka County office. Unfortunately, in his position he doesn't get into the level of things we need to access."

"Shucks," I said, disappointed.

Then Bob said, "The good news is that I talked directly with Larry Williams and have an appointment with him this Saturday afternoon."

I was surprised at this revelation. "Hey, nice work, Bob. Be sure to let me know how that comes out."

"You'll be there, Mike. I told Larry I wanted to bring a director to the meeting, and he thought that would be fine."

"How did you ever arrange that? Do you know him?"

"Yes. We know each other from banking conferences and such. He lives out here in the area, and expressed how happy he is we have a local bank in the community. Wants to do what he can to help."

"That's great, Bob. So we'll get together on Saturday, then?"

"He's stopping by here at the bank at twelve-thirty."

"I'll be there."

"Oh, by the way, Mike, Owens and I chatted a bit about the death of John Payton."

"Did you bring it up, or did he?"

"I did. The official word from the bank is that Payton committed suicide due to problems at home. However, friends of his wife . . . his widow that is, say that's not true. It seems she's been paid off to go along with that fabrication. Mrs. Payton hinted to those confidants that there wass something bad going on, and John could no longer handle the pressure."

"Wow! Does she mean at the bank?"

"Yes."

"Did you find out what it was?"

"My sources aren't enough in the know for that, but it sounds like a real rats nest."

"Well, thanks for trying, Bob. See you Saturday."

That news about Payton was really a shock. If Payton was that agitated by whatever it was, then Williams could be stressed out, as well. It was beginning to look like the problems were with his work and not another woman. What I couldn't understand was why the man would want to meet with us under those circumstances?

Well there was no point speculating. I would see what happened when we met. Nonetheless, I was intrigued.

~14~
A BIG MOVE

WITH ANOTHER WORKDAY behind me, I hurried home to change clothes. It was golf league night, and I was anxious to get out onto the course. After collecting rust all winter, my game was finally coming around, and I was thankful we hadn't had another rainout. My clubs and shoes already were in the car, so I headed out to the local club.

With a cloudless sky, it should be light until nearly nine-thirty. I would easily get in my eighteen holes, even with the normally slow league play.

My round began with a bogey and concluded with a par. I was generally pleased if I could play bogey golf. Tonight I beat it by one stroke. That led me to extending my round at the nineteenth hole. After refreshments, I was still okay to drive, I hoped.

There was a lot of activity on my end of town when I arrived home. Cruise boats were unloading, and customers were streaming up the sidewalks to where they had parked their cars. The usual crowd at the bar signaled a successful night for them. This was all normal activity for this time of the year.

What was unusual was the moving van I spied parked in front of my building. I pulled into my garage stall and returned outside to check out the activity next door. It was at the Thompson place, and I wanted to make sure it was legit. Someone could be cleaning out the place. I resisted calling 911.

After a mover came down the front steps with a box, I peeked inside and then went on into the Thompson place. Wandering about a bit, I ran into Sherrill Thompson.

"Sherrill. I'm glad it's you. I thought it might be thieves."

She turned and saw me. "Mike."

Sherrill was dressed in cutoff shorts and a short-sleeved shirt. She was wearing tennis shoes without socks. A white headband held her hair in place. She looked harried.

I asked, "Sherrill, where have you been? Everybody's been looking for you."

"Listen, Mike. I can't talk now. I want to get everything out of here and get the truck on the road. Unless you're going to bed early, can I stop over later?"

I was surprised, but said, "Sure."

I walked back over to my place thinking about her getting the truck on the road. She must be moving and not just to the other side of town. I wondered where? I decided to shower. It had been a warm night, and my clothes were clinging to me. A shower would be refreshing. Then I fixed myself a snack. I hadn't eaten dinner prior to heading out to golf, so I was feeling hungry. I turned on the TV to catch the news while I ate a sandwich. Liverwurst made a great meal and went well with beer. I just hoped it wouldn't keep me up all night.

When the doorbell later rang, I turned off the television and went up to let Sherrill in. Looking outside, I saw that the truck already had departed.

"Want anything to drink?" I asked after we had descended the stairs.

"No thanks, Mike. I'm driving tonight. Maybe just a glass of water. I packed all my glasses."

"Coming right up. So you're moving?" I asked, as I poured the cold water.

"Yes."

"Were you aware that everyone's been looking for you?"

"No. Why should they?" she asked as she took the glass.

"You didn't show up for work for a number of days, and somebody there called your husband. Apparently he was your emergency contact. After that, he came over and was rummaging around your place, so I called the cops. I had no idea who it was inside."

She smiled. "A tempest in a teapot. I sent my notice in to H.R. Apparently someone forgot to tell my supervisor. They probably remembered to do it when I called to tell them where to send my last check."

"Oh. So you're moving out of town, then?"

"That's right. I'm making a clean break of it."

"Can I ask you why?"

"Mostly to get away from Jack. He's . . . he's been abusive."

"No!" I was really startled by this admission, but uncertain as to why. I had not really known the couple. You just didn't expect things like that to happen to folks you knew.

Sherrill answered with a grimace. "I'm afraid so."

"You mean he's hit you?"

"Plenty. He's cute about it though. Mostly in places that don't show. Finally, I told him to get out or I'd call the cops and he did. Moved in with his girlfriend. But she eventually kicked him out, and he wanted to come back here. That's when I decided to run. If I don't, I know he'll try to weasel his way back in. He's good at making promises, but he can't keep them."

"Gee, I'm sorry, Sherrill. I had no idea."

"No need to be sorry. It's certainly not your problem, and I'm dealing with it. I've got myself set up in a new town, have a new job, a new life. That's where I've been, getting it all arranged."

"That's really good, Sherrill. I'm happy for you. What about this place?"

"I bought a new house in a bank foreclosure sale in the town where I'm headed. As soon as I close on that home, I'm going to sign over this place to Jack and declare bankruptcy. He'll be stuck for everything. I'm filing for divorce. It'll be a fresh start."

"You've got an attorney handling all that for you."

"Most certainly."

"I take it you don't want your husband to know where you're relocating?"

"That's the plan."

"You afraid of him?"

"I am, and after this all goes down, most decidingly so."

"Do you need a place to stay the night? You could get a fresh start in the morning."

"Thanks, Mike, but I want to put as much distance between here and my destination as soon as possible."

"Makes sense. Do you want to take some coffee?"

"No, but thanks anyway. I'm going to be on the freeway. I'll stop every couple of hours to pee and get fresh coffee. That'll get me through the night, and by daylight I'll be juiced up."

I did not understand why, but I was sad to see her go. I think it was the circumstances. I said. "Good luck, then, Sherrill. Drop me a line or call if you need anything." I gave her a hug.

Then I stood by my door and watched as she made the short U-turn to her own front door. Standing there, I watched her go inside and close the door. I closed mine. I felt finality with those doors closing. Suddenly I was tired, or was I depressed? I figured it was one more human relationship on the rocks. I guess I could relate. My success rate lately had not been so hot.

Sherrill was leaving to begin her drive out of town and into a new life. She'd said she didn't want to chance running into Jack by hanging around any longer than necessary. I didn't blame her. Who needed confrontation.

I would have to think about it, and decide if I wanted to tell the local police she was safe. I didn't want them looking for her. That would just help out her husband.

Now I was too keyed up to go to bed so I turned on the Late Show and watched that for a while. Then I finally hit the rack.

~15~

COMPLICATIONS

WEDNESDAY MORNING I was at work savoring a cup of coffee while Janet and I had our usual pre-work confab. I was relating to her my encounter with Sherrill Thompson from the previous evening.

"Do you know the Thompsons?" I asked.

"Thompson? Yes, I know of some Thompsons, but not the ones you're talking about." Janet put a finger to the side of her head. "No, I don't think so. Have they lived there long?"

"Next to me, no. I don't know where they lived before that. They might have been new to the area."

Janet shook her head. "Too new for me. There's lots of new folks in town I've never met. Area's growing too fast to keep up."

"That's so true," I responded. "So true."

Janet had lived in the Excelsior area all her life the way I had and always had prided herself on knowing just about everyone who lived here. Now things were becoming less stable.

"Do you know if they worked local?" she asked.

I threw up my hands. "I actually have no idea what either of them did for a living here, but I do know they both worked. The husband hadn't been living there with her for a while, and I didn't even know that." I shook my head, disgusted. "It shows you how much I know about them, about my neighbors in general."

Suddenly my statement made me feel somehow inadequate. It felt as though all the blood suddenly had drained from my face. I felt weak.

Apparently I had sounded disconsolate because Janet asked, "Mike, you okay?"

I sipped my coffee. "Just a little lightheaded for a second. I'm fine."

Janet looked concerned, but I continued. "Yah know, it's kind of tough living in those units there. If you don't see someone outside on their deck or down on the boat dock, you don't see them," I said. "It's not like when you own a house and are out in the yard working. Since we have no yard, everyone pretty much is on the patio or stays indoors or is on the lake or about town."

"I see your point. Even in an apartment building you'd see people in the halls."

"Right. But here everyone has their own door and large partitions between outdoor decks. If you don't meet in the garage, when would you? I probably walk past my neighbors on the sidewalks downtown and don't even know them."

I had to wonder if I was making excuses to myself for my lack of interaction with people. Now I was beginning to feel really bad. My face began to heat up as remembrances of the loneliness I suffered this past winter enveloped me.

Janet read my expression and tried to be upbeat. "Well, all's well that ends well. Right?"

I nodded in agreement, and went to my desk where I sat staring at my computer screen. I was having difficulty concentrating and getting anything done, so I called Bill Rehms. He wasn't available, but I was told he would return my call. I didn't really know why I was calling. It was a struggle to know if I should call or not. Finally I decided if I were to say that Sherrill was all right and safe, maybe everyone would leave her alone.

I worked pretty steadily until Bill returned my call.

"You called, Mike? You didn't leave a message."

"No, I wasn't sure what to say."

"So say it now."

I told Bill about my encounter with Sherrill the previous evening at her home, and what she had told me about the mix up at her workplace. "I think she's trying to get lost, Bill."

"Okay. I'll pass the word. No point in us wasting time unless we're forced into it."

I was glad he had taken that attitude. Just leave the poor woman alone.

We disconnected and I continued working until noon. After lunch, I considered skipping my walk about town. I wasn't in the mood. The blues had returned and their hold was strong. I realized I hadn't felt this poorly for at least the past couple of months. Something had set me back, and it wasn't a place I wanted to be. I decided if I weren't better in a couple of days I'd schedule an appointment with my shrink. He had helped me over the winter, and I shouldn't be afraid to ask him for his help now. Maybe I just needed to talk.

I even considered breaking my evening engagement with Sandra, but couldn't summon the energy to do that. I was wallowing in despair, or caught in an eddy that wouldn't let me escape. I decided on doing the walk after all and the exercise helped improve my outlook.

I returned to work feeling better. A good workout always left me feeling better, but even a brisk walk helped. Thus, I was in a brighter mood when about two o'clock I received a call from Bill Rehms. I hoped he wasn't going to heap more trouble on me. I didn't need more just now.

"Mike."

"Yes."

"We've got a problem." He sounded concerned.

I sighed. "We as in the police department, or we as in you and me?"

"Maybe both. Jack Thompson called in to us this morning and said a lot of furnishings from the condo are missing, as is one of his cars. I just saw the report a few minutes ago, or I would've said something to you earlier when we spoke."

"Okay, what's the problem?" I asked.

"The problem is he wants to file a theft report."

"I see, so you're going to get caught in the middle of a domestic dispute?"

"I guess."

I decided to fill Bill in on some of the facts. "Listen, Bill, I told you I talked with Mrs. Thompson last night, and that she was moving."

"Right."

"Well, there's more."

"Great. Go ahead." His tone told me how little he wanted to hear my information.

I related to Bill about Sherrill's intentions with filing the divorce action, and financial moves she intended to make. When I was finished, I said. "She really doesn't want to be found by her husband, Bill."

"I see that, Mike, but if her husband files a complaint like he says he's going to, we'll have to follow up. Have to let the court settle it."

"I understand. That's what makes your job shitty, right?"

"Right. So you say there was a moving van?" he asked.

"More like a flatbed with storage containers."

"Like Pods?" Bill questioned.

"Well, yes. That's a trade name, and it wasn't that, but same idea. They were unloaded onto the ground, filled, then loaded back onto the truck."

"Did you get the name of the company?"

Here I hesitated. I really did not want anyone looking for Sherrill, but it would not be hard for Bill and his gang to find out who did the move. I answered. "There was nothing on the containers themselves. Maybe on the truck cab. Let me think on it. Maybe it'll come to me."

I could almost see Bill smiling on the other end of the line at my futile diversion.

"Okay, I'll look into it," he said. It won't be hard to find out. There aren't that many moving companies around."

I felt stupid in my efforts to dissuade him. "So you'll have to follow up then?"

"I may be able to drag my feet a couple of days, but if the husband complains, we'll have to let the divorce court settle it. Pull the goods in and let the legal system do its thing."

"What if she's out of state?" I asked.

"That'll complicate things. Our department probably would be out of it."

"Then I think you'll be out of it."

"You think?"

"That's the sense I have," I said.

"Okay, Mike. I'll keep in touch."

"Bye, Bill.

I hung up and managed to plow on through the day. When five o'clock arrived, I struggled home. Up until today, I had been looking forward to this get together with Sandra. Now I wasn't so sure. I was obviously beset by doubt. The woman was far too young for me, and there didn't seem to be that feeling of sexual attraction I thought there should have been.

I knew better than to make a decision in my current state of mind. What had possessed me to ask her out? Lord Fletchers. I would like to go there, but not alone. Maybe she could snap me out of this fog.

~16~

DINNER FOR TWO

I HAD RESIGNED MYSELF to my fate. Thus at the appointed time I drove to Sandra's apartment building to meet my commitment. Surprisingly she was ready, with no phony making me wait routine.

I had to admit she did look nice, wearing a black-and-white striped top, and black Capris. She had all kinds of silvery bracelets on one wrist, and a brightly colored beaded necklace around her neck. A barrette held back part of her bangs.

Sandra appeared to be in a jovial mood as we walked to the car. My car was no Audi, but it did get me from point A to point B. When I approached the car and put my hand on her door, she stood for a moment looking over the ride.

"This is such a cool car. How long have you had it?" she asked.

"It's a '95. That's the fourth generation of the Mustang. I bought it new."

"You've had it for quite a while then."

"Yes."

"Kept it in good shape. Can I drive?"

At first I hesitated, and then said, "Sure, why not?"

She wore low heel shoes, so driving shouldn't present a problem. I walked her to the driver's door and opened it for her.

"Do you want the top up or down?" I asked.

"Highway or back roads?"

"Back roads."

"Let's leave it down, it's such a nice evening."

I had to agree with her on that.

"How's the clutch?" she asked.

108

"About standard. Let it out slowly."

I was half turned in my seat ready to rescue her if she had trouble shifting.

She looked at me quizzically and nodded. Then she proceeded to exit the parking lot like she had driven a clutch before. She moved the shift lever smoothly, letting it seat itself rather than forcing it. I let out a sigh of pleasure and faced front.

Sandra laughed. "What? You thought I was going to hurt your baby?

I laughed in return.

She glanced my way. "Grew up on a farm. Drove everything."

"I can see that." My admiration for her was growing.

I gave her directions, and we drove slowly past Navarre before reaching Lord Fletchers. We parked and walked around the volleyball courts to view the casual dining area near the water.

"This really is more for the bar and burger crowd off the boats," I said. I then pointed up to a second level. "That's a screened in area where we might sit, or they have the more formal dining area."

"It'd be nice to sit outside. We have so few days to enjoy this weather."

"I agree."

We went up to the screened portion of the building and were shown to a table. A waitperson arrived almost immediately and I asked Sandra, "Would you care for some wine?"

"That'd be nice."

"Red or white?"

"Maybe a nice pinot."

"Sure."

I looked over the wine list and ordered a bottle of wine. Then I smiled at my date. Now that I was here, I realized how much I had been looking forward to tonight's date with Sandra. It had been more than a year since I had been to Lord Fletchers, and the food here had always been great. I realized what I had been missing. Sandra had been my excuse to come here, and I thought perhaps tonight I would get an indication of what was possible for the two of us going forward.

That said, I knew that, deep down, I wasn't sure what I wanted to happen with us. I certainly did not want to make a decision while in the funk I had experienced earlier in the day. If I had learned anything over the past year it was not to make important decisions when I was down in the dumps. I'd only regret it later.

Our wine arrived, and I made a big production of tasting it. It tasted just fine. I never could understand the formality of checking the bottle to see if it was spoiled. I never had run into a bad bottle yet. I had to admit I would have preferred scotch, but I didn't want to get sloshed on this first date. That could easily happen in this melancholy mood of mine.

We silently toasted one another and each took a sip. Sandra was looking at me. "What's the matter? You seem to have lost your smile."

"Does it show?"

"A bit. What's happened? Bad day at work?"

I told her about my neighbor woman moving out in the middle of the night. "I really didn't know those people," I said. "The guy I saw maybe once or twice. The wife I wouldn't have known any better if the patio door hadn't come off the track."

"What was that all about?" she inquired.

I told her about my door rescue in the rainstorm.

She laughed at my description of events. "You sure seem to get yourself involved in weird situations."

"I agree."

I had finished my wine while Sandra had barely touched hers. I took the bottle and filled my glass half full.

Then I continued, "The thing is this woman was trying to be secretive about leaving, but she told me her husband had beat her. I had no clue why she told me that, and I wish she hadn't. That bit of information just hit me hard for some reason. After that revelation, I saw her as vulnerable. Women are vulnerable."

There was silence for a moment. I thought Sandra was waiting to see if I was finished. Then she said, "Most people would feel compassion in circumstances such as those as you surely did. There isn't anything wrong with your reaction. It shows you're human."

She reached across the table and placed a hand on mine. It felt reassuring. I shook my head and bit my lip before answering, "No, I understand that." Nodding to her I said, "It's the association with past events I made afterwards that did me in." I could feel a tear form in my eye and I quickly blinked it away.

Sandra looked quizzically at me. "And what association was that?" she asked.

I told her about the previous summer, my involvement with Grace, and what the police thought had happened to Grace.

"Wow, you sure get in deep when you get involved. So when you heard the sad news from your neighbor, you dredged up all the misfortune from last year."

"I must have. Hey, listen. It's my problem. I don't mean to ruin your evening."

"You're not. It's nice to meet a sensitive man for once. I certainly can understand what you must have gone through."

I wasn't sure how to take that. Just then the waiter returned and we ordered dinner.

Grace . . . sorry, I mean Sandra. How did you end up in the Navy? You said you were in R.O.T.C."

"That's correct. I couldn't afford college, and the Navy paid something for my duty, then paid for dental school. So it was a big deal for me."

"How was it being in the Navy?"

"I didn't like it a lot, not really. It's populated by a bunch of male chauvinist pigs. They still don't think women belong in uniform, and they're not afraid to let you know it. They treat it like it's their own private club."

I stared at her and was momentarily concerned, wondering if anything had happened to her while in service. I knew I did not want to go down that road tonight. Then I laughed. "You shouldn't hold back," I said. "You should be more direct with your comments."

That brought out a smile on her lovely face. "I tell it like it is."

She did do that. No little wallflower there.

"So, Mike, why is it that an eligible bachelor like you isn't married?'

I was dumbfounded by her directness. I looked for help from a waiter, but our dinner had not yet arrived.

"I don't know how to answer that," I said. "Maybe we're getting too personal here."

Sandra looked over her wine glass at me, never blinking. "I don't think so. It's merely an observation. What are you, forty?"

"Only thirty-eight, if you please. Don't make me older than I am."

She smiled. "Gosh, girls must have been throwing themselves at you."

There was a lull so I said, "Not so much. I'm not that great to look at."

She cocked her head at me. "You're maybe not pretty, but there's more than that for a guy."

"Like what?"

"Personality."

That got me to laugh. "Personality," I roared.

People around us stopped talking and looked at me. I was laughing so hard tears were flowing.

I said more quietly. "Personality. Thanks a lot. That's what we always said a girl has when she's really ugly."

"I know, but you have rugged good looks *and* personality, pardon me. You have a career, a home, and a jewel of a car. I don't get it."

"Don't forget the boat."

"Right, and the boat."

I sat musing. I really did not want to get into my sordid past, but she did not seem to be backing off. I got serious for a minute. "As a matter of fact I was married for a short time," I said.

"Oh, you were?"

"Yes. My last year of law school. We met at school. The girl, Nancy, came from a wealthy family out East, and I think she expected me to be the next Clarence Darrow. When she found out that was never going to happen, and I wanted to move back to Minnesota, she dumped me like a hot potato and ran home to daddy. Daddy saw to it she got a quick and easy divorce."

"I'm sorry, Mike," she said in a soulful tone.

"Don't be. It had been a mistake. We weren't suited for one another."

We sat there for a minute and looked at each other before Sandra said, "So that was a long time ago. Afraid to try again?"

I shrugged. "It's tough as one gets older. Maybe because of the fact I did go to law school, and I went out of state, so I lost contact with a lot of old high school chums. By the time I came home, a lot of girls already had paired up with guys. Twenty-four, twenty-five is getting old and spintery for some women, and they begin to panic."

"Well thank you very much."

I realized what I had said. "I guess you must be over twenty-five, then," I squirmed.

She seemed to enjoy my discomfort.

The waitress brought our salads, and it gave me a break.

I tried to salve the situation. "Actually, it's difficult to meet people in a small town. People who settle here mostly are married. Unless I were to hit the bar scene . . ."

She looked up. "There's church."

"I guess, but that's not my thing. I'm not going to go there just to meet women. There's something wrong in doing that." I finished by saying. "I just haven't met the right person."

"So you're not gay, then?" she asked with a straight face.

She broke me up again. I think all the emotion that had built up in me now broke loose. I began laughing and barely could stop.

"Want me to show you?" I choked out.

She smiled demurely.

Sandra suddenly had become quite attractive to me. I did not know what it was, and I didn't understand her. She was a force.

We enjoyed our dinner together and I was a little more respectful of the diners around us for the remainder of our meal.

After dinner, I drove us around the lake to Wayzata where we stopped and gazed over Wayzata Bay for a few minutes. The waterfront was busy there also. Then we drove home taking back roads. When I walked her to her door, she didn't offer to have me come inside.

"I had a lovely time, Mike. Thank you."

She reached up and kissed me on the cheek. I thought of that kiss as the brush off. Suddenly I wanted more. "I wanted to show you I wasn't gay," I blurted out, although I said it with a smile on my mug.

She smiled. "I hadn't thought you were. Next time it's my treat."

Then she was gone behind her door, and I stood there like a sap.

I scratched my forehead and slowly walked to my car, thoroughly confused. This woman was different.

It was only a short drive home from Sandra's apartment, but it gave me time to reflect. The woman had opened old wounds for me by bringing up my failed marriage, and then questioning my lack of dating success.

I had to wonder where the time had gone. It had been twelve years since my divorce and where had I spent my time? I had dated for sure, but I never had become serious with anyone. Perhaps I she was correct, and had difficulty committing.

Now here I was dating someone a lot younger than myself. How old would she be, twenty-six or seven? Why was she not married? Was she gay?

~17~

A NEW INVESTIGATION

O N FRIDAY AFTERNOON I received a phone call from Officer Bill Rehms. I was sitting at my desk staring at the computer screen and frankly the call was a welcome interruption. It had been a long week and I was ready for the weekend.

"Mike Connelly here."

"Mr. Connelly, could you come down to the town homes?"

"You mean my place?" I asked.

"Yes. Could you come on down here?"

I was surprised at the request and said, "I guess I could, when?"

"Would now work for you?"

"Yeah, I think so." My mind was churning with ideas as to why Rehms wanted me. "Care to enlighten me as to why?"

"I will when you get here. Okay?"

"Sure, I'll be right there."

I had absolutely no idea what Rehms wanted, but he appeared to need me for some reason, so what could I say? Suddenly I woke to the realization that someone might have broken into my place, or done something to my boat. A wave of anxiety swept over me. Obviously something had happened or why else would the police want me there? Now I really began getting nervous. I could feel dampness forming under my arm. Why had Rehms not told me anything? Then I recalled he had addressed me as Mr. Connelly, not Mike. He was being officious. Apparently something had happened, and others were listening.

I turned off my computer and monitor. Then I put everything away where it belonged and exited my office, moving quickly over to Janet's desk. She was busy checking a column of figures. I waited until she looked up, then said, "Listen, Janet. I've got to go home. The police want me over at the town homes. Maybe someone's broken in or something. I'm not sure, they wouldn't say. Why don't you close her up now and start your weekend? Nothing much doing here this late anyway."

"Oh, Mike, I'm sorry. Okay, sure. We're doing fine here." Suddenly Janet was flustered. "I hope it isn't serious. Do you want me to come along in case I can help?"

I thought for a moment. "Well, since I don't know what has happened, I think it would be a waste of your time."

"Okay, Mike. Let me know what's going on. Call me at home. I'll just finish up here, then take off. Remember, call me."

I was distracted and did not immediately answer. When I saw Janet staring at me I said, "Yes, yes, I'll call."

"Want a ride?"

"No, I'm good. Thanks. Have a nice weekend."

I breezed out the front door and quick-walked towards home. When I reached the corner of Water and Lake streets, I saw a police cruiser parked by the garage entrance to my building. Two more crowded the street in front, and a State Crime lab truck was there as well. Oh, oh, this had to be big trouble.

I was uncertain what I should do or where I should go. Bill Rehms hadn't indicated where to go, so I entered my own place. Before inserting the key, I checked the front door. It was properly locked and didn't appear tampered with. I quietly let myself in the door, standing just over the threshold. Everything seemed normal from the landing.

"Anyone here?" I hollered with a break in my voice. Nothing. It was so quiet I could hear a pin drop. Apparently nothing was wrong in my place. I hurried downstairs and opened my blinds to the patio. No one was outside on my deck and from what I could see no one was down on the dock either, and my boat seemed to be riding normally. Good, the problem wasn't here.

That was when it hit me. I bet this was all about the so-called stolen furniture and missing car from next door. I shook my head. I really could not believe this affair had gotten to be such a big deal. That asshole

Thompson had pushed everything beyond all belief. I actually was disappointed in the local police for pursuing his complaint as aggressively as they appeared to be doing.

All of a sudden with my concern assuaged, I noticed how warm it was in my place, due to the fact I normally set the thermostat at eighty during the day while I was at work. I shut off the air, and opened the house both up and down to fresh lakeside air. Then I changed clothes, putting on a pair of shorts, knit shirt, and sandals.

Returning to the lower level, I went outside onto the deck and peeked around the barrier to observe what was happening next door. The blinds on the patio door were drawn, and I was unable to observe any activity taking place through any of the windows. However, the action had to be next door, so I mulled over the situation as I lit up a stogie.

My immediate neighborhood was daytime quiet. It wasn't quite time for people to return home from work, and I didn't see my neighbor on the other side, Walter, outside on his deck. Maybe he was out fishing. I couldn't see if his boat was docked or not.

I considered my options. Rehms had asked me to come here, but had not said where exactly here was. Was I supposed to come to my place and wait for them to find me, or were they expecting me to go next door? He had not been very clear on that point. Obviously everyone was next door, so I determined I might as well stick my head in over there and find out what was up. Thus I trudged upstairs and went out front, approaching my neighbor's door. I rang the bell and waited expectantly.

The afternoon sun was beating down on the front of the building creating an uncomfortable heat pocket. I didn't want to hang out there for long.

When an auxiliary officer unknown to me opened the door, I informed him Officer Rehms wanted to see me. He instructed me to wait and closed the door in my face. No thank you for coming. No please wait a minute. No nothing. This whole affair was getting me pissed. I was hot and tired and annoyed. Fuck this I decided. I had left work early, came home as I was instructed, and now I was getting jacked around. I decided I had endured enough crap from those people and went back to my place.

I felt the asshole could look for me if he wanted me. This investigation or whatever it was was not about my place so what did I care? It fried me they were pursuing Sherrill, as if the poor woman had not had enough trouble with that jerk-off husband of hers.

When my front door slammed behind me after entering my abode the noise startled me. I took a deep breath and cautioned myself to control my temper. Perhaps I needed to put myself in their shoes. I took a few more deep breaths and tried to relax. My neck and shoulders felt tight. But I considered that, if they wanted my assistance, at least they could have told me what was going on.

Still pissed off, I grabbed a beer from the refrigerator and went out onto the deck, leaving a trail of cigar smoke throughout my place. I was afraid to put the beer to my lips; it might boil. I was that mad. But then I raised that thin, brown-colored bottle neck to my lips and tasted the nectar within. The liquid was so cold and refreshing it caused me to initiate an attitude change. Very slowly I could feel the tension flowing away from my body.

I was uncertain why I had become so upset. Yes, maybe I did know the reason. This upheaval of emotion had happened all too frequently to me since my old girl, Grace Adams, abandoned me last year. A lot of seemingly inconsequential things had gotten blown out of proportion over that timeframe. For a while I thought I'd been getting better at controlling my temper. Apparently not. I'd have to keep working on it. A new appointment with my shrink might be a good idea after all.

That first beer was great, and I swallowed it right down. I slowed down on the second. With the aid of the alcohol, I had cooled down a bit by the time my doorbell rang. At first I ignored the noisy entreaty out of pure spite. When the bell rang a second time, I got up to answer it, grumbling. Stay cool, big guy. Don't burn any bridges here today.

When I opened the door, two officers stood in the heat to greet me. I knew them both. One was Rehms, the other a woman named Nancy Bishop. I had met her the previous summer when I had been embroiled in another mess. I had considered asking her out on a date back then, but life got complicated for me and I never did.

Both officers had grim expressions. Obviously this wasn't a social call.

"Mr. Connelly, may we come in?" Bishop asked.

Mr. Connelly was it? This must be serious business, then. I thought for a few seconds. If I said yes, then I opened my entire place to a free search. I had nothing to hide, yet I had no idea what's taking place.

"Well, may we?" she repeated.

"What exactly is the purpose of this visit," I asked.

Bill spoke up. "We'd like to discuss with you your meeting with Mrs. Thompson on last Tuesday. The one you already discussed with me."

I thought for a moment. "Okay," I responded carefully. "You have my permission to join me on my deck."

The two officers looked at one another. Then Bill shrugged. Both officers stepped inside as I backed away with the open door. Three of us in the small foyer created a crowd. I was barely able to swing the door shut, as I said, "Follow me."

I squeezed past my guests and walked downstairs. When we reached the living room, I paused and said. I'm having a beer, either of you care to join me?"

Bishop shook her head, while Rehms said. "Not while we're working, Mike."

So it was Mike again was it? All friendly and social? *Cool it, Connelly. Give the guy a break. I know he can be a jerk, but you did not have to be one.* I could have offered the duo something to eat, but wasn't in a convivial mood, so I neglected to extend the offer. My razor-sharp senses told me that this wasn't going to be a pleasant call.

I slid open the screen door to the deck, and the two officers went through. Following, I slid the door shut and walked over to where I had been sitting. My beer bottle and cigar were placed in front of my seat. My territory had been staked out. We sat in chairs opposite one another, each marking our terrain.

Both officers were in uniform. Officer Bishop was a medium size woman, standing about five-foot-six. She was a little thick in waist, but voluptuous in form. All that hardware hanging around her waist had no slimming effect. I had thought previously I might like to see her in a dress, or better yet out of it, but time had dimmed that desire.

The woman was light-complexioned, which had made me wonder if her dark hair was natural or dyed. It was longer than I remembered from last summer because she had it pulled behind her head into a bun. Last year it had been cut about chin length. Her lips were full, and her dark eyes were staring at me. I remembered after seeing her lips last summer that I wondered how well she kissed. I still could ask her out.

I remained a little hot under the collar so before I could control myself, I blurted out, "Still pursuing that poor woman on the stolen furniture angle, I see."

Officer Bishop searched Officer Rehms's face for an explanation, so he answered, "I'm afraid it's gone beyond that, Mike." He crossed one foot over a knee and held it there with a free hand.

"How so?" I asked, slightly taken aback. I wondered what the asshole Thompson had done now.

Rehms leaned forward slightly. "Let us ask you some questions and maybe that'll answer yours," he said.

I resigned myself to the ordeal. "Okay, shoot." I leaned back in my chair and crossed one leg over my knee, mimicking Rehms.

"Mind if we record this?" he asked.

"Why?"

"I want to get it right and don't want to have to bother you again with the same questions."

"Makes sense. Go ahead," I said.

Officer Rehms placed his recorder onto the table between us and turned it on. Then he spoke into it with the date and who was present for the interview. Then he indicated the interview concerned the disappearance of Sherrill Thompson.

I was surprised at the last statement because I had surmised he would have tracked her down by then How hard was it to find the shipping company? Besides, if she did go out of state, why the big effort to find her? He knew she wasn't a missing person, at least not in the strictest sense. With the recorder running, I kept my mouth shut. When speaking with the police, it was best to speak when spoken to and not offer more information then asked for.

A gust of wind blew along the building and felt refreshing. It had been a warm day, and I thought I still could feel residual heat radiating off the building's siding from earlier exposure to the sun. A drop of perspiration trickled down past my nose, and I touched my forehead with the cold bottle. "How about some water, guys?"

"Maybe later," Officer Rehms spoke. Then, "Earlier this week on Wednesday you told me you had seen Sherrill Thompson on the previous night. That would have been Tuesday night."

I nodded.

"That's a yes, then."

"Oh, excuse me. Yes, Tuesday night."

Officer Bishop was sitting on the edge of her chair looking at a notebook.

"What were the circumstances of that meeting?" he asked.

He already knew this, but I played along. "I came home from golf, and saw people entering and exiting the unit next door. Since I knew the occupant was supposedly absent, I went over and checked to see if everything was kosher."

"And you saw Sherrill Thompson at that time?"

"That's correct. She said she was too busy to talk at that moment, but would try to stop by my place before she left town."

"Why do you suppose she said that?" Bill asked.

"That she was busy?"

"No, that she would stop over to say goodbye?"

I shrugged. "I really don't know. You'd have to ask her. Being neighborly, I guess. She was putting me off at the moment so wanted to stay friendly. It's all a guess on my part. Ask her."

Rehms grimaced.

"Did you know the woman very well?" Officer Bishop interjected.

I turned my head and looked her in the eyes. I tried to figure out their exact color, but the light here didn't help. I answered, "Know her well? No, as a matter of fact, I barely knew her at all. My only real interaction with her was an occasional hello across our decks or in the garage. I never had done anything together with her and her husband socially. Actually the night I put her patio door back on track during a rainstorm was the most interaction we'd ever had." Boy if they knew the interaction we had that night, I'd probably be in hot water!

Officer Bishop interrupted my reverie. "Explain that if you would."

I had to get my mind back on track. Rehms knew what had happened, but I suppose they wanted it on tape, so I went through the whole story. I dragged it out as long as I could with as much detail as I could just to be an ass. I wondered who would have to type this up? However, neither of them interrupted, so it must have satisfied both of them.

"So you're saying that, in all the time the couple lived next door, you never interacted with them?" she asked looking surprised.

I thought about that statement, and it revived my earlier guilt about not knowing my neighbors. I had to wonder if these two were purposely trying to make me feel shitty?

I sucked it up and said, "Seldom it would seem. These units are set up in such a way that we have a lot of privacy. We don't really see our neighbors. You can see that sitting here. There's a partition between each deck. One would have to go down near the water to view inside them. There isn't any common area, so unless we meet going out our front door or on the dock or in the garage, we don't meet. I don't think those folks have a boat, so that limits things somewhat there. Apparently they both worked, and I didn't see them on weekends. I'm a boat guy, and I don't know what they did with their spare time."

"Apparently his brother had a cabin in Wisconsin. He went there a lot," Rehms answered.

I nodded. "There you go," I said. That explained a little of it. I felt somewhat better about my lack of interaction with the couple.

"Mike, err Mr. Connelly, you told me that Mrs. Thompson told you about her reasons for moving, but you never said where she was going," Rehms said.

"That's correct. She said she was trying to get lost, at least where her husband was concerned."

"Did you infer anything from that?" Officer Bishop asked.

"I didn't have to. Previously she had told me her husband physically abused her. To me that made it obvious why she would want to flee."

"I thought you didn't know her well?" Bishop said.

"I didn't."

"Then why would she tell you that? It's pretty personal information, isn't it?" she asked.

"Well, she had asked me to help her with her door, right? I had asked her how the door came to be off the track. They don't just fall off by themselves, big heavy doors like that." Here I laughed. "She admitted to me that, in a fit of temper, she had slammed it shut, and it had banged so hard it jumped off the bottom rail. Out of curiosity I followed up with a question of what had made her that angry and she broke down crying and told me about her husband."

"What did you do?" Bishop asked.

"I suggested she work through her attorney and cut off contact with him."

"Logical," Bishop said, leaning back in her chair.

"Fine, that answers that." Rehms said. "Do you recall what time you got home Tuesday night?"

"Home like in here, or home like over there?"

"Either."

"I think I got here about ten-thirty. I went up and took a shower, then came down and fixed a snack. The local news was long over, so I put on E.S.P.N. to catch the scores. Pretty close to ten thirty, ten forty-five."

"And what time did Mrs. Thompson leave?"

"Here?"

"Yes."

I tried to think, but nothing definite came to mind. "It must have been after eleven, maybe even eleven-thirty. I just didn't pay attention. She hadn't been here more than five minutes, but I really hadn't paid any attention at all to the time. There had been no reason to."

Rehms looked at Bishop. She shook her head.

"What's going on?" I asked.

Rehms answered. "We have found out that Mrs. Thompson was headed for Vegas. She was going to live with her sister and brother-in-law out there until she closed on a house she purchased in that town. There's no indication she ever arrived there, and there's been no word from her since the sister spoke with her Tuesday night before she was to leave here."

"What time was that?" I asked.

"Ten-thirty our time."

I realized she must have talked to her sister before we spoke at her place or before coming over to mine.

"So you think she had an accident on her way out there?" I asked.

"I'm afraid not. Her auto was towed from the downtown lot here in Excelsior on Thursday morning. The vehicle was registered to Mr. Thompson, so we didn't tumble to the connection immediately, but the impound lot caught it from the list of wanted vehicles."

"Oh," was all I could say.

This whole thing was getting weird. Something dreadful had happened and to someone I knew. I thought about our night in the shower. I finally came to. Both officers were staring at me.

"So you're looking for her?" I asked.

"Yes. Anything more you can add that might help us?"

I shook my head. "I'll let you know if I think of anything."

"Do that," Bishop said.

Rehms turned off the recorder and put it in his case. They both stood though I didn't notice. I sat immobile, overwhelmed by the news. How could she have just disappeared?

"Mike?"

I jerked and stood. Then I led the way to the front door. I let the officers out and then went back to my deck where I lit up a new smoke. I tried to think of what might have happened on Tuesday night but could think of nothing. I just wasn't very creative when it came to that type of thinking.

What I did know, however, was that when Sherrill left my place, she had intended to get right in her car and beat it out of town. She had not wanted to hang out for any reason. So what could have delayed her from leaving? Other than using the bathroom at her place, what else would she have needed to do?

Had her car been parked down in the garage? It must have been. I had no recollection of seeing it on the street that night. Did someone attack her in the garage? How could they? No one could get in unless they lived here. Of course someone could have walked in behind a car that was entering. Who knew what the movers were doing. Were the movers gone when Sherrill came over? Yes. There had been no one on the street. What could have happened? Was it possible she was dead?

Now that they had found her car at the impound lot, why would she have parked it where it would be towed? She wouldn't have done that. She was leaving town. Was she hijacked before she left? On an Excelsior street? My god!

A shiver came over me. I had a bad feeling, but there was nothing I could do.

~18~

A Busy Saturday

I HAD NOT INTENDED to stay up very late on Friday night because I wanted to rise early on Saturday morning to drown some worms. However, it seemed to take forever for me to finally fall asleep. Even after I had dropped off, I slept fitfully.

There hadn't been much of a breeze through my open window, since what wind there was came from in front of the building. Thus it had remained warm in my room well into the wee early morning hours. The humidity also appeared elevated and that caused me to toss off my covers. I almost gave into turning on the air conditioner, though I wasn't sure I would have slept any better.

While trying to doze off, I lay motionless on my bare sheet with closed eyes listening to the faint sounds of talking and laughter, as the soft hum of human activity drifted across the still water to me from the nearby restaurants. Boat motors seemed particularly obnoxious when, otherwise, I never would have noticed. I was extremely on edge, and slept badly as a result.

When four-thirty arrived, I was roused from a dead sleep by the clamor of my alarm clock and felt as if I had just lain down. I certainly felt far from rested. Because I intended to go fishing, I forced myself out of bed. After dressing and organizing, eventually I found myself on the lake and somewhat ready to fish by 5:00 a.m.

The humidity this early morning remained high and caused a halo to form around the sole light illuminating the dock. I fiddled with the gate to gain access to the boats, then carried my gear to my craft. I had taken the effort to make coffee since I felt I might need a jolt of something before I was done.

126

Most of my fishing gear already was in the boat. I had the foresight to prepare that equipment in the light of day. However, this morning I removed my worms from the refrigerator and carried those along with my coffee and a lantern on the shadowy trip onto the dock.

It was soothing to my psyche to be able to get onto the water in the early morning when I had the lake nearly to myself. Decidedly, I needed this quiet time alone on the water this morning to clear my head of all that was spinning around in there. My mind had been working overtime since last evening with the Thompson mess front and center, and I needed a complete break from normalcy to gain some perspective. The shocking news had come so suddenly and had in turn been such a surprise, that I was having difficulty comprehending the scope and ramifications of what I'd heard.

Then too I had my scheduled meeting at the bank later this morning and in light of everything else, I wasn't sure I was looking forward to that. I had such superficial knowledge of banking that meeting with two experienced bankers was intimidating me to no small degree.

Just a sliver of a moon shown off to the west, and dawn was breaking slowly. By five-thirty I could see a glow of yellowish orange that was tinting the eastern horizon from below clouds. That was about the only way I could sense direction while on the water. Very few lights from homes or businesses on shore were on, and once I motored away from Excelsior, streetlights were few and far between. Of course I had carried my lantern flashlight down to the boat with me to aid me in my work at least until the sun came up. To do otherwise probably would have resulted in my baiting the hook with my thumb rather than a worm.

No other boats were on the bay when I pulled away from the dock. It would have been easy to spot their lights. A warm breeze blew out of the south and kissed my bare skin. It was strong enough to create a slight chop on the water, which I decided wouldn't hurt fishing.

I stayed out on the lake until nine, by which time I had used up my supply of worms. The pan fish were there, but merely nibbling at the bait, expertly stripping it off the hook. The fish must have been quite small. I didn't mind though. It was action and that was why I was out on the water. If I caught a couple of decent-size fish to eat that was fine with me.

Once the sun had risen, I saw more activity along the shore. Home-owners were at it early mowing grass and preparing boats for a weekend of activity. As I passed by one particular dock, two boys were cannon-balling off the end. I smiled as I remembered how much fun that was when I was a youngster.

By the time I returned home, the chop on the water had grown some, and in the open bay it would have been sufficient to allow a float-plane to easily break free from the surface on takeoff. They needed choppy water like this to allow their floats to escape the surface tension that the water provided. Still, it promised to be a fine summer day, and the lake eventually would be crowded with boats.

By returning home early I generally missed most of the weekend boat traffic. That would come later in the afternoon. In addition, getting home early this morning allowed me to prepare for my meeting at the bank. I left my tackle in the boat since I hoped to go out fishing again Sunday morning. I just had to remember to get more bait. My refrigerator was empty. I had shocked more than one woman when they opened a container from the fridge wondering what was in it only to find leaches or worms. I never knew why they were so surprised, after all it was a man's domicile. What had they expected?

The remainder of the morning was spent doing laundry and house-cleaning. Though I had a service come in and clean once a week, there were always things that needed to be done in between those visits. I did most of my own laundry, but acquiesced to having the laundry across the street do my shirts and suits. I drop a suit off every Friday with five shirts. I wasn't into ironing. When I finished my chores, I showered and shaved, put on a dress shirt without a tie and pulled on a sport coat. Looking in the mirror, I declared myself presentable for the public.

When the time came for our meeting, I walked to the bank. It was only three blocks away, the location being a small building on the corner of George and Water streets. A filling station once had this location, but it had morphed into many uses over the years. That original building had been removed for the construction of the small bank building. An adjacent property had been commandeered, and that had provided space for a drive through.

Weekends always brought plenty of visitors to town, and I noticed on my walk that already the curbside parking was mostly taken. Soon the back lots would be crowded to overflowing.

It was going to be a warm day and most people were dressed accordingly. It made me feel conspicuously overdressed as I passed by them wearing a sport jacket and long pants.

Yet it was a glorious day for a walk. The sidewalks supported many shoppers, and the streets were crowded with cars. However, once I passed Third Street on my way through town, the number of people diminished. There was less commerce on this end of town.

This banker's meeting at one time had seemed immensely important to me, but after my visit with the police on the previous evening, Katie's so-called problems, considering what might have happened to Sherrill, my need to meet with Bob had diminished in significance. I even had considered canceling, but upon reflection I could not very well do that to Bob after he had stuck his neck out and made this appointment with Katie's old man. Besides, as I had indicated to Bob, this would be a learning experience for me. God knows I had a lot to learn.

Furthermore, I had wondered what kind of person Katie had fallen for. She had come from modest circumstances as a young girl, and I couldn't imagine her even today as a social climber. But then I hadn't known her beyond high school and couldn't fathom what influences might have swayed her in college and beyond. She had seemed immensely normal, though, during our first visits.

Hopefully I would be able to extricate myself from this chore very soon now and would have no further need to analyze Katie and her lifestyle. If I were fortunate, I might learn all I needed to about Larry Williams today and that would put an end to my research. I merely had to propose something plausible to Katie to get her off my back. I no longer wanted her fantasies to be my problem.

When I stood before the bank building in the mid-day sunshine, I realized I should be grateful for another wonderful summer day in Minnesota.

I chided myself to concentrate on the positive and not dwell on the negative. The forecast for this week was for more of the same. I let out a sigh, realizing it should be a great Fourth of July holiday.

The bank lobby was open only until noon on Saturdays, but Bob apparently was watching for me. He was standing with the front door partially open, and I heard him say to a woman standing there, ". . . but the bank is closed now, Gail."

"I know, but I got held up at church and lost track of time. I need to get this deposited or my checks will bounce. Can't I leave this with you, then?"

I inched closer, not wanting to invade her space, but near enough that Bob noticed me. He did and nodded. Bob had a perplexed look on his face, but then he reached out and took the woman's offering. Then he smiled. "Sure, Gail. No problem, and don't you worry. We won't let any of your checks bounce."

"If the checks I wrote come in on Monday will it cover them?"

"Yes. Don't you worry. I'll handle it personally."

"Then that's okay. Don't forget now." The woman put her hand on Bob's arm and squeezed. "Thanks, Bob."

"I won't forget," he reiterated. That was small town banking for you.

The woman turned and saw me for the first time. She smiled at me and I reciprocated. "The bank's closed young man."

"Thank you," I said, and I watched her walk away.

Bob smiled as he admitted me. Larry Williams already was inside, standing by one of the kiosks. My first impression was positive. He was a good-looking man. Katie had chosen well. He stood erect with an elbow on the writing desk. His face was inscrutable. I tried to imagine Katie and Larry together, but my imagination left something to be desired. I more readily saw her on my arm. I was pulled from my reverie when Bob said my name.

We completed the introductions, and then Bob stopped momentarily to write a note and clip it to the deposit left in his care. Then he showed us the way to his office. He had provided coffee and donuts for the meeting, and I was glad I had eaten before coming here. There would be no need to work off the calories from those beasties later since I wasn't tempted.

I had not worked out last night, and I needed to do that this afternoon after our meeting. I really didn't want to let it go another day. I never felt good missing a workout. That alone gave me the resolve to stay away from the flour/sugar combination.

The three of us stood in Bob's office. This was the first time I had met Larry, and I didn't recall having ever seen him around town. Apparently he was not a member of any local organizations to which I belonged. That was understandable since his work wasn't here in town. I was sure he was involved in plenty of organizations elsewhere, and probably on a much grander scale than I ever contemplated.

I was standing a mere three feet from Larry, which allowed me to see him very well indeed. He was handsome in a manly sort of way, though upon closer inspection, he looked haggard. He stood just short of six feet tall and had a trim build. He appeared to be in his mid to late forties, about Bob's age. He didn't appear overweight, but neither was he in shape. Working out regularly would have corrected that in no time. He was just a little squishy around the edges. The man suffered the curse of the typical well-fed but under-worked populace.

Larry's dirty-blond hair was stylishly cut and slicked back. The hairline was receding slightly but not excessively so. A strong jaw anchored a thin, somewhat emaciated face devoid of facial hair.

I saw plenty of worry lines, and I noticed a slight twitch below his right eye. He occasionally moved his index finger up to it and gave it a quick massage. I don't think he even realized he was doing it.

With today's economy, the man probably had plenty of worries. A steady workout regime might help relieve some of that tension, though I decided not to offer that advice. I had no way to know or understand what pressures the man was under, and it certainly would be presumptuous of me to prescribe a remedy.

I thought of Katie though and had a momentary pang of regret. For such a lovely lady, I could only wish the best. Having her husband in distress diminished her chance for happiness. That troubled me somehow. Perhaps I was doing the right thing in trying to help her.

Today Larry was dressed in casual slacks, dress shoes, and a shirt and tie. From that I surmised he had been at his office and had stopped here to accommodate us on his return home.

On such a great summer day I was pleased he found the time for us. I was certain he would be spending the afternoon on that yacht of his probably entertaining clients.

Bob on the other hand was dressed more casually, with just a short-sleeved white shirt and a pair of khaki slacks. I knew Saturdays were casual dress days here at the bank, and Bob's attire reflected that.

Bob had a round coffee table in his office and invited us to sit in the comfortable swivel chairs around it. They not only swiveled, but reclined as well.

Larry smoothed out a crease in his slacks and asked, "Is it Michael or Mike?"

I was looking out the window, but turned at his inquiry and said, "Mike is fine, Larry."

"I wondered," he said noncommittally while he picked at a fingernail with one from his other hand. "Katherine keeps mentioning this Michael she knows. Perhaps that's you?"

I nearly blushed but realized there was nothing of which to be ashamed. I answered, "I don't know, Larry. Of course I know your wife, but can't imagine why she'd mention me. It must be some other Michael."

What I had said was true. I hadn't thought our previous meeting was a secret, though just the same, I wondered why Katie would mention it to her husband. It could possibly open a whole can of worms as to why we met. Upon further reflection I determined perhaps the man was fishing. Maybe Katie hadn't mentioned my name to him, and he was looking for a response on my part to confirm a suspicion of his.

While I was considering all this, Larry was eyeing me as he poured himself a cup of coffee. He apparently wasn't ready to let the subject drop. "Did you go to school with Katherine?" he asked, as he crossed one leg over the other.

I leaned back in my chair testing how far it would go. Then I crossed one foot over my knee as Larry had done and said, "No. I only knew

Katherine because she used to baby sit for my family when she was in high school. I really had lost track of her since those days."

He nodded while he played with a tooth with the tip of his tongue. "How old were you then?" he asked.

I pursed my lips as I recollected. "Let me think. I must have been eight or nine when she graduated high school. She stopped babysitting for us then."

"Help yourself to the coffee, Mike," Bob said.

"Thanks, Bob." As I poured myself a cup, I asked. "Are you from around here originally, Larry?"

He reflected for a moment as though trying to remember. "No, I grew up in Illinois. Down around Champaign. Are you familiar with that area?"

I shook my head. "Not really. Good farm country I understand."

"Very much so."

I wanted to learn as much as possible about Larry to determine Katie's problem so I continued to make small talk. I asked, "How did you and Katherine meet?"

Again the man looked off into space as if trying to remember. Later I would put this down to a preoccupation with weightier matters, but at the time was perplexed. "Let me think. I believe she was ushering at the Saturday night symphony here in downtown Minneapolis, and she showed me to my seat. I was smitten by her and seem to recall having someone introduce us, then me asking her out after that." He nodded as if satisfied with his answer.

Larry's careless response surprised me. I personally thought a guy would remember when he first met his wife, but who was I to judge? Perhaps this was indicative of what Katie had considered inattentiveness.

I wondered if it was anything about which she should get so emotional.

~19~

ECONOMIC MELTDOWN

U P TO THAT POINT in our conversation, the topics had been of a general nature. Then Bob jumped in. "Larry, I know you're busy, and I don't want to keep you too long. I appreciate you taking the time to meet with us. We had an F.D.I.C. exam here last fall, and I heard you're being examined now. I thought we could compare notes. Maybe you could share some insight."

I thought it a cute ploy for Bob to bring in the Federal Deposit Insurance Corporation as an excuse to query Larry. I had wondered how he'd go about it.

"Sure, Bob. Maybe your experience can help us with our audit," Larry answered. "How was your exam?"

Bob shook his head in disgust. "I've never been through anything like that before," he answered. "It was worse than a rectal exam." Here Bob did grin slightly. Then his face grew serious once more. "We ended up having over fifteen pages of findings, observations, and recommendations, Larry. We were faulted for lack of control, lack of separation of duties, and lack of oversight. I think the examiners were making it up as they went along. I'm not so sure there were laws on the books for everything they were quoting."

Larry nodded as if he understood. He kept a straight face. I did remember the exam. With my limited experience, I had thought the team of examiners would be in a couple of days, but they were around for well over two weeks by my recollection. I had inquired of Bob every two days how things were going and had been unable to get any answers. The examiners had played it pretty close to the vest until the exit interview. I had never seen Bob so rattled.

Bob continued, "We aren't big enough to have a person in each job. Most employees wear several hats. That makes it difficult to have separation of responsibilities between several people." Bob shook his head. "But the examiners weren't very sympathetic to our situation I'm afraid. It makes it really difficult. We'll have to figure something out. If Congress keeps passing all the regulatory rules they've been passing, all us little guys will be out of business. We can't keep up with it all. Can't afford it."

Bob had hit his stride and clearly was upset.

Larry jumped in. "I don't know if it'll ever ease up, Bob, but they're just covering their asses. Ever since Lehman Brothers went down, the hammer has come down from Washington. Consequently, none of those inspectors wants a bank to fail under his or her watch, especially after they've reviewed the bank and given their approval to the bank's actions. That would reflect badly on them as examiners. Going forward, if it's going to fail, they want to be the ones to decide that."

I was surprised at the statement. "You think?" I asked.

Larry looked at me. "Damn right," he answered. The look on his face was pure malevolence.

This was enlightening. Bob previously had said banks were highly regulated, but I really never had paid that much attention to the situation. I did remember him telling me we didn't own the bank, just leased it from the government. I had always thought that sounded funny, but now with all the regulation I could see the truth in it.

"What do think, Bob? Just covering their asses?" Larry questioned.

"That's my sense, Larry. They left no stone unturned."

"Did you contest the final review?" Larry asked.

"We considered it. We hired legal counsel, and they advised us that we could but weren't terribly optimistic it would do any good. So we decided to take our licking and do what we could to comply."

"I don't suppose you'd want to disclose your rating?" Larry asked.

Bob hesitated. The bank rating was supposed to be a secret. "We got a two," he murmured.

Larry nearly jumped out of his chair. "Well, damn, man. What have you got to complain about? We're happy with a two most any time."

"You are, really?" Bob asked.

"Sure. If you get a one, you're not managing your finances properly, being too careful. The more you leverage your capitol the more money you make. Probably leaving money on the table, otherwise."

Bob squinted and nodded. "Yes, I see that. What you say makes me feel better. But it gets hairy if you leverage too highly, doesn't it? I hate to take chances. Isn't that what got most banks in trouble?"

Larry smiled. "That's the reason why so many institutions are in trouble today, gentlemen. Consequently why the F.D.I.C. has decided that every bank needs to increase capital by roughly fifty percent. Hell, just about every community bank in Minnesota that's been examined this year has gotten a *four* rating. As you know, that's not very good. That puts the bank on the edge of being closed. Of course in most cases it's because the ratio of their capitol compared to the combination of their deposits and bad loans wasn't high enough."

I had to think about that for a minute. I knew banks had to have money to charter. That would be their capitol. It was understandable the more they grew, the more money had to be put in capitol as a safeguard against losses.

Then Bob said, "I hadn't heard that. I mean, about so many banks getting four ratings."

"And the thing is many of them aren't doing anything about it, at least not rushing out panicking," Larry replied. "They're treating it like it's a joke. Maybe they think this recession is going away overnight, I don't know. We were proactive though. Last fall we raised our capital base by quite a bit. Put in over fifteen million. We may have some bad loans, but at least the extra capital injection will give us the cash if we need it to pay out to our customers. We've been touting that to the examiners. I hope they're listening.

"Remember the old saying, gentlemen? 'You can't go broke with money in your pocket.' That's the case for adequate capitol. If every loan fails, can you still pay off on your customer accounts."

"That's true," Bob said.

I was struck by this information. I'd always thought banks were loaded. But if businesses were suffering, and they were, and they weren't paying on their loans, banks also would suffer. They could not print money.

"I don't want to imply anything," Larry continued. "But you know your F.D.I.C. insurance premium takes a big jump if you're given a four rating. With all the money that's been paid out on insured accounts for failed banks, do you think maybe the bureaucrats are looking for ways to recoup some of that money by handing out four ratings?"

I was astounded that Larry would imply such a thing, handing out fours to secure a higher insurance premium, but I guessed that at one time or another I had seen just about everything. I decided to keep an open mind on the subject. He sure sounded cynical and bitter, though. I wondered how his exam was coming along?

Then I questioned myself as to whether any of this was helping me with my problem. So far I had not heard anything to help me evaluate Larry and his relationship with Katie. My mind jerked back to the subject at hand and I asked, "What exactly happens if a bank gets a four rating from their exam? Besides insurance, I mean?"

Larry made a teepee with his fingers and said, "When you don't meet certain preordained requirements on such things as capitol, assets, and liquidity, you used to get what was called a Cease and Desist Order, but they've softened the language a little nowadays. Now they call it a Consent Order. The bank in jeopardy is required to consent to make appropriate changes. It's the same basic thing, just a different name."

Larry paused and looked off into the distance. Then he jerked to attention and continued. "Perhaps the examiners are going into the audits with the idea they'll be giving fours to everyone regardless of how poor the situation—"

Here I interrupted. "Why would they do that?"

Larry cocked his head. "Maybe the bank doesn't deserve a four rating. Perhaps last year they might have received a three with the same financial numbers, but in today's world those numbers are going to produce a four rating. The examiners want a lever to force banks to take the appropriate steps to recover. This is it."

I digested, or attempted to digest what he had said. It made sense, though I didn't fully understand it.

Larry continued, "Then on the worst side of the spectrum, perhaps the examiners realize there are so many banks in trouble they can't shut them all down. Instead they'll work with those capable of recovery. The softer language of the order gives them latitude to decide. Maybe.

"You choose. My personal thought is that they don't want to rattle the public, so they've softened the language. The effect is the same, though. Of course they're closing some banks either way. You've certainly read in the papers where a bank closes on Friday and opens Monday under a different name."

I had seen that but had paid little attention. After all, it had not affected me directly, though I had wondered at the process.

Larry continued. "Most of those cases of failed banks have been smaller out-state community banks that got into real estate deals in an effort to grow. Now they can't get their money out of those deals. You know, development loans."

"Who loses in a case like that?" I asked.

"Everyone eventually, but mostly the stockholders. Remember, though, everything eventually trickles down to the consumer, the ultimate source of money. Of course the customer accounts are insured unless the depositor has an amount in the bank higher than the insurance limit."

"What are the banks doing who get a Consent Order and have decided to comply?" Bob asked.

Larry turned toward Bob and said, "You're given a list of what you have to do to get yourself squared away. That might include anything from restructuring your staff to deciding which customers you have to cut loose. Most of the time it'll require the bank to raise additional capital. Either you do what you're told to do or fail. Not much of a choice."

"Cutting loose struggling customers is certainly not serving the community," Bob said. He paused and reflected for a moment. Both Larry and I watched him, knowing he had something to say. Then he looked up and said, "We had this problem loan where the value of the building through the appraisal process turned out to be less now than what still is owed on the mortgage. The building's value in the three years since we gave the loan has dropped by a third."

138

"Just like eighty million homeowners today," Larry interjected.

"Yes," Bob continued. "Just like that, and they wanted us to foreclose on the customer if we couldn't get more collateral from them." Bob looked down at his feet. "There's nothing more to get, we got it all out front. Heck we started these guys out. They're hardworking. They own a carwash. The town needs them. I'm not going to put them out of business without giving them a chance. Besides why would I want to run a carwash? I have enough headaches as it is."

I could hear the anxiety in Bob's voice.

I remembered that particular deal well enough. A local fellow, Jack Goodman, started the carwash. Jack's family had lived in the area for at least four generations, and Jack was not only hard working but also an all-around good guy. Then his young daughter, Sarah, broke her leg in a biking accident this past spring. Jack had been carrying no insurance because he couldn't afford the premiums with business being so bad. He had been putting everything he could into the bank payment. After the accident, his church held a bake sale to help pay his hospital bill, and raised three hundred and fifty dollars against a bill of nearly two thousand. It has been a tough situation all around. I was certain there were many more stories like Jack's.

My thoughts were interrupted when Larry asked, "So, what did you do?"

Bob began talking with his hands. "Instead of shutting them down, we got creative and got a government Small Business Administration loan on the building. The S.B.A. has some good programs for small business. With an S.B.A. loan, the money we loaned comes first, ahead of the government money in case of a default. Because of that, our portion of the total loan amount now is only fifty-percent of the building's value. So it's no longer considered a troubled loan for us because our loan is only fifty percent of the appraised value. Plus we get to keep a good account and help a worthy member of our community."

"That's smart banking, Bob," Larry said. "Keep that up, and you'll grow. Word gets around when you treat people right. I wish we could do that on our land deals. Individual lots just aren't selling. Builders can't afford to build on spec because they have no cash. Look what happened to Centex Homes. One of the biggest homebuilders in the country, and they went bust. Ran out of cash. Just didn't see the bottom falling out. Who did?

"We've had to get creative to help sell those lots to get our money back," Larry continued. "We had already loaned the developer the money to put in the streets, curbs, and sidewalks. They installed all the utilities. To pay us back, they needed to sell the lots to builders who would put up the homes. Selling improved lot gave them the cash to pay us.

"Hell, we had one client who'd been developing around the cities for years. Some pretty darn nice golf course developments. They had a huge project and we backed it. A large national builder was going to build all the houses. Then the bottom fell out of the market, and the nationally known builder backed out. Our developer was stuck. He didn't have the kind of cash resources to pay off the development costs, and he couldn't get anyone to start building in this climate. There's not a single house completed. No clubhouse, no nothing.

"We stuck by him for more than two years, but now we're forced to foreclose."

"What do you want with the land?" I asked.

Larry laughed a sickly laugh. "We *don't* want it. We were left with only two choices, since we weren't getting paid anything. We could charge off the entire loan from our books and go back against the company later for any possible recovery. In an instance like that any holding costs still would belong to the developer. Or we could foreclose and take the land ourselves. If it were a building we might be reluctant to take it back because we'd be stuck with the upkeep and taxes, and all that. That gets expensive fast. Not so much on raw land.

"In this case the land still is considered undeveloped for tax purposes and our cost of holding it remains low. We'll start looking for small builders who want to put up a few houses each. We'll see what happens."

"Couldn't the developer have done that?" I asked.

"They've been trying for two years, but they wanted to discount the selling price of the lots. We wouldn't let them discount the lot price or they wouldn't pull in enough money for us to get paid. We'll have to discount a couple of those same lots to get things going. Then later maybe we can get full price after a few houses get started. It's like putting up a model. People won't buy unless they can see something," Larry said.

I couldn't follow the reasoning because, if the bank was going to discount the lot price, I didn't understand why they wouldn't let the developer do it? I guessed that was why I was not in big business.

"You're going to take a loss on the loan then?" I asked.

"Potentially, yes," Larry said. "But there's two things to consider. First, by going this route we'll get revenue returning to us we can reloan and earn income from. Secondly, in our tax bracket, for every dollar we lose, Uncle Same picks up fifty cents. The quicker we get this behind us, the sooner we get back to business as usual."

Here Bob interrupted. "So the key is to have enough capitol behind you to get through the downturn."

"The cash in your pocket," I said.

"You've both got it, "Larry said. Then he added. "The builders don't have the money to put up a spec home, and shoppers generally can't see what things would look like without that parade home. Most people can't read a blueprint. You've both been to the Home Parade. Which would you rather see? A home painted and bare on the interior, or one fully decorated with window treatments and furniture? The second one, right?"

We both agreed.

"So now we're paying builder's costs to put up the parade home so people will see it, buy a lot and build, so then we can get paid on the lot sale. It's tough sledding."

"You have a number of those?" I asked.

"That and commercial developments that aren't filling. Plus condos that no one's buying. A hotel or ten. A waterpark. Housing developments in Nevada and Florida. We're spread around. We lost a bundle on Ramsey Town Center right here in Anoka County a couple of years back."

"You were in that?" Bob asked.

"Yes, for a piece."

"There was fraud there, wasn't there?" Bob asked.

"Yes, but that won't help us get our money back."

I was not sure what that deal was. I would have to try to remember to ask Bob later. Another deal gone sour.

"I've heard that Las Vegas and parts of Florida are really bad," I said.

"That's an understatement. Bob, be very careful getting into participating with other banks in these kinds of things going forward. Stay at home and in things you know," Larry said. "We have crap in both those states."

He could see the question in my eyes and said, "When you're trying to grow, you need loans. Participations are a way of getting them. Maybe twenty banks each take a piece of the action. It spreads the risk around and gets us more loans, thus more income. However, when the whole country tanks . . . well you know the rest. In some extremely hard-hit areas, home values have dropped to twenty percent of what they originally were selling for."

Those developers must be hurting pretty badly," I said.

"Not only them. Remember trickledown economics? This is real trickledown economics. Think about it. The builder isn't building. Who does it affect? The excavator isn't digging. How does he pay for that dozer he bought when things were going crazy? The concrete block maker has no customers, so he lays people off. Same with the carpenters and framers. What about the roofers and sheetrock people? Painters and floor covering people as well. These are mostly small businesses that end up carrying employees for a while and then lay them off. All these people are out of work, and they stop buying anything but the bare necessities. You can see where this is heading. A third of the country is affected because of the housing bust."

"There's plenty of pain to go around," Bob said.

"Amen to that," Larry added.

I was overwhelmed with the reality of the difficulty affecting the country. I looked at both Bob and Larry. They were thinking.

Then Larry spoke up with renewed energy. "I'll say though as far as your F.D.I.C. exam, you don't have enough people to gain separation, but you can accomplish it in review. Have an officer review and initial the documents. That will give you separation in review. Try to make it someone not in charge of that area."

"Thanks, Larry. We'll try that."

"Well, I've got to be running along gentleman. Thanks for the coffee, Bob. Nice to meet you, Mike. You guys keep up the good work."

"Nice to meet you, Larry," I said as I stood. I reached out and took his hand.

"Thanks for coming by, Larry," Bob added.

The three of us walked out of Bob's office, heading toward the front door. I hung back, and Bob let Larry out. Turning to me, Bob said, "Well, that went well don't you think?"

I had heard so much information my head was spinning, and I was not sure what if anything I had learned about Larry himself.

~20~

A Time for Review

LARRY WILLIAMS HAD LEFT US, and as Bob locked the front door, I returned to his office where I refilled my coffee cup. Sitting back in my chair, I thought how totally overwhelmed I was by all the information I had just heard. I thought that perhaps Bob could clear some things up for me, if not today then over time. I found I was so immersed in the detail, just trying to understand what was said, that I had completely forgotten to think of it in the context of Katie's perceived problem. I'd have to do that later when I had time to mull it over without distraction.

From what I could tell, on the surface at least, there didn't seem to be a problem with Orion Bank, particularly due to the timing of the capital injection Larry had mentioned. I'd have to look elsewhere to find the reason for Katie's concern.

My thoughts then went back to our opening greetings. I had to wonder what the circumstance was of Larry bringing up my name. Would Katie actually have been bantering my name about? Why the clandestine meeting if that was the case. I think perhaps I had read the situation incorrectly. Apparently she kept no secrets from her husband and that could be the root of the problem if he were keeping secrets from her.

Perhaps it was just a circumstance of being too busy to be in love. If a person didn't remember how he met his wife, how much attention was he paying to her twenty years later? That was more than likely the real cause of any actual or imagined problems.

Bob silently entered his office behind me. "What did you think, Mike?" he asked, interrupting my reflection.

I was startled and flinched. "Bob, I'm not the man for this job. I think you should get someone else to be a director. I didn't know half of what you guys were discussing, much less even a beginning of understanding any of it."

Bob laughed. "You will in time. Just stick with it. You aren't expected to know everything, certainly not at first or all at once. Just provide oversight and sound council when needed."

I thought about what he said for a minute, and Bob left me alone to contemplate. Then I spoke up. "You know, Bob, I didn't know things in the economy were so bad."

"People have been suffering, Mike."

"But housing. How'd we get that bad? Things have always seemed good relative to home ownership."

Bob reflected for a moment, before answering. "You could fill a room with experts, Mike, and never get a consensus. Many things contributed to what happened, though."

"Like?" I asked.

Bob poured himself some coffee and joined me in his previous chair. Then he said, "Well, for one thing, our parents never would have played Russian roulette with their home."

I pictured holding a gun to my head, but that made no sense. "How do you mean?"

"The previous generation cherished the ability to own a home. It was really a big deal for them, something they worked for their whole life. Conversely, I believe many people today take home ownership for granted, like it's a right, not an earned privilege. If you recall, home ownership didn't become wide spread until after World War ll. That's when the suburbs grew up and home ownership ballooned. You've been in south Minneapolis and St. Louis Park, right?'

"Sure."

"Look at those homes, Mike. Compare them to what's being built in the suburbs today. The homes built back then were small, compact homes. There were no vaulted ceilings, no foyers the size of gymnasiums, no audiovisual rooms. Not even two-car garages. The places were similar to the apartments the owners left behind. The key back then was that they were affordable homes, and the people who bought them loved them. The home was theirs.

"They never would have put their home in jeopardy by borrowing against it for anything other than the original mortgage. People were conservative back then. Many had been through the Depression and then the war. They knew they could lose everything in a heartbeat." Bob stopped talking and took a sip of coffee.

"I get all that, Bob, so what caused the housing crises?"

"Well, for my money it was two things. One was a desire by some misguided individuals to get just about everyone and anyone into a home they could call their own. That turned out to be a mistake. Even when a certain economic group of people was able to put very little down on the purchase, they still had to pay the mortgage payments, and they were marginal. It didn't take much of a hiccup in their life for them to miss payments and default. Illness, loss of work, whatever. When things started going bad, that marginal group was the first to suffer. They just didn't have enough personal equity to get themselves through a rough spot."

"Sorta like us needing capitol to get through a tough period for our bank."

"Exactly, savings."

I rotated my shoulders to give my neck a break. I had been sitting too long. Then I asked, "You mean that marginal group should have continued to rent instead of buy?"

Bob shrugged. "I'm not passing a moral or value judgment here. All I'm saying is that hindsight shows that a large group of people had no reserves, and when something unfortunate happened in their lives, they lost their home.

"Now you've read about all the fraud that took place in north Minneapolis some time ago with flipping homes on sales, and phony appraisals, and all that, but there were plenty of hard-working folks who just got lost by the wayside when times got tough."

"Yes, I remember those fraud instances," I said.

Bob nodded. "To answer your question honestly though, Mike. Maybe they shouldn't have been into home ownership, but who am I to deny the American dream to anyone. If everything had broken just right . . . but no one saw the downturn coming. Or if they did, certainly never imagined anything as bad as what we've seen. It had been so good for so long. Everyone thought there'd never be a downturn. Folks expected property values to keep rising forever."

"Yes, but now lots of folks are under water since prices fell," I said.

"Ah. There it is, finally. Underwater. What does that mean exactly?" Bob asked me.

I looked at Bob to see if it was a trick question. His look didn't give him away. "That their house is worth less than the mortgage owed on it," I said.

"Correct, but so what?"

I tried to figure out what Bob had asked me. "I don't understand?"

"Think about it, Mike. What does it matter if your home is worth less than the amount of your mortgage? It's only relevant if you're selling or trying to refinance." Bob pointed down the block. "Do you know what your place is worth?"

I was caught off guard and realized I wasn't sure what a current valuation would give me. I answered, "Not exactly."

"Correct. You only need to know that when you offer the place for sale and someone buys it. Only then is the true worth established."

"I know what my tax statement says," I said a little too defensively.

"Okay, that's a starting point. How long have you lived there?'

"Let me see. About thirteen years."

"Is it worth more than when you bought it?"

"Sure," I answered without hesitation.

"Is it worth more than it was worth two years ago?" Bob had an evil grin on his mug now.

I half laughed. "I don't think so. I've heard owners in our place say values have dropped in the area twenty to twenty-five percent."

"Fools. It's only worth twenty-five percent less if they bought four years ago at the highest valuation and sold yesterday at the nadir. Don't you see? Paper gains and losses don't mean a thing. It's all a fantasy," Bob exclaimed. He was very animated.

147

I was almost sorry I got him started.

Bob continued. "It's only if I need to sell my property and the selling price is less than my mortgage balance that there actually is a loss. If I'm underwater as people say, and I hold the property for another ten years living there and enjoying the home as planned, I'll sell it for far more than I owe. The whole discussion is a Trojan Horse."

"But the news people talk about it all the time."

"Sure and that boosts their ratings. They get people all excited. Besides, when did you ever believe anything they said?'

I laughed. "I guess. Let me think for a minute. "There's lots of people losing their homes, though."

"Sure there are, and sometimes through no fault of their own. Maybe they were laid off and can't make the payments. They followed the rules and had a year's worth of payments in the bank, but . . .'"

"Yes, I see. There are a lot of tough stories out there."

"And there are many more where the people lost their conservatism and lost out because of it. I call it greed."

"Explain."

"You know about the H.E.L.O.C.?"

"Sure, the Home Equity Line of Credit."

"Right. Here's a common case we see a lot. Someone takes out a H.E.L.O.C. Maybe to buy a car, maybe for home improvement. That way they can deduct the interest expense on their income tax where they otherwise could not. But by doing that, they might be putting their house at risk. If something happens and they can't pay, the bank has a right to foreclose. This is where we banks contribute to the whole problem. We created the loan vehicle and allowed it to run amuck."

I was listening carefully.

"What if that guy with the H.E.L.O.C. on top of a mortgage loses his job, and now because of the original mortgage and the added H.E.L.O.C. he's underwater. Now what does he do? He can't sell, because the return on the sale will never pay off the total debt. He often today walks away from the home and says to the bank, 'Here take it.'"

"I've heard about a lot of that happening."

"You know what has become common practice?"

"What?"

"Say you're under water to use your term. You sell your home, and as soon as the agreement is signed, you stop making any more payments. Nothing to the bank, nothing on the taxes, not even the utilities. If the seller isn't getting any profit out of the sale he figures why put more skin in the game. There is simply no sense of obligation with the populace today. It's a whole new world out there, Mike.

"I could go on all day but let me give you one last example. A man consults a financial advisor. He's looking for an investment. He is advised to invest in condos at ski resorts. Why? Because he can generate an income stream to pay expenses, claim depreciation and make money when he sells because of eventual appreciation in the value of the property while he has owned it. Minimum down and an A. R. M. mortgage. You're familiar with those, right?"

"That's when there's a low rate up front and maybe five years down the road, the rate jumps to a high rate," I said.

"Correct, an adjustable rate mortgage. There are variations, but that's the gist of it.

"Only thing is the locations chosen for the scheme might not that great, so the places he invested in only fill when it's high season when everything else also is filled. All the good properties go first. He gets the overfill, or overflow if you will. Thus, the units aren't occupied enough to provide enough revenue and don't cash flow even with the depreciation for tax purposes. Now here's the kicker.

"Down the road the A.R.M comes due and its time to either refinance everything with a new loan, as they originally had planned; or they stick with the original loan and be forced to pay a hefty monthly payment from here on out. The original plan was to refinance, perhaps with another A. R. M., but now they no longer can refinance. Why? Because the values of the condos have fallen off the proverbial cliff. Can't afford to make the payments, can't refinance without throwing cash in that they don't have. What to do? Walk away. That's what's happening."

"It's no easier being a lender than it is being anything else, is it, Bob?"

"Not on your life."

We were both silent for a minute. Then I said, "Let me change the subject for a minute here, Bob. What did you think of our meeting? Do you have confidence in Williams?"

Bob pursed his lips. "I don't see why not, but I'll leave you with a note of caution. Wait for the exam to conclude. Larry made it sound like a piece of cake to work out those bad loans of his. It's not. I'll bet every one of those real estate ventures out of state is a pure loss. That will eat up capitol quickly.

"Then there are the commercial real estate deals. I know of at least a dozen that they're in. If they can move the properties, it will be for sixty cents on the dollar if they're lucky. That's after sitting on them for two to three years, or maybe ten, and absorbing all the costs for that amount of time.

"Besides that, there are all the commercial customers whose businesses are suffering. Those guys all are asking to reset the interest rates lower on their loans and also extend the terms of their loans so they might lower their payments. That's happening all around town to every bank. Margins are shrinking and profits are down. Cash is tight.

"Orion may not make a profit for the next three years. I know a person only can earn at most two percent on bonds today, but at least they have the security they'll have the money back with the sale of the bond to reinvest again later. Lose it on a bad investment chasing return and it's gone forever. Think about what you learned today. Be very cautious, and tell your friend to be cautious."

I nodded in agreement with what Bob had said. "Thanks, Bob. You've been a great help. See you Thursday for the board meeting."

"No. Thank you, Mike. You've become much more valuable to the bank now with this increased knowledge."

I left for home with a lot on my mind. I wasn't the kind of guy who made up his mind quickly. I needed to think about things for a while. Though I wanted to help Katie, I now was unsure what I might be able to accomplish on her behalf. I regretted now more than ever saying I would help.

~21~
MULTIPLE REFLECTIONS

FTER SAYING GOODBYE to Bob Lindgren, I strolled the main street toward home. It felt much warmer now than earlier in the morning. I reached into my inside pocket for my sunglasses, only then remembering I didn't have them. I was glad I had the bright sunshine at my back, though some squinting still was required. The sidewalks were crowded with people hustling here and there or merely looking in windows. It appeared to be a good shopping day in Excelsior.

I briefly considered stopping in at the wine bar for a sandwich, but decided to fix myself something once I got home. I remembered I had some summer sausage. I thought it might go good with a beer.

Once I crossed Second Street, I had to slowly weave in and out of pedestrian traffic in no hurry to get anywhere. My end of town was a sought out destination this time of day. We were in the height of summer activities, and Excelsior was a draw for many out-of-towners on the weekends.

I realized I had not spotted a familiar face on this end of town, and I mused over that. Then I realized much of the crowd was younger than I. Where had the time gone? I saw a steady stream of customers at the liquor store. Why not? A beer or two was a nice way to celebrate a hot summer day.

After arriving home, I opened the house to the summer breeze. I changed clothes, putting on nylon shorts and a tee shirt. Then I poured myself a large tumbler of ice water.

I went out to the deck with a Tobascos Biez and sat in the shade with my feet up. The wind was warm and brisk, though refreshing. Winter would be here soon enough to sequester me indoors. If possible I would try to enjoy every day of summer out in the fresh air.

The activity on the bay was increasing. Boats cruised every which way, and the restaurants appeared to be a favorite destination. Even the resurrected streetcar boat was sailing today. It was just leaving its dock on the opposite shore as I sat and watched.

My brain remained burdened with financial talk. I decided to try to let that subject rest for a bit. Bottom line was banking in general and Orion in particular were having a rough go of it recently. It wouldn't surprise me in the least if there weren't tremendous pressures on Williams, and all his key people to solve the dilemma. Would that have been enough for Larry's associate to commit suicide?

Everybody had his or her own problems. I had mine. My situation was getting better though, I hoped. My outlook since winter had brightened. I just had to keep climbing that hill.

Then a memory I wished forgotten invaded my consciousness. What about Sherrill Thomson? She'd had her problems—bad marriage, an abusive husband. Her problems sort of paralleled what I went through emotionally last winter. I wondered where she was? I still couldn't figure out how her car got into the parking lot by my office. Even if she had taken a plane . . . But she had said she was driving, hadn't she? That was what I remembered anyway. Said she'd stop every two hours to pee and get coffee. Yes. She definitely had planned to drive. Was there another car? Wait, had the cops said her stuff was in the car? That I couldn't remember, or hadn't paid close enough attention. It had been such a shock to find out that the police were really searching for her, not just following up her husband's request.

I slumped forward in my chair and rested my elbows on my knees, cradling my head. Something had to have happened to her, but what? I shivered as a chill came over me with that thought. It was one thing to read about a missing person in the paper. It was another entirely when you knew that person.

I heard something that made me sit up. There was no one there. I played with my cigar and watched the smoke tail away. Then I reflected back to when the F.B.I. agent had told me about my old girlfriend Grace's disappearance last fall. I was beginning to feel an anxiety attack coming on just as I had suffered back then. *Shit, why does this always have to happen to me?* I wiped my mouth with the back of a hand and took a couple of deep breaths. Then I lowered my head between my knees. It seemed to help. I sat up and rotated my neck to relieve some tension. Then I took a long drink of cold water. I had to learn to control my emotions.

I had to get practical. The Thompson woman being missing had nothing to do with me, did it? I hardly knew the woman. I couldn't be responsible for everybody in this god-damned town! I had myself to worry about. I had to get on with my life. I had to blot this event from my mind!

Sandra. Concentrate on her. She was in my life now. I wondered if anyone called her Sandy? She really was not a Sandy, though, was she? She was a good listener. That was for sure. She had a nice personality. Attractive, but not in a super-model style. I thought perhaps she was too short for me. Hell, she might be too intelligent for me, too! Maybe this was just one of those guy-gal friendships I had heard about.

I took another drag on my cigar. What was with that no good-night kiss crap? Did I have bad breath? A friendship kiss? I hadn't expected hot and sweaty sex, but a peck on the cheek was a definite signal. Not one I had wanted either.

Then it dawned on me what had happened, and I shook my head disgustedly. That response was entirely my fault. All night long I had gone on and on about my lost love, and how I was down in the dumps, how I had been down in the dumps all winter. Did I expect the poor woman to jump in bed with me after that soliloquy? I should be surprised she hadn't gotten up from the table and left me sitting there alone in my misery. No wonder I was single. I was a narcissist. All I thought about was numero uno. Oh well, it wasn't necessarily that bad being single, and alone. All alone.

If we did go out again, I'd have to pay a little more attention to her, and listen to her story. If I were in her place, I probably never would accept another date. I studied my cigar ash, and twirled the tobacco tube in my fingers. I was set in my ways; there were no two doubts about that. Someone would have to be pretty forgiving to hook up with me.

Now I felt hungry, since I hadn't eaten since coming in from fishing. I also needed to do my weekly shopping, so there wasn't much in the larder. I considered my sausage, but decided to save it for snacks. I opened a can of sardines and slapped those bits of herring between two pieces of buttered bread. Then I cracked a beer. There was a ball game on, though the Twins wouldn't be playing until later this evening. I sat and watched the game for a bit.

After eating, I threw on a load of laundry and grabbed my workout gear. I decided to head out to the health club. After the workout I'd do my grocery shopping at Shorewood Center. Maybe a good workout would clear my brain. We would see if anything helped that feeble mass of tissue.

The club was practically empty when I arrived, which shouldn't have surprised me if I'd thought about it. It just was too nice a day to be indoors. Most people probably got in early to leave their day free for other activities. I decided it would be nice to get back out onto the water later today just to do something. After my warm up, I did my weight reps and then did a half hour on the elliptical. It felt good. It even sharpened me mentally.

After showering and changing, I raced through the grocery store, returning home with two bags of groceries that cost me ninety bucks. Man, everything was getting expensive. I stored away my purchases, and once again returned to my deck, this time with a scotch to accompany my cigar. I had my iPad with me to make notes from my noon meeting.

For the longest time I sat thinking, but nothing came to mind. I realized I had no idea what Katie wanted from me, and not enough knowledge of her and her husband's relationship to figure things out on my own. I was uncertain how to classify today's meeting or the information learned from it, or how it pertained to Katie's perceived problem.

Since I wasn't able even to get started, I finally decided that a one-on-one meeting with Katie was appropriate at which time I planned to kiss her off. I wouldn't call her on the weekend, though. Larry might answer.

I was so immune to boat noise due to constant exposure that the activity near me went on without my notice. But now a water skier was coming close to the shore. I was surprised they were skiing so close to the docks and with all the boat traffic. They obviously were not locals. There were quieter waters in St. Albans Bay or around the point to the east. Whatever, it wasn't my problem. If they got hurt, they got hurt.

I swirled the remaining ice in my glass and appraised my drink. The ice nearly had melted. It was warm out here. My shirt was sticking to my back. I began laughing because I knew that, if I were married, I wouldn't be able to sit around like this and relax. I most certainly would have to be doing some chore. Maybe I did have it good after all.

Now I wondered if Katie had her own free time, or if hers was always spoken for? I had no idea how the other half lived. I had seen her house from the lakeside, but never from the road. Three stories faced the lake, but with the inclined bank alongside, it must be two stories roadside. I had seen it by boat. Quite a castle.

After all the thought I had put into it, it seemed pretty simple to me that either Larry was having an affair or he had just lost interest in his wife. I cogitated for a moment on which answer was worse. If it was the latter, I wouldn't be surprised. From what I had heard it wasn't unusual for those highly successful types to be married to their work. Maybe it was as simple as that.

I was friends with a Pillsbury exec who had an assistant who ran his life for him. That person kept all the appointments and schedules, had all the reports waiting. Gary just showed up and led. What a life. Maybe that was what Larry's life was like. They could have it.

If Katie wanted to know exactly what was bothering her husband, she'd have to go elsewhere for assistance. Hell, why not just ask Larry? Maybe that was what I should have done. There was no way for me to find out anything further. All I could figure was that it was the pressure of the economy and the bank exam.

But Larry had not seemed unusually stressed at our meeting, or at least had not shown it. Maybe he was on tranquilizers. He knew things were bad with the economy; he enumerated the issues for us. He knew some of his customers were in trouble. He seemed to have a plan for turning things around. If I garnered anything from the meeting, I knew that increasing Orion's capital base, bringing in the cash, as they had done should help solve their problems.

If Katie wanted love, she best look elsewhere than at home. I choked back a laugh. I was always available. God she was beautiful. There I go thinking with my dick again. That was what had gotten me into this mess in the first place. I had let myself be taken advantage of. I walked right into it. All Katie did was bat her long lashes, and I followed like a lovesick teen.

I would have thought I was more mature then that, but actions proved otherwise. Now that I had an exit strategy, I better not blow it.

~22~

A Putrid Discovery

SUNDAY MORNING FOUND me once again on the water drowning some bait. Since it was always chilly before daylight, I motored out into the lake wearing a warm jacket and jersey gloves just in case. I have to admit they felt comforting. I hate cold hands. For some reason the damp cold had seemed to cut right through me this morning even as I was dressed. I also had brought along a thermos of hot coffee. All the comforts a man could ask for. The warm cup in my hands felt comforting.

Recreational boaters were usually a little slower to venture out on Sunday mornings, and as a result I could usually get three hours of quiet fishing in before I was driven off the lake by the fast runabouts. It was a lot tougher to fish when passing boats stirred up the water creating large wakes. Sometimes they nearly bounced me out of my boat.

My eyes were a little droopy this morning as I again had spent somewhat of a restless night, and was hopeful that some time relaxing on the water might help my psyche. So far today it had not, but I was willing to make the effort. Generally when I went out fishing, I tried to keep my mind clear of business problems. Fishing was my time to get away from reality. My quiet time alone.

However, today I was beset by a myriad of problems I was having difficulty shaking. I was unable to keep Katie and her circumstance out of my head, nor could I forget the situation with my former neighbor, wondering where she had gone, or what might have happened to her. On top of that, I was trying to more fully understand everything Larry and Bob had been discussing on our Saturday get together. I knew I'd need to review things with Bob to keep it all straight. I was just glad I had been afforded the opportunity to have the learning experience, as overwhelming as it had been.

By the time the sun finally crawled up over the horizon, I already felt chilled. Not even the coffee seemed to help. It was said the coldest time of the day was that period just before sunrise, and this morning I believed it. At the same time I wondered if it was all psychological? I closed my eyes and faced directly into the rising sun. I could feel its warmth on my face. Gosh I love the out of doors.

This morning I was fishing out near a weed bed that had grown up over the summer months. Now that it was getting light, I could see spider webs dripping with dew hanging from the weed stalks. Those industrious little buggers must have worked all night creating that masterful scene. I wished I had brought my camera or my phone.

I had caught and released two small mouth bass before I called it quits. Then I returned home, and succumbed to my favorite Sunday breakfast of bacon and eggs. I understand it wasn't the healthiest of meals, but I only occasionally ate this way and only on Sundays. Besides I needed something substantial to help warm me. However, as good as the meal tasted today it left me with a bloated feeling. Comfort food.

What I needed now was exercise. Although I had been there just yesterday, I decided to go to the club. I had done weights and the elliptical on Saturday, but today I thought I would use the treadmill and work myself to exhaustion. Maybe that also would help clear my head of all the conflicting thoughts. I wished I could discuss all this.

I gathered my gym gear and went down to the garage. It was quiet this morning in the bowels of the building. Many people were at Sunday services. Others perhaps were sleeping in late. I reflected for a moment on days growing up and Sunday service. Maybe I should consider getting back into that church habit. I had attended occasionally during the winter months when I was looking for something, but eschewed formal services for Mother Nature during our short summer season.

Approaching my car I wrinkled up my nose. There was a putrid odor in the basement this morning. I wondered if the exhaust fans were working. I would hate to be overcome by carbon monoxide. At first I had thought it might be an automobile's catalytic converter gone bad. It smelled something like that, but not the same. I sniffed around my car, but did not notice anything in particular. I would keep tabs on my vehicle to see if the smell went away.

When I arrived at the Shorewood Shopping Center, I popped the hood on my Mustang and perused the engine compartment, thinking perhaps with the engine was heated up I might find something. I hated the thought of a rodent making a nest in there. I couldn't see anything, nor did I smell anything. Good, it apparently wasn't coming from my vehicle. That was one less thing for me to worry about.

Once inside the club, I encountered a surprising number of people working out, but there was a treadmill available. I hated it when I drove all the way out here and could not do the workout I had planned. As an added bonus, a really cute blonde walked on the machine ahead of mine and I watched the action of her butt. She was wearing spandex shorts, and the sight made me feel young. All I needed was for her to go a couple of hours and then I'd have the incentive to do a long workout.

No such luck. She finished her workout only five minutes into my stint. She wiped her face with a towel as she climbed off the tail end of the belt, and I smiled at her. She smiled back and departed for the weight machines. *She's probably still in school, what am I doing looking at girls that young?* Heck, Sandra was not that much older, was she?

What a loser I was for chasing those young girls. I increased my pace to punish myself. After an hour I began to get sore. I had done enough. It was hell to get old. I decided to shower at home, using the ride home with the top down as a cool down. Instead of jumping back onto Highway Seven, I went over to Yellowstone Trail. It was a much slower journey home and the wind would not be taking my head off.

When I'd parked in my stall and got out of the car, I smelled that same peculiar aroma again. I couldn't quite define what it smelled like. Shaking my head, I went up to my place and contemplated a shower. But first I grabbed the key to my garage storage locker, located high on the wall and protruding out over the hood of my car. It wasn't a large space, only six feet wide by two feet deep, but it allowed for each tenant to store things we would not want in the house. I kept paint cans and car and boat supplies in mine.

I backed my Mustang far enough to access the locker and then removed the padlock on the double doors. I swung those open and looked inside. Nothing inside seemed to smell in that space, and nothing had spilled. After checking all the lids, I closed up and relocked the compartment. Then I pulled my car forward up to the wall.

Puzzled, I climbed out, wondering what could be done. Then a thought struck me. I wondered if the Thompsons had left some crap in their cabinet, which was adjacent to mine? I walked over to their empty stall and the odor got stronger. So that was where it was coming from. I'd better notify the management company that something needed to be done about it. I'd call Thompson himself, but I didn't have his number, and I didn't know what his reaction might be to a call from me. Anyway that was what the management company was for.

I returned up to my place once again where I showered and shaved. I was feeling refreshed. It was such a perfect day with bright sunshine that I decided to sit on the deck for a bit. I'd recently downloaded a Harry Bosch novel onto my Nook, so I grabbed a beer, my reader and a cigar. Then I settled into a comfortable chair and began to read. I wasn't a big book reader, but I plowed through about a book a month. It probably took me as long to read one as it did for the author to write it.

Of course it was a murder mystery, all of Bosch's books were. What else would it be with him being a homicide detective? I read for about a half hour and then put down my reader. A nagging thought had flooded my subconscious, maybe because of the story I was reading.

Suddenly my stomach was in turmoil and my head felt too heavy for my neck to support. Terror overtook me. I quickly leaned forward and almost vomited. After holding my head between my knees for several seconds, I slowly stood and walked over to the screen door. Holding onto the wall for support, I slid the door open and walked to where I had set my phone.

My hands were shaking while I tried to punch the numbers. The first attempt was wrong, and I tried again. I was forced to leave a message, but was assured I would hear back shortly. I returned to the deck where

I leaned on the railing and tried to catch my breath. I could not concentrate enough to read any more of my story. I would not have remembered anything if I had attempted to do so. I tried a taste of my beer but that left a fowl taste in my mouth, so I abandoned the remainder of the bottle. Finishing my cigar was about the only thing left for me.

It seemed like a lifetime before I got a return call. It was Officer Nancy Bishop on the phone. I explained to her what I'd like her to do and she agreed. A half hour later she was at my door.

"Drive around to the parking garage door and I'll let you in," I instructed.

She nodded and turned back toward her squad car.

I stumbled into the basement and over to the pull cord for the outside overhead door. As that door rose I walked back toward my stall. Here I leaned my backside against my car for support. I was feeling lightheaded and fairly queasy.

Officer Bishop pulled her car up to me and looked at me inquiringly.

"Park it there for now," I said, pointing to an empty stall. "Did you bring the bolt cutters?"

"Yes."

I pointed to the appropriate storage cabinet.

Officer Bishop climbed out of her vehicle and approached the box. She hesitated momentarily, as she sniffed the air. Then she turned to me with inquiring eyes. I shook my head.

"I'm going up to my place. Let me know what you find," I managed to squeak out. "You going to cut the lock?"

Officer Bishop paused. "No, I think not. Not without a search warrant. If there's anything in there of importance, I'll need to maintain the proper chain of evidence. You go ahead. I'll find you if I need you." Then she was on her phone.

I nodded toward her and moved to the door leading up to my townhome. My legs were like rubber as I climbed the stairs, pulling myself on the handrail. I grabbed another cigar and plopped down in a comfortable chair on my deck. The lake was active with boaters now, and I took refuge by watching the action before me. I glanced at the abandoned beer bottle I had left earlier and decided to give it a try. The liquid was warm, but wet. I finished the contents and went inside to get another. That one was icy cold and went down too easily. I realized I'd better be careful or I might get drunk. I had learned last winter that it didn't work for shutting out the world.

Sometime later I heard sirens. They were coming closer. Shit, I hated it when I was right. I would've liked to know what was happening below, but at the same time I had no desire to see what I thought was there.

It was more than two hours before my doorbell rang. When I gathered the courage to answer the entreaty, I found both Officer Bishop and Rehms.

"May we come in?" Bishop asked.

"Social call?"

The two officers looked at one another. "Yes," said Rehms.

"Come on down. You know the way."

I lead them out onto the deck. I had prepared a pitcher of ice water and now took that with glasses on a tray with me. I placed it on the small round table between us. I had a fresh beer and I caressed the neck of the bottle like a drowning man hanging on to flotsam.

We all sat, and I could cut the tension with a knife. I was hunched over with my elbows on my knees caressing the neck of the bottle. I looked up into both their faces, knowing the answer. Officer Rehms had a firm set to his jaw. Officer Bishop looked worn and bedraggled.

"What did you find?" I asked with a quiver in my voice before staring down at the deck.

"She was in there," Bishop answered.

I shook my head and lowered it down to my knees. I felt sick again. It was hard to face the truth. The officers gave me time.

"Could we impose on you to make the identification?" Bishop asked.

I slowly raised my eyes to look at her. "I don't think so."

"You'd be doing us a favor," Rehms said.

I shook my head. "I can't do it. Besides, I really didn't know her that well. I'd probably recognize her on the street, but now after being in there . . . no, I can't do it. That should be her husband."

"We haven't been able to contact him," Rehms said.

I shook my head again.

"Then we'll transport her as a Jane Doe," Bishop answered. "Don't worry, Mr. Connelly. This happens all the time. I fully understand your feeling on this. It isn't easy looking at someone who's dead."

There was silence for a minute and then finally. "You didn't know her well, then?" Bishop asked.

"I looked up with tears in my eyes. "No, but she seemed nice. She certainly didn't deserve this."

"No one does," Rehms answered.

Then it was quiet for a couple of more minutes, as the officers let me recover somewhat.

"Can we ask you a couple of questions?" Bill Rehms asked.

I shook my head. "Not today. I wouldn't know what I was saying. This is all too familiar to me. After what happened last year, I don't think I can go through this again."

"I understand," Nancy said. "But we do need to get on this as quickly as possible."

"I already told you all I know."

"But this is different," Rehms said.

I didn't answer right away, but then croaked, "Is it?"

"There's been a murder." He replied.

"I know, but that doesn't change what I know. How'd it happen?"

"That's for the medical examiner to determine," Bishop replied. "We will need a formal statement from you."

I grew wary. "Why?"

"It's customary in this situation. You were perhaps the last person to see her alive."

"Except for her killer," I corrected.

Neither police officer said anything.

I was watching the lake now, looking for solace, but turned toward the two officers. "Look, I suspected something was amiss in the garage and I notified you. That's all I know."

Bill Rehms cleared his throat. "Mike, we understand that, but we have a job to do here. Being the last person to see the victim alive, logically you're considered a suspect."

Blood pounded in my temples. I became enraged. "Me a suspect?" I shouted. Officer Bishop recoiled and reached for her sidearm. I stood up. "I see. So you're at it again, Rehms. You're going to take the easy way out again just like before and try to pin this one on me. I'd thought you'd grown up and learned something by now, you twerp."

Both officers were now standing and taking defensive positions. Officer Rehms looked at me red-faced, but before he could say anything, Bishop said. "Not true, Mr. Connelly. You have to understand you're a suspect until we're able to clear you. We can't clear you until we have your story."

"That's bullshit. You have my story. I gave it to Rehms here this past week. There's nothing to add. Instead of hanging around here, why don't you do some real detective work and find the killer of that poor woman?" I'm sure they could hear me across the lake in Wayzata.

I was shook by the news of my neighbor's death, and fatigued by all that had taken place in the last week. I was in no mood to be cordial. A couple of neighbors who were walking up from the dock stood and stared at us. Officer Bishop waved them along.

"Would you prefer to have us take you out to the police center and talk there?" Rehms asked.

"Fuck you, Rehms!"

Bishop seemed annoyed at the escalation of the dialogue. It showed on her face and the way she shifted on her feet.

"Why take me to the station? So you can use your rubber-hose techniques on me?" I asked. "It'll look real good for the department when I write a series of columns for the paper on local police brutality and their propensity for tromping on citizens' rights. Then when I start a petition to reduce payments from the contributing cities to the department, how will that look? Will you bozos like that? Maybe I'll add how you couldn't find your ass last year until the F.B.I. bailed you out."

"Okay, that's enough," Bishop said. "We need your statement, but we needn't get it now. Let's set a time for tomorrow at the station."

"Let's say five o'clock," I answered. "That'll give me time to alert my attorney and have him present."

"You certainly have a right to counsel," Officer Bishop answered. "We'll see you at five then." She had lost her cordiality too. Could I blame her? I was being an ass, but didn't give a damn.

I walked toward the patio door, which signaled that the meeting was over. I escorted the officers to the front door and slammed it shut behind them. I hope they got the message.

MONDAY MORNING I CALLED my attorney, Ford Crouch. We'd gone to law school together, and I had used his Minneapolis firm ever since I graduated. I found out the firm didn't do criminal defense work, but Ford recommended someone who did. An hour later I received a call from an attorney by the name of John Steil.

I laid out the situation for him, and he suggested I write up a statement, which I did. I faxed that statement to John, he made a couple of changes and sent it back. I printed it out and took it with me when John and I went to the police offices that afternoon.

John had me sign the statement in the presence of the officers and I passed it over to them. He wouldn't let me answer any questions at all. That brought an end to it for now.

When we were back at my office, John asked. "Is the statement you signed today true?"

"Absolutely."

"Do you know any more about how the woman disappeared?"

"No."

"That doesn't mean the police won't try to pressure you. If they haul you in, don't answer anything without me being there. Don't even tell them your name. Understand?"

"Yes."

"Good. A large part of their tactics are muted once you have advice of counsel. Remember no talking."

John reflected for a moment, then said. "You're either going to be considered a suspect in this killing or a valuable witness. Either way the police will want to talk to you. As a witness you will want to cooperate, but that doesn't give them the right to hassle you."

"I know."

"Good. We'll have to see how they operate. If we can schedule meetings, then I can work my schedule and be present without any inconvenience to you. If not, they could pull you in at any time, and you'll have to sit there till I can get free and come out."

John thought for a moment, then said, "Is there an attorney in town you trust?"

I reflected a moment. "There's Jim Davis."

"Where's he located?"

I looked up the relevant information.

"Good. I'll talk to him and see if he's qualified to assist you in case you are pulled in. That way you won't have to sit around for hours at a time if I'm not available. I'll get back to you on that."

"Okay."

We parted and I went home where I crashed into bed.

~23~

NEW COMPLICATION

WHEN I WENT TO WORK on Monday morning, my personal sense of gloom was matched by the weather. The sky was overcast as if threatening rain, and my surroundings were ashen and cheerless. I had not paid attention to the forecast earlier and now was surprised at what I was encountering. Several times I looked up at the clouds while making my normal journey into work. The one bright side was that the higher humidity level made my cigar particularly aromatic.

Reaching the office, I saw that Janet was eager to learn what had happened to Sherrill Thompson. Apparently the local grapevine was alive and well, and she had heard of the gruesome discovery. The way the woman sat expectantly in her chair told me everything. I would have been a fool indeed not to understand. I knew I might as well spill my guts before we got busy with work or she'd bug me about it all day long.

Janet was dressed in her typical work uniform: a dress, bare legs and comfortable shoes. She kept a sweater on the back of her chair in case the air conditioning got too chilly. Her hair was neatly combed and tidy, while her cheeks held a glow of anticipation.

Maybe deep down I was happy to have someone in whom to confide. I yielded to Janet's inquiry. It turned out that telling her all I knew was easier than I had imagined. Maybe getting it off my chest to someone I knew well and cared about was cathartic. To speak about those horrible events wasn't easy, but I managed to get through my dialogue without tearing up. That wouldn't have been manly.

"So you're a witness then?" Janet said, nodding her head.

"Of sorts, I guess, and maybe the only one." I thought about that for a moment. The police were going to have to depend on my story for any insight into what might have happened. I roused myself and continued. "What I mean is I did see her go into her place, but I saw no one hanging about in the street at the time. And the movers had gone by then."

I thought for a moment. "Someone could have rung her bell after I went downstairs. How would I know?" I shrugged. Then I looked up at our ceiling as I reflected back to that night. "Someone had to have gotten to her either through her front door or the garage when she went down to get into her car. She'd said she wanted to leave immediately and put some miles on before morning. I just don't know. What happened to her had to have happened pretty quick after she said good-bye to me or she would have been gone."

Janet waited a bit to see if I was going to continue. Then she chewed on the tip of a fingernail as she said, "Perhaps she could have been stopped on the street. By someone she knew."

"Hmm." I gave that thought. "Maybe if she knew the person. I don't see her stopping for a stranger, though."

Janet got out of her chair and refilled her coffee cup. She stood looking at me. "Right. Or if someone had car trouble or something like that, and she stopped to help."

I shook my head at the potential theories. "The possibilities are endless, Janet. It's better to let the authorities do the speculating."

Janet nodded. "They'll have a tough job trying to figure out what happened and who might be involved."

"Yes," I said. Then I could feel my face heating up. "That's what worries me."

"What worries you?" she asked.

"The fact they might have a tough time figuring it all out. When that happens, they take the easy way out."

"Which is?"

"Going after yours truly."

"You don't—"

"Yes I do. That's why I've hired a good attorney to represent me."

"Gosh, Mike. I certainly hope they don't go that route."

"We'll see."

We looked at one another and neither of us spoke for a full minute. Meanwhile I walked over to the coffee maker and poured myself a cup. I had the feeling Janet wasn't yet finished with the subject. She turned away from me and faced her workstation, then said, "Sad, Mike. Very sad. You'd think we'd be immune to that sort of thing out here in the country like we are."

"I'm afraid we're not in the country anymore, Janet. The city's moved out and taken us over."

She shook her head. "I guess you're right."

I took my cue and headed into my office to get started on the day.

Later that morning, I received a visit from our local journalist, Bobby Green. I went out front to meet him. "Greenie, how are you?"

"Good, Mike. You?"

"Recovering," I answered as I bobbed my head.

"Good. Yes, that's good."

Bobby looked up at the threatening sky. "Is it supposed to rain?"

"I didn't think so," I speculated.

Bobby nodded. "Could we talk?"

"Sure, Bobby. What's on your mind?" I asked.

"I wanted to interview you about the murder."

"Oh, the Thompson woman."

Bobby nodded.

"Have you talked to the police?" I asked.

"I just came from there, though I didn't learn much of anything from them. Seems like it's still early on in their investigation."

I tilted my head toward my office. "Come into my office, Greenie, and we'll talk."

Bobby took a chair, and I asked, "Want any coffee?"

"No, thanks. I already had my quota for the day."

I sat adjacent to Bobby rather than behind my desk. "We can talk in here without bothering Janet."

"Fine."

I enjoyed talking to Bobby. He was a real intellectual with a great sense of humor. I tried playing Scrabble with him once, and for every three-letter word I made he was making five-, six- and seven-letter words. I put it down to luck. You have to have the letters, right?

"Care to tell me what you know?" Bobby asked.

I sighed. "I'll do what I can."

I spent the next half hour chronicling everything I knew from the time when Sherrill Thompson had disappeared the first time to when the police made their gruesome discovery of the body. That ate up a good half hour. Bobby sat quietly listening, taking notes the entire time. It looked like shorthand, and I was surprised he hadn't chosen to record our conversation. I imagine he was putting down just what he considered relevant. His expression was serious.

Bobby Green was a thin drink of water, standing just less than six feet tall. His dark hair was cut short on the sides, but spiked on top, and he was clean-shaven. A rather pale complexion accentuated a narrow face and protruding jaw. A small mouth sat under a long, thin nose. I knew he couldn't have weighed over one hundred fifty pounds.

I concluded my narrative by saying, "That's all I know Bobby. What have you heard different from that?"

"Not much. In fact not even that much detail, more of a summary." Here he hesitated. "I guess I can tell you, Mike. I talked to Officer Bishop first out at the police office, and then followed up with Officer Rehms. When I talked to Rehms, he seemed to imply you were the main suspect. Care to comment on that?"

I nodded. "Off the record?"

Bobby smiled. "Off the record," he replied.

I could feel my face turning red with anger, but I was committed to holding my temper with Bobby. He was not the enemy. In fact, he could be valuable in any confrontation I might have with the police. "Rehms. The guy has a real problem, Bobby. He's out to get me this time just like last summer, maybe because he failed in his attempt last time. The guy's mentally lazy and has tunnel vision, He couldn't find the prize in a Cracker Jacks box."

Bobby laughed. "That's funny. What you're implying isn't. You know, over the winter I reviewed that entire file from last summer. We were lucky the F.B.I. broke the case. It seemed like our locals never had a clue what was going on? It was just too large and involved for this small department. They don't have the manpower or the expertise to pursue a case that magnitude. The question now is, can they handle this one?"

"I agree with everything you've said, man. The police here were a step behind the whole time last year and acted like bulls in a china shop. But heck, Greenie. What do they know about murder? How many murders has Rehms ever solved or even been involved with? If they don't call in the state this time, maybe nothing will get done on this one either."

"Hey, that's a good angle, Mike. Getting the State Bureau involved. I may write something on that. At least they might look at things with an open mind rather than harassing the people who helped break the case."

Bobby was on a roll. When he got his teeth into something, he didn't let go.

"Go for it Greenie."

We talked for a few more minutes, but I could add nothing new to the case file.

After Bobby Green left, I went to work. Most of the morning already was shot, and I hadn't done much of anything productive.

~24~

KATHERINE

BEFORE I HAD LEFT the office on Tuesday, I phoned Katie Williams, asking her for a face-to-face meeting sometime soon. I needed to update her on what I had found out concerning her husband's activities, and perhaps, more importantly, what I hadn't learned about her husband's work situation.

In addition, once that meeting was completed and my assessment delivered, I intended to close out this commission I so foolishly had undertaken. That was a task best done in person. I felt there was little more I could accomplish to satisfy Katie's original request. If she wanted more information, she'd need to employ someone far more gifted than I.

Consequently when Katie suggested lunch at the Wayzata Country Club for Wednesday, I readily agreed. I'd never been to the club before and had a desire to see the establishment as well as the clientele associated with the place. I surmised that might give me a window into Katie's personal life.

Thus, on Wednesday, after I parked in the club's lot, I perused my surroundings, leaning momentarily against my vehicle while finishing the last few puffs of my smoke. My Mustang was a poor cousin to the cars parked nearby.

Nonetheless I finished off my cigar, not daring to carry that offensive little stick inside with me. One last puff, and then I pushed the stub of tobacco into the car's ashtray, grinding off the glowing ash.

When I stood again, I studied the building, but could see little of it from where I had chosen to park. The visitor's parking lot was not prime real estate. Maybe I would be able to see the building better as I approached it.

Reaching into my pants pocket, I removed a stick of gum, unwrapped it and slipped it into my mouth. At least with this improving my breath, I wouldn't offend anyone, though I doubted I'd be kissing-close to people inside. I fetched my blazer from the back seat, shaking out the wrinkles.

Bright sunshine blanketed the parking lot, forcasting little danger of immanent rain. I left the car's ragtop down. I straightened my jacket and began crossing the parking lot to the building entrance. Squinting against the glare of a bright mid-day sun hindered any appraisal of the building's exterior. Not wanting anything protruding from my shirt pocket, I'd left my sunglasses in the car. A raised hand turned out to be an inadequate substitute for a cap bill to aid in warding off glare. With scant cloud cover today, I barely could see until I neared the door. However, I wasn't one to complain, since I'd been able to leave the car's top down and enjoy a nice summer morning's drive.

In Minnesota we're so starved for summer weather that it wasn't unusual to see people on a sunny April day with their convertible tops down while driving wearing a parka and blasting their heaters full force. No fooling. I'd take today's weather anytime. Even with the glare.

No other patrons were entering the building at that moment, though the parking lot held numerous cars. I was curious to see if the restaurant was crowded. If so, that would be less conducive to a privileged conversation. I sighed, as I could do little to control the circumstances of our seating. I'd find out what the situation was soon enough. Katie must have had something in mind when choosing this location.

As I stood inside the building's entrance, I suddenly felt my apprehension rising. Over the past few days I'd struggled to maintain some footing in this quest to help Katie, even though I seemed to be wasting my time. I never should have said I'd help. Clearly in over my head, I was bound to disappoint the poor woman with my meager results.

I was remiss in thinking this was all about me and my failure. I totally was disregarding the woman's needs and her vulnerabilities. After all, she was the one without any solid contacts, cut off from all Orion Bank's advisors. Katie was adrift and alone. She'd needed someone even if it turned out to be only me. Obviously, she was depending on me to show her the way, but I hoped she wouldn't expect me to hold her hand moving forward.

I glanced at my watch. I was late, and that also ramped up my stress. Road work on County 15 had been at fault. County 15 wound around the lake's many bays, but had only two lanes, and when one lane was being repaired, it left few options. I'd hd to wait my turn to bypass the construction.

After locating the dining room, I was told Mrs. Williams was expecting me. I spotted her as I was being guided to her table. The dining room was spacious, but not well attended. Individual parties were scattered about in a haphazard fashion. A sea of white from unoccupied tables had the room taking on the appearance of a checkerboard halfway through a game.

The room was formal, and the clientele appeared sophisticated, and well dressed. From the look of the patrons, the minimum age for attendance here for a meal must have been fifty-five, Katie excluded. I was the only gentleman present, if one cared to call me a gentleman. Conversation in the room was subdued, but heads did turn as I was escorted to my seat.

Our table appeared to be far enough away from others to be private without whispering. Perhaps that was by Katie's design. One worry eliminated. Now all I had to do was lay bare my failings to my friend.

I was shown a chair, but I first reached out for Katie's hand. I gave it a light squeeze before moving around the table to sit. The cloth-covered tables had cloth napkins configured into the shape of a hat marking the table setting, and a small bud vase with flowers sat strategically in the table center.

Before I could say anything, someone from behind me was pouring me a glass of water. I focused on Katie. I moved the flowers out from between us. It was as though they were defining each of our territories. I needed no restrictions.

The two of us sat quietly across from one another looking into each other's eyes. She blinked first, and the spell was broken. I shifted in my seat and unfolded the napkin, placing it onto my lap. Then I smiled. So far I hadn't made a social faux paux. Chalk one up for the good guys.

I remembered my mother telling me to use my inside voice. "Is this the ladies dining room?" I inquired softly.

Katherine showed me her smile, then turned her head to scan the other diners. Nodding she said, "I see what you mean. You may become quite popular here. The room may be filled with cougars."

I let that comment settle, then said, "There aren't that many people in here today."

"There never are for lunch."

"Why's that?"

Katie shrugged. "Those playing golf use the bar for lunch either before or after a round. This is more of a dinner location."

"Oh," was my only reply.

Remembering my manners, I said. "You look nice today, Katherine."

"Thank you. You do as well, Michael."

I had chosen a light-blue dress shirt, striped tie, and blue blazer. Katie was decked out in a sleeveless white dress with a low neck. I could only view her from the table up, so I was missing some good parts. Her hair was nicely done. Every strand appeared to be in place. Her makeup again was flawless. If she was wearing lip rouge, it was very neutral.

A thin, white-gold chain hung from her neck, and a small sailboat with a not-so-small diamond in the sail hung from that and rested against her chest. I counted four rings, two on each hand. Diamond studs were the only ear decoration.

"Would you like a drink, Michael?"

"I think not, just iced tea."

She nodded. "May I order for us?" she asked.

"Sure."

She filled out a ticket and laid it near the edge of the table. Then she folded her hands in front of her.

I smiled my goofy "what am I doing here" smile. I wasn't entirely sure what to do or say. Suddenly a thought arose. "How was the Symphony Ball? Did you attend?" I asked. I'd read about the ball in the paper.

She brightened. "Very nice."

"Was it well attended?"

"Yes, it was a sellout as usual."

"You didn't bid on conducting the orchestra, did you?"

She laughed and blushed slightly. It looked good on her. "I would be too embarrassed to get up there, even though it'd be an invitation only affair. I never was very good with music. I would surely look the fool."

"Weren't you in high school band?"

"If you want to call my participation as being in band. I couldn't play an instrument very well, and I couldn't carry a tune in a bucket."

I laughed quietly.

"My father used to say that about me," she said.

I was happy to see Katie had not disavowed everything from her past. After my first visit with her this past month, I formed the impression she had become a whole different person from the girl I had known growing up, which I had felt somehow diminished her. I now was feeling somewhat better about her.

"Do you play golf here?" I asked.

"No, I never learned. I'm not very athletic I'm afraid."

It was funny how people rarely had all the gifts. If they were smart, maybe they were not as gifted athletically. Or if they were beautiful, they perhaps were lacking somewhere else. Upon self-inspection I realized I was sort of mediocre in everything.

A waitperson had taken our drink order and now placed a glass of tea before me accompanied by various sweeteners. I dumped in a couple of packets and stirred vigorously. I played with that, making it abhorrently sweet.

I was not sure when to get to our business. The previous time we had met, Katie had held off until after lunch. I decided to do the same unless she broached the subject first.

Searching my vast repertoire of knowledge, I asked. "How are your folks?"

"Father passed away a few years ago. He was sixty-nine. That was in 1999. He didn't see the millennium."

"I'm sorry, Katherine. I wouldn't have brought it up had I known." Now I was feeling even more uneasy.

"Not a problem, Michael. I'm long over the initial loss."

"Dare I ask about your mother?"

"She's doing fine. She lives in an assisted living home. I think she likes it there."

"Does she have medical problems?"

"Not anything serious. Aches and pains. Her eyes are bad, so she can't drive anymore. Being homebound really frightened her. Living where she does alleviates a lot of the problems. She can take her meals in the community room if she wishes, or cook in her kitchen. They have a lot of activities, and provide transportation to doctors or grocery stores, or just shopping."

"Sounds nice. Did you ever consider having her live with you?"

"Yes, we talked about it," Katie said. "Heaven knows we have the room. But we're stuck out in the middle of nowhere there on Howard's Point. As I said, she doesn't drive, and she'd have to be chauffeured everywhere from our location. There's no bus nearby. She's always been sort of independent and decided to go this route instead."

I nodded and again tried my tea, hoping it had mellowed. The sweetness nearly made my teeth fall out. I dumped in some water from my water glass, sloshing some onto the tablecloth.

Katie gave me a quizzical look.

First mistake goes to the bozo.

"I hadn't thought about that aspect of her being with us," Katie continued. "But when we broached the subject to her, she laid it all out for us. She decided that if she was going to sell her house, she'd move closer to the city. She said she was tired of living at the end of the world."

"Since when was Minnewashta Heights the end of the world?" I asked.

"Ever turn to the west leaving Minnewashta Heights?" she asked.

I thought for a moment. "Not too often."

A couple of women in their fifties walked by and stopped to say hello. Katie introduced me, and I stood.

They stayed only momentarily, then left.

"Friendly," I said.

"No, inquisitive," Katie responded. "They want to know who you are. I bet they go right home and Google your name. If they had an iPad or iPhone, they'd be doing it right now."

"Probably want to see if you're playing around."

Katie laughed. "This certainly wouldn't be the place to do it."

"No. We're a little exposed, aren't we? But then, who'd suspect?" I said with a smile. She smiled as well. I wondered what it would be like to carry on a relationship with someone like Katie. I hoped my face was not betraying my thoughts.

I took another sip if my tea and asked, "Do you miss the old life?"

Her face showed mild surprise. "What old life?"

"I just meant living the more simple existence like your folks did and you did while you were growing up."

Katie looked over my shoulder into the distance and didn't immediately answer. Then she said, "I don't think much has changed for me."

I had a mouthful of tea and nearly spit it out. My napkin quickly went to my mouth before I dribbled down my chin.

"Are you all right?" Katie asked, looking frightened.

I coughed and then managed to say, "Yes, just went down the wrong pipe."

There was a lull in the conversation while I regained my composure. Then I asked, "You don't think your life has changed?"

"No." Katie shook her head slightly.

I thought for a minute and then asked, "Do you have a garden at home?"

She brightened. "Yes, several."

"You mean flowers?" I was looking for clarification.

"Of course. What did you mean?" she said.

"Vegetables."

"No, of course not."

"Why of course not? Your folks did when you kids were growing up, and you worked in it."

"Yes, I did," she answered, taking a sip of water.

"You don't do that now."

She looked offended. "Neither do you, do you?"

"No, but I'm just trying to point out how your life has changed, Katherine."

"I don't see that it has. I merely have different interests. We all grow up, Michael, and put away the things of our youth."

I squirmed in my seat. "I wasn't expressing myself well, perhaps," I mused.

"What is it then that you are trying to say?" she inquired.

"It's just that your lifestyle has changed a lot from when you were growing up."

"My lifestyle? Certainly it has, Michael, if you mean standard of living. But I haven't changed. Besides, aren't you better off than when you were young? Did your father go to college? No, but you did. Was he an attorney? No, he wasn't. Should you have been a factory worker because he was?"

I appeared to have touched a nerve, but Katie had trumped my ace. I was doing such a poor job of presenting myself I decided to quit.

Katie continued, though. "Michael, you make the mistake that a lot of people make. They assume that because someone has money they live their lives differently. Maybe some do, I don't."

"I bet some of the women who belong here do," I said softly.

She didn't answer right away. Then, "Certainly it's possible, if they're new money. Don't automatically group me with them. I'm lucky to be here."

I did not understand. "Why's that?"

"This is old money that belongs here, Michael. There are exclusive clubs in town where your lineage is more important than your wealth. In other words, it's who you know, not how much money you have. Larry has family connections back in Illinois that got him into this club. It didn't help with the Minneapolis Club, however."

"I hear that it's tough to gain admission there," I said. "It was that tough here, also?"

"Yes."

I sensed disappointment in her voice, so I abandoned the line of discussion.

"So what is it that you like to do, Katherine? I mean with your life."

"Oh, many things. I love classical music. We have tickets to the Minnesota Orchestra and I enjoy attending the concerts. I have a gazillion CDs at home to listen to."

"Do you go to the concerts often?" I inquired.

"About once a month. Larry uses the occasion to invite business associates."

"Do you always know those folks?"

"Larry does, of course. Me, mostly no. We meet the couple at Orchestra Hall, listen to the concert and then go to dinner. It's not too bad to make small talk for a couple of hours, even if you've never met. Generally you find a subject of interest and let the guest talk. People love to talk about themselves. I merely have to get them started."

I laughed at that and said, "I see. So you don't find yourself living a lifestyle much different than if your husband hadn't been successful?"

"Heavens, yes. I never said that. There is a very large difference between living a certain lifestyle and pursuing the interests that mean the most to you."

I thought that perhaps I was beginning to understand. "So you have to do certain things because you are successful, but you don't let them conflict with your interests."

"Maybe even combine the two as is the case with the symphony," she said.

"Okay. Now I'm beginning to get it. Pardon me for being so obtuse, Katherine, but I don't mix much in your circle."

"You'd fit in just fine, Michael, especially if you were just yourself and didn't put on airs."

I thought about that. I could not see myself being comfortable in her circle, but . . .

Then our meal came. While we ate, I asked, "How did you meet Larry?"

Katie finished chewing and put her napkin to her lips before responding. "We were introduced at a party by a mutual friend. Larry was in town for a weekend, and I became his date for a Saturday night. It was a favor for a girlfriend."

I found the disconnect between Katie's and Larry's memories about their first meeting intriguing, but I wasn't about to bring up the subject yet.

Instead, I said. "I understand you live out on Howard's Point."

"Yes."

"Large house?"

"Pretty large. You've never been out there?"

"I've been by on the lake. I haven't been out there on land for a few years. I wasn't sure who lived in what house, though, when I saw them from the water."

"We're the gray one." Then as if remembering, she said. "That's right, you said you own a boat."

"Yes."

"Use it much?"

I smiled. "I spend my summers on the water. I love to motor to all the restaurants, and I fish a lot."

"I haven't been fishing since I was a kid."

"Want to go sometime?"

"Sure."

"I'll call you about it."

Then I switched subjects again. "You don't take care of that large place by yourself, do you?"

"You mean the house? Not alone. Larry has a lawn service once a week. I have a cleaning service come in twice a week. I do what needs to be done in between. Normal housekeeping chores, cooking, laundry, making beds."

"Are you gone a lot?"

"You mean out of town?"

"No, just like this today."

"Maybe three times a week. We sometimes entertain at home on weekends."

"That's nice."

We finished our meal, and the waiter took away our plates. We both declined desert. I took a deep breath. Now it was time to talk business.

~25~

Down to Business

WITH LUNCH OVER, I initiated the business portion of our meeting by asking. "Do you have a schedule to keep this afternoon, Katherine?"

"Yes, I have another appointment later."

"Okay," I answered. "What I have to discuss should only take a few minutes."

Katie nodded. She was studying me, while she fingered the napkin before her on the table. Her look was inscrutable. Then she said in a rush, "I've set in motion some things you suggested when we last met, Michael."

"Oh?" I answered, somewhat surprised.

"Yes. I'm acquainted with an attorney here in St. Paul from my college days. She's quite good on financial matters, and I decided to work with her." Katie's face took on a serious look. "On her advice, I'm selling all of the Orion shares I hold personally. She wants me to position myself in a defensive posture in case Larry is found to be fooling around."

This revelation caught me by surprise. I scratched my jaw. I thought the move was a little drastic, but said, "That's smart. Besides, we've all seen what happens when people's retirement is all in their company's stock and that company fails. They lose everything. Yes, that's probably a smart move, Katherine."

I was uncertain that I totally agreed with Katie's decision, but I realized there was nothing that I could do about it. What puzzled me, though, was her taking the action that she had. Here I had been thinking she was this wallflower and badly in need of my help. Apparently that wasn't entirely true. I wondered if perhaps I'd been spinning my wheels this whole time while Katie had been out making her own moves.

Katie looked as if she was about to say more, then just nodded. Her mood had lightened, and she had become more animated. She was talking with her hands.

She said, "That's what my attorney advised. We've opened an off-shore banking relationship. The money from the stock sale will go there. That way Larry can't access it in case we have a falling out. The transaction is set to close the day after tomorrow."

"That was quick."

"We had the opportunity and went for it. I'm willing to sell at a discount to get a quick sale. I want this behind me."

I wondered what the hurry was. "Will there be quite a tax bite?"

"None."

"How can that be?" I asked totally surprised.

"The bank is a Sub Chapter S Corporation and under those rules if the stock had been held ten years or longer, there is no capital gains tax."

I marveled at her knowledge. "Good. You sure know your business."

"Thanks. I've had good advice. By the way, is that e-mail address on your card a good one?"

"Yes."

"Okay. I just wanted to double check in case I wanted to reach you by using it."

Our table now was cleared of everything, but our beverages.

Katie seemed done with her revelations so I asked, "Are you ready to talk about our business?"

"Yes."

Katie sat up. She looked small and vulnerable, though that probably was merely an illusion. I was glad I had nothing detrimental to tell her.

Katie's revelations had put me off my stride, but I regained my composure and began. "I haven't got anything shocking to tell you. I should say that up front."

That seemed to make her relax. Her shoulders seemed less tense.

"As I said at our first meeting when you discussed the situation with me, I could see two possibilities for what you described as your husband's unusual behavior. Now I'm able to add a third."

Katie listened without speaking, but her brow wrinkled.

"The most obvious situation that appeared to me would be a case of Larry cheating on you."

Katie looked like she is about to speak, so I held up my hand in a stop signal.

"You didn't think that was a possibility, and quite frankly, I wouldn't be able to find it out if he were cheating. I wouldn't even know how to go about it. You'd need a good private inquiry agent to research that. However, I'm willing to discount that as a possibility if you are."

She nodded. "I am."

"Good. The second possibility I considered was work-related pressure. I don't know if you are aware of this, but I actually met with your husband for this inquiry."

She looked surprised. "You what?"

"Yes. Bob Lindgren from the local bank and I met with Larry and discussed banking issues. Did he tell you?"

Katherine shook her head. "No, he never said anything. Why would he?"

I reflected for a moment, then asked, "Did you ever tell him you and I met that time on your boat?"

She looked surprised. "No, I never said anything. I wanted to keep that between the two of us."

"Our little secret, huh? Well, someone told him."

"Why do you say that?"

"Because when I met him, he acted as if he knew about me."

Katie's eyebrows pinched together. "Why's that so strange? You're local. You do a lot in the community. Your name gets in the paper. He could have heard about you. You've done a lot about town."

I considered what she had said. "Yes, maybe, but he wanted to know if he should call me Michael or Mike."

"How's that significant?" she asked.

"Other than my fourth-grade teacher, you're the only person to ever call me Michael. Now why would he have said what he did unless he heard from someone that my name was Michael?'

Katie reflected for a few moments. Then, "The boat works. They told Larry I took the boat out."

"And he checked up on you and talked to the driver," I added.

"Probably. I thought I was being so cute."

"I've thought about it, and it could be totally innocent. Your husband's talking to the marina and they just mention it in passing. His follow-up, however, is indicative of something. He either doesn't trust you or he's being very paranoid about something. Any ideas?"

She shook her head, but looked disconsolate. "I don't know what's going on, but I don't like it."

I continued. "I was willing to discard the thought of his distrusting you because of other factors at play. I think what's really happening is that he was being paranoid and was acting that way because of pressures at work. He's playing the game close to the vest. I just don't understand what the game is."

I paused as I gathered my thoughts. "You know the bank's being audited, don't you?" I said.

"Yes, it happens every year, either by the state of the feds."

"Okay, but this time it's different."

"Why? What do you mean?"

I spent a few minutes explaining the facts of life to her about the economy and the state of banking in general. After that I explained to her how Orion was suffering from failing loans. Then I threw in the death of John Payton, the controller.

"The death appears to be relevant to me in this affair," I said.

"Relevant how?'

"You said his wife told you it had nothing to do with any situation at home, that it was work related."

"Yes, that's correct."

"Then things at the bank have to be pretty bad for an executive to commit suicide. I mean really bad. The question is what could be that bad?"

Katie's expression was blank. Obviously she has no clue as to what might be going on at the bank even though she was a major stockholder.

I changed the subject. "I'm not trying to be indelicate here, but has Larry had problems performing?"

"What?"

"In bed."

Katie's expression hardened. "You've crossed the line, Michael."

"It sometimes happens when men are under a lot of pressure."

Katie seemed like she'd withdrawn from the conversation. If I was not careful she might actually get up and leave. But what would I care? After today I would be out of this.

"Well, just think about it as a possibility," I said in a soothing tone. "Then consider it in the context of Jerry's personality. Is he generally a loving and caring person?"

"What has this to do with anything?"

"You told me how you two met. Are you sure of that?"

"Of course I'm sure. A woman doesn't forget things like that."

"Well, that may very well be true, but Larry doesn't remember how you met."

"You asked him?"

"Yes, in general conversation. Getting to know one another. He wanted to know how you and I met, so I asked him the same question."

I paused to take a drink of tea. All of a sudden it tasted less sweet. The waiter had refilled my glass. Katie was becoming morose, and I was feeling guilty for causing it. I considered getting up from the table and placing my arms about her. Then I remembered where I was and what gossip a move like that might engender.

I went on to explain. "I've met people like Larry before, Katherine. His work is all that matters to him. He's driven and successful. Everything else becomes secondary. Did he come home and play with the kids or did he work, secluded in his den?"

There was a faraway look in Katie's eyes.

"I'm not passing judgment here, honey. I just want you to explore the facts. I'm no expert, but I think the pressures of work have guided Larry to be more, well more Larry. That is less affectionate or interested in anything not work related."

"Thank you, Michael. That will be enough."

"Whoa. Are you shooting the messenger?"

Tears had found the corners of Katie's eyes. "Sorry, I guess I am."

"Don't look at it that way. Keep the faith and keep supporting your husband. When the economy begins to improve, maybe things will get better. This isn't the end of the world."

"If I want to stick around that long."

Now I was silent. What did she mean by that? What was she contemplating anyway? Things could not be that bad or could they? Why had I ever gotten involved? I had plenty to do at work. I didn't need this hassle. Why did I always fall for the good-looking babes?

I decided to play it cool. "I'm not sure if this has helped you?"

"I don't know yet. I have to think about it."

I wanted to help her think. Maybe a quiet room some place. *Stop it, dummy. It was not professional.*

"You're covering your bases, then? Selling some stock, getting your affairs in order in a defensive mode?"

"Yes."

"That's appropriate, even without this drama."

"Drama? You call this just drama?"

"Yes, Katherine. And if you take a step back and look, you'll see that also. Consider everything for a moment. All you've given me so far is a statement that Larry seems different, maybe a little more distant. Do you realize how shallow that sounds? It appears that you're looking for trouble. You have way too much time on your hands."

I had lost my temper, and I could not take back what I had just said.

Katie looked at me with a shocked expression. "Michael, I didn't deserve that."

I chewed my lip. "No you didn't, but I'm not sorry for what I said. Katherine, you're spoiled. You're used to getting everything you want and used to having your perfect little world. Ever since you were little, you got a free ride because you're beautiful. You were always treated special. Do you deserve that? Have you earned that? Now that you can't have what you want, you don't know what to do."

I paused here and then said in a low voice. "Maybe you should have a talk with your mother."

Katie looked shocked, too shocked to move.

"You . . . you're insolent."

"Above my station, maybe?"

Katie shook her head. "I'm sorry. I don't mean that, Michael." Tears formed in her eyes. "I don't know what I'm saying."

I repeated. "Talk to your mother."

"Why do you keep saying that?" Her face hardened.

"Because you need a dose of reality. Ask your mom what her life was like raising a family and what she had to do without to give you those dance lessons and cheer costumes. Your folks didn't have a lot of money. She didn't have it that great, but maybe she was content with what she had."

Katie now was staring off into space. I decided I'd done enough damage for one day.

"Thanks for lunch. If I learn anything more, I'll let you know. Otherwise I think I've done all I can. I hope it's done you some good."

I stood and walked around the table. I took her hand and kissed it. I do not think she even knew I was there.

~26~

A BRAZEN ATTACK

S A GENTLEMAN, I should have offered to escort Katie to her car, but I realized she probably would have declined considering the state in which I had left her. I probably was just as confused over the meeting as she had appeared to be. It was difficult for me to ascertain with any degree of accuracy who she was. Was she that girl with the country background I had known many years previously or some hard-bitten egomaniac elitist? If I ever cared to determine that answer, it would take time, time I had no intention of spending, as I wanted out of this affair.

Katie had said she had begun looking out for herself. I believed I had cautioned her to think of herself on a previous meeting, but she certainly had taken the bull by the horns, so to speak. I just shook my head in wonderment at the change I had seen in her. Or was she a chameleon? Had she fooled me the first time we had met with that "I'm so helpless" act?

I availed myself of the men's room on the way out the door and then stood by my car studying a building cloudbank over the lake. The weatherman had called for rain later today, and I was probably looking at the leading edge of that system. I estimated I should be home well before it rained, though. I decided to leave my top down.

Pulling out my phone, I called Janet and alerted her that I was just about to leave Wayzata and return to the office.

"Do I need to do anything on the way in?" I asked.

"No, everything's okay. See you when you get back."

"Bye."

I stuffed the phone back into my pocket before reaching into my car to remove my half-smoked cigar, which I then lit. A slight breeze floated the smoke away from me off into an evaporating vapor. The aroma of the burnt sulfur clung to my nostrils from the spent match. I tossed it casually onto the pavement. That act probably would get a member expelled.

Then I wondered if there was a prohibition against smoking on the grounds? The rules were becoming much more restrictive all the time. Oh, well, what did I care. What were they going to do, revoke my membership? I could get Katie into trouble, though. It was time to leave and reenter my familiar life.

Then I saw Katie walking along the walkway toward the parking lot. Her head was down and she appeared to be punching numbers into a hand-held device, probably her phone. She had said she had another appointment.

Apparently her car was on the opposite end of the lot from mine, because her course was angling away from me. She apparently had not seen me leaning against my car in my cool guy pose.

I wondered what she was driving, since I had never seen her car. I decided to wait around until she had reached her vehicle before I left for home. I concentrated on her walk because it was a nice walk. Her dress clung nicely to her hips and came just above the knee. She was wearing open toe white heels, which give her just the proper amount of waddle as she proceeded into the lot.

Then, before she has gone far, a man dressed in a dark suit approached her. Even from a distance I could see that the suit was well cut and not inexpensive. The man's hair was short and neatly combed. He wore dark glasses. He was almost my height and seemed very fit.

Katherine initially seemed startled by his sudden appearance. She jumped slightly and stopped walking. I moved a bit away from my car to see what is going on. The two of them conversed for half a minute and then the slick-looking gent took Katie by the right elbow and led her toward a dark-colored Mercedes with tinted windows parked a few feet away.

Slick opened the back door of the vehicle and indicated with his free hand for Katie to get in. She bent over and looked in, but did not enter. I could hear conversation, but did not understand what was being said. Finally Katie climbed aboard and Slick shut the door.

Now he took a step forward away from the vehicle, and turned his back to it. That was when he spied me watching. We were about forty feet apart in the lot. He was one row ahead of my car with no cars adjacent to his. I had a couple of vehicles still in my row, but not crowding me.

I took a long draw on my stogie and remained standing in place. I was curious as to what Katie was doing, but not particularly concerned for her welfare. Slick was watching me, but neither of us could see each other's eyes, since we both had on our shades. I decided to hang around.

Apparently I was making the other guy nervous because he unbuttoned his jacket and took a step toward me.

"Don't you have anywhere to go, fella?"

I didn't respond. I was trying to analyze why he had opened his coat. If this were a movie, he would have a gun under there and would be wanting to provide quick access.

"Do you hear me fella?" he said.

I nodded. "Just waiting for someone."

"Why don't you wait somewhere else? We don't need an audience."

I considered moving away and calling the police. On what, a business meeting? I was getting wacky. I could walk over to him, but what if we got into a scuffle? That would look pretty silly in the parking lot of a high-tone club. I never would get invited to join, then.

I decided to take a different tact. I was not about to leave until I knew Katie was okay. I turned and reached back into my car where I removed another of my cigars. Then while smoking mine, I walked toward Slick with the wrapped offering in my hand. What was he going to do? Shoot me in the parking lot?

"You smoke, fella?" I asked, after I closed the distance between us by half.

He held up his left hand in a stop sign.

"This is a private party. You're not invited."

I noticed his voice has an educated quality. This wasn't some goon who got by on violence for his answers.

I slowed my pace but did not stop.

"I have business with Mrs. Williams. Did you have an appointment?" I said.

He did not respond, merely slid his right hand inside the left side of his jacket. I stopped walking at this provocative gesture. Now I put my hands in front of my shoulders in a surrender posture and then with one hand unbutton and remove my jacket. Throwing it over my left arm, I did a pirouette showing my adversary I was concealing nothing in my back.

"Have one on me," I said as I approached closer.

"No thanks. Please keep your distance. I may have a cold."

I had no doubt he could hurt me, but not by passing a virus. It did not appear that Katie planned on this meeting, but it may be harmless. At any rate, I didn't think they'd try anything with witnesses present. At least I hoped not. I had not seen a copy of the script.

At that moment I heard soft-toned conversation and saw two ladies approaching from over my left shoulder.

I turned and did a slight bow. "Good afternoon, ladies. Did you have a nice lunch?" I asked in a bright and cheery voice.

They looked as though they had just stepped in something smelly and didn't understand the question, or at the very least wondered who we were, standing there as we were in their parking lot.

The braver one asked. "Do you belong to this club young man?" Her tone was casting call snooty.

"No, ma'am. I'm a guest of Katherine Williams. She was just about to exit that black bus over yonder," I said, pointing at the Mercedes. "I think she told me she wanted to talk to you about something."

That statement garnered looks of puzzlement from both women, but only I knew I was lying, and now I had put Slick in a box. He thought momentarily before turning and walking to the car. He rapped twice on the window and stepped away. While the gathering crowd watched, the door opened and Katie emerged. She appeared to have been crying.

Katie stood outside the open car door as if bewildered. Then she smoothed her dress and walked away toward her car. Slick closed the rear door of his vehicle, nodded to me, and climbed into the front seat. The Mercedes slowly left the parking lot.

The two women shook their heads and went about their business. I followed Katie. She had a hand to her face when I caught up with her. I took her by the shoulder and spun her around.

"What's going on?" I asked.

I took out a handkerchief and allowed her to use it on her face. She had two red marks on her chin. I was getting mad.

"Are you all right?"

"I'm . . . I'm not sure. Oh, Michael, I was so scared I peed my pants. I'm so embarrassed." She began to cry and buried her face in my shirt.

I was trying to figure out what was going on. So far I had no idea.

"Can you drive?" I asked.

"I hope so."

Katie's hands were shaking and she hasd the smell of urine about her.

"No you're not going to drive. Let me have your phone."

She dug into her purse and removed her phone.

"Do you have a number Larry will answer?'

Katie scrolled to a number and handed me the phone. I connected to the number and listened to it ring. A woman answered.

"I need to speak to Mr. Williams," I said.

"I'm sorry but Mr. Williams is tied up this afternoon."

"Well, untie him because his wife has had an accident."

"What? Hold on just a moment."

I was good at causing panic.

In less than a minute, Larry was on the phone. He sounded cool. I would like to tell him what happened, but I did not know myself.

"Larry, this is Mike Connelly. I don't know if . . ."

"Sure I remember you. What's going on?"

"I was having lunch at the Wayzata Country Club with a client and as I was leaving I saw your wife come out. She appeared to be accosted by a man in the parking lot. She's not badly hurt, but certainly is shaken."

"Did he, I mean did he . . ."

"No. She might have a bruise or two, but I don't think anything else. I would have seen."

"You intervened?"

"Yes."

I know that made me sound like a hero, but how else could I answer?

"Do you know who it was?" Larry asked.

"No, my immediate concern was with your wife. Do you think you could come here and pick her up?"

"Gosh. I'm right in the middle of a meeting with the F.D.I.C. Could she maybe take a cab?"

Now I'm wondering what kind of a guy this was. What an asshole. I'd never make it in big business because I wouldn't put my job above my wife, especially one as lovely as Katie.

"Look, Larry. I don't think she should drive. I'm on my way home to Excelsior anyway, so I'll take her home. You get there as soon as you're able."

"Right. Thanks, Mike. Should I call the police?"

"No. I don't want to put Katherine through that right now. They can be updated later."

"Sure thing. Thanks again, Mike. I'll get home as soon as I can."

What a schmuck I was. I had not even got the plate number off that car.

~27~
TAXI SERVICE

I COULD HAVE LET KATIE go home alone in a cab, but then I was such a softy where she was concerned, it just was out of the question. I didn't wanted her to be alone because of the uncertainty of her mental state. At the moment she appeared very vulnerable. One look told me that. I guided her by the arm over to my car. She looked at it as if it were some strange beast.

Standing by the passenger door I said, "Katherine, I'm going to drive you home. Larry will meet us there. Okay?"

Katie did not immediately answer. She looked over her shoulder to where the altercation had taken place and shivered. Then she asked, "What about my car?"

"Someone will retrieve it."

That seemed to satisfy her. Once I had Katie seated in my car, I started the engine and put the top up. It threatened rain, and I thought it better to do it here rather than on the road.

Then I pulled up to the main entrance. "I'll just be a minute," I said. "Let me have your keys." I took her car keys and went inside. I told a club official that Mrs. Williams was ill, and asked him if he would arrange for someone to deliver her car. He assured me he personally would take care of it.

Then I returned outside. Katie had her knees pulled up to her chest with her bare feet on the seat. Her shoes lay on the floor. She appeared small and vulnerable. I was glad I'd made the decision to help her home. I told her to buckle up, and she looked at me as if not understanding what I had said. Then I pulled on my own chest harness, and she got the picture.

Besides my concern over the distraught woman's ability to drive, there was the selfish desire on my part to find out what exactly was going on. That was no ordinary business meeting in which she had been involved.

With the top now up on the Mustang, I extinguished my cigar. I was not about to toss it, so I stuck it in the ashtray and pushed it closed. I had hoped it was out.

"You okay, honey?" I asked.

She nodded, but then added, "Is it cold in here?"

It wasn't, but I realized she might have been suffering from mild shock. I considered my options, then turned on the heater to the lowest setting and directed an air vent right onto her. I may have to suffer from the heat, but the ride would not be that long. I could take it.

When I turned back forward I took her hand and kissed it.

"I'll have you home soon. Larry will be there," I said softly as I buckled up.

"You won't leave me. Will you?" She looked at me with soulful eyes.

I pursed my lips, then said, "I'll stay till Larry arrives home."

There was no answer, but her body appeared to relax as she nodded her head in acknowledgement. There was no quick way home from there so I reversed my route from this morning's travels and ended up waiting at the same spot on County 15 for our turn to move. I purposely let the conversation wane since Katie appeared less than talkative. It was advisable for me not to say anything that might push her over the edge.

My route took me along the Lake Minnetonka shoreline back to Navarre and then through Tonka Bay and again along the lake to Howard's Point. I spied a few fishermen standing along the shore, but little boat activity on the water. It was a pleasant enough summer afternoon, but the clouds definitely were building. The storm that had been forecast for this evening perhaps was arriving earlier than expected, and the impending weather had warned off casual boaters.

We definitely could use rain for the agricultural crops, but we didn't need wind or hail. My friends in farming had told me it was to be a great crop this year if only rain arrived at the critical times. I wasn't sure when exactly that was, and I wasn't much of a gambler, so I wouldn't have made a very good farmer.

In the silence of the drive, I racked my brain trying out various theories as to what had taken place in the parking lot. All my machinations accomplished exactly nothing. I had wanted to ask Katie several times what had taken place, but decided to wait until she was in more familiar surroundings and feeling more comfortable.

We finally reached her house. I had never driven here before, but there was a nameplate by the drive. Turning in I spied a three-car garage to the right between the house and road and a small circle that approached the front door. I chose that.

When I stopped, Katie sat in the car looking straight ahead without moving. Then she spoke very quietly and thanked me for my help without turning to look in my direction. I had the impression she was ashamed of her present condition. She fumbled for the door latch and finally swung the door open only to be trapped by her harness. I reached over and popped the latch, and she was free. I likewise exited, and we stood looking across the top of the car at one another.

"I'm not leaving until Larry arrives," I announced authoritatively to relieve any anxiety.

Katie gave me a dead-eyed look and shrugged. Then she turned toward the house without closing the car door. I grabbed my jacket from the back seat and walked around to close the door before following her. I noticed the billowing thunderheads were closer, and I thought I probably would see rain before I reached the office. Katie then entered the house, leaving the front door open behind her.

"I'm going to clean up," she announced without turning around.

"Okay."

She began moving off toward one end of the house. "Help yourself to a drink," she said with a little more energy. "The liquor is there," she said pointing at a cabinet. Then she disappeared.

I found the glasses all right and the liquor. Ice was another matter. Since I had no desire to wander all over the house looking for ice, I took my scotch neat. Then, when I was seated and looking back in the direction of the bar, I realized I had missed seeing a mini fridge right at the bar. I moved back over to that and dropped some ice into my drink. Since I was there, I poured myself a little more scotch.

I sipped from my drink as I stood in the middle of the room looking about. The area was spacious and had vaulted ceilings, which gave it an airy feel. Lakeside, the wall was comprised of all-glass panels. I wandered in that direction and stood looking out. I was far above the ground when standing here. This actually was the second floor on the lake side.

Katie had gone down a hallway so I assumed the master suite was on this level. I didn't see a kitchen and assumed that and the eating area was a floor below. Looking around I saw an open staircase near the front entrance. That must have been the access to lower level.

Now I remembered that I had never called Janet back to alert her to my delay. By now she must have been wondering where I was. I phoned the office and told her I had seen an accident and had to wait to give my report. I was getting to be a regular little liar. Pretty soon I could fool my mom. Yeah, like that would ever happen.

I sat on a small sofa that faced the lake. At first I thought the windows were tinted, but then realized the sky was darkening. Yes, the rain would be coming soon. I should have brought an umbrella. Perhaps I could borrow one.

Before long Katie rejoined me. I had never seen her looking like she did now. Her hair was obviously still damp and was combed straight down. She must have wiped it briefly with a towel and then just ran a comb through it. She was devoid of makeup, and was wearing a terry cloth robe that reached to her calves. We were in air conditioning and she must have needed the robe to keep warm. Her feet were bare. She sat on the same couch I had chosen and curled her feet under her. She was turned half toward me. She smelled of soap or shampoo.

Katie's eyes were downcast and she was playing with the fabric of her robe with her right hand.

"How are you feeling?" I asked.

"Better."

I could see bruises beginning to show on either side of her jaw.

I reached out to touch her face, and she pulled back. I did not push it. Instead I said, "Care to tell me what happened?"

She hesitated, as if telling the story would once again overwhelm her with the original events.

She looked at my hand. "Could I have a drink?"

"Sure. What would you like?"

"What are you having?"

"Scotch."

"I'll have that."

I got up to pour her a drink, and remembered she had told me she wasn't much of a drinker. I put a single shot of liquor over ice with a splash of water. When I stood before her to hand over the glass, I could see down inside the parting of her robe. I lingered. Then I got a hold of myself and moved to my spot on the couch and sat. I briefly considered a chair across the room to protect the woman from my leering, then I chided myself to grow up and show a little restraint.

I watched as Katie threw down a slug of whiskey, causing her to choke. Her eyes began watering, and she wiped tears away from her alabaster cheeks with an oversized sleeve. Then she imbibed once again. Obviously she needed something to quiet her nerves. Whatever she had experienced must have been traumatic, though I hoped she wasn't going to make herself sick, at least until after I was gone. I was not much of a caregiver.

A clock was ticking loudly somewhere nearby, otherwise there was silence.

"You were saying?" I encouraged, keeping my voice low.

"About what?"

"About what happened back there."

Katie gazed off into the distance. "Do I have to talk about it?"

"It might help."

She twisted the glass in her hands before saying, "Oh, yes. Back there." Katie was staring at the floor. "All right. After we ate, I was leaving the club . . ." Her voice was raspy. I was not sure if it was from the whiskey or from her experience.

I knew this part, but decided to let her tell it her own way.

". . . and all of a sudden there's this man standing in front of me."

I nodded for her to continue, while I tried to maintain a neutral expression. I found myself leaning forward in anticipation and forced myself into a more relaxed pose.

Katie continued, "I don't know where he came from. I was looking at my phone not paying attention . . . then, suddenly, there he was."

Her eyes were wide with fright. I didn't want to stress her but knew her telling the story to me would help her come to grips with the event. It would be less frightening to relive events here in the security of her own home. The whole incident illustrated to me how easy it would be to nab someone. Nobody paid attention to his or her surroundings.

Katie tried to inhale an empty glass, the ice resting on her lip. Then she held the glass out to me. "Get me another drink, will you please?"

I was hesitant, but she held the glass out toward me shaking it, with that doe-like look in her eyes. It was easy to see why men fell for women like this.

I sighed. "Sure."

I pushed myself off the couch once again and walked slowly to the bar. Then I fixed a short one with more water this time and returned to Katie. She was sitting on the couch staring out the windows toward the lake with a faraway look in her eyes. When she saw me she reached out for the glass. I handed it to her she looked at me with a quizzical expression and said. "I'm not driving you know."

It took me a moment to realize what she was telling me. I went back to the bar and dropped in a few more cubes and a lot more scotch. I handed Katie the cold glass and she took it in both hands. Then she took another quick drink and grimaced, shaking her whole body. I let her sit and think without me saying anything.

Regaining her thoughts, she said. "I don't know what his name was."

"The one who first spoke to you?"

"Yes. He spoke very nicely to me, and said an associate of Larry's needed to speak with me. I asked him who and he said, 'Mr. Runyon.' Yes, I think the name was Runyon."

Runyon, Runyon. The name meant nothing to me.

"Did he have a first name?" I asked her.

I could see her thinking. "Yes. It's a funny name. Something like Kale."

"Kale Runyon. Does the name mean anything to you?" I asked.

She shook her head softly. "No, I never heard it before."

I watched her face carefully and then asked, "Did he put those marks on your chin?"

She felt her face. "Yes, he grabbed me with his hand and squeezed. I begged him to stop. It really hurt." Tears once again made an appearance.

I did not want her to sit and brood so I said, "Okay, go on."

Katie took a long sip of her scotch and shivered once again. I was sure it was not because she was cold.

"He said he was a business associate of Larry's and something like he didn't like the fact Larry was ignoring him. I told him I didn't understand. And he said that Larry would, and I was just to give him the message."

Katie took a deep breath and let it out slowly. I could see this story was taking something out of her, but I felt it was important for her to continue. When she told Larry later, it would be easier.

She chewed her lower lip and said, "He told me to tell Larry to get the feds off his back or there would be consequences."

"Did he say what he meant by that? What were the consequences?" I asked.

"He . . . he said he would hate to see my pretty face all sliced up."

Now the tears flowed. The scotch glass was trembling, and amber liquid was splashing out and dotting the white robe.

I moved closer to Katie and took her drink, placing it on the floor next to me. Then I put my arm around her shoulders. I hugged her, and she buried her face in my chest, wetting my shirtfront. She grabbed the lapels of my jacket like they were her lifelines.

Katie's robe now had split open down from her waist where a tie held it from coming completely apart, and I could see she had not bothered to wear anything underneath. Her legs were spread apart on the cushion in a way that had caused the robe to part. Her pubic hair stood out like a dark island in a pale white sea.

I looked away, but the desire within me exploded as the warm feel of this woman next to me continued. I was getting hard and could not will it to stop. My face flushed and my ears began ringing. I wondered if I was having a heart attack. My breathing began coming in rapid gasps.

Katie lifted her head and placed her face in front of mine. We were only inches apart, her eyes pleading. Salty drops of liquid had left streaks on her cheeks. I could feel the heat of her body radiating off my face. Then her lips parted ever so slightly and she kissed me. I had quickly grown hard, but just as quickly I knew that this was wrong. I couldn't take advantage like this. I pulled my lips from hers, cursing myself the whole time. I knew I had to leave, but I was just as sure I didn't want to abandon Katie until Larry arrived.

However, she didn't give up. While hanging on to my jacket, she slid her leg across my groin, caressing my hardness with the softness of her inner thigh. My body was racked by desire. I put my arms around her back and felt her small frame. Her beauty was engulfing me, and I was too weak to resist.

"I'm not sure we should do this, Katherine," I croaked. Desire was overwhelming my body. I couldn't believe what I heard myself saying.

She kissed me again. Her soft mouth captured mine. Her leg moved back and forth against me. I found my hand slipping inside her robe where I found a breast hardened with pleasure. I worked it until it had softened, and then I bent down and kissed it.

Soon I was between her legs tasting her sweetness. We were both out of control and neither of us now wanted to stop or could stop. Later when I had climaxed within her, we both lay exhausted. I had fulfilled my ultimate lifetime fantasy.

I was totally spent, but I didn't want this to end, so I kissed Katie again and again all over her body. Only then did I finally suggest she get her robe on. "Your husband could be home at any minute. I might have a hard time explaining."

"She smiled. "A hard time?"

I smiled back. I did not know when I had felt so good.

"It's been so long since someone made me feel this way," she said quietly. "Thank you, Michael.

I now was embarrassed. Shit, what had I done? When could I do it again?

~28~

RETREAT

I KNEW LEAVING KATHERINE now was the correct thing to do, even though I felt as though I was abandoning her. It was just too embarrassing to remain any longer. I certainly didn't need to compound one unfortunate incident with another. I'd counted on Larry being home by now, so I was perplexed what to make of his absence.

I let myself out the front door and immediately noticed the sky. It had grown much darker, and the wind has picked up while I had been inside. I smelled rain. I was glad I already had put up my car top.

On my way to my car, I met a dark-blue Mercedes entering the drive. For a moment I anticipated trouble. Was this the same car from the country club? Then I realized that it wasn't the vehicle Katie and I had encountered this afternoon. Apparently it was Larry Williams arriving home as promised. It was a good thing for both Katie and me that I chose to leave when I did. I got lucky this time, in more ways than one.

Larry parked his car in front of the garage and stepped out, facing me. "Mike, can you come in and visit for a minute?"

"Larry, I need to get to work and cover some things. I've tried to quiet Katherine, and I believe I've succeeded. Why don't you see what you can do to console her, hear her story. Then if you want to get together this week and discuss things, let me know."

"That sounds like a plan. Is she all right?"

"I believe so. She was frightened, of course. This Runyon character appears to have tried to get to you through her. I think she'll have a small bruise on her chin where he held it. Again, get things under control and then we can talk."

"Thanks for looking out for her, friend."

204

Larry surprised me when he approached and gave me a bear hug. "Again, thanks."

I nodded to Larry and got into my car. I watched as he entered his car, opened the garage door and drove in. Larry was thanking me. If he only knew. I felt like such a heel.

I looked at the dashboard clock and saw it was almost four o'clock. I'd missed half a day's work. I was thinking about what I still had to do that day when it began raining. That was okay since my route to work was on slow roads, and the rain should not be a problem. I switched on my defrosters and drove slowly.

While waiting at the nearby stop sign, I placed a call to Janet. "I'm ten minutes out and it's raining."

"You're quite the forecaster. Did you put your hand out the window?"

"Smarty. See you in ten."

There were no parking spots available near my office when I arrived in Excelsior, so I parked as close as possible and ran for it. Needless to say, I was a bit damp when I entered the office. Janet just shook her head and laughed.

"Ever hear of an umbrella?"

"It's at home."

"Good place for it."

I checked to see if there was any coffee left and emptied the pot. That would warm me some, as the air conditioning working on my wet shirt was giving me a chill.

"How was lunch?"

"Pretty fancy place I can tell you. But there was construction on 15 and I had to wait both times."

I dug into my work. It was difficult. I had a kaleidoscope of images floating through my mind. The confrontation in the parking lot and the scene on the couch keep revolving. Concentration was definitely a challenge. I did my best to block those thoughts and get some work done.

Janet left me alone for a bit, then came into the office with a copy of the local rag, which came out every Wednesday. She handed it to me and said. "There's an article in here about the murder and an editorial by your buddy, Green. You might find it interesting."

I took the paper and looked at it. Janet had it folded open to the editorial.

Freedoms Suspended
By Bobby Green

The essence of our freedom is that as a society we respect the freedom of the individual over that of the collective group. As a nation we are nearly alone with that concept.

When we allow the government to trample on that freedom, slowly, but inexorably that freedom is eroded. Oftentimes the excuse used to chop away at this personal freedom is that the common good requires it.

What common good surpasses this one above all other rights? Can we use the excuse that it is necessary to get at the truth? Never! Every person has his or her version of the truth. That is too nebulous of a reason. We cannot, we must not let our local government, our local officials, or our local police usurp our rights in the name of expediency.

How many people have been wrongly accused and convicted of a crime, only to be freed from death row when better technology became available?

Don't let that happen in our town.

Stand up! Stand up my fellow citizens and demand respect for your individual rights.

Don't let the police run amok!

Well, I'll be damned. Bobby was on fire with this one. I wondered if this was going to hurt me or help me. I would have to wait and find that one out.

"What do you think?" I asked Janet.

"I'm not totally sure what he's saying. It sounds like he's criticizing the police."

"Sounds like," I agreed.

"How will that affect you?"

"I hope it gets them off my back."

"Right."

Janet returned to her desk, and I again dove in to my workload. I had some catching up to do. I worked straight through until six to make up for my afternoon absence. Janet had not inquired further about my delay before she left at five, but she probably would pursue things further tomorrow. I could usually take her mothering me and wanting all the latest information on my problems.

When I drove home the two blocks to my place, it was still raining, though not hard at the moment. Still I was glad to have my car. I did not get totally wet running to retrieve it. After parking in the underground garage, I went upstairs to my bedroom and changed clothes. Shorts and a tee were a welcome change to my more formal attire. Before tossing my shirt into the hamper, I smelled it. I smelled the scent of a woman. I wondered if Larry had noticed when he was close to me.

I had second thoughts on my damp clothes. I decided to hang them up in the bathroom to dry. I didn't need moldy clothes in the hamper. Then I went downstairs. With all I had been through this afternoon, I decided a drink was in order. I took care of that immediately. What I had at Katie's had worn off long ago, and I had a need.

I was not really hungry since I had eaten a late lunch. I decided to see what my mood was later and perhaps make some popcorn. Watching TV and eating popcorn. That would work. Besides I had nothing in the refrigerator that could be fixed in short order, and I was trying to cut down on ordering pizza. It had become too easy to do too often and with too many calories.

The schedule said the Twins were home, but I was doubtful there would be a game if it kept raining. This was becoming a real soaker. From what I understood, the new field drained well at least from what I had read, but there were limits. I laughed at my thought that if they did play, cleaning the uniforms would be a major challenge. I shook my head. They should have put on a retractable roof.

After refreshing my drink and staring into the refrigerator for five minutes to confirm my dinner decision, I put on a rain jacket, took my drink, and went down to my boat. The dock could be slippery when wet, but there was a traction strip down the middle. I was careful to walk on that. I didn't need to slip and have them find my body floating in the water tomorrow. An autopsy would show I had been drinking and what a legacy that would leave.

I removed part of the rain cover and climbed aboard. My boat had a large canvas sunscreen overhead, so sitting under it I was covered, but I more or less was checking just to make sure the sump was working. I decided to just sit under the covered area for a bit and watch it rain. As long as the wind did not blow hard, I'd be okay. It was quiet out there. No one else was about in the dock area, and I couldn't see any activity on the patios. I laughed when I realized I was the only dummy out in the rain.

Looking out over the water was like looking into a closed closet. It was darker than I remembered it could get at this time of evening. It wasn't even sundown, but the weather was a major contributor and not particularly welcoming. The lake also was devoid of activity, which was probably good as I saw a nice healthy chop on the water. It wouldn't be easy going for a boat. Speeds would necessarily be slow. I glanced over to the end of the bay to the diminished lights. There wouldn't be many boats at the local restaurants tonight.

I sat alone with my thoughts and stared out over the bay. Fog was rising off the water. I could see it close in where the light over the dock aided my view. That was when I first noticed the chill in the air. Already damp and with the breeze, I felt the drop in temperature quickly. I hadn't given it a thought until now, since I had other things on my mind. I wasn't dressed for this weather. Yet I remained. I had things to work through.

A ton of ideas ran through my head. First of all even with what Katie had told me, I had no idea what took place in the parking lot at the Wayzata Country Club. It obviously was an attempt at intimidation, but why? Katie hadn't seemed to have any idea what was happening. Whoever this Runyon character was, he seemed to have a unique way of doing business. How did he know Katie? How did he know Larry?

Larry was the obvious answer. He must know what this incident involved. The question was, had he put his wife in jeopardy or was this event a surprise to him as well? If we talked further, I intended to ask him that directly. What kind of man would put his wife in harm's way.

I took a large swallow of liquor. I needed to salve my conscience. Of greater concern to me was what had taken place on the couch in the Williams home. I know I was way out of line there. I preferred to think that it was an accident, that Katie was distraught and looking for comfort from whomever had been there. I realized, however, how I had taken advantage. I did not feel good about that, though I seem good at it.

To fantasize as I had been doing since first contacted by the woman was one thing, to act out that desire was something completely different. I understood that both now and at the time, but what scared me was that I believed I really wanted to lose control in that situation regardless of what I knew was right. Really, really wanted to. That bothered my sense of personal responsibility.

I couldn't get the thought of Katie's naked body out of my mind, try as I might. My pulse quickened just thinking about it. I decided the only course of action open to me was to avoid getting together with her again. I didn't trust myself. It sure was sweet, though. I unconsciously drained my glass with that thought.

I was weak when it came to women, and I admitted that. Moving forward I had to get my thoughts on other things. The Fourth was coming up in a week, and I was looking ahead to the parade and fireworks. The Fourth itself was a terrible time to get around town, with so many visitors, but I could watch the parade from my front stoop, and the fireworks from my deck. I just needed to lay in enough provisions ahead of time so I wouldn't need to go out much on that day. Driving that is.

Maybe I would invite a few friends over to join me. Steve and Cindy Anderson for sure. Maybe the doc will come also. I wonder if Larry and Katie would care to come? Now that would be novel. They had their own boat, though. They might go out on that and come out front of my place to watch the festivities. I wondered if Katie would be looking for me on shore.

I attempted to take a drink and realized my glass was empty. It was time to leave the boat. I was cold. Maybe I'd take a hot shower. Returning inside, I first called Steve, and invited the two of them for the afternoon and later the fireworks on the Fourth. They had been here before, so the decision was an easy one for them. They were familiar with the program.

Getting off the phone I determined I needed a refresher on my drink. I dumped my ice trays into a bowl, made some more ice, poured a drink and went into the living area. Then I called Sandra Gross. Apparently she wasn't yet home from the office, or maybe she was out to dinner. I left a message and told her I was at home for the night, and that I'd try back later or she could call me. That was a really decisive message.

An hour later, Sandra answered my follow up call. "Hello, Sandra. This is Mike."

"Hello, yourself."

"Say listen, Sandra. This is your first summer in Excelsior, and you maybe don't know about all our activities here. In case you hadn't heard, we have a big Fourth of July celebration in town. I always have a party on that day, and I'm having a few friends over again this year. If you could come, it would give you a chance to meet a few people. That is if you could join me."

"That would be great, Mike. It would be a great send off for me."

My heart sank. "What do you mean?"

"I go to summer training for two weeks. Remember? I'm in the Reserves?"

I brightened and tried to sound positive. "Oh, right. Let's make it a big sendoff then."

I felt good about the call. Tomorrow, I'd call Bob and remind him of the party. Then, I would be set.

The rain was still coming down as I stood and looked out the patio door. My vertical blinds were wide open and all my lights were on. It was still gloomy inside. Not enough light comes down the stairs from the front door, and on dark days the room required indoor lighting.

I was still not very hungry after my larger than usual lunch, so I decided on some cheese and apple slices. I figured popcorn and scotch might not go well together. I munched on that repast as I sipped my scotch. Sitting in my favorite chair, I rehashed my earlier meeting with Katie, the part before all the drama.

I felt comfortable with what I had told her about her husband and my suspicions of the issues at hand. I think I had things worked out pretty accurately. Only time would tell. The wild card in the equation was Katie herself. I wasn't sure what motivated her. What she recently had done totally surprised me. There was something going on there I didn't understand because why else would she have come to a virtual stranger in the first place to seek answers to such private matters. She may not be all that bright.

I decided at this point to let things with the Williams's family play out, and get on with my life.

~29~
CALL A SPADE A SPADE

WHEN I AWOKE the following morning, the rain had stopped, the sky had cleared, and I felt a refreshingly cool breeze invigorate me on my walk to work. I looked forward to a good day's productivity without interruption from outside influences. There had not been many of those lately. I could only hope I'd get two full days in before the weekend, or I would be working Saturday.

As I had suspected, when Janet and I sat down with our coffee to discuss the day's business she began with what she considered business.

"Tell me about the accident. Was it anyone I'd know?"

"Gosh you look lovely this morning, Janet. Did you do something new with your hair?"

She gave me a sly grin. "Okay, big boy, what's going on here?"

I knew I should tell the truth. Actually there was no reason not to.

"Listen, Janet. There was no accident yesterday. I made that up, but for a good reason. Remember I had lunch with Katherine Williams."

"Yes. The new woman in your life."

I frowned, but went ahead. "Well, as I was about to pull out of the parking lot after lunch, when Katherine came out to get into her vehicle and was assaulted right there in the parking lot."

"What?" she exclaimed. "At the country club?"

"Yes. Right there in the lot. But it's probably not what you envision, so let me fill you in."

I told Janet the whole story up to when I took Katie home. I obviously left out the details of our tryst.

When I was finished, she asked, "So you think it was done by someone who knows the banker husband?"

I nodded while chewing my lower lip. "Undoubtedly. That's what I was led to believe."

"And they actually threatened to cut her face?" she exclaimed.

I nodded. "That's what Mrs. Williams told me while she was crying. I have no reason not to believe her."

Janet slowly shook her head. "I can't believe this could happen here."

"Me neither. That's why I hadn't wanted to explain what happened over the phone with her listening. She was pretty upset and mentally fragile."

"I understand." Janet thought for a minute. "Maybe there's something weird going on at that bank."

I pursed my lips. "You may be correct, Janet. I have slowly been coming around to that conclusion. You don't see what I saw yesterday every day of the week."

Janet looked concerned. "What have you gotten yourself into, Mike?"

"I wish I knew. I hope nothing. I do know, though, that I'm going to get out now. Listen, Janet, like I said, the reason I told you there had been an accident was that Katherine was in the car with me when I called, and I didn't want to subject her to any more stress at that time by rehashing the story in front of her. I knew if I told you what had happened, you would have wanted to know more, and I hadn't wanted to discuss it just then. Sorry I lied to you."

"That's okay, hon. I understand. I think you did right by not talking in front of her. So you talked to the old man before you left?"

"Not really. Just to say hello and goodbye. I wanted to get clear of the place as fast as I could. By the way, that's a real castle they live in."

"Big huh?"

"Huge. I think I'd get lost in there. Want more coffee?"

"Sure."

I got up and poured us each another cup.

"What did you think of the editorial?" Janet asked.

"Bobby's prose is so flowery, I'm not sure anyone will get it."

"Only the police will have to get it. Maybe only one policeman will have to get it," she said.

I thought about that for a moment. "Perhaps."

We sat thinking, then. "Have you heard any more from them?" she asked.

"From the police?"

"Yes."

"Nope. My attorney said I would, but so far nothing. Have you heard anything on the jungle drums?"

"The rumor mill is suspiciously quiet, Mike. I heard that the police were checking out the husband, but that he had an alibi." Janet looked down at her cup. Then she said tentatively, "I see why you may be a suspect, though."

I was surprised by her comment. "Why?"

"Process of elimination. Good thing Bobby wrote that editorial or you might already have been arrested."

You think?"

"Yes. I've been going over your story and have tried to think about it from the point of view of the police trying to find the killer. Okay?"

"I don't see it."

"Okay then. You said you went over to see her, correct? I mean the night she purportedly was moving out."

"I went over to check on things. To see why the movers were there. To make sure nobody was raiding the place."

Sure. But she threw you out."

"No, she didn't throw me out. She didn't have time to visit just then."

Janet shook her head. "She threw you out so you came back later after the movers had left and intended to punish her for rebuffing you. It got out of hand and you accidentally killed her. Then in a panic you hid the body and moved her car."

My face had heated up by now. What was Janet doing? "What are you saying?"

"Point of view of the police, remember?"

"But I told them that she came over to see me."

"Any witnesses?"

"No. No, I don't think so."

See, the police only have your word that she came over to your place. It could all be a fabrication to cover up the crime. And anyway, you could just as well have killed her at your place as at hers."

"There'd probably be her fingerprints at my place proving she'd been there."

"Could have gotten there anytime, Mike. You were neighbors after all. Maybe the week before when you lured her over to seduce her."

"Shit. What are you saying?"

"I'm saying that you have to be damn careful. Don't talk to the police without your lawyer."

"That's what he said."

"Then listen to him. Your story has more holes in it than a sieve."

I took a drink of coffee. "Ah ha. Then why would I find the body? Tell me that."

Janet took a sip of her coffee and thought. "You wanted credit for the murder, but couldn't get it until the body was found. The police weren't doing it, so you had to make the find. Big hero. You needed the psychological fulfillment."

"What a crock." I nearly spilled my coffee I was so agitated.

Hey, I'm just telling it the way the police might look at it. The good thing is they have no proof against you, right?"

"Right."

But now I was worried. What did the police have?

~30~
LARRY WILLIAMS PAYS A CALL

I WAS NOT TOTALLY SURPRISED when I got a phone call at work later that Thursday morning from Larry Williams. He seemed to have wanted to talk to me at his place when I brushed him off the previous afternoon. Apparently he was not going to let it go. Perhaps he knew what had happened between Katie and me? No, I'd hope he trusted her more than that. Maybe he had no one else to talk to.

He began the conversation, "Mike. I want to thank you again for interceding on behalf of Kate yesterday. Who knows what might have happened otherwise."

I felt my chest tighten. "One does what one has to do," I replied. "How is she today?"

"She was distraught last night. The thought that someone would invade her personal space and make threats against her is just not in her vision of the world. I'm not sure how long it'll take her to recover. She may need counseling."

I had not envisioned that deep a scar, but Larry knew his wife better than I did, or did he? I said, "I can understand that, Larry." I did understand. I knew firsthand after my trauma the previous year, I was now more sympathetic to others and their problems. I really felt for Katie now.

There was a pause, then Larry said, "Perhaps you could come visit her sometime this weekend. I think she looks at you as her knight in shining armor who came to her rescue. You may be able to soothe her."

That was not what I wanted to hear. I couldn't trust myself with her. I said, "Let's see how things play out."

"Fine. Mike, could we get together and talk?" The neediness in his tone unnerved me.

I answered, "What did you have in mind, Larry?"

"I don't want to bother you at work. Could I perhaps drop by your place on my way home tonight?'

Larry had done me a favor by meeting with Bob Lindgren and for that I had violated his wife. I decided I owed him one . . . maybe even two.

"I think that would work," I said.

We worked out the details for our meeting, and I finished out my day.

Later when I was at home awaiting Larry's arrival, I puttered about straightening up the living area. It had been a great day weather wise and I also had accomplished a lot at work. Yesterday's rain had brought clear skies and slightly cooler temperatures, which I had appreciated on my noontime walk. There was little breeze now, and the sun still felt warm. Puffy white clouds dotted an azure sky. A perfect Minnesota day.

While I waited for Larry, I refrained from fixing myself a drink, though I had lit up. When the doorbell rang, I climbed the stairs and answered it.

Larry was silhouetted in the light of the doorway, his face in shadow.

I pulled open the door and stepped back. "Hi, Larry. Any trouble finding the place?"

"None. I can park out there, right?"

"As long as you plug the meter," I said. "Come on down."

I stepped past Larry and led the way down to the living room.

"Two levels huh?" he asked as we descended the stairs.

I turned my head slightly. "Yes."

"How many bedrooms?"

"Two. Both up, with a bath both up and down."

"Nice," he said.

The patio door was open, and the blinds drawn completely open. The room looked its largest this way, bringing the out of doors to us inside.

Larry looked around the living space. "I like that fireplace. Do you use it much?"

"It's gas, but has a nice ambiance. Yes, I use it quite a bit."

"Was the stone work original with the place or did you do it?"

"I had it done. It's river stone."

"It goes well with the room," he commented.

"Thanks."

Larry walked over to the oak slab mantle and picked up a trophy. "So you play golf."

"I play at it. I'm no threat to anyone."

Larry laughed at that and placed the trophy back on the mantle. He slid his hand along the back of the couch as he returned, and said. "I like this leather furniture."

"It's very comfortable. Can I get you something to drink?"

"What have you got?"

"Anything," I answered.

"Beer?" He inquired.

"Sure. Do you want a glass?"

"Bottle's fine, or can as the case may be."

I got both of us beers and led the way onto the deck. "Okay if we sit outside?" I asked.

"I prefer that," he answered.

We both chose chairs facing the water with a small table between us. Larry was dressed in an expensive, well-cut suit, white shirt, and silk tie. His loafers were Italian. He had opened his suit coat and made himself comfortable.

I could see the man's face better now. In the daylight it appeared strained. Dark smudges rested on baggy skin beneath his eyes, giving him a tired appearance. Maybe he was. He looked older than when we had last visited at the bank.

"You have a nice view of the bay. Have you lived here long, Mike?" Larry asked as he sipped his beer.

"Quite some time now. I guess nearly thirteen years."

"You live alone?"

"I'm afraid so," I answered.

"Confirmed bachelor, then."

I hesitated momentarily while thinking about the question. "Not by choice. My marriage didn't work out and I haven't met anyone since."

"Sorry to bring it up."

"No problem."

We sat silently watching the lake.

"I never get tired of sitting on the water," Larry said finally. "There's something so peaceful about it. I think I could retire on some remote lake and spend my entire summer there."

"I agree, though I'm probably not very good company for myself."

We both laughed.

After a few moments of silence, Larry asked casually, "So how do you know Kate?"

I turned my head and looked at him. I wondered what he was after.

"Like I said before, I've known her since we were kids, but not really since then."

Larry nodded.

I continued, "Yes. We were neighbors in Minnewashta Heights. You know where that is?"

"On Lake Minnewashta off highway seven, right?" Larry said.

"Yes. She babysat me and my sister for a couple of years."

"How old were you then?"

"Oh, I guess about eight or nine."

It seemed like we had been over this before.

"Do you see much of one another?" he asked before taking a sip of his beer.

I shook my head. "I hadn't seen her for more than twenty-five years until this summer."

"Oh."

"In fact, I hadn't seen her until we had lunch together a couple of weeks ago. On your boat, actually. Nice boat by the way."

"Yes. Yes, it is. So you're very old friends."

He sounded like a broken record the way he was repeating himself. "I guess we are," I finally answered."

How'd you happen to be at the Club with her?"

219

I wasn't sure what Katie told him so I decided to be ambiguous. "I had a client lunch and afterwards had walked to the parking lot—"

"Do you belong?" Jerry interrupted.

Do I belong? That was a really good question. No I don't think I belong with that crowd. However, I answered. "No, I was a guest."

"Sorry, you were saying?"

"I ended my meeting and had walked to the parking lot to leave. I removed my jacket and had placed it into my car. I was just lighting up a cigar. Excuse me one minute."

I walked into the house and returned with two cigars. Do you smoke?"

"Some."

"Try this. It's Jamaican."

Larry unwrapped the cigar, bit off the end, and I lit it for him.

"Nice draw," he said, after inhaling a lungful.

I nodded.

Larry drew the smoke through the tightly wrapped tube and said. "Cool smoke."

"Yes, it's a nice cool smoke."

"Jamaican you say."

"Yes."

"Thanks."

"You're welcome."

I continued with my story. I was assuming Katie has not said we were at lunch together when I said, "As I was saying, I was in the parking lot considering the weather and wondering if I should put up my car's top when I saw Katherine walking into the lot. I don't think she saw me because of where I was parked, but I was pretty sure it was her."

"You couldn't tell?'

"Well, she was walking sort of away and I had only seen her once in those many years."

"But you noticed her?"

I shook my head. "Larry, a man would have to be dead not to notice her."

He paused for a moment and then nodded and half smiled.

"You haven't been married that long that you don't see what you've got, have you?"

"Go on," he said in a perfunctory tone.

"Okay, sure. Well, I really didn't think anything of it and was about to get into my car when this nicely dressed dude walked up to her. I think he surprised her because she sort of jumped. Then they spoke for a half-minute or so, and he guided her by the arm to a car parked nearby. He opened the door for her, and she got in."

"So what made you hang around?'

Here I paused for a moment. Then I said, "I don't really know, Larry. There was just something in the guy's manner I didn't like. He was too slick."

Larry continued to ask me a few more questions, then said. "Kate was really shaken."

"I know."

"Did she tell you what went on in the car?" he asked.

"Yes."

"Was it understandable to you?"

"More or less. She didn't discuss the actual deal you're involved in, just the outline."

"So you know?"

"Pretty much."

"Are you going to say anything?'

"To whom?'

"To the feds."

"No. That would come better from you, don't you think?"

The conversation has taken a turn into territory where I was totally unfamiliar. I actually had no idea what the Runyon character wanted with Katie, nor what deal he was involved in with Larry. Although I had no idea what Larry was talking about, I decided to play along. Maybe I would learn something useful. It was total bluff on my part.

Larry leaned over with his elbows on his knees. "I don't think I can. I still have hopes I can pull us out of this mess."

I didn't say anything. This went on for nearly five minutes as we both studied the lake. Finally, I broke the silence. "Larry, I don't know this Runyon guy. I Googled him and got a brief biography, but from what I saw yesterday, he doesn't seem like the kind you want to fool around with."

"No, he isn't."

"What does he do then?"

"He's in a lot of things. He owns condos, parking lots, a car dealership, some gas-convenience stores."

"So you got involved with him on the deal?"

"Yes. He was willing to help out. I didn't have a lot of options."

"Did he know what was going to happen?'

Larry hesitated. "No. No one did. It didn't turn out the way it was supposed to. I thought it would be okay. We just needed some time to get things back on track. Who knew the recession was going to be a depression, and that we'd be audited when we were."

I had an inspiration. "That's what led to the suicide of your comptroller?"

Larry looked at me with startled eyes. Then he looked down at his cigar. "Yes. So you know about that also. Did Katherine tell you?"

I shook my head. "I don't think she has clue one about that, Larry."

Even with this admission, I really have no idea what Larry was alluding to, but it sounded serious.

"Then how do you know all this, Mike?"

"It's not that hard to figure out, Larry. Stuff like this is tough to hide."

He mulled over my statement while playing with his cigar. "Yeah, I guess you're right. I thought I was being real cute."

"I'm sure not that many people know," I answered.

"Perhaps not, but one is enough if it's the wrong person."

"You mean like the regulators."

"Yes, the regulators."

"Maybe you should consider getting Katherine out of town for a while," I said.

He looked up at me with a surprised expression. "Why?"

"Because Runyon thinks he can get you to do his bidding through her."

"He can't."

"Will that stop him from trying?"

"I don't know."

I was heating up at the man's cavalier attitude. "Don't be a pigheaded fool, man. He threatened to cut her up. Do you want to see that happen?"

"No. I mean I know." Larry looked me in the eyes. "Maybe you're right. That's a good idea. Get her away until this works itself out."

I nodded my approval and sat back in my chair, more relaxed now.

We sat quietly for a few moments. Larry would be a good boat partner. He did not need to talk all the time. The sun was behind the building and we were in the shade. The breeze off the lake had cooled. With low humidity and a lack of sunshine it now felt cooler. We sat quietly while we both contemplated.

I broke the silence when I asked, "Would you like another beer?"

Larry looked at the bottle in his hand as if he hadn't known it was there. "No. This is fine."

We continued to just sit and relax.

"Do you own a boat, Mike?"

"Yes."

"Which one is yours?"

"The Chris Craft Catalina with the blue canvas top."

"Sweet. Can we take a look?"

"Sure."

We got up and left our bottles on the table. We both trailed smoke while walking out onto the dock.

"This boat looks pretty maintenance free," Larry said.

"It is. Just hose it down unless I've got fish guts all over it."

Larry smiled at that. "What size motor?"

"It's a 300."

"Okay, I see that now. Do you like the center console?"

"Yes. It works well when I'm alone in the boat."

"Does that electric work pretty well for fishing?"

"Pretty much unless it's real windy."

Larry nodded.

We sat in the boat and smoked for a bit. Then Larry said." I want to thank you again for helping Kate, Mike. She's going to need someone to help her some more later on. She'll have professionals to advise her, of course, but she'll need someone she can trust to confide in. Can she, could we count on you?"

I wasn't following. "I don't understand, Larry."

Larry stifled a laugh. "You will soon enough, Mike. You will soon enough. Please say you'll look in on her occasionally." Tears formed in the corners of Larry's eyes. He took out a handkerchief and blew his nose.

I had no idea what I was getting into, but now I was becoming concerned. I answered, "Yes, sure I will, Larry. You can count on me."

"Thanks. You're right. I'm going to get her out of town. I wonder . . . I mean she shouldn't go alone, should she. We . . . she needs someone we can trust to get her safely there. Do you think you could do it? I can make it worth your while."

"Do what exactly?"

"Go with her and get her settled, of course."

"I don't know, Larry. When will she leave and where is she going?"

Larry shook his head. "I don't know that either, yet, but I want to get her out of town as soon as possible, maybe tomorrow."

Wow, this was hitting me awfully fast. "Listen Larry, slow down a bit here. Formulate a plan. Then let's talk. I have no idea what you're thinking here. Besides, Katherine may not want me to accompany her."

"Why wouldn't she?"

"She doesn't know me, man. Maybe it should be someone she knows better and trusts. Maybe some lady friend."

"I trust you, Mike. That's what counts. You've got a head on your shoulders and can think on your feet." The man scared me, as he looked me in the eyes. "I know you would do the best for her."

"Of course, but . . ."

"You're right, Mike. Let me get it figured out first."

The thought of him trusting me after what I had done behind his back made me sick to my stomach. Now he wanted to throw the two of us together. I was getting nowhere with Larry trying to talk him out of it. He appeared to be panicking, though I agreed with him that getting Katie out of town was a priority just now.

Maybe he would change his mind after he had a chance to think on it. "Think about it, about what you want to accomplish and call me either here tonight or at the office tomorrow," I said.

"Okay, thanks. Look, I've got to run. I'll call. Thanks again for everything."

Every time he said that I felt like a heel. I wondered what would happen if Katie and I went off together. I was excited just thinking about it. Could Larry see that on my face?

We climbed out of the boat and walked back up to my place. Larry thanked me for the beer and cigar. Then I walked him to the front door. Misery followed the man. I could see it in his slumped shoulders. Whatever battle he had been fighting was getting the better of him.

He reached for the doorknob and pulled open the door. Then he paused and turned. Reaching out his hand, he said. "Thanks again for everything, Mike."

Then he turned and walked away. I watched him. His gate was unhurried and deliberate. The phrase "dead man walking" came to mind. Why, I didn't know? I watched his car disappear around the corner as he headed home.

I returned to the patio with my cigar. Now that Larry was gone, I had to try and figure out what had just happened.

~31~

MEETING WITH THOMPSON

AFTER SEEING LARRY WILLIAMS OFF, I sat on the patio for a while and thought about what I might want for supper. With the turmoil from the most recent meeting grinding in my stomach, I wasn't hungry now, but I knew I probably would be later on when my emotions had settled down. I entered the kitchen and looked over my stock of groceries. From that perusal I decided to make chili. I had a pound of fresh hamburger in the refrigerator, so that insured I had everything that I needed for the meal. Even if I decided later not to eat, the chili would keep.

Fifteen minutes later I was adding all the ingredients to the browned burger, and the chili was simmering on the stovetop. I cracked open another beer and exited back outside to the deck where I chose a chair facing the lake. Activity was growing down on the docks, as residents home from work prepared to head out onto the water for an evening sojourn.

I would have liked to join them, but I was beset by inertia. The conversation with Larry had robbed me of all my energy. Consequently, I sat and quietly watched the lake activity, trying to make sense of our dialogue.

Evidently I had bluffed Larry with my evasiveness to the extent he thought I knew more about his affairs than I actually did. That bluff, however, did nothing to increase my knowledge of what had been and was taking place. All I could say for certain was that it involved Orion Bank and Larry himself.

The best I had been able to figure out was that Larry and this Runyon character were in some sort of business deal together. Larry had not said what sort of deal it might have been, but he was a banker and the purpose of a bank was to lend money. It stood to reason that Larry's bank might have loaned money to Runyon or to one or more of his businesses. Fine, so how was that bad? I mulled that over for a bit without a resolution.

My next door neighbor, Walter Johnson, walked on past my deck on his way to the dock and waved to me. I waved back, and Walter kept on walking. Walter was a gregarious sort and often stopped by to chat. I was grateful he hadn't chosen to do so tonight since I had a lot to decide.

My thoughts drifted back to Orion. Perhaps one or more of the loans Runyon had was not performing. That wouldn't be unusual in today's environment, but it certainly would get the examiners' eyes. Then what would the examiners do? From what I remembered of my meeting with Bob and Larry, they might want the bank to acquire more collateral, or they might even want the loan called. Regardless, I couldn't see why that would elicit the kind of action Runyon had taken against Katie. Runyon would be asking for help with the financing, not telling Larry to get the feds off his back. I pondered that scenario and sipped my beer. I wished I were smarter.

No, Michael my boy, there had to have been something else, something that I had not yet recognized. There was something out of the ordinary going on and whatever it was, it had to be dramatic, and dramatic enough to cause John Payton to take the suicide route. Larry had admitted to that fact. What could it be?

I sighed and shook my head in frustration. Then I realized I could take solace in the fact I had successfully tied Payton's death to the current problem whatever that was. Yet that didn't give me an answer to my current conundrum.

I tried moving in a new direction with my thinking. If something illegal had taken place relevant to the association of Runyon and the bank, then Runyon may be worried he could be drawn into the investigation, or perhaps he already had been drawn in. Thus the cryptic comment about getting the feds off his back. If it was one of Runyon's companies that was miscreant, then he might not want his association with the bank looked at too closely. It might reveal something untoward. That could be it. He wouldn't want to be involved in any investigation, nor scrutinized too closely by law enforcement. Particularly if he had any shady deals going on elsewhere.

However, since I knew nothing of Runyon's business affairs. That angle got me nowhere. If Larry wouldn't tell me more about what was taking place I wouldn't be able to solve that one. And why would he tell me more? He assumed I already know everything taking place. I outsmarted myself this time. He even asked me how I had put it all together. But I need not solve the mystery. All I had to do was to help protect Katie.

The salient question here was would he send Katie out of town? Would she agree to leave town? Could he convince her to go? I nearly retched thinking about her with a scarred face. What kind of an animal would hurt a woman? This Runyon must be a real scuzzball. I realized that some people would do just about anything to get what they wanted.

I had worked myself up into a frenzy and was breathing hard. When I realized it, I paused in my machinations to view the activity taking place on the lake. The water and lake activities always had a soothing affect for me. I needed that just now. I noted that in contrast to the previous evening when it had rained, tonight was a beautiful boating night and everyone with lake access must have had the same idea. Boats by the dozens were heading for the lakeside restaurants in my view. I smiled at the fun those parties were having. I had to laugh to myself. They all were having fun while I sat and brooded.

Now I found myself slipping into a foul mood. Why had I been so quick to wash my hands of Katie's misfortune? I thought back and realized I had never even suggested any alternatives for Larry to consider. But then it wasn't my responsibility, or was it? Maybe I had made it my responsibility when I made love to her in her own living room. No, I couldn't keep beating myself up over that, as unexpected as it had been. The decision was something for Larry and Katie to decide. She could visit friends or family somewhere until Larry straightened things out with Runyon.

Anyway, I didn't know where I stood with her after the way I acted at her home. She had been vulnerable and hurting, and I took advantage. It didn't matter that she said it was the best sex she'd ever had. That was the moment talking. She probably hated me today.

I meant it wasn't like she could stay here with me or anything. They, whoever they were, would figure that out. There was no need for me to get involved. I just hoped Larry could carry the day with Katie, and I would not be involved. I prayed he didn't call me back.

If he did call though, I simply could say I was too busy at work to take time off to travel. Actually it was the truth, particularly with the holiday coming up so soon. Why would Katie need an escort anyway? She was a fully capable adult. If it was protection Larry was after, there were far better choices than I was. An off duty policeman would serve her better than a middle-aged lothario. Of course Larry might be thinking that Katie is too much of an emotional basket case to go by herself. I could see that being the understanding. I'd be a smuck to not want to help out.

My legs were cramping so I stood and walked around in a circle a couple of times. If my head was spinning with all this information, I might as well also be spinning. What I wanted more than anything was to forget the whole mess and get on with my life.

Besides, could Katie leave? She'd said she had the stock deal brewing. I couldn't remember when it would close but knew it was soon. Had she said it would close on Friday? No, she'd said the next couple of days, but that could be tomorrow. Perhaps she needed be here for the sale. She might have already signed over the certificates. Her attorney could collect the check. Yes, it would be best for Katie to disappear for a while, for her own good.

I went indoors and turned on the news as I waited on the chili to finish cooking. There was a brief follow up report on the mysterious death of Sherrill Thompson of Excelsior. The murder suddenly seemed to have taken on new life. Stories about her mysterious death had been all over the Twin Cities news these last few days. It definitely was a ratings war and this apparently was prime news material.

From public reports I had heard, Jack Thompson had been questioned by the police in connection with his wife's death, but no charges were pending. The televised news had been portraying him as the distraught husband who had been twice wounded, first by being kicked out of his home by a vindictive wife, and later by the wife's death. I was sick of hearing about the skuzzball. I turned to E.S.P.N.

As I reviewed the slate of ballgames for the evening, I reflected on still not hearing any more from the police about my involvement in the affair. I hoped that was good news, because I knew they had gone over the townhome with their Crime Scene Unit. It appeared from several rumors that the word was Sherrill had been killed in her home and then moved to the storage unit. The car then must have been driven over to the municipal parking lot and abandoned there.

As I thought about the car, I wondered why it hadn't been left in the garage? The fact it had been moved wasn't good news for me. My attorney told me moving it was made to look as if the person who committed the crime knew Sherrill was moving and hadn't wanted the car seen to call attention to her not having left as planned. Had anyone else known of the move besides me? I hoped so. Coupling that situation with the scenario Janet had presented to me earlier made me nervous.

In talking to my attorney, John, I could expect to be grilled again sometime soon by the local constabulary. That probability would remain hanging over my head. I hated to go off half-cocked, but Jack Thompson was on the top of my list for the murder, regardless of the police letting him go free. There was motive, and he had ready access to the place. Maybe proving it was the hard part. I guess just because they hadn't arrested him didn't mean he wasn't a person of interest.

I sighed. I had tied myself up in knots. What I needed was a workout to relieve stress, but I didn't want to go soon after eating. I jumped out of the chair and entered the house. A workout it would be. I turned off the chili and covered it. Then I locked up, gathered my things and went down to the garage. I hated each time I had to go down there the past few days. The memory of finding the body still was too fresh in my mind.

I motored out to my club without bothering to put the top down. I just wanted to beat my body into submission and couldn't even take the time to remove the roof, I was so anxious to get there. Once at the club, I did a nice long workout on the treadmill. Being tired felt great. Since spring, I'd been more consistent with my routine. As a result I was feeling better because of it. I think I was looking better also.

On my drive home, I wondered if I'd hear from Larry tonight. I'd like this whole mess resolved one way or another soon. When I pulled into the garage, I noted a car parked in the adjoining space. The driver was just removing a duffle from the trunk. I recognized the man as Jack Thompson. I thought I had only said hello to him a couple of times since they, or rather he had lived there.

Though I hadn't known the man well, Jack looked as though he had lost weight. He'd always had a thin face, but it now appeared stark to me. Perhaps he had been ill. He had a pale cast anyway, but looked more so in the garage lighting and with his dark hair slicked back. A bushy mustache appeared too large for his small mouth, and there was also a small scraggly patch of hair on his chin. All together it wasn't a pleasing picture.

I hoped he'd leave before I exited my car, but the man waited for me. As I climbed out of my car he said, "You're my neighbor, right?" He held out his hand. "I'm Jack Thompson."

I hesitated, and then shook his hand one time. It was moist and soft. "I'm Mike Connelly. If you're Thomson, we must be neighbors." I tried not to let my feelings for the man show on my face.

He dropped his duffle and I looked at it.

As if sensing my question he said. "I'm moving back in."

"Ah. They've turned the place over to you then?"

"Yes, just today."

There was an awkward silence.

"I hadn't anywhere else to stay, and I'm stuck with this place," he offered unsolicited.

I was curious by that statement so I asked, "How so? I mean how so stuck?"

He warmed to the question. He apparently liked to talk with his hands. "We bought at the high water mark it seems. Now I'm told it's worth twenty percent less than what we paid for it. Heck, maybe it's thirty percent. Anyway, I owe more on my mortgage than I can sell the damn place for, and I can't afford the payments with just my income, now that Sherrill's gone."

Hearing her name sent shivers down my spine.

The man lowered his head and wiped a hand across his eyes. The move made me ill. Instinctively I didn't like the guy. It was as though he was playing a part. I wanted to get away from him.

"Hell of a fix. Can't afford to stay and can't afford to sell," he said.

I had heard the tale too often lately, and had felt compassion for people in that position. I wanted to get away from the man, so I said, "Why not rent it out?"

"Huh?"

"Yeah, rent it. You can hire a firm to do it all for you. It'll provide cash flow, and you can continue to pay down the mortgage. When the market recovers, you can consider selling or continue renting."

He played with the hair on his chin. "I never thought of that."

I started to move away. "Well, it might work. Check into it. Listen, I've got to take a shower. Nice to see you."

I continued walking and headed into my place.

I thought it awfully funny meeting the guy like that. I'd hardly seen him since he and his wife moved in last November, and now I meet him right after I suspected he killed her. Tough spot not being able to pay his mortgage, though. As Bob Lindgren said, "There's a lot of pain out there."

Listening to his sob story, I almost forgot he was a prime suspect in his wife's death. He hadn't been arrested, though. I wondered what evidence the cops had that might go against him? If only they'd heard from Sherrill, as I had, that he beat her up, they might work harder to implicate him. I shook my head at the whole mess.

LARRY WILLIAMS DID CALL me later that evening while I was watching the Twins Game.

"Mike, Kate says she's capable to travel on her own. In fact she already contacted her travel agent before you and I spoke. Fancy that will you. When I suggested to her you'd be willing to accompany her, she said it was a nice idea but not necessary, that she was fine, having done it before. So, that's that. I guess we tried though didn't we. The woman has a mind of her own," he said.

"You think she will be all right then?" I said. "I mean going by herself?"

"Kate's traveled extensively on her own previously. I think she'll do okay. She told me she'd keep in close contact."

When's she leaving?" I asked.

"Tomorrow afternoon."

"I guess that's settled then."

"I guess."

We signed off and I went about my dinner making. The chili now sounded like a good idea. Later I went to bed thinking about what I might have missed out on.

~23~

PARTY TIME

THE FOURTH OF JULY always had been a marker of sorts for me, since its arrival reminded me we were well into our summer season in Minnesota. Once we got to State Fair time at the end of August, warm temperatures quickly would succumb to fall's impact. There'd still be nice days, but fewer nighttime cruises on the water, at least not unless warmly attired. But, hey, that was still two months away. There was no sense in hurrying summer along.

I needed to be a glass-half-full kind of guy, and forget the half empty stuff. That thought brought me up short because there had been so much turmoil in my life during the last twelve months I wasn't really sure how I was be as stable as I felt I was. Help from my friends, I guessed.

I was stable now, wasn't I? I went to work each and every day. I actually accomplished something when I was there. I had begun dating. I couldn't have done that last fall. I was having friends over for this big party. Yeah, I was getting back to normal.

It was unfortunate the murder had to happen next door and to someone I knew. If it had been one more unit over, I wouldn't even have cared. Shit. No, that's not right. I can't in all honesty say that. Certainly I would have cared, regardless, but maybe not to the same degree, since I wasn't well acquainted with those folks. I can't even understand why I felt for Sherrill as much as I did. I hoped it wasn't because I was transferring this recent death, this loss of life, to my loss last year of the first love in my life? Had Sherrill somehow become a surrogate Gracie for me? My shrink would make a fortune off me if I kept thinking this way.

Shaking my head, I removed myself from this hurtful reverie and looked over my list of things yet to do to prepare for the party later today. I appeared to be in pretty good shape. Pre-planning had served me well.

234

A little get together at my place on the Fourth had become my tra-dition, and this year I had prepared a special surprise. If the forecast was only partially correct, the weather should cooperate, giving us a perfect backdrop for the planned activities.

I purchased a beef tenderloin, which I sliced into two-inch thick steaks. I considered that thickness perfect for grilling. Sweet corn, which I picked up yesterday, would accompany the steaks. Homemade bread from my handy dandy bread maker completed the main portion of the meal. I also laid in a tub of butter for the corn and bread. I knew it wasn't the healthiest of meals, but I felt we could survive once a year. *We'll all diet tomorrow.* I laughed as I considered that the watermelon I provided would count as fruit, allowing for a balanced meal.

I was busy whipping up a batch of homemade strawberry ice cream. I bought the berries and was using my mom's old recipe for the ice cream. It was basically milk, cream, and eggs. The salt and ice did the freezing somehow. This was my first time serving homemade ice cream at my party so I hoped it went well.

My liquor cabinet was well stocked. A large cooler sat on the deck with equal parts beer and ice. Liquor and mixes were placed on the counter that divided the kitchen and living space. I'd add an ice bucket there later when the guests began arriving.

I told Sandra I'd pick her up at two and set the party time for every-one else to arrive at three. That should give us a couple of hours to drink and socialize before dinner, and then a couple more hours of socializing before the air show and then the fireworks. They had been doing the air show for a couple of years now, and it was getting bigger each year.

My place was a great spot from which to watch the action, and not just that up in the sky. So many boats crowded Excelsior Bay, they were a show all by themselves.

Steve and Cindy Anderson always parked their vehicle outside of the main downtown area on Yellowstone Trail, since they lived on the west side. Then they rode their bikes to my place. That way after the fire-works were over, they avoided the traffic tie up that took an hour or more to clear town.

Bob Lindgren and his wife, Betty, lived in town. They would walk here. Janet and her husband, Dick, would be joining us for fireworks. They had a family gathering earlier in the day.

The subject of my dead neighbor should never come up, since both Steve and Bob knew how current events had affected me as well as my recovery from last fall's tragic events.

Sandra asked me about the murder when I had called her to set up a party time, and I explained I'd discuss it with her sometime in the future. I hoped she would respect my feelings on that subject.

I was surprised when she called me in the middle of my preparations. "Hi. What's up?" I asked.

"I don't know. You called me."

"I did. When?"

"A few minutes ago. I was in the shower."

I looked at my phone to the list of made calls. Sure enough I had called.

"I must have butt called you when I sat on my phone," I said laughing.

"Well, that's a pretty thought. My number must be pretty high on your list."

"Numero uno."

Sandra laughed. "See you later, then."

"Right."

I went about my tasks until it was time to pick up my date.

Once I've gathered Sandra and returned home, she helped me put a woman's touch on things before the others arrived. She thought to bring a bouquet of flowers along to my place, and that brightened things considerably. Fortunately we were able to find a vase that would work. I didn't have a lot of that kind of thing around. I believed this one had come with some flowers when I was in the hospital the previous year.

Together, we hung some bunting on the inside of my deck railing, and of course my flag was flying from my back wall. I used to buy festive party hats, but dispensed with that this year. I had a red plastic tablecloth on my picnic table, and Sandra got some tape and secured it so it wouldn't blow away.

"Once we get some plates and stuff on the table, it'll be okay," she said.

I agreed with her logic.

When Cindy arrived, she rushed up to me and gave me a big hug. Then she began to cry.

So much for ignoring my troubles. Steve looked at me with that "I give up" look and just shrugged as we both laughed. I introduced Steve and Cindy to Sandra, and Sandra took Cindy by the arm and out onto the deck. Girl talk. Cindy was wiping her eyes as she walked through the house. I looked at Steve and we both sighed.

Cindy was a firecracker of a personality. Always ready for anything, she usually was the life of the party. In great physical shape, she could out do me at everything except eating.

I had known Steve for quite a few years now. He stood three inches taller than I, had a solid build and chiseled good looks. Stylishly cut dark hair complimented penetrating hazel eyes. Steve dressed well, and today had picked blue shorts to accompany a white polo shirt. I didn't know where he found the red belt.

Shortly thereafter Bob and Betty Lindgren arrived. Betty was a petite blonde. She could not be taller than five feet. She wore her hair short and her blue eyes sparkled. I loved her ever-present smile.

After everyone had a drink and we were sitting around enjoying the sun, Steve asked, "Bob, what's with all the failing banks?"

This generated a lengthy discussion that we guys took down onto the dock, since the women were busy with their own conversation. I handed out cigars, and we spend some time enjoying our guy time together with our smokes.

While Bob gave Phil a banking 101 course, I thought of the Orion situation, and particularly Katie's impending journey. I wondered if she'd be celebrating the Fourth wherever she was. Larry probably was entertaining on his boat and may very well be out front of my place tonight watching fireworks. I wondered if he'd be looking onto my deck as I sat in the dark?

When the women thought we had ignored them long enough, we were summoned to return.

"Did you solve the world's problems?" Sandra asked.

"We did," Bob answered with a smile. "We were just working up an appetite."

I can take a hint," I said, and I went into the kitchen. Sandra followed. I turned on the gas below my large kettle full of water. If you'd let me know when the water boils, I'll put the corn in."

"I can do it."

"I don't want you to burn yourself."

She put her hands on her hips and scowled at me. "I grew up on a farm you know."

"Okay, okay. Corn's in the fridge, already husked."

She laughed. I took the platter of steaks outside and started the grill.

"Help yourselves to refreshments," I said. "Beer's in the cooler, hard liquor on the kitchen counter." Everyone seemed satisfied.

There was a good deal of friendly banter both before and during the meal. It did a lot to lift my spirits. I couldn't believe how Sandra had taken over the kitchen. The day went as planned, and the fireworks were worth the wait. The community always did a nice job with the festivities.

Janet and Dick made it for the show, and we all oew'ed and awe'ed for twenty minutes or more. Janet had pulled Sandra aside and was talking animatedly with her, which gave me some concern. I couldn't figure out what they were discussing. I hoped it wasn't my shortcomings. That would have taken all night.

Later when everyone had left but Sandra, the two of us were sitting on the couch talking. She looked very feminine today in a pair of Capri pants and cotton top. She smelled good too when I sat close to her. I reprised my juvenile ploy of putting my arm first over the back of the couch and then around her shoulders. The result was her placing her pretty red head onto my chest. I took advantage of that to lean in and kiss her. Her lips were warm and tender. When she responded by putting her arms around my neck, my body stiffened. Her breasts pressed against my chest and one leg slid across my lap.

I was really hungry for her, but my mind was telling me to go slow. She didn't seem to have any roadblocks, though. After a few minutes of immense pleasure, I pulled away and said. "Shall we give it a go to get you home? It's nearly eleven-thirty."

She smiled. "That late already. I don't work tomorrow, and I leave town Friday for two weeks. When I get back I close on my house and will be busy moving."

I wasn't sure what she meant and didn't verbally respond.

Finally she said. "Rather than fight the traffic back to my place tonight, I could return home in the morning."

So that was what we did.

~32~

A Two-Way Grilling

THE FOURTH WAS A SUCCESS on many fronts. The party went well, and I seemed to have taken a leap forward with Sandra. I hadn't thought of it at the time, but Steve had commented that she was really cute, but kind of young.

Was he criticizing our age disparity? Or was he just happy I was getting out and seeing people? I wasn't sure which. The difference in our ages was something that concerned me, as well. Frankly, I couldn't even understand why she was going out with me, and didn't know why she had spent the night. Was there a dearth of males in her age bracket around town? I would have been surprised to learn that fact, and I hadn't considered myself that great of a catch, especially for someone like Sandra.

I came into work on the fifth because it was a habit. Not much was going on, but I didn't need another day off. I'd rather be caught up than behind and under the gun.

As I stared at my monitor, I thought a little about dating Sandra. I didn't want to lead her on. After some reflection, I decided we'd take it a step at a time and see what happened. We'd parted this morning with no commitment and no further plans. Of course she was leaving for two weeks of training in a couple of days, so planning something would have been difficult.

My main concern was to see how things played out with the Thompson investigation. No one connected with that inquiry had contacted me. Did that mean I was in the clear? I should be, but the way the police thought, one could never be certain.

I put in about two hours, mostly cleaning out my desk, arranging files and organizing. Then I walked home. There was a lot to do there. I had left the cooler with beer on the deck, so I had that to take care of. Only six cans were left, so I stored those away in my fridge. Then I dumped the ice water into the lake and left the cooler open on the deck to dry out.

I had a bunch of those little chores to do, but they didn't take long. It afforded me plenty of time to get in a workout later at the club, and then fix a light supper. I had eaten enough yesterday to last me a while, and didn't need that much food today. Instead of eating, I decided to fix myself a drink and go down to my boat. There I could relax and feel a part of the lake activity.

I spend an hour on my boat, just taking in the atmosphere. The lake certainly was a lot quieter than on the Fourth. Hardly anyone was on the water, at least by my place. It was almost like everyone was burned out.

When my drink was gone, I decided to go in and see a little of the Twins game. I was returning from my dock with a cigar between my teeth, when my neighbor, Jack Thompson, hailed me.

"Mike. Could you come over for a sec?" He was standing on his deck, facing me.

I stopped walking and looked up toward his voice. Since I had no good reason not to do so, I climbed up to his deck rather than mine. I could hardly avoid him. Jack stepped back to welcome me.

"I'm really sorry about your wife, Jack," I said for something to say.

I felt funny calling him Jack, since I really didn't know him well, but Mr. Thompson seemed a little stiff and formal.

"Thanks for your condolences. You know it's really strange. It almost like nothing has happened."

I didn't understand. "How so?"

"We were separated, you know."

I played dumb. "No, I didn't know."

"Yes. Well, I made an ass of myself and was running around with this little honey from work." Jack made a self-deprecating gesture. "Sherrill kicked my ass out. I've seen so little of her these last six months, I really don't know she's gone."

"I see," I acknowledged.

"A cigar and a drink. So that's the bachelor life, then?" he asked. "I'll have to reinvent myself now, I guess."

I smiled slightly, but then wasn't sure how I should take his comment. Was he trying to be light hearted or soulful? I wasn't sure. His facial expression gave me no clue.

"You had a little party yesterday," he stated.

"Did we bother you?"

"No, no. I just noticed it when I went out last night to watch the fireworks. I was alone."

I nodded.

Jack then said, "I wanted to thank you for the suggestion about renting out the place. I have an agency lined up, and you're right, it should cash flow for me."

"I'm glad," I responded.

"Here, take a chair," Jack said.

"Thanks." I didn't really want to stay, but wasn't sure why. I sat on a fold-up chair.

Jack joined me.

There was a pause, then. "I was talking to my attorney today," Jack said. "You wouldn't believe it, but I'm a suspect in my wife's death. The cops have questioned me twice about where I was that night."

The change of subjects caught me off guard. Why was he telling me this? I wasn't sure if he expected an answer, but I said. "Do they know when she died, then?"

"I don't know. Nobody ever said. They just asked me to account for my time the day she was to leave town."

"I see. I wondered because you said they wanted to know where you were that night. They must think she died that night," I said.

"Oh, I see what you mean," Jack replied. "They told me they believe she died sometime Tuesday night. The night the movers came. Wasn't she headed out of town? That's what they told me anyway. I wouldn't think she'd have been killed two days later."

"I have no idea," I answered, "but I guess you're right. Isn't the husband usually a suspect? I don't know it's necessarily something to worry about."

"I suppose, but it's pretty farfetched," he responded. "I mean why would I kill Sherrill. I loved her?"

"Well, don't feel lonely, I'm also," I stated matter of factly.

"You're also what? You loved her?"

I laughed. "No. I meant I'm also a suspect."

"You? Why?"

"I guess because I live next door and probably was the last person besides the killer to speak with her."

Jack looked interested. "I didn't know that. How'd that happen?"

I explained how I had arrived home when the moving van was there.

"So you were the one who called it in? The cops told me someone had reported her there but didn't say who it was."

I nodded.

"So you're a suspect just because you talked to her?"

"I guess."

"Then what about the moving guys? Why couldn't one of them have come back? They would have known she was alone."

I thought about the possibility. "What's the motive?" I asked.

"Sex." Jack shrugged. "What's yours?"

I shook my head. "They're looking for an opportunity for a quick resolution. They'll take what they can get."

Jack screwed up his face. "That's pretty cynical on your part, isn't it?"

"It is what it is," I said, shrugging.

"I take it you're not a cop lover," Jack stated.

"I don't love lazy ones," I answered.

We both sat and looked out over the water. The early evening breeze had freshened. It felt good. After a few moments Jack looked at me and said, "They want to pin it on me, but the cards are stacked against them."

"How's that? I mean why you?"

"Like you say, the husband is always a suspect."

I nodded in agreement. I realized he would be, especially with the spousal abuse.

"Any particular reason for them to suspect you?" I asked, fishing for information.

"Like what?"

"I don't know. Was she cutting you out of the family inheritance or something?"

Jack laughed loudly. "Neither of us has a pot to piss in. No luck there."

Neither Jack nor I spoke for a bit. It looked like Jack was thinking.

Then I spoke up. "There's a rumor around the building that you were physically abusive toward her," I said softly.

"What!" he shouted. He came half out of his chair.

I put my hands up in a gesture of surrender. "Just telling you what I heard. Thought you'd want to know."

Jack wouldn't look me in the face. "Lying bitch. Somebody's just trying to get me into trouble."

I was surprised at his short fuse. "Could be," I answered.

"So, why do you think they'll have a difficult time pinning it on you?" I asked to change the subject.

Jack seemed to have simmered down somewhat, but I now had seen that quick temper I was sure Sherrill had seen all too frequently.

He answered my query. "I lived there. Any of my fibers or D.N.A. belongs there. They'd have to like . . . find my skin or blood under her fingernails or something like that to have a case. Of course they don't have a case since it wasn't me."

I thought about that scenario, and realized there was no evidence like that to link me either. I grasped the fact that under certain circumstances we could have engaged in one last coupling that night before she departed. Wow, what would that have caused? Killed with my D.N.A. all over her. A crime of passion. I was glad I kept it zipped up for once.

It was as though Jack had read my mind. "They would have had that from you as well, unless you signed a confession." Jack laughed and I smiled in return.

I wondered if he knew she and I had fooled around? "I guess," I responded lamely.

"Talking about it isn't too hard on you?" I asked.

"No. Honestly, I think it helps. Like I say, with not seeing her much these last six months, it's almost like nothing's changed. Can you see that?"

I agreed with him.

"I mean if I had seen her body in the garage or something . . ."

"Did you have to identify the body?" I asked.

"Yes. That was a bitch. I don't want to go through that again."

"Any idea when the funeral is?"

"No idea. The cops aren't saying when I can arrange things. Soon I hope. I have to figure out how to pay for it."

My cigar was finished, so I dropped the butt into my glass.

"You know what I can't figure out, Jack?"

"What?"

"Why put your wife's body in the storage container? If she was killed upstairs, why not leave her there?'

"Or why not put her in the car trunk?" he said.

"Right. Why move her?"

"No idea. I hadn't thought about it. Maybe they wanted to give themselves time to get out of town."

I shook my head. "Doesn't make sense to me, unless they wanted to make it harder to pin an exact time of death."

"I don't know what good that would do. I mean if I killed someone and had an alibi, I'd want the cops to know when she died, wouldn't you?"

"I guess."

"Whoever put her in there certainly didn't think she'd remain hidden forever."

"I never thought about it before now, but don't see any sense to it," I said.

I stood and prepared to go, and Jack said. "Thanks again for the lead on the rental deal. You saved my bacon."

"Glad to have helped," I answered.

Then I retreated to my place. I thought over what Jack had said about evidence. He would have marked himself all over their townhome. Finding a trace of him would be obvious. What about me? If they found a trace of my being there, was that evidence for murder? I worked on the carpet and door, but they knew about that. What did I touch when I went in the other night? Nothing I thought. I wonder how many more times they would drag Jack in for interviews? How many for me?

~34~
A Surprise Visit

Two days later, Wednesday morning, I was diligently working in my office when Bill Rehms came calling. He was dressed in his civvies and exhibited a cordial demeanor. Although I was apprehensive about his purpose, I waved him in. He entered my office, laying a package onto my desk.

I lifted one edge of the brown paper sack and peeked inside. I recognized the contents. Looking up at Bill, who remained standing before me, I said. "What's this?"

"A peace offering."

I nodded. "You didn't have to do this. Have a seat. Is this an official visit?"

"No."

Bill pulled up a chair and sat. Meanwhile, I walked around the desk and shut my office door. Janet, who had been watching us, gave me a look of inquiry, but I did not respond. I returned to my chair, sat and leaned back before saying. "Thanks for the treat. Do you want some? Maybe some coffee?"

"I'll take some coffee."

I went out and poured each of us a mug of coffee. While there I reassured Janet. When I handed Bill his cup, he said, "Thanks."

Then he grimaced and said. "I thought we were friends."

His comment startled me. I had to think about it. Were we friends? I hadn't thought about our relationship in those terms. Not friends in the sense of doing stuff together, but cordial nonetheless. I wouldn't argue with his statement.

"And you say that why?" I asked.

"You embarrassed me in front of a colleague."

I remember now that Bill hadn't been alone when we had our little tiff. "You mean Bishop?"

"Yes."

"Is she your superior?" I asked.

"Yeah."

"Sorry, I didn't do it intentionally," I said. "I was defending myself."

Bill looked down at his hands, which were rubbing the knees of his khakis. "I thought we'd buried the hatchet last fall. Is this still about what happened then?"

Bill's questions were getting under my skin. Was he trying to lay a guilt trip on me? Was this some new interrogation tactic? I decided to be blunt. "Maybe we had, I thought we had. But you can be a real ass sometimes."

"What do you mean?" Bill looked shocked.

"Like when you were ready to throw me under the bus for the Thompson killing," I said.

His expression was grim. "I think maybe you exaggerate," he responded.

I didn't say anything more. I wasn't ready to start a fight, and could see no value in continuing along this line.

"You say you're not here officially?" I asked.

"No, just visiting."

"Okay. So how did I hurt you? Besides your pride, maybe."

"You tried to make me look the fool in front of Bishop. Made her think I can't handle a simple interview."

I tried to think back to what was said, but I honestly didn't remember. I told Bill that.

"What did you want me to do, confess?"

Bill grinned. "That would have been all right."

"That's what I figured. Are you in hot water?"

"No, but I'm told I have to improve my interviewing skills. The department is sending me to a class on that."

"So, they have stuff like that?" I asked.

"I guess."

"That's not all bad then."

"I guess not," he answered.

Then I changed the subject. "I saw Thompson recently. He suggested that I confess."

"Why would he say that?" Rehms asked.

"He didn't say it in those exact words, but he said that's the only way the police will find the killer, if the killer confesses."

Bill nodded and took a sip of coffee. He was skirting the issue I had raised.

I thought some more and then said. "Getting back to the interview, you have my statement so there's nothing more I could have said to help you."

Bill sat and shook his head. "You really don't get it do you, Mike?"

"Get what?"

"How this works. That you were a prime suspect on this case when I did my interview with you."

"What? Why? I was the one who told you Sherrill had been at her place that night. I was the one who found what turned out to be the body. Do I have to find the killer too?" My face felt heated up.

Bill laughed. "Now don't get your pants in a bundle. You finding the killer might help, though. Save me some trouble.

"Look, Mike. Besides the other two thousand residents in Excelsior, we have a small number of suspects. The husband usually is number one, but he wasn't living there at the time. We have no witness placing him there that night. He says he was at home at his hotel, and we have no way to disprove that statement. There's no forensic evidence on the body to connect anyone to the killing. No one. Anything we found in the townhome is useless if it belongs to someone who had a reason to be there at one time or another."

That statement caught my attention because it helped my case.

"The movers would be suspect, but you yourself cleared them. You said you saw them leave, and you said the victim was alive after they left. They vouched for one another after that, and they clocked in at the depot when they came back with the load. We don't see how they could have been involved."

I nodded. "Didn't they run the load out of town?"

"No. The next morning the crates were off loaded and reloaded onto a truck heading in the direction of the destination."

"Which was?"

"Vegas."

"So the movers are in the clear?'

"That's correct."

"So, why aren't I?"

"You just happen to be now, but you weren't then. Think about it. You're the last person to see the victim if you hold to your story. The two movers saw you at the place earlier, but you say the victim came over to your house later. That gives you opportunity."

I didn't like what I was hearing. "But no motive," I reminded him.

"Maybe you tried to make a move on her and she resisted, so you killed her."

I laughed. "Nice try, but if I'd made a move, there'd have been no resistance. You should try writing science fiction."

Bill smiled, but said, "You were as good a suspect as her old man."

"I don't think so. He had motive."

"What motive?" Bill asked.

"She was leaving him."

"How's that motive? Most guys would welcome the wife leaving."

I shook my head. "Yes, but her leaving put him in a financial bind."

"Explain."

I explained the economics of the home ownership. "He can't make it on just his income. If she left, he'd be stuck."

"So how does it help to kill her?" Bill asked.

"It doesn't really, but in a rage maybe he wasn't thinking straight. Say, did she have life insurance?"

"A small policy. Not enough to kill her for. Maybe enough to bury her."

"So, there you go," I said, hopefully.

"Maybe." Bill rubbed his jaw. "But we have nothing to tie him to the scene that night."

I mulled that over without seeing anything new.

Then I said, "Say is it privileged info as to when she died?"

"We can't pin it down exactly."

"Why's that?"

"Because it was up to five days before her body was discovered. We have no idea of her schedule before you saw her moving out. We don't know when she last ate. The confined space she was in makes things difficult for the medical examiner since it was so warm in there.

"But to answer your question, it seems it might have been Tuesday night right after you saw her. That makes the most sense. Her car was towed the next day."

"Does Thompson have an alibi for the time of the murder? For Tuesday night?"

"Yes and no. He was living at a motel in Chanhassen, but no one pays attention to comings and goings. The security cameras are digital, but only keep the data for two cycles. We thought we might have seen him go in or out. But even if he had gone out, we couldn't say where he went. It's a dead end. We'd have to prove him at the murder scene.

"The bottom line is that no one saw him there."

I bit my lip on that one. "He's moved back in now, though," I said.

"I know."

"So, you say I'm still a suspect?"

"Yeah, I'm afraid so, but not a good one. The marks on the victim's neck from the choking she got line up with a much smaller hand than yours. That's one thing in your favor. I'd personally like you to come in and take a lie detector test for us to clear you."

"I didn't think those were reliable?"

"They tell us stuff."

"I'll check with my attorney."

"Okay. Just let me know. We can do it at your convenience. It'd just be justification if we cut you lose, and someone squawks.

"I'd like to be cleared. Being a suspect would hang over my head always."

"It's not like we're going to broadcast it. No one will know."

"Thanks, but people do know."

There was a moment of silence, then. "The chief's thinking of pulling in the state to investigate."

I nodded.

Bill stood to leave.

"Where did you get the Kringle?" I asked.

"I was in Racine over the weekend visiting my brother.

"Thanks again," I repeated.

"No problem. Let me know about the test."

Bill left and I brought the kringle out to Janet and told her to take it home. Her eyes lit up.

Back at my desk I sat and thought about how it was being a suspect. I'd like to be cleared. If they didn't solve this case that'd never go away.

~35~
FINANCIAL NEWS

ON A THURSDAY EVENING a little more than two weeks after the Fourth, I was in my kitchen preparing my supper, while the local television news droned on in the background. I had not been really listening.

Suddenly I heard the name Larry Williams and turned my attention to the screen. Unfortunately I had missed much of the spot, but the sense I did get was that he had resigned from the Orion Bank. I quickly changed channels, hoping to catch the story elsewhere, but either the other outlets weren't carrying the story or it already had run. I took out my phone and searched the name, but no story was logged on yet.

I was left to wonder why he would resign? I thought back to his visit here at my place. What had it been, about three weeks ago? Had he given me an inkle of this? I didn't think so, but really couldn't precisely remember the conversation.

I stewed for a bit, then considered the problem in conjunction with Katie being threatened. Maybe that was why Larry left the bank. Would I have done the same thing to protect someone I cared for? Probably.

If that was the case, I couldn't blame him for leaving. In the scheme of things, maybe his family was more important than a job, even a high paying job. Even after he had built the bank up from next to nothing to what it was today.

If I had known what had gone on between Larry and the Kale Runyon character, I'd been better able to understand what caused Larry's actions. Since I didn't know, I couldn't judge.

Then too, everyone had a breaking point. Maybe Larry had reached his. Someday I might have occasion to ask him. The pressure from Runyon may have been overwhelming, especially if Larry had no answer to Runyon's threats.

All a person could do was control certain things. All the threats in the world wouldn't change that. If I were Larry, I would leave town for a while. Meet up with Katie and get away and out of Runyon's reach. Maybe that was Larry's intention. But he didn't need to quit the bank to do that. He could have gone on an extended vacation, or even taken a leave of absence.

Maybe there was something more going on. Maybe.

SATURDAY MORNING FOUND ME with two buddies out fishing on Lake Minnetonka. Late July wasn't the best time to fish, but I liked to go anyway. The water had warmed up and the fish had dispersed, looking for the optimum water temperature. Luckily, through persistent scouting, I knew a couple of holes next to raised flats where the walleye sometimes hung out in late summer. We tried those spots for a few hours. Just getting out on the water was the real object, at least for me. Maybe it was the beer for the other two. Either way I didn't mind.

Since we were lazy fishermen this morning, we rigged up slip bobbers and still fished. I had anchored the boat by the bow, which caused us to slowly swing on the anchor rope in an arc of about thirty degrees when the early morning breeze caught us and moved us back and forth. This gave our bait just enough movement to be effective. We caught a couple of nice-size walleye but returned them to the lake. I figured that by doing so I could catch the same fish again at some future date. I was not really a meat fisherman.

About nine-thirty we headed home. I said goodbye to the guys who had a noon golf date to catch. I cleaned up the boat and brought my remaining bait into the house and put it in the refrigerator.

Because of my Saturday morning plans, I had missed any Friday night news updates. I had spent my time getting the boat and gear ready for the next morning. Thus a message left on my phone from Saturday morning while I was on the water surprised me. It must have come pretty early.

The call was from Bob Lindgren, and he simply said to call if I wanted info on Orion Bank. It was nearly three in the afternoon before I saw the message, since I was notoriously bad at checking my messages. Janet did it at the office, and I never got into the habit at home. Even with the blinking light on my home phone, I missed them half the time. Friends who understood me usually called me back a second time, or called my cell.

By now the bank must be closed, so I phoned Bob at his home. When he answered, I said, "You called, Bob?"

Yes, this morning. Were you at work? I hadn't thought to call you there."

"No, I was out fishing."

He laughed. "Do any good?"

"Drowned some worms. That's about all."

"Sounds about like my luck. Say, I was wondering if you heard about Orion?"

"You mean Larry's calling it quits? I was going to ask you about that."

"No. The regulators shut it down last night."

"Shut down Orion?" I wasn't at all familiar with the process, and didn't understand what Bob had said. "What do you mean shut it down?"

"They took control and sold the assets to another institution."

"No shit. Why would they do that?" I asked.

"They usually only do that when the bank's insolvent," Bob explained.

"Which means what exactly? Tell me in terms I can understand. Dumb it down a little."

"That's when the assets won't cover the liabilities," Bob instructed.

I was thinking now. "Bob, the assets are the loans the bank has made. Kinda like accounts receivable, right?"

"Right."

"And the liabilities are the savings accounts, checking accounts?"

"Yes, that's correct. The money owed."

"Okay, I get that part now. So how'd it happen?"

"I can't say for sure. Apparently there were enough bad loans so the amount of money in good loans if paid back to the bank no longer covered the money owed to customers in their accounts, and capitol wasn't adequate to make up the difference."

"Wow, they're a big bank. A lot bigger than us."

"No shit."

"So, how exactly does the whole process happen?"

Bob said. "After analyzing everything and seeing there's no chance to remain open under the current ownership, the feds find a willing bank to take it over. In this case I believe it's a Missouri bank called Prairie View Bank and Trust. The bank will reopen on Monday under that name."

"So the regulators must have known for a while this was going to happen?"

"Yes, it seems to work that way."

"I wonder how long Larry Williams has known?"

"Unless he's stupid, and I don't think he is, he probably had indications when we all sat down together," Bob said.

I thought about it. In that case he knew for sure the day he and I met and talked about Katie. Did he give me any indication? I couldn't remember the conversation well enough to say.

"Does anyone get hurt?" I asked.

"I don't know the details. We may not know for weeks. Most accounts are covered by insurance. Some aren't of course, and large accounts are covered only to a certain limit."

"Doesn't pay to have too much money in the bank."

"Gosh, don't say that to our customers. The secret is to have it in different accounts. Then each is individually insured," Bob advised.

"Oh."

"The stockholders are out, though," Bob said.

"You mean like my stock in our bank?"

"Right. They'll lose everything."

I thought of Katie and wondered how she would make out. If all the assets for the family were in the bank stock, they would be broke.

Katie said she sold some stock, though. Would the government attempt to claw that back? Could they take the house? What a mess. I wondered if Katie knew about recent events wherever she was hiding out?

Then a really disturbing thought arose. Would Larry be able to get another job in banking? When you're the head of a failed bank, that's not exactly a prime recommendation.

There might be some changes in store for the Williams family.

~36~

A Pleasant Reunion

ON WEDNESDAY MORNING I phoned and left a message for Dr. Sandra Gross at her dental clinic, asking if she wanted to go out to dinner that evening. I felt like getting out, kicking up my heels a little. I also wanted to find out how her Navy training tour had gone. The Fourth at my house was the last time we had seen one another, and I found I was missing her bubbly personality.

With that task accomplished, I busied myself with work. When Sandra returned my call just after twelve, I was out walking, but it was only a couple of minutes later when I entered her office. She came out to greet me, and she looked great.

"I didn't want you to see me like this," she said, running a hand through her hair.

"Like what?"

"In my work outfit."

"Oh. You look nice. Did you get a haircut?" I asked.

"Yes, before I left."

I nodded. It probably had to be regulation length for her tour.

"So, will tonight work for you?" I asked.

"Yes. That'd be great. I called, but you were out walking I guess."

"Yes, I walked over here on the chance I might catch you."

"Great."

It was somewhat difficult to talk because a patient arrived, so I cut it short. We set up a time for me to pick her up, and I informed her that the attire was casual.

At exactly six o'clock I pulled my Mustang into the apartment parking lot when I noticed Sandra waiting for me under a nearby shade tree.

I have to say this for the woman, she didn't stand on formality. I swung the car around toward her location and stopped.

When I began opening my door to get out, she said. "Stay where you are. I can get it."

She opened the passenger door and slid in.

"Or were you going to let me drive?"

"I'll drive there and if you're sober, you can drive home."

"Who judges?"

"Me."

Sandra was dressed casually, but nicely with a patterned skirt, dressy sandals and a collared top. A choke necklace showed in her V-neck blouse. She was sporting a pair of sailboats for ear adornment.

"What are you doing outside?" I asked.

"It's such a nice day, who wants to be inside? I was stuck there all day."

"Don't you get a lunch break?"

"I'm supposed to, but if I have a patient scheduled late, that throws everything off. Or if things take longer than they might with a patient, I don't get much free time, maybe just enough time to wolf down a sandwich."

"Not enough to get out, then," I said.

"No. In the armed forces people are more punctual for their allotted time. I'm going to start spreading my schedule some and account for these delays. Otherwise I'm constantly working under the gun.

I shook my head in agreement.

I reflected on how lucky I was to get my noontime walk nearly every day. I surmised I couldn't do that if I worked for a large law firm. I wondered if my defense attorney, John Swenson, had that freedom of action? Probably not. You can't bill hours unless you're working, and that was a big thing in those firms. A guy might as well be on an assembly line. Professionals today were nothing more than glorified assembly line workers in my mind. That was how insurance companies seemed to view it anyway.

Since Sandra enjoyed fresh air, I took as many back roads, as I could for our drive out west. That way we could motor as a reasonable speed, and didn't have to be blown out of the car like we would be at highway speeds. This took a bit longer, but was a much more pleasant experience, and we had all the time in the world.

We reached Waconia and drove down to the lakeshore where our restaurant of choice was located. I was uncertain of the building's lineage, but my guess was at one time it might have been a warehouse, or used for boat storage. In today's edition, lots of windows faced the lake, and panels like garage doors even opened up to expose the inside diners to the great outdoors. Leave it to entrepreneurs to be creative.

It was such a pleasant night we chose to eat outside on the deck. This placed us closer to the water, anyway. We could only hope the bees stayed away. It was getting to be that time of year where they began to swarm around either food or drink. We each ordered a tall gin and tonic and then relaxed, turning our chairs slightly, and looking out over the water.

After a long silence, I asked. "Glad to be back home?"

Sandra smiled. "Yes, I am. It was a very interesting two weeks for me, but being away from work for as long as I was, I got a little rusty on the dental work with the Fourth and then my tour."

I nodded in understanding. "What did you do? I mean on your tour."

"We had a week of classroom, studying electronics, and then a week of sea duty where we actually got to use what we learned."

"So you did what exactly?"

Sandra hesitated for a moment. "Let's just say I worked in the shipboard command center."

"Oh! Classified stuff, huh?"

"Yes. I'm never sure what I can say and what I can't, so usually I don't say anything."

"Makes sense," I answered.

The waitress brought our drinks and glasses of water. The drink tasted good and hit the spot on this warm night.

"Want a hors d'oeuvre?" I asked.

"No, thanks. I'm not that hungry, unless you want something."

"Maybe something to nibble," I decided.

Sandra took a sip of her drink and said, "That was a nice party you had on the Fourth."

"Thanks."

"I really enjoyed myself."

"I'm happy you could join me."

I tried to read something into what she was saying, but wasn't sure I was on the mark.

Just then the waitress asked if we wanted to order dinner. I ordered a snack and said we'd wait a bit on dinner. Then I said, "Give us a few more minutes to enjoy your wonderful ambiance and please bring us another round."

The waitress acknowledged me, and then turned to leave. "Trying to get me drunk, huh?" Sandra suggested.

"They're not that strong, are they, especially for a sailor?"

She laughed, as did I.

"I found the conversation at your party interesting, especially about the banking stuff. I learned a lot just listening," Sandra said.

I nodded. "Bob knows of what he speaks."

"So you're a bank director, I understand?"

"That's correct."

"Wow, big shot."

I snorted. "Hardly. I'm glad you spelled that with an O and not an I," I said laughing.

"So you know this fellow who ran the bank they closed? The one they were discussing."

"Yes, a little."

"Must be tough to have your business taken away like that? That's what they did isn't it? Just took it away?"

I thought for a few seconds. "Bottom line, that's what happened."

I hadn't thought about it in those exact terms, but Sandra hit the nail on the head. "Really hard I'd say," I replied. "And they're nice folks too. Just ordinary down-to-earth folks. I knew the wife, Katie, when we were kids."

260

"No fooling."

"Yes. She used to baby sit for our family."

"That must have been brutal for her," Sandra said, with a smile.

"The closing . . . oh, you mean the babysitting." I started laughing. "You know me so well."

The waitress brought a second round of drinks and removed my empty glass.

"I think it may be hard for Larry to get another position," I suggested.

"Is that the husband?"

"Yes. Who will want to hire him, especially in this environment?"

Sandra nodded in agreement.

"They live here, locally," I said.

"Where? In town?" she asked.

"Out on Howards Point. Know it?"

"No."

"Nice place. I'll take us by there on our way home."

The waitress was hovering, so I suggested to Sandra that we order. I decide on a burger and Sandra has a fish sandwich. We both ordered salads.

When we had ordered, I said. "How's your dental practice coming?"

"Slowly building. I'm getting a lot of kids."

"The mothers like you."

"Maybe."

"The dad's would love you."

Sandra blushed at my statement.

Our salads arrived and we dug in. "Do they have a lot of money?" Sandra asked.

"Who?"

"The banker. I forget his name."

"Williams. Yes, I would think they're in that upper one percent we hear about. Though I don't know what this business closure will do to their finances. I can assume that a lot of their wealth was tied up in bank stock."

"How does that matter?" Sandra asked.

"Bob Lindgren said the stockholders are out of luck. They won't recover anything."

Sandra took a sip of her drink and then said, "Brutal."

"You said it."

"They'll have to live like us then," she said.

I thought about it and realized she could be right. "They both grew up that way, so maybe they can adjust back." I recalled Larry's visit to my place when I said, "The little I know about him, I could see he appreciated simple things. Larry was at my place once, and he seemed to like it. He loved my fireplace and fell in love with my boat. I think perhaps he'll land on his feet."

"Won't he go to jail?" Sandra asked.

I had wondered about that point myself. "Why do you ask that?"

"I heard someone speculating about it. They said that might happen."

"I really don't know anything about it," I answered, but I was chagrinned I hadn't considered the eventuality. Perhaps I had been more concerned for Katie than for Larry.

Our main course arrived, and we ate in silence for a short while.

"I think it would be harder on the woman than the man," Sandra offered.

"What?"

"Losing all your money."

I was surprised at her evaluation. "Why's that?"

"Because while the man's working hard all the time and accumulating things like a nice castle and boat and cars, his focus is still his work. The things he buys are just things. They really don't count for anything. His deal is the success he achieves in business. If he fails one time, he can start over and achieve success again. There are many examples of that. Heck, the JC Penny guy went bankrupt three times before it stuck with the department store. Those guys just don't quit because things get tough."

I thought about it and wondered if she was correct.

Sandra continued. "Now the wife's another matter. What's her name?"

"Katherine."

"Katherine? Not Kate?"

"I guess."

"That's sort of an affectation, isn't it? That supports my point."

"What point?"

"I haven't made it yet," she laughed.

"Okay."

"Anyway. The wife now, she lives on the prestige of what her husband's built. It's a status thing with her. Do you think that's the case here with Katherine, or Katie?" she asked.

I chewed my lip for a moment. "Golly, I don't know. I never thought about it that way, and I guess I don't know Katherine well enough to really know. Could a person change that much from when they were young?"

"Change how?"

"I mean she grew up just ordinary hard-working folk. Does that change when you grow up?"

"I guess one's personality would help determine that," Sandra replied. "Does she do a lot of volunteer work? Does she work in the food kitchen or get her hands dirty?"

"I have no idea, but maybe with her position she could do more by organizing benefits on a higher level. Maybe she's active at the legislative level. I just don't know," I replied.

"You're right there. She could perhaps accomplish much more using her position and influence rather than as one person serving up soup. The question is does she?"

I shook my head. "I really don't know, Sandra. "That's a very good question. I guess time will tell."

"Yes, it will," she said.

We finished our meals and I asked her if she wanted another drink.

"No, thanks," she replied. Two's my limit. I have to practice tomorrow."

"Coffee then? We can sit here by the water or go back to my place and sit out on the deck."

"Let's do that," she said.

We drove a circuitous route that took us to Birch Bluff Road and then to Howard's Point. I drove slowly past the Williams estate and pointed it out. No one was outside in the perfectly manicured yard. I pulled into the drive just far enough to back around and then headed out.

"This doesn't look so big," Sandra said.

"That's because of the lot elevation. On this side the house looks like its two stories, except for the garage wing. But it's a walkout on the lower level. It's actually three stories on that side."

"Oh."

"Say, when do you close on your new house?" I inquired.

"Friday. I'm moving in this weekend."

"Need any help?"

"I have a mover doing it. It's seamless that way. I hope."

"Be sure to invite me over to see it when you get settled."

"I will. The place is in pretty good shape, but I'll want to paint some inside, and sometime I'll remodel the kitchen. There's a bunch of flowers there in the yard. What do you know about flowers?"

"Nothing."

"You're a big help. What are you good for?"

"I kiss good."

"Prove it."

I was getting nervous. Was this just mindless banter or did she expect something? I just smiled a nervous smile and continued driving toward home.

"Do you mind coming up through the garage," I asked.

"No, of course not."

We entered my place. I had left the air on and set at seventy-six, so it was cool inside.

"Okay to sit on the deck?" I asked.

"That'll be nice."

"Coffee?"

"Do you have decaf?"

"No."

"What else do you have that's non-alcoholic?"

"Lemonade."

"Yes. That'd hit the spot."

I poured two large tumblers of pink lemonade for us and returned outside. I've turned off the air so I left the patio door open.

We sat outside enjoying the lake until well after dark, and then I suggested we return inside. When we're both in, I put my arm around her and gave her a kiss. It lasted a long time, and when we were finished, I said. "See, I'm good at that."

"Fair. Better give me a longer sample."

Much later I drove Sandra back to her place.

~37~

An Unexpected Visitor

THE NEXT EVENING, I had returned home from work, and after pouring myself a beer was in the process of evaluating my dinner options. I had not planned very well with last weekend's grocery shopping, so there wasn't much enticing in either my cupboard or freezer.

I briefly considered making an omelet, but the only ingredients I had were eggs and cheese. Pretty bland. I would have preferred to add some ham, onions, mushrooms, and peppers if I were going to go to the bother.

Thus, I took my frequently used option and decided to order a meat lovers pizza from the joint out in Shorewood. I almost added an order of wings but decided that would be too much. My order was placed on line and the response said it would be a half hour. They knew me by now, or at least the delivery driver did if it was Freddy. He should remember me, since I had always tipped him well. He had always delivered my platter here nice and warm, and normally early. I think he delivered here first on his route.

I was just connecting my phone to call Sandra, when the doorbell rang. "Wow, that was quick service," I said to no one in particular. Looking at my watch, I knew it couldn't be my pizza that quickly. I wondered who it might be at this hour, since I hadn't been expecting anyone. I disconnected my call and shoved the phone into my back pocket. Trudging up the stairs, I opened the door. Standing there on my front stoop looking up and down the street was Jack Thompson.

He turned toward me and looked at me with a faraway expression. He said, "Could I drop in for a minute?" The man looked nervous and edgy. I briefly wondered if he was on something.

I hung my shoulders because I really didn't want anything to do with the man at this moment and my hesitation must have shown.

"I'll just be a minute," he said.

"Okay, just for a minute, then. I haven't had a chance to make dinner yet." This turned out to be a decision I would regret.

The only person I might be less pleased to see right now would have been Bill Rehms. I motioned for Jack to go downstairs and I followed him down. He was carrying a piece of white printer paper in his left hand, folded in half, but not creased. His right hand was in his jacket pocket. I wondered what was with wearing the jacket, since it was seventy some degrees outside?

When we reached the living room, Jack set the piece of paper down on a table and began taking off his jacket with his back toward me. When he once again turned around, he was holding a gun in his right hand. Now that had been unexpected. I stared at the weapon. The hole on the end of the barrel looked awfully large, as it swung to and fro. Jack obviously was nervous, and now I was too.

"Whoa there, Jack," I pleaded. "What's this all about? Careful with that thing. Is it loaded?"

He didn't respond immediately. Instead, he walked over to my patio door, which he slid closed and locked. Then he drew the blinds. That created an atmosphere that approximated my new mood.

I tried to keep things light. "Hey, what's up, Jack? Put away the gun. Somebody could get hurt." I had a difficult time looking away from the barrel. I didn't know much about guns, but surmised this was an automatic, since I saw no cylinder that would revolve. I couldn't see how that knowledge could help me, however.

"Sit down, Mike," he instructed, motioning toward a chair with the gun. The only relief was that the gun temporarily was not pointed at me. When I failed to move, he pointed once again at my overstuffed chair with his gun. I decided to do as he said, giving myself time to see exactly what he wanted. The guy looked really stressed out or maybe even nuts. I doubted this was a robbery attempt. It had to be something much more sinister.

My mind was casting for possible options. I couldn't come up with anything.

Jack's eyes darted around the room. "Are you alone?"

"Sure."

Jack looked about as if weighing the veracity of my statement. "Sit."

I had moved over to the chair as instructed and now I sat. When I did so, I apparently sat right on my phone. I heard it beep. I was butt calling someone. Maybe this was something that would work in my favor. To cover any noise of the phone dialing or of the person answering, I quickly said quite loudly, "So, what's up, Jack? Want a beer? I have plenty in the fridge. Why don't you join me?"

"Cut the host crap. This is serious business."

I nodded in agreement with him on that note and had no desire to increase his level of agitation. Maybe the plan should be to quiet him down. I put my hands out in front of me momentarily to acknowledge his statement. Jack showed no change in demeanor. I concluded that he apparently had not heard the phone dialing. I didn't know if it made a difference, but if I had reached someone, it was possible they might hear our conversation.

I spoke loudly so my phone could pick up my voice. "What's with the gun, Jack? You planning on using it? My apartment isn't a very good shooting range." I smiled at him, eager to defuse the situation.

"Shut the fuck up," was his only reply as his head swiveled on his thin neck.

I decided to heed his advice until he showed his hand. "Okay," I replied. Then casually I leaned to my left to expose the phone in my right rear pocket as much as possible.

Now that I was seated, Jack Thompson strode nervously back and forth in front of the patio doors. He looked like he was about to lose it at any moment. I needed to keep him talking.

"Take a load off, Jack, and tell me what the problem is, neighbor. How's the rental going?"

Jack didn't answer me. The man's eyes were wild with nervous energy. He swung the barrel of the gun up toward the ceiling and waved it around in a circular fashion. Wiping his face with his free hand, he said,

"I'm sick and tired of being accused of killing my wife. Even if they don't say anything, I can see it in their faces. People are constantly looking at me funny behind my back. I tell you I can't take it anymore."

He was shouting now, but tears were dripping down his cheeks.

When I tried to paste a look of concern on my face, it was difficult to move my muscles, they were so taut. "Who?" I asked.

"Who what?"

"Who's looking at you crazy? Are you sure? You're a good looking guy. Maybe they're just looking at you."

"Everybody's looking at me. It's not my looks. It's because of what they think."

The guy wasn't making much sense. Was he delusional and imagining things? If he really had killed his wife, it could be his conscience at work.

I decided to try once again to change the subject. Maybe it would calm him down. "I thought you were going to rent out your place and move to a smaller joint?"

Jack stopped pacing and turned his head toward me with an inquiring expression. "What's that got to do with anything?"

I had to keep him on this subject. "You can live anywhere you want, man. Move to Eden Prairie or even Hopkins. Better yet, how about out to Prior Lake. People won't know you over in those places, won't know anything about your wife. You can live in peace, start over, create a new life for yourself."

He shook his head. "No good. People at work would still know. They'll still treat me like something smelly they stepped in."

"I hear you. So, what's the plan? New job?"

Jack waved the gun. "Jobs aren't that easy to come by, bozo."

"Maybe I could help you find something," I said hopefully.

"No good, but if someone confesses to Sherrill's murder, then I'll be cleared and people will stop looking at me funny."

The man was obsessed with the thought of being cleared of his wife's murder, something that probably wasn't going to happen. I said, "Ah, no doubt. Got anyone in mind?"

Jack's face took on a toothy grin. "You just volunteered, you supercilious twit."

Supercilious twit was I? Yeah, this guy was nuts. I'd need to take a chance. I shook my head at him. "That won't work, Jack. Pinning the murder on me, I mean because then you wouldn't get credit for the murder yourself, credit for being so smart. The police have no evidence against you. You covered your tracks too well."

Jack thought briefly and then said while shaking his head, "I don't want credit."

The gun dropped to Jack's side as if it was getting too heavy to carry. "Sure you do," I said. "I mean, think about it. How many perfect crimes are there? You pulled off the perfect caper. No proof who did it. Pretty darn clever. Don't you want people to know that? Know how smart you are?"

"No, of course not. Then I'd have to go to jail."

"Yeah, sure, but people still would know, Jack. They'd know how clever you were to cover your tracks. They'd respect you for that, Jack. Anyway, jail'd be better than how you're living now, right? Nobody in jail would be looking at you funny. You'd be their hero, the guy who pulled the perfect crime."

Jack reflected for a moment and then said, "Shut up. You're going to confess to killing her." He once again pointed the gun at me.

That was not what I had wanted. I answered, "Me?" My voice reflected my surprise.

"Yes, you, lawyer man."

"How's that going to work, buddy?"

Jack picked up the paper he had carried in with him. This is your confession. You're going to sign it."

"What then?"

"Then you'll shoot yourself."

"I see. You worked this all out by yourself?"

Jack said nothing.

I assessed the situation and couldn't believe how calm I was. Time seemed to move in slow motion. It was as if I already knew the outcome. Maybe things were preordained?

Jack now handed me the paper and a pen. I read aloud:

I no longer can live with the guilt of having killed Sherrill Thompson. My life this past year has been miserable. I can't go on. Please forgive me.

Nicely done, Jack. I see a few problems though."

"What?"

"My printer's broken. See it's out for repair," I said, pointing into the corner where my desk stood. "So you see, I couldn't have printed this. Plus, this isn't the kind of paper I use. You can compare it to what I have over there on my desk." I rubbed the paper between my finger and thumb. "Then there's the printer itself. You see, any expert worth their salt would be able to tell that the printing on this paper didn't match my printer head. No, Jack, it won't work." I made a big point of shaking my head back and forth.

Jack was getting agitated again. I could see it in the way his mouth twitched. I decided to let him quiet down. He leaned his backside against the couch across from me. Then suddenly he rose and began his nervous pacing once again. Finally, after several more trips back and forth in my living room he said. "Fine, we'll just do it without the suicide note."

That was not an outcome I had considered. We sat looking at one another for a few seconds. Then I said, "Okay, but am I right handed or left handed?'

He stopped and looked at me. He clearly was perplexed. "What the hell difference does that make?"

"Shit, Jack, it makes all the difference in the world, man."

Jack had opened his mouth and was about to say something when the doorbell rang. We both looked in that direction.

"You expecting anyone?'

I shook my head. "I don't think so. Wanna check?"

"No."

In a few seconds the bell rang a second time. I was hoping it was Freddy, but then thought better of that. I did not want him hurt. I put my hands up in front of me, and shrugged to signal I had no idea.

"God damn it, go away," Jack whined. Nobody's supposed to come now." He looked like he might cry.

The bell tolled thrice. I hoped Freddy would leave. I did not want him involved in this.

Then my landline rang. By the third ring, I said. "Want me to answer it?"

Jack stood still, too shocked to move.

"I can get rid of them," I said without moving.

Jack stood frozen as if he had not heard. Then he nodded.

I got up slowly and went over to pick up the phone.

"No funny business or you'll get plugged right now," he shouted in a high-pitched squeal.

I nodded to Jack and answered, "Hello."

It was Freddy. He was telling me he was outside trying to deliver my platter.

"Oh, hi, Ma."

I had Freddy confused.

"Everything's fine. Say, Ma, could I call you right back. I'm tied up just now."

Freddy wanted to know if I was okay.

"Not so much tonight, bye." I hung up.

"Ma calling," I said. "You want to sit outside?" I asked.

"No. Sit back down there." He pointed to the chair where I had been seated.

I considered rushing Jack while I was still standing, but that was an iffy proposition. I still hoped I could talk him down. Maybe someone heard my phone, or maybe Freddy would understand and get help.

"We'll do it without a note," he said.

"Right or left."

"What?"

"Right or left. We were talking about how important that is. Am I right handed or left handed? It makes a difference. A righty doesn't shoot himself with his left hand or visa versa."

"Tell me."

"Why should I tell you? You aren't very well-prepared on this. Not like with your wife. I'm not going to do all your work for you, Jack. You aren't being professional. What else have you forgotten? What else have you fucked up?"

Jack was thinking. I had him confused.

How about gunshot residue? Have you forgotten that?" I asked.

"What's that?"

"The powder and whatever that's left over on one's hand when the gun's fired. Don't you watch TV?"

"I don't have time for that shit!"

"Damn right you should because if I shot myself, I'd have powder residue on my hand and arm. How you going to accomplish that if you shoot me?"

I hoped this would set him back.

Jack thought for a moment. "I'll fire a second shot with your hand on the gun after you're dead."

I hadn't thought of that one. "Don't you think the cops'll figure that out?" I asked.

Jack laughed a maniacal laugh. "No, the cops are stupid."

"Don't you believe it, Jack. You're making a mistake if you think that. They'll tumble to that right off."

Jack was wearing a hole in my rug with his nervous walking.

"Sit down for a minute, Jack. I have a few things to tell you. Stuff you should know."

To my surprise, Jack sat opposite me holding the gun on his lap.

"What's the reason I'm supposed to have killed your wife?"

Jack put his hand to his chin and reflected. Then he took his hand away and said, "You forced yourself on her and she rebuffed you, so you killed her."

"What evidence is there of that. Remember, I barely knew the two of you. How often have you and I spoken in the time you've lived here. Pretty thin story, Jack. Let's talk about that for a minute. First off, your whole plan here is shit."

"No, it's not."

"Yes, it is. I've already been cleared by the police in Sherrill's death.

"What? How?"

"Well, first of all, last week I took a lie detector test. Ever hear of those?"

"Sure."

"I came out clean as a whistle."

"Those can't be used in court."

"No, but they tell a lot. Mine said I was innocent."

"Fuck that," he snarled.

"Okay, so you say, but hold up your hand for a minute."

Jack gave me a puzzled look. I held up my right hand with my fingers pointed toward the sky. "Like this," I said.

Jack held up his left hand.

I reached out my hand so it nearly touched Jack's. "Whose is bigger?" I asked.

Jack looked at his hand and then mine.

"Yours," he said tentatively, not knowing what I was after.

"By quite a lot, right?"

Jack nodded. "I guess."

"That's important, Jack. There are marks on your wife's neck where she was choked. Those marks indicate the size of the hand that went around her neck and squeezed and squeezed and squeezed until she was lifeless, Jack."

"So?"

"Those marks weren't made by a large hand like mine, Jack. They were made by a hand more like yours, Jack. The police know that. They've already cut me loose as a suspect. You'll have to get another fall guy. Someone more your size."

Jack looked dazed.

"Why'd you do it, Jack?"

The man was totally defeated. He hung his head and tears filled his eyes. His chest shook, and his voice quivered when he said, "I didn't mean to. I loved her. She just made me so mad. She was going to run off and leave me with all the bills, all the debt. I'd have drowned in that debt. I was just going to punish her, but then I kept squeezing and squeezing, and her eyes got bigger and bigger, and then she stopped moving. I tried to revive her, but I think her throat was crushed. Nothing worked. There was nothing I could do. It wasn't my fault."

He stopped talking, and the silence in the room was deafening. I said in a low voice, "Why didn't you call 911?"

"I was too scared. I knew no one would believe me that it was an accident. I didn't mean to do it, Mike. Really I didn't. You've got to believe me."

"I know," I said softly. "I know you loved her. She told me she knew it too."

He stared at me. "She said that?"

"Yes."

"When?"

"When she was leaving town. She said she knew you loved her, but she needed a fresh start."

Jack nodded up and down.

I stood slowly and walked over to my neighbor. I grasped the barrel of the gun and pointed it away from my leg. At first Jack held tight and then finally his hand relaxed. The gun slipped out of his hand into mine.

It was over.

"We'll get you some help, Jack. We'll make the nightmares go away."

The man sat slumped over, sobbing.

Just then the door to the basement garage flung open and Bill Rehms jumped out, his gun at the ready. "Freeze," he yelled.

I raised my hands with the gun in my palm and said. "All over, Bill. You're just in time, though."

Apparently two calls had gone out to the police. The first came from Sandra, whom I had butt dialed. Someone had gotten hold of Janet who had provided the keys to my place from my office desk. Bill had used those to crash my basement door after listening to our conversation.

The second call had come from my good buddy Freddy. He hadn't known what was wrong, but knew something was amiss. A guy can't miss with friends like those.

Before the police left with Jack, Sandra showed up. She was crying, tears streaming down her face. She said she couldn't believe I was okay after having heard most of the conversation. Then Janet and Dick Brown arrived. Janet had called Bob Lindgren. He and a crowd of maybe twenty people were outside on my front sidewalk. More police arrived, and they weren't letting anyone else inside.

After a few minutes when my heart stopped racing, I went outside and told everyone I was all right and thanked them for their support. I said I'd talk with them as soon as the police got things under control. Then I went back inside where I sat on the sofa with my arm around Sandra and answered police questions for an hour.

Freddy had left the pizza, even though it had been getting cold, and I told him to bring four more of various flavors and half a dozen jugs of soda. I knew people would be in and out all night. For me I couldn't eat a thing. I was just happy to be alive.

~38~
FAREWELL

GOING TO WORK the next morning was difficult for me, but sitting at home alone would have been worse. Experts would say it took time to get over a shock, and I guessed I certainly had experienced a shock. Now I had to find out how long it would take me to recover. Everything had seemed so normal and under control at the time of the intrusion, but I certainly crashed back into reality afterwards when the truth of my close call settled in and the adrenaline rush ebbed.

This morning I had to drag myself out of bed, having gotten little sleep by the time everyone had left. The smell of fresh brewed coffee helped jumpstart me, though I wondered if I'd experience a crash later.

Something about my neighbor hadn't seemed right. I realized that now and took little satisfaction in being proved correct. I needed normalcy in my life. Work would help bring that to me.

Once safely ensconced at my desk, I thought I was set. However, there were more than the usual interruptions throughout the day. I felt sorry for Janet. She did her best not to mother me, but I could see she was on edge and barely able to contain her emotions.

The police made a couple of visits to wrap up loose ends. Then Bobby Green inquired about coming over to interview me for a large piece he was planning. I was resigned to let him come. Sandra seemed completely on edge, calling me at least twice that first day. I think she couldn't believe I was all right. Then too, as the days went by, friends would stop by just to say hello. Somehow I got by, and Janet and I were able to settle into a somewhat normal routine.

Late the following week, one of our local churches held the funeral for Sherrill Thompson. I felt I needed to go, and I volunteered to be a pallbearer. Closure was what I was seeking. I asked everyone I knew to attend and asked each one of them to spread the word. As a consequence, the church was filled to overflowing. Sherrill deserved a big send off and I was grateful for the community support. Bobby Green was there snapping photos and taking notes. He had promised me the obituary of the century for Sherrill.

At the cemetery after the reading, I placed a mixed bouquet on the casket before it was lowered into the ground. Tears formed in my eyes, and I shook with emotion. Strange behavior for someone I barely had known. Sandra was there to hold onto my arm to steady me.

When the minister had finished speaking and the coffin slowly was being lowered, I spoke softly to the angels. "Farewell, my sweet." I blew a kiss to the coffin.

Then I went home to wallow in self-pity alone. The poor woman had not deserved to die and had come ever so close to escaping a brutal relationship. What had happened to her diminished my vision of the human race. I knew it was going to be struggle for me to not slip back into depression. Over the next few weeks, Janet helped me immensely by having a soft heart, and Sandra did also with a soft shoulder.

~39~
TIME TO PAY

IN EARLY AUGUST the F.B.I. announced that Larry Williams, former majority stockholder and president of the failed Orion Bank had been indicted for conspiracy and fraud. The newspaper article I was reading went on to say that Orion Bank had made eighty million dollars in loans to a straw borrower, and that fifteen million of that loan had been returned in an illegal stock purchase into the Orion Holding Company.

Kale Runyon was named as the individual involved in the fraudulent transaction. Charges against him were pending. So I finally found how this Runyon character was involved with Williams. Now the attack on Katie made some sense.

I didn't really understand this straw borrower stuff, so as usual I called Bob Lindgren for an explanation.

"Hi, Bob," I said when he answered.

I heard laughter on the phone. "I thought I might be hearing from you," he said.

"Why's that?"

"The Orion announcement."

"Got me there, Bob. Can you explain it? What's a straw buyer or borrower or whatever?"

"Well, everything hasn't come out yet, Mike, but apparently Orion loaned money to a person who already had borrowed the limit the bank could legally lend to one entity or person. Thus the person got a fake entity or person to borrow it for them. This stooge sort of stood in for them. This Runyon guy apparently was behind it with a friend of his being the stooge. Someone at the bank had to have been in on the phony deal to make it work. It probably was Larry or perhaps he and his financial man. Anyway, fifteen million of it was then invested back into bank capitol so someone inside had to have been involved."

There was a pause, then Bob said, "Remember Larry saying he had raised additional capitol when we met with him?"

I thought for a moment. "Yes, I do remember that, now that you mention it. At the time he made it sound like such a sound move."

"Yes, he led us to believe he had everything under control."

I had a sudden thought. "Say, Bob. That would mean that Orion Bank really invested its own money to buy its own stock, right? I don't see where that would help anything."

"That's right, Mike. It wouldn't really help the situation. They phonied up the whole stock investment to put the F.D.I.C. off the track during their audit. They took the money from one pocket and put it in the other."

"But the feds caught it, huh?"

"They usually do, Mike. Pretty sharp guys you know. Well then . . ." Bob apparently was looking to go.

"One more thing then before you run, Bob. The comptroller committed suicide. Maybe that was the reason, then? I mean he was in on the deal or found out about it."

"It sure could have been, Mike. If he was in on the illegal transaction or knew about it, he probably was sharp enough to know they'd be caught. He couldn't handle the pressure of ruin and jail time."

I sighed and shook my head. "Sad, so very sad. So that's the fraud they're talking about in the paper?"

"It seems so. They haven't yet released any details, but they will eventually. This is a really big deal you know, so the news outlets will be all over it. It seems obvious Larry tried to fool the regulators into believing the bank was stronger than it actually was at the time with the fake capital investment. He probably hoped he could get the bank back on track and profitable before the next audit. Very few of us expected such a tough recession."

"No we didn't. Pretty cute, though. They invested their own money, in effect," I said.

"In effect," Bob replied.

"What do you think will happen to Larry?"

"I have no idea. He may get a slap on the wrist or may get jail time. My guess is jail time isn't out of the picture." Bob paused for a moment, but before I could say anything, he added, "The initial estimate I heard is that this bank loss will cost the F.D.I.C. six and one-half million dollars."

"Wow!"

"Wow is right. They'll try to get as much back from Williams as they can, but I don't know how much he has. House of course, cars, retirement savings. I'm sure it won't add up to 6.5 million."

"So, because the bank has no money, the insurance has to pay the depositors?"

"Correct."

"That's the six and one-half million?"

"Yup."

"Wow again."

Bob let that idea settle and then added, "On another note, you understand, Mike, that the stockholders will lose everything. You realize that, don't you?"

"I kind of figured that," I said.

"Okay, chew on this for a while. The directors may be personally liable as well. Financially liable, Mike. Their directors and officers insurance will cover them if they used their best efforts to guide the bank and weren't privy to the fraud, but that's always subjective. Just thought that as a director of our bank you should know."

I laughed into the phone. "Boy, that makes me feel good. You sure know how to make a guy's day. Say, Bob, hear anything about Mrs. Williams? Was she dragged in this whole mess?"

"That I don't know, Mike. I don't know a lot about her involvement, but I understand she was a major stockholder. She'll lose all the value of that stock. She probably wasn't involved in the day-to-day operations of the bank, so I don't think charges would be brought against her. We'll have to wait and see on that. The government probably will try to claw back anything of value they can lay their hands on that she might own separately from Larry, though."

As Bob spoke I thought of the stock sale Katie had conducted. She had said the proceeds were going off shore. Had she known?

When Bob finished speaking, I said, "I suppose."

"You've heard, Mike that she left town?"

"Huh?"

"Mrs. Williams has left town."

"Oh."

I knew Katie had gone into seclusion when there was a threat from Runyon. I had expected she would have returned by now. I asked, "What do you mean by left town?" I had not heard anything from Larry since we had met and had no current information.

"She took off a few weeks ago according to what I recently had heard. Rumors were flying even before these bank problems came to light that there were problems at home. But you know how rumors are. Recently, though, I heard from someone in her family that she had settled in Argentina if you can believe that. It might not be true, though. One has to be careful with this kind of information. You know how those rumors get started. I spoke with a cousin of hers, though, so it might be accurate."

Argentina. I could not imagine why Katie would be in Argentina. I said, "Yeah, I guess. Well, Bob. I've taken up enough of your time. See you next week at the board meeting."

The information I got from Bob puzzled me. I grabbed a stogie, went out onto my deck and lit up. Sitting there, I puzzled over the news that Katie might be in Argentina. I realized she must have taken the money from her stock sale and beat it out of town. As I had thought previously while talking to Bob, she must have had an inkle that something at the bank was amiss. Or perhaps her legal advisor had cautioned her to go that route. Regardless, if her money was safely ensconced off shore, would the government be able to retrieve it?

It was either pure dumb luck or brilliant planning that got Katie into her current situation. Then too, was choosing Argentina chance or part of a grand plan? With relations such as they were between the two governments there was little likelihood of any kind of extradition, or money claw back.

Who was this woman I thought I had known? Had I been played for the sap? Was Katie an ordinary country girl as I had hoped or some elitist snob? If the latter, she was a hell of an actress. I certainly had been fooled, but that was easy when I thought with my dick.

I slumped back into my chair and contemplated getting plastered. I sighed and studied the lake. What a beautiful sight. The water on the bay was relatively calm today I noted while breaking out of my reverie. There was little wind, but what breeze there was cool. It was a sign that summer was already waning. I shook my head and felt morose that everything about me seemed to be dying with the season. My neighbor lady was dead, her husband was in jail awaiting trial, Katie apparently had made me a fool, and finally, fall was fast approaching. My days on the water were becoming limited. I shrugged thinking I had better take advantage of every last one.

Here is where Larry Williams would be if he had his chance. He loved the solitude of the lake. He even had said he liked my place. It surely wasn't much, not anything like what he had acquired, but he said he really liked it. Katie on the other hand had thought it small and tacky. I shook my head at the remembrance. Perhaps after all I had been wrong about her.

My thoughts now were on the woman I had fanaticized over for so many years. I wondered how I could have been so wrong about her? Circumstances of which I was not aware had compelled Katie to act as she had, taking the money and running away. That was another of my fantasies about her. When would I ever learn?

However, I had to admit to myself that with Larry's problems, a divorce of convenience probably had followed or was soon to follow, though I would never hear about it. I laughed. My chances with Katie now might be slim to none.

~40~

CLOSURE

DURING THE WINTER, I saw a newspaper article that stated Katherine Brancel, formerly of the Excelsior area and divorced wife of disgraced banker Larry Williams had wed wealthy Argentine banker Ramiro Garcia.

That news certainly came as a surprise to me, but then again perhaps it should not have. It merely was the next chapter in the story. Actually, I should have been able to predict it. It appeared that Katie had landed on her feet after all. When I said farewell to the good, kind person, Sherrill, at the funeral, I could have envisioned saying the same thing to Katie when she exited my life. I had so long thought of her as my dream girl. However, now that I had seen how the woman had schemed and planned and perhaps used me, I no longer could think those thoughts. Now it was to be good riddance.

I guess you weren't the person I had imagined you to be, Katherine.

Author's Note

On Friday November 13, 2009, the Florida Office of Financial Regulation shut down Orion Bank of Florida, and the Federal Deposit Insurance Corporation was named Receiver.

On the same day, the Federal Reserve Bank released an order firing Orion's President and CEO, Jerry Williams, while describing the bank as "critically undercapitalized."

Williams was later accused of loaning money illegally and lying to regulators to make the bank appear in better shape than it was. Orion Bank had grown to be one of Florida's largest community banks.

However, it was alleged that Williams made sixty million dollars in illegal loans to "straw buyers" who were fronting for a borrower who already had reached his legal allowable loan limit. Williams was alleged to have known that fifteen million dollars from those loans would be used to buy stock in the bank to prop it up. The bank was near failure due to excessive non-performing loans brought about by the worsening economy. When the bank did fail, it cost the F.D.I.C. 615 million dollars in insurance payouts.

Williams, who had been chairman of the Florida Bankers Association in 2006 and had been voted banker of the year that year, was charged with conspiracy and fraud. He was sentenced to a six-year sentence in an Alabama prison after pleading guilty to bank fraud and conspiracy. Williams also was ordered to pay thirty-one million dollars to the F.D.I.C.

This book is a work of fiction based on these actual Florida events. Any resemblance of characters or events in this book to anyone in real life is purely coincidental.

Acknowledgements

I wish to thank my editor, Corinne Dwyer, for the help in keeping me on track, and making my story readable.

Thanks are due to Tom Beck, Minnesota Banker of the Year, for teaching me a lot about the banking business which I have woven into this novel.

Finally, thanks to my wife, Mary, for having faith in me and encouraging me over the years.